Acclaim for Stuar

'Cracking! At last British
Pawson's past books are
If you like Jack Frost, you'll love DI Charlie Priest'
ETLife

'The character of Charlie Priest is a winner; a good and intelligent man in a hard world, fighting the villains on his patch with a mixture of common sense, determination and, above all, humour. Highly recommended'
Crime Time

'Totally engrossing. A classic whodunit with the best bit of misdirection I've seen since Agatha Christie. A truly brilliant book, but don't start reading it in the evening or you'll never get to bed'
Sherlock Holmes Magazine

'A very welcome return for DI Charlie Priest...who keeps a sense of perspective as well as a ready eye on the one-liners'
Good Book Guide

'One of the least tortured, most engaging cops on the shelves at the moment'
Morning Star

'Enough to satisfy the most ardent lover of crime fiction'
Yorkshire Evening Post

'Manages to combine a spikily dry sense of humour with a fast-paced story...far outranks the usual police procedural. Pawson has a great future'
Yorkshire Post

Some By Fire

Stuart Pawson

Allison & Busby Limited
13 Charlotte Mews
London W1T 4EJ
www.allisonandbusby.com

This paperback edition first published in Great Britain
in 2006 by Allison & Busby Ltd.

A CIP catalogue record for this book is available from
the British Library.

10 9 8 7 6 5

13-ISBN 978-0-7490-8255-0

The paper used for this Allison & Busby publication
has been produced from trees that have been legally sourced
from well-managed and credibly certified forests.

Printed and bound in the UK by
CPI Bookmarque, Croydon, CR0 4TD

STUART PAWSON had a career as a mining engineer, followed by a spell working for the probation service, before he became a full-time writer. He lives in Fairburn, Yorkshire, and, when not hunched over the word processor, likes nothing more than tramping across the moors, which often feature in his stories. He is a member of the Murder Squad and the Crime Writers' Association.

www.stuartpawson.com

Available from Allison & Busby

In the DI Charlie Priest series

The Picasso Scam
The Mushroom Man
The Judas Sheep
Last Reminder
Deadly Friends
Some by Fire
Chill Factor
Laughing Boy
Limestone Cowboy
Over the Edge
Shooting Elvis
Grief Encounters
A Very Private Murder

To Doreen

Many thanks to the following for their help: Christine Elliott, John Vessey, Dennis Marshall, John Crawford, John Mills, Hazel Mills, Paul Cockerill, and TRACKER Network (UK) Ltd.

Chapter 1

The ferocity of the blast shocked him. He'd barely started to stuff the burning newspaper under the door when, with a roar like a jet engine, a blade of flame scythed his feet and hands, sending him staggering backwards down the stone steps and out on to the pavement. His gloves and plimsolls were on fire, his bare ankles stinging with pain. He jumped up and down in a wild dance, slapping the flames until they were extinguished, and swung a still-smoking leg over the Claud Butler racing bike that had cost him most of his first year's grant. Panic is a defence mechanism given to us by nature, in spite of protestations that we should never succumb to it, and it had served him well. The paint on the door was already bubbling with heat and the glass panel cracking as he turned out of the cobbled street and on to the main road, expertly spinning the pedals to locate his toes in the clips.

Duncan Roberts was twenty years old, a student of chemistry at Leeds University, and in trouble. Correction. He had been in trouble. Now, hopefully, his tribulations were behind him. He snicked the Derailleur gears up five sprockets and stood on the pedals, swooping down towards the city centre on the traffic-free road, the cool morning air chilling the sweat of fear that had drenched him in that terrifying moment when it looked as if his well-laid plan had gone wrong.

He was behind with his rent, his studies and his overdraft, but so were most of his friends. They survived by bumming meals and beer, dossing on floors and copying each other's lecture notes. Then Melissa, his girlfriend, had announced that she was pregnant.

'A hundred quid,' she'd said.

'A hundred quid!' he'd echoed. 'Where do you think I'll get a hundred quid? Can't you get rid of it, you know, locally, sort of thing?'

'Get real, Duncan. I'm not having some old biddy poking a coathanger up me, and I'm not drinking a bottle of gin while sitting in a bath holding a nutmeg between my knees. There's this place, like a clinic, where someone I know went. It's in London. What with the fare and a room for the night it'll cost a hundred pounds, and that's all I'll settle for, so you'd better get used to it.'

Duncan glanced over his shoulder to check for traffic and made a sweeping right turn across the empty junction that took him into Buslingthorpe Lane. He stopped once, to dump the empty petrol bottle in a litter bin, then chased his shadow, flickering and dancing over cobbles and kerbs, back to student bedsit land via a maze of streets of blind terraced houses. The only other people he saw were early-morning dog-walkers and muscle-bound paper-boys, cursing the advent of the Sunday supplements. Behind him, a hundred years of desiccation had left the woodwork in the house drier than a hag. The flames ripped and tore through the building like an enraged tiger loosed from its tormentors. Floors, staircases, linoleum and furniture were devoured in its rampage, exploding into incandescence as the flames reached them until the very walls themselves were ablaze.

Melissa had come up with the idea that Duncan should advertise in the Other Paper for work. He thought it was crazy, but went along because it was the line of least resistance and he had nothing better to suggest. 'Student requires work. Anything considered'. Slip in a *legal* or *within limits*, of course, to imply that you weren't bothered if it wasn't, and wait for the offers to plop on to the doormat. Students did it all the time, but he suspected that the only replies they received were from sexual deviants or fellow students with underdeveloped senses of humour. Which meant any of them.

The reply came the very day after the advert appeared. It was neatly typed, reasonably written and on good paper. The best bit, though, was that enclosed with it were four crisp five-pound notes. Duncan's teeth rattled as the hard racing tyres bounced unforgivingly on the much-repaired tarmac of his own back street, and he cocked a leg over the saddle as he freewheeled to rest, front wheel against the broken gate. He lifted the bike easily on to his shoulder and let himself in. Nobody was about.

He'd memorised the note, then burned it. It said:

Dear Desperate Student,

I am sorry to hear about your troubles, but am sure that they are nothing compared to mine. No doubt a few pounds are all you need. I need a few thousand. Perhaps we can help each other.

I own the house whose address is at the top of this letter. Tomorrow I am going abroad for one week and the house will be empty. It would be very convenient if it burned down while I was away. I would suggest that Sunday morning, say between six and seven, might be the best time to strike. Petrol through the letter box, a match under the door. I'm sure you can work out how to do it. Wear gloves and take the normal precautions.

If the house is gone when I return, I will immediately post you two hundred pounds in cash. I am putting a lot of trust in you. I hope you feel you can trust me. Who dares wins. The twenty pounds is a non-returnable bonus.

Good luck.

Duncan leaned the bike against the wall of the hallway, the brake lever settling into the groove it had made in the plaster, and chained the front wheel to the frame. He peeped round the door of the downstairs room. Two strangers were asleep on the floor, one of them no doubt having abandoned the settee in the middle of the night when the itching started. He tiptoed upstairs, stepping gingerly between the cans and bottles, and skirted the rucksack, broken record player and surplus coffee table on the landing.

His room was a dump, but it was home. The job was done. He flopped on the bed and closed his eyes. The place smelled, even to him. That's what going out in the fresh air does for you, he thought, and made a mental note to avoid it in the future. He giggled to himself, and wished Melissa was with him. He was wide awake, thanks to the adrenalin coursing through his veins, with nowhere to go.

Melissa was in London, arranging her appointment and creating an alibi for the two of them. He hadn't thought it necessary, but she'd insisted. She was six years older than he was, and he'd given way to her experience. If there was one thing he loved doing, it was giving way to her experience. They'd recced the house together and decided it was a piece of cake. It was the end one of a Victorian terrace, a bit like the flat, with a small yard in front overgrown with willow-herb and brambles, transferred from the park via the alimentary canals of the local pigeons.

'Nothing to it,' she'd said, putting her arm through his and smiling up at him. They'd celebrated by spending some of the twenty on a curry and a few pints.

Duncan rolled on his side and embraced an armful of bedsheet, burying his face in it. In one week he would have two hundred pounds, and their troubles would be over. He fell asleep dreaming of what he could do with the remaining hundred, and never heard the sirens of the fire engines as they charged across the city.

It was early afternoon when he awoke. He peeled his cycling gear off and changed into his normal uniform of jeans and Hawkwind T-shirt. One of the strangers was in the kitchen, making toast, accompanied by Radio Leeds from a cheap transistor on the window-sill.

'Hi, I'm Duncan,' Duncan said with exaggerated *bonhomie* as he entered the room. 'Where are the others?'

'Oh, er, John, hi. Gone to Headingley on a demo. D'you live here?'

'Yeah. Any coffee made?'

'Coming up. Pete said it was OK if I helped myself. Hope I haven't taken your bread.'

'Don't worry about it. What is it, anti-apartheid again?'

'What's what?'

'The demo.'

'No idea. Not my scene.'

'Thank fuck for that.' Duncan nodded towards the radio. 'Anything on the news?' he asked.

'Yeah,' John told him. 'Some heavy shit up Chapeltown. House burned down. Didn't you hear the engines?'

Duncan was looking in the fridge, lifting out and inspecting cartons of milk and half-eaten packets, but not really seeing what he was doing. 'Mmm,' he mumbled, as if uninterested. 'Anybody hurt?' The toaster popped behind him, and the smell of burning bread set his saliva flowing.

'Shit!' he heard John exclaim.

'It burns at anything over number one,' Duncan informed him.

'Thanks.' John started to scrape carbon into the sink, trying to rescue his toast.

'So?' enquired Duncan.

'So what?'

'I asked you if anybody was hurt.'

'Where?'

'In the fucking fire!'

'Oh, yeah, sorry.'

Duncan hesitated, a carton of milk halfway to his lips. 'Who? Did they say who?'

'Not really. Just that it was some sort of hostel. There were three women and five kids in it. They were all burnt to death.'

Duncan reached his free hand out to steady himself, not realising that he was squeezing the carton and its contents were running down his jeans and over his plimsolls and soaking into the threadbare rug.

God, it was a long time ago. I was just coming to the end of my first week of night shifts at Chapeltown, Leeds, where I'd been transferred after making sergeant. I was tired, hungry and out of my depth. The radio in my clapped-out blue and white Vauxhall Viva burst into life. Something about a fire at a dwelling in the Leopolds, wherever they were.

'Alpha Charlie to XL,' I said into the microphone. 'The intruder at the health centre was the caretaker, come in early to prepare the place for some function. PC Watson had it sorted.

Tell me where this fire is and I'll take it. Over.'

'Thanks, Sarge,' came the reply. 'Where are you now? Over.'

'Halfway out of the health centre gate, pointing at Roundhay Road, over.'

There was some background noise, it sounded like laughter, then: 'Turn left up Roundhay Road, right at the traffic lights, and the Leopolds are on your left. It's Leopold Avenue. Over.'

'Ten-four, out.' We were big on ten-fours in those days.

The lights obligingly showed green as I approached them and I swung right across a road that was freer of traffic than I'd seen it in the two weeks I'd been there. A good scattering of people were walking the pavements, though, in a variety of shapes, colours and modes of dress. I saw yashmaks, jellabas, and severe old gentlemen wearing yarmulkes. In Heckley, where I come from, we have plenty of Asians who came to work in the textile industry, but nothing like the mix I was witnessing here. The sun was already high and warm, adding to the illusion that this was another country. We were heading for a scorcher, and I was going to spend it in bed, once I'd sorted this fire.

I found the Hovinghams, the Dorsets, the Sandhursts and the Chatsworths, but there was a definite lack of Leopolds. They were streets of back-to-back terraced houses, built by hard-nosed industrialists in the nineteenth century and given inspirational names by their wives between bouts of swooning and fundraising for the vicar's latest campaign to save the heathens. Indoor toilets and hot water came much later. The heathens themselves later still.

I was weighing the embarrassment of radioing in for further instructions against the indignity of asking a pedestrian when I saw the fire engine coming towards me. He went by in a bedlam of noise and flashing lights and I made a U and raced after him. As soon as I turned round I saw the smudge of brown smoke over the chimneys, an affront to the morning. We crossed the main road and there it was, on the left – Leopold Avenue.

I went past the fire tender and swung in next to one of our mini-vans that had beaten me there. A big PC I'd only seen at shift-change times was standing in the road, looking up, shielding his eyes from the glare of the sun with both hands. As I got out he dashed through the gate in front of the house and leapt up the three steps to the front door. He held his head low, away from the door, and smashed the glass with his elbow. I looked up at the windows but I could see only smoke. The PC was groping inside the door, feeling for the latch, as more smoke swirled around him.

He got the door open as I reached him and went inside, head down, arm raised across his face. 'What's happening?' I shouted at him.

He looked round at me, his face bunched with pain. 'I saw someone!' he yelled back.

'Where?'

'The roof window.' He dashed into the hallway towards where he knew the stairs should be, stumbled into them and started climbing. The smoke was yellow. I went back to the door, took a deep breath, closed my eyes and dashed into it. I caught him halfway up the first flight, doubled up and coughing. I grabbed him round the waist in a rugby tackle and dragged him back down the stairs. An oblong of light marked the position of the door. I smothered his flailing arms and bundled him towards it and out into the morning

'What the fuck are you playing at?' a fireman shouted at me as the big PC leaned on the wall of the yard and coughed the chemicals out of his lungs.

'He saw a face,' I gasped. 'Up at the roof window.'

'Right.' He yelled the information to his colleagues, then told me: 'A couple of lungfuls of that and you're a goner.' He nodded towards the open door and dashed off towards the fire tender as another one came hee-hawing down the street.

Firemen were running all over the place in a well-rehearsed ballet. 'You OK?' I said to the PC.

'It was a l-little g-girl,' he spluttered.

'It's out of our hands now.'

'I could have got to her.'

'Maybe.'

I put my hand on his arm, saying: 'Come on, we're in the way here.' He pulled his arm out of my grasp but followed me across the road. We stood against the low wall of the house opposite and watched the professionals. They ran a ladder up to the attic window and pulled a thin red hose from the tender. A fireman in full breathing gear readied himself to go up, his mate adjusting his equipment for him while another ran down the street looking for the hydrant. Two more engines arrived. Word had got back that this was a big shout.

'You OK?' I tried again.

He nodded and tried to stifle another cough.

'Want a whiff of oxygen?'

'No.'

Right, I thought. Please yourself. My left hand felt sticky. I looked down at it and saw blood. I gave myself a quick once-over and decided it wasn't mine.

'Are you bleeding?' I asked.

'It's nothing.'

'Let's have a look.'

'I said it's nothing.'

'And I said let's have a look.' Because I'm the sergeant and you're a PC, right?

He held a bloody fist towards me.

'Open your fingers.'

He opened them. It looked as if a sliver of glass from the door had sliced into the ball of his thumb.

'That needs stitching,' I told him. 'Let's get you to the Infirmary.'

'It'll be OK.'

'It needs stitching.'

'I'm not going for it stitching.'

He was a stubborn so-and-so, no doubt about it.

'Well, it needs a dressing,' I insisted. 'Let's see what's in the first-aid kit.' I strode towards my panda without waiting for a reply and after a slow start he tagged along.

Not much, was the answer. A couple of dressings, a one-inch bandage, some rusty safety pins and the inevitable triangular bandage. The one from his van was worse. The neighbours were standing in little groups, watching the action, and an old lady let us use the sink in her kitchen. It was a deep porcelain one, streaked brown by a century's drips, its spindly taps encrusted with verdigris and dried calcium. A galvanised peggy tub stood in the middle of the room with a handle sticking out of the lid for agitating the clothes. Automation had arrived. I washed the wound with cold water out of the hot tap and smothered it with some Germolene she found. A big ginger cat jumped up to inspect my handiwork and sniffed the open tin. The cut was deep and really needed stitching. I put a dressing on it and told him to hold it there with his thumb across his palm. No blood came through so I covered the lot with a bandage.

'It's Sparky, isn't it?' I said as I tied it off.

'No, Sarge,' he replied. 'My name's Dave Sparkington. I don't like being called Sparky.'

'Fair enough.' I pulled the ends tight, saying: 'That should do it. Keep that on for as long as possible, or until a proper doctor sees it. Have you had a tetanus booster?'

'Yes.'

'When?'

'Yesterday.'

With some, you just can't help them.

The fireman in the breathing apparatus never made it into the attic bedroom. He was nearly at the top of the ladder when the window exploded outwards and a ball of flame blossomed from it, rolling up over the roof. He hesitated, took a few more rungs and called for the water. Two more in breathing gear went in the front door, carrying powerful searchlights, and others came running up the street unreeling canvas hoses, having connected them to the mains hydrant. You could tell they'd done it before.

An hour later they brought the first body out and I sent for assistance.

The house was a smoking, sodden shell when the duty undertaker's van left for the last time. 'That's it,' the assistant divisional fire chief told me. 'There's no one left inside.'

'Three adults and five children?' I said.

'That's what I made it.'

'Jesus.'

'Multiple occupancy,' he explained. 'Only one means of egress. These places are death-traps.'

'The neighbours say it was some sort of hostel.'

'That fits.'

'Any thoughts on the cause?'

He pulled the strap from under his chin and rotated his helmet forward and off. There was a white line of clean skin between his face and his hairline. He rubbed a hand across his head, unsticking his hair from his scalp. 'It almost certainly started at the foot of the stairs, just behind the door. An accelerant was used, probably petrol. You were first on the scene, weren't you? Did you smell anything?'

I shook my head. 'Only smoke.'

'The yellow stuff's from the furniture filling,' he told me. 'You were lucky, Sergeant. It's deadly.'

PC Sparkington had gone back to the station, so I'd have to ask him later if he'd smelled petrol. 'Was . . .' I began. 'Did you . . . did you find any of the bodies down where the fire started?'

He'd put his hat back on. 'No,' he replied. 'You're wondering if one of the kids was up early, playing with matches.'

'Something like that.'

He smiled at me like a benevolent uncle. 'They were all upstairs. I've got the details.'

'So it looks . . . deliberate. Arson?'

'I'm afraid so.'

'But . . . who'd want to do something like that?'

'That, I'm pleased to say, is your province, not mine.'

'Right,' I mumbled, adding: 'We'd appreciate your thoughts in writing, as soon as poss.'

'You'll have them, Sergeant.'

'Thanks.'

The DCI arrived, closely followed by the SOCO and the forensic boffins from Weatherfield. I was centre of attention until I'd told them what I knew, and then they closed ranks and left me out of it. I'd always wanted a big crime, and they took it away from me. Ah well, I thought, if that's how it goes I'll just have to join them.

Melissa Youngman had been the star pupil at the East Yorkshire grammar school she'd attended. Her parents were a trifle disappointed that she hadn't made it to Oxbridge, but assured their friends and neighbours that it was because Essex University had more modern facilities for the study of Melissa's chosen subject – palaeontology. It was also much nearer – the only Oxbridge Daddy could find on the map was in Dorset, on the south coast.

Mr and Mrs Youngman decided to invest their life savings in property. After several excursions south they took out a mortgage on a modest semi not too far from the university and proudly presented the keys to their daughter. There were three bedrooms, so two other girls could share with her, which would take care of the bulk of the mortgage. Their only stipulation was that the cohabitants be female. Mrs Youngman knew all about students, she said, and the antics they got up to. Another girl from Melissa's school, Janet Wilson, had also been accepted for Essex, so she was offered one of the rooms.

Melissa took to university life like a dog takes to lampposts. Towards the end of the first week one of the lecturers from the psychology department, Mr Kingston – 'Please, call me Nick' – saw her reading the noticeboard and drew her attention to an extracurricular talk he was giving about Aleister Crowley, the self-styled wickedest man in the world. It was in a smoky back room of a pub, and Nick introduced Melissa to the acquired pleasures of Courage bitter. Later that evening, on the sheepskin rug in front of his guttering gas fire, he eased her legs apart and introduced her to the more readily appreciated delights of casual sex. Melissa stared at the lava lamp on his bookcase, watching the globules of oil in their ceaseless monotonous dance, and said a little prayer of thanks that she hadn't made it to Oxbridge.

Next day, Saturday, her waist-length hair went the same way as her virginity, and a week later she had it cropped into stubble and dyed scarlet. The metamorphosis of Miss Youngman had begun. After the hairdresser's she visited a tattoo parlour and asked to see some samples of his work. The first tentative butterfly on her breast was soon followed by a devilish motorcyclist on her shoulder blade and a sun symbol, better known as a swastika, where only a privileged, but extensive, few would ever see it. Her modest nose stud was considered outrageous in those days; far more so than the nose, eyebrow, navel and nipple rings she acquired in later years.

Mr and Mrs Youngman grew worried about their daughter. They'd had the telephone installed so she could keep in touch, but after the first week the calls ceased to come. There was no phone in her house, so they couldn't call her. They received a Christmas card, with a note added saying she was staying in Essex for the holiday, but there was no other contact between Melissa and her parents until, desperate with worry, they made a surprise visit on her in the middle of April.

Janet Wilson answered the door. As Mr Youngman was the mortgagee there was little she could do to prevent him entering.

'Is Melissa in?' he demanded.

'Er, yes,' Janet admitted as her landlord pushed past her, closely followed by Mrs Youngman.

'Which is her room?'

'First on the left,' she called after them as they mounted the stairs, and stifled a gulp and a giggle with her fingers as she dashed into the kitchen, all the better to hear the imminent commotion.

Melissa was in bed with her latest conquest. They'd met at a party the night before and arrived home just after daybreak, which comes late at that time of year in Essex. Melissa had worn her full war paint and had not had time to remove it before jumping into bed, so it had become somewhat disarranged by the subsequent activities.

Mater and pater would still have been unimpressed with the poor man in whose arms they found their only child if they'd known that he was a pupil barrister with a highly promising future. They would have been even less moved to learn that he was a full-blooded prince, and back in his homeland was entitled to wear a red feather in his hair to demonstrate his royal connections.

He pulled his Y-fronts on and jumped out of bed. He pleaded with them, for he was princely by nature as well as breeding, and a natural diplomat. He said he loved their daughter, had known her for a long time, wanted to marry her. His only mistake was to call her Miranda.

The middle-aged couple stood transfixed, unable to speak; Mr Youngman horrified by his beloved daughter's appearance, his wife hypnotised by the bulging underpants, which confirmed everything she'd always known about 'his sort'.

Voices returned. Insults were hurled. Below them, Janet Wilson held cupped hands over her ears and listened in horrified delight at first, and then in sorrow as things were said from which there was no going back.

It was a short visit. They didn't even have a cup of tea. No further words were exchanged between Mr and Mrs Youngman until their car juddered to a standstill, drained of petrol, just south of Doncaster.

A week later Mr Youngman transferred the mortgage on the house in Essex to his daughter and posted her the documents. That was the last correspondence he had with her. Mrs Youngman finished off the bottle of sherry left over from Christmas, and took to walking to the corner shop to purchase another bottle, even when it was raining. The following August she died after an overdose of barbiturates and alcohol.

Melissa never slept with her Swazi prince again, although

his performance was the one by which she measured all others. She left Essex at the end of the year, to read modern languages at the Sorbonne. From Paris she went to Edinburgh, Manchester, UCLA, Durham and Leeds. She never stayed longer than a year, never sat an examination. She played the impoverished student, but her fees were always paid in full, in advance.

When Melissa came into his life Duncan Roberts had been slouching in the students' union, hoping to con a pint out of a friend, or maybe earn one for collecting empty glasses.

'Things can't be that bad,' she'd said.

'How would you know?' he'd growled.

'Because I have magical powers. I can read your aura.'

He'd seen her around, wondered if he'd ever be able to afford a woman like her. Over the years the rest of the world had done some catching up, but the zips and pins holding her clothes together were gold-plated and the leather was finest calfskin. Her bone structure was as good as ever and the just-out-of-bed hairstyle cost more than a student could earn in a week waiting table.

'As long as you don't expect me to cross your palm with silver,' he'd replied.

'Why?' she'd asked, sitting beside him on the carpeted steps that were a feature of the bar. 'Do I detect a cash-flow crisis?'

Her face was close to his and he could smell her perfume. 'Not so much a crisis,' he'd told her. 'More like a fucking disaster.'

She held her hand out in front of him, palm up. On it was a collection of coins. 'Well, I've got two pounds and a few coppers,' she'd said. 'So we can either have a couple of pints each here, or buy a bottle of wine and take it somewhere more comfortable. What do you say?'

He looked at the coins, then into the face with its painted eyes, only inches away. That perfume was like nothing he'd ever experienced before and her arm was burning against his. 'Right,' he'd croaked. 'Er, right. So, er, let's go find a bottle of wine, eh?'

By the time I'd finished all the paperwork, that final night shift had lasted until three o'clock in the afternoon. I was supposed to be looking at a flat, but I hadn't the energy. I drove back to my digs and went to bed. The thin curtains couldn't compete against the afternoon sun, the landlady's beloved grandson was kicking his ball against the back wall and the man next door had chosen that particular Sunday afternoon to install built-in wardrobes twelve inches behind my headboard. And then there were all the other things chugging and churning away inside my mind. I didn't sleep.

I was up at seven and the landlady kindly allowed me to have a bath, even though I hadn't given prior notice and it wasn't really my day for one. She didn't do meals on the Sabbath, but guests were allowed to cook their own food in the kitchen, as long as they left it as they found it and didn't use metal implements inside the non-stick pans. And didn't leave any dirty crockery around. And didn't leave a tidemark inside the bowl. And didn't stink the place out with foreign food. And didn't . . . Oh, stuff it. I got in the car and went looking for a Chinese.

I knew there wasn't one in Leopold Avenue but I went there just the same, returning to the scene of the crime like a magpie to a roadkill rabbit. Tugging at the entrails. A police Avenger was parked outside the burnt-out house, the bobby deeply engrossed in the back pages of the *Sunday Mirror*. Dave Sparkington was sitting on the wall opposite, gazing up at the blackened brickwork and the charred ribs of the roof. He was wearing a short-sleeved shirt and his left hand was encased in bandage.

'How is it?' I asked as I climbed out of my elderly Anglia. It's hard to imagine that most of us couldn't afford cars in those days.

He held his fist up for inspection. 'OK, Sarge, thanks.'

'That looks a better job than I made of it.'

'The inspector made me get it fixed, but it's just the same as you did it. My thumb's still inside, somewhere.'

I said: 'Did you know there's a judge in Leeds who's lost both his thumbs?'

'Justice Fingers?'

'That's him.' I sat on the wall alongside him and stared at the house. The smell of wet soot hung heavy in the warm evening. It should have been pollen and new-mown grass, but we got chemical fumes, carbonised wood and sopping carpets. And a memory of something else.

'She was called Jasmine,' he said. 'Jasmine Turnbull.'

'Was she?'

'Mmm. They had a bedroom upstairs. And the attic. I bet it was the first time she'd ever had her own room.'

'Don't personalise it, Dave,' I heard myself saying, as if quoting from the textbook. 'Something like this happens every week somewhere. It's just that we were here this time. That's not a reason to feel any worse about it.'

'You could smell them,' he said. 'When we went inside . . .'

After a silence I said: 'They sent me the wrong way.'

'Who did?'

'Control. They told me to turn right at the lights. Not left.'

'It wouldn't have made any difference.'

'It might have done.'

'It's an easy mistake to make.'

'It wasn't a mistake.'

'So what will you do?'

I thought about it for a few seconds, then said: 'Nothing, I suppose. But I'll remember. I bear grudges.'

'That'll learn 'em,' he said.

'Why don't you like being called Sparky?' I asked, changing the subject.

He shrugged his big shoulders. 'To be awkward, I suppose. I've a reputation to maintain.'

'For being awkward? I'd noticed it.'

He grinned and nodded.

'Well,' I went on, 'I don't like being called Sarge. It's Charlie, OK? Charlie Priest.'

'If you say so,' he replied.

'How long have you been in the job?'

'Nearly five years. You?'

'About the same.'

'Is that all? So when did you get your stripes?'

'A fortnight ago,' I admitted.

'Honest?'

'You mean it doesn't show?'

'I thought you were an old hand.'

'Bullshitting doesn't become you. I prefer it when you're being awkward. My dad's a sergeant at Heckley; it runs in the family.'

'Is that why you joined Leeds City? To get out from under him?'

'I suppose so.'

'What did you do before?'

'I'd just left art college. I've a shiny new degree in art, if you know anyone who needs one. So far it's earned me commissions for two police dance posters. What did you do?'

'Three years in the army. Waste of time. Me and discipline don't go.'

'I can believe that.' Something over the road caught my eye. 'Come and look at this,' I said. We walked across the street to the burnt-out house. The number, thirty-two, was written in chalk on one of the bricks beside the door. A patch of peeling paint showed where it had originally been.

'That's been done recently,' I said, examining the numbers.

'To help the postman,' Dave suggested. 'Maybe they received a lot of mail. It was a hostel . . . court papers, that sort of thing. Important stuff.'

I walked to next door. The number thirty was neatly painted on the wall. 'Postmen can usually count in twos,' I said. 'Maybe someone chalked the number nice and clearly so someone else knew they'd found the right house.'

'You mean . . . the arsonist.'

I sighed and felt myself deflate. 'Nah,' I admitted. 'It's just crazy guesswork.'

'It might not be,' Dave said, interested. 'Just suppose someone did come and write the number on the wall. What would they do with the chalk?'

'Get rid of it.'

'Right. Would you say chalk carried fingerprints?'

'I doubt it. No, definitely not.'

'So you might as well just chuck it away?'

'As soon as you'd done with it.'

'Right, but if you *lived* here you'd take it inside and put it back wherever you found it.' Dave stood facing the door, pretended to write the number, turned around and mimed tossing a piece of chalk into the little garden.

The soil in every other yard was as hard as concrete, but this had recently absorbed a few thousand gallons of water and firemen's boots had trampled all the weeds into it. We didn't see any chalk.

'Let's look at the other side,' Dave suggested.

And there it was – a half-inch piece of calcium carbonate, just the size teachers hate, nestling under the wall where the stomping boots couldn't reach it. I braved the mud and picked up the evidence between my finger and thumb. 'Exhibit A,' I said, triumphantly.

Dave repeated his mime. 'Maybe it's at that side because he was left-handed,' he concluded.

'Possibly.'

'And not very tall. I had to stoop to do the number.'

'You're as tall as me.'

'I know, but it's written two bricks below the painted number. I reckon he suffers from duck's disease.'

'Or he's a she,' I suggested.

Dave nodded enthusiastically. 'Or he's a she.'

We gave the piece of chalk to the PC in the car and told him to invite CID round. We left it at that, not going into our leaps of conjecture about the culprit. They're supposed to be the ones with the imagination, not we poor woodentops.

'Fancy a pint and a Chinese?' I asked Dave, smiling with satisfaction as I dusted the mud and chalk from my fingers.

'I'd prefer a curry,' he replied.

'Awkward to the last,' I said. 'Curry it is. Let's go.'

In the car I asked him if he came from Leeds. He just said he didn't.

'So, is it a secret?' I asked.

'Heckley,' he responded, and I could sense the amusement in his voice.

I glanced across at him. 'Really?'

'Really.'

'I don't remember you.'

'I remember you. I wasn't sure at first. You played in goal for the grammar school.'

'That's right.' I grinned at the memory. Recognition at last.

Dave said: 'I played for the secondary modern. We beat you in the schools' cup final.'

I was nearly laughing now. 'Only by a penalty,' I replied.

'You let it in.'

'It was a good one. Unstoppable.'

'I thought it went between your legs.'

'No it didn't!' I insisted, indignantly. 'It was a cracker, straight into the bottom left-hand corner. I didn't have a chance.'

'Thanks.'

I pulled into the kerb and looked across at him. 'Was that you?'

'One of my finer moments.'

'You big sod!'

We both ordered vindaloos. In those days it wasn't curry unless it stripped the chromium plating off the cutlery. I took a big gratifying draught of lager and said: 'So, how are you finding the job?' I wanted a moan, so I thought I'd invite him to have first go.

He bit off a piece of chapati, holding it in his good hand, before replying. 'It's OK. I've never really wanted to do anything else. Just be a copper, ever since I was a kid. A detective, preferably, in the suit and the white socks . . .' He fingered his imaginary lapels. 'But after this morning . . . now, I'm not so sure.'

'I don't think there'll be many days like today,' I said.

'One's enough. Let's just say I learned something this morning, about myself. What about you?'

'Me?' I thought he'd never ask.

'Mmm.'

I tipped some more pilau rice on to my plate. 'I don't know,' I replied. 'Do you want this last bit?'

'Please.'

I passed it across to him. 'To be honest, I'm having second thoughts. I only came into the job to make my dad happy. Family firm and all that. I wasn't under pressure or anything, but I knew that was what he wanted, not an art student for a son. And I didn't want to be a teacher, nuh-uh. In a way, it was the easy option. My ambition was to make inspector, prove I could do it, but I don't know if I'll stick it that long.'

'You make it sound easy.'

I shrugged and wiped my mouth. 'That's just the plan. Maybe I'll fail. So why didn't you join East Pennine?'

'I tried. They wouldn't have me.'

'Oh, I'm sorry.' As an afterthought I added: 'Perhaps they were full.'

'Perhaps.' He caught the waiter's attention and ordered two more drinks.

'Just an orange for me,' I said, almost apologetically. I felt a prat, and deservedly so. I'd taken for granted what Dave had struggled for, but I never gave another thought to the lesson he said he'd learned that morning, not for another twenty-odd years.

The waiter placed the drinks in front of us and asked if we'd enjoyed the meal. We nodded profusely and mumbled our thanks. When he'd gone I said: 'Have they given you a sick note?'

'Yeah. Just for a week,' he replied.

'It's my long break.' Four blessed days off and the weather was set fair. 'Have you ever done any walking?'

'Walking? You mean up mountains?'

'We call them fells.'

'Not since a couple of school trips. Ilkley Moor, Simon's Seat, would it be?'

'I was thinking more like Helvellyn, in the Lake District.'

'I've never been to the Lakes. Would I be able to do it?'

''Course you would. And I'll tell you something else: you don't half enjoy a curry and a pint on the way home.' I didn't mention the aphrodisiac properties of a day's pleasant exertion in the fresh air. He could discover that for himself, in different company.

And that's how the West Yorkshire Police Walking Club was born, all those years ago.

Melissa wasn't in London when the litre of petrol ignited, sending a fireball up the staircase of the hostel and instantly consuming all the oxygen in the sealed-against-draughts building. The fire had faded briefly, starved of fuel, until the windows imploded and dense morning air rushed in to meet vaporised hydrocarbon in a conflagration of unimaginable ferocity. The news reports said that the eight occupants were overcome by fumes. They were being kind; fire is not a gentle executioner.

Melissa was in bed at the time, in the finest hotel Biggleswade had to offer, in the arms of Nick Kingston. They learned of the fire on Radio Four's *The World This Weekend*, sandwiched between a story about Lord Lucan being wanted for the murder of his child's nanny and one that they didn't hear because they were dancing on the mattress. They lunched in the dining room and took a bottle of champagne back to their room. Melissa wanted to make love, but Nick was discovering, to his dismay, that sometimes it took a day or two for the well to fill up again. And he preferred them younger.

Three weeks later they met again, at the same hotel. Duncan had received his two hundred pounds, as promised, and Melissa had told him that she was booked into the clinic for the abortion. After dinner, in the safety of their room, Nick handed her a thick envelope.

'I'm to tell you well done,' he said.

'How much?' she asked, glancing at the contents.

'Normal rates. Two for the job, plus a bonus of a hundred each for the bodies. How's your boyfriend?'

'A cool thousand pounds. Thank you very much. How's Duncan? I'm worried about him.'

'Did he take the money?'

'Oh, he took the money, no hesitation.'

'He'll be all right then. Don't forget you'll need a hundred from him for the abortion,' he told her, grinning.

'Well, let's make sure they've got something to look for, Dr Kingston,' she whispered. She put her arms round his neck and kissed him, then lowered her hands and started to undo his belt. Nick Kingston grasped her hair, pulling her head back, and explored her mouth with his tongue. If he imagined she were the nineteen-year-old maths student he'd shagged last night, he might just about manage it. He was beginning to find Melissa repellent and sensed it would lead to trouble between them.

Chapter 2

I made inspector bang on schedule, but by then I had a wife, Vanessa, and a mortgage, and had been sucked into a way of working that wasn't negotiable with much in the outside world. I'd had a brief spell in CID and enjoyed it, so when the opportunity came to head the branch at Heckley I grabbed it with enthusiasm and outstretched arms. The job fell into them and Vanessa fell out. My dad was dying of cancer at this time and I desperately needed a rock to lean on. I rang Dave Sparkington.

'Could I speak to Sparky, please?' I said when he answered.

'Hiya, Shagnasty,' he responded. 'Congrats on the move. Sorry I didn't make the bash but I wasn't invited.'

'We haven't had it yet. Do you still want to be a DC?'

There was a silence, apart from his breathing, then he said: 'Are you serious?'

'Deadly. There's an aideship coming up. Interested?'

'You bet!'

He did six months as a CID aide and sailed through the twelve-week course at Wakefield training college. The day he joined us he came into my office carrying six pairs of white socks and insisted that we change into them, right there and then.

Slowly, I built up the team I wanted. Gilbert Wood arrived as our new superintendent and gave me a free hand to run the show my own way. We rewarded him with the best arrest rate in the division, and some of them were big fish. I'd worked for Gilbert before. He was one of a dying breed – the old school – who believed that we were there to catch villains and protect the public, and if this meant we upset a few local politicians, or failed to keep within budget, so be it.

Trouble was, Gilbert had no time for meetings, either. Somebody had to go, which was why I was now sitting at the bottom end of the long polished table that graced the conference room at City HQ, while he cast a fly across some lake filled with tame but hungry trout. It was nearly six o'clock and the deputy chief constable was drawing proceedings to a close.

'As you know . . .' he was saying, '. . . this will be my last Serious Crimes Operations Group meeting, so I'd like to take the opportunity . . .'

'Let's have a look,' Les Isles whispered to me, leaning closer. Les is another one of my protégés who leap-frogged past me in the promotion stakes.

I'd spent nearly three hours doing sketches of the DCC on my note pad, and the last one had his likeness to a T. He was leaving at the end of the month and I knew that the day before he went somebody would ring me and ask for a cartoon illustrating some inglorious moment from his past. They thought I could churn them out like Barbara Cartland novels. I slid the pad across to Superintendent Isles.

'Brilliant. Can I have it?' he hissed.

'Mmm,' I mumbled.

'Sign it.' He slid the pad back my way.

With a few deft strokes I gave the DCC a quiff of black hair falling over one eye, added a Penny Black of a moustache, scrawled *L. Isles* across the bottom and pushed it in front of him again.

'Was there something, Inspector Priest?' the DCC was saying, his head tilted forward so he could see me all the better through his bifocals.

'Er, not really, sir,' I improvised. 'Superintendent Isles was just commenting that you'll be sorely missed.'

A murmur of amusement ran round the table and the assorted chief supers and bog-standard supers who represented their divisions at the SCOG meeting took it as a signal and closed their notebooks. They eased their chairs away from the table to notify the chairman that he was pushing his luck if he thought he was going to keep them here much longer.

'Before we finish . . .' the boss remonstrated, determined to show us that he wasn't gone yet, '. . . could we just wind up by going round the table. Anything you'd like to raise, George?' he asked the person sitting on his immediate left.

'No, I think we've covered everything,' George replied, clipping his pen into his inside pocket for emphasis.

'No,' the next in line added.

Shakes of the head and various negative expressions answered the DCC's query as his glance moved round the table, towards me.

I couldn't resist it. Not often do I have so many bigwigs hanging on my words while slavering in anticipation of the pre-prandial gin and tonic that the little lady was no doubt mixing at that very second. The bifocals flickered in my direction and moved on, but not quickly enough.

'There is just one thing, sir,' I said.

They stopped, hesitated, swung back and settled on me like the searchlight at a PoW camp finding a luckless escapee. There was a rumble of groans and the clump of chairs falling back on to four legs. I had them in the palm of my hand.

'If we could go back to item seven on the agenda . . .' I continued. Papers were retrieved from executive-style briefcases and shuffled impatiently.

The DCC said: 'Item seven? Retrospective DNA testing? I thought we'd given it a good airing, Mr Priest. You made it quite plain, if you don't mind me saying so, that Heckley was way ahead of the rest of us in reopening unsolved cases where DNA evidence was available.'

'Yes, sir, and with a certain amount of success. As I told the meeting earlier we were able to associate two rapes with a villain already in custody, and a murder with a dead suspect. However, if we examine the statistics, I believe they lead us to consider new lines of enquiry.'

The person on my left sighed and tapped his pencil, but the chairman leaned forward on his elbows and Les Isles said: 'Go on, Charlie.'

Nothing would have stopped me. 'If I could just invent some figures, to illustrate my point,' I responded. 'If we go back, for convenience, for, say, twenty unsolved major crimes – murders – in the Yorkshire region. There might be four of those where old DNA samples are available which were of little significance at the time of the offence. The new techniques allow us to link crimes in a way which was unheard of just a few years ago. Our experience at Heckley indicates that of those four crimes with DNA availability, it is highly probable that we will find links. Supposing, for example, we link two of the crimes to the same villain. All well and good. We rope him in, present the evidence, and he gets a few more years on his sentence, probably running concurrently with what he's already serving if he's in custody.'

There were murmurs of approval at my disdain for concurrent sentences. It proved they were listening.

'But!' I went on, raising my hand as if plucking a plum, as I'd seen the Prime Minister do. 'But what about the other sixteen cases where there is *no* DNA evidence? The statistics indicate that eight of those crimes could quite easily have been committed by the same person. Maybe we should be taking a new look at all of them. DNA testing isn't the only new tool we have.'

They were silent. They had been listening, unless they'd fallen asleep. 'Profiling,' someone mumbled.

'Is that what you're thinking, Charlie?' the DCC asked in an uncharacteristic show of intimacy. 'That we should set a profiler loose on the files?'

'Some call it profiling, sir,' I replied, resisting the urge to call him Clarry. 'I prefer to call it good detective work.'

'But that's the sort of thing you have in mind?'

'Yes, and computerisation of all the information.'

'Going back how far?'

I shrugged my shoulders. 'Thirty years?'

I sensed a collective *Sheest!* In theory, unsolved murder inquiries never close, but it's in our interests to conveniently forget the occasional one, and staying within budget earns more medals than pinning a forgotten murder on some old sod who is in a nursing home in the advanced stages of Alzheimer's. I could see the cogs going round in the DCC's head. A serial killer would be a fantastic high note to go out on, but he was already on notice, and I was talking about results in three years, not three weeks. There was nothing in it for him.

'Right, Charlie,' he concluded as the wheels ground to a standstill. 'It looks like you've got yourself a job.' He gave his famous smile, like a chimpanzee threatening a rival, and closed his file. Everybody laughed.

'You walked into that,' Les Isles told me as we strolled out into the sunshine.

'I'll never learn,' I concurred.

'Mmm. You could have a point, though.'

'I'm sure I have. It'll give Sparky something to do.'

'How is the big daft so-and-so?'

'Just as big. Slightly dafter.'

'Mr Priest!' Someone was calling my name. I turned to see a PC following us out of the front entrance. 'Telephone!' he shouted at me.

'See you, Les,' I said, turning to go back.

'Tell him he's missed you,' he urged.

'It might be a woman,' I replied.

'Fair enough. S'long.'

It wasn't, of course. It was Nigel Newley, my brightest sergeant. 'There's been another,' he told me, as I leaned over the front counter, the telephone cord at full stretch.

'What, a burglary?' I asked.

'Yes. Old couple tied up and robbed, some time this morning.'

'In Heckley?'

'That's right.'

'Who rang in this time?'

'The BMW showroom on the high street, about fifteen minutes ago. An ambulance is taking them both to the General for a check-up. I'm going straight to the house, while it's daylight.'

'Have you done the necessary?'

'Had a word with traffic about the videos; told the woodentops to keep off anything that might take a tyreprint; sent for Scenes of Crime. Maggie's on her way to the hospital.'

'Good show. Give me the address, I'll see you there.'

I knew what to expect. Not the details, just the overall picture. This was the sixth robbery of its type in as many months; three outside our parish and now three inside. Elderly couples, well off, living in comparative luxury in large, secluded houses. Two villains drive up, pull balaclavas on and threaten them with baseball bats. They tie the terrified householders into chairs and steal anything of value, loading their own vehicle and, in two of the robberies, also taking the victim's car. They grab all their cash cards and force them into revealing the PIN numbers, threatening to come back if they don't work. Several hours later, when well clear of the scene, they telephone someone from a callbox and suggest that the police go to such-and-such an address.

They didn't risk calling us themselves, choosing to ring small firms that had switchboards but wouldn't be expected to record calls. So far, they'd been lucky. The people who received the calls had been responsible and passed the information on. It was only a matter of time before some dizzy telephonist, chosen for her off-the-switchboard talents, put it down to an ex-boyfriend taking the piss and hung her nails out to dry. Then two people would have a lingering death.

The target this time was on Ridge Road, between the house where our football manager lives and the home of Heckley's only pop star. He sprang to fame with a song called 'Wiggle Waggle' which earned him third place in the Song for Europe contest. The following year he destroyed his career by winning it with 'Jiggle Joggle', or something. He's a nice bloke, but alcohol and fast cars have earned him a few hours of contemplation in our cells. Nigel was waiting outside the grounds.

'They're called McLelland,' he informed me. 'Audrey and Joe, late seventies. He ran a printing business until about five years ago. Sold out and came to live here.'

'McLelland?' I said. 'They had a shop in town, and a couple more in Halifax and Huddersfield. Sold stationery, artists' materials, that sort of stuff, and did small printing jobs. We used them now and again. Have you been in?'

'No, not yet.'

The PC who'd answered the call and found the couple came with us, explaining exactly where he'd been and what he'd done. The house was mock Georgian, with pillars flanking the entrance and windows that would be a bugger to paint. Four bedrooms, two en suite, and what estate agents describe as a minstrels' gallery. They have the monopoly on midget minstrels. It wasn't your average retirement home.

'I can imagine you living somewhere like this, Nigel,' I said, casting my gaze towards the chandelier and flamboyant Artexing as we stood inside the doorway.

'Cheers,' he replied, with a scowl.

The PC showed us the two chairs in the dining room, at the back of the house, where the couple had been tied. Bundles of string lay on the floor between the chairs' legs. 'You cut the string,' I said, bending down to examine it.

'Yes, sir.'

'Good.' The knots were evidence. 'Did you touch anything else?'

'In the kitchen, sir. I took a knife from a drawer. And I found a dressing gown for the lady, from the bathroom.'

'This would be about, what . . . five thirty?'

'Five thirty-seven, sir.'

'Cut out the sir, please. You make me feel like Mr Chips.'

'Sorry, er, Mr Priest.'

'Charlie will do. So Mrs McLelland was still in her nightclothes?'

'Yes, she was.'

'So they could have been here from, say, eight this morning. Ten hours.'

'It looks like it.'

'How were they?'

'Bad, I'd say. In shock.'

Nigel returned from scouting the rest of the house. 'It's been well and truly turned over,' he announced. 'Just like the others. Stuff lifted out of drawers in a bundle, almost neatly. Mattresses disturbed. Circles in the dust on the sideboards and suchlike. We won't know what's missing until we talk to them.'

I looked at the chairs, imagining two frail people tied to them all day. He'd risen early, perhaps, like he usually did. Made a pot of tea to take to his wife. A little ritual they'd fallen into after they'd retired. He'd have heard the tyres on the gravel drive; maybe thought it was the postman with a parcel. When he answered the door he was bundled aside as they rushed in. They roughed him up a bit – terrifying the victim was part of the *modus operandi* – and then one of them would dash upstairs to find his wife. We could never imagine how she must have felt when he burst into her bedroom, masked and armed.

I stood in the doorway to their lounge and let my gaze run round the room. A lifetime's accumulation was there. It wasn't to my taste, but everything was good quality, some of it old, some newer. Mrs McLelland's mark was on the place. She liked frills and bows and flowery patterns of pinks and lilacs. His pipe sat in an ashtray on the hearth, within reach of his favourite chair. This was their home.

'We've got to catch them, Nigel,' I said softly. 'Before they kill someone.'

'How do we know they haven't?' he replied, coming to stand next to me. 'All it takes is for someone not to pass on the message. Somewhere, two people might be sitting in chairs like these . . .'

'In that case,' I interrupted him, 'we'd better give it all we've got. Why isn't that bloody SOCO here yet?'

* * *

Maggie Madison, one of my DCs, had no luck at the hospital. Audrey and Joe were sedated and in no condition to speak. 'Perhaps,' the doctor told her, 'after a good night's sleep . . .' At least it looked as if they'd survive. They had friction burns from the string on their ankles and wrists, and bruises on their arms from manhandling, but no other damage. No other physical damage. I dismissed the troops and arranged for a full meeting at eight a.m. On my way home I stopped at the fish and chip shop, but it was closing. I settled for a bowl of cornflakes and went to bed.

The meeting was informal, in the CID office, with me at the blackboard making notes on it and everyone else sitting around in rapt attention. SOCO had found a tyreprint where a vehicle had turned round in the drive and run on to the garden. So far all we knew was that it wasn't from Mr McLelland's elderly Rover which stood in their garage. He'd collected a few fingerprints but it was looking as if they all belonged to the householders. We hadn't expected it to be otherwise. 'The string used to tie them,' he informed us, 'is the same gardening twine as from the Woods End robbery, and the knots were simple overhands, three or four on top of each other, as at Woods End.'

'They used clothesline at the first four,' I added, 'but the knots were the same.'

'They ran out of clothesline?' someone suggested.

'Probably,' I agreed. 'The point is, we can assume it's the same gang.' I turned to DC Madison. 'Hospital duties for you, Maggie. Ask if there's any next-of-kin they'd like informed, then if they saw the vehicle. Most importantly, what time did the villains leave and who do the McLellands bank with? Take one of those consent forms with you that we created after the last job, so we can talk to their bank. Find out what you can, but let me know if either of them is fit enough for a proper statement.'

'I'm on my way.'

'Jeff,' I said, looking at Jeff Caton, another of my sergeants. 'Liaise with our neighbours, let them know we've had another and keep them informed. Tell them about the tyreprint – one was found at the Oldham job, I believe. Collect whatever videotapes Traffic have to offer and have someone look at them. Maggie'll let you know the time frame. It's a pound to a pinch of snuff they use the motorway.' So did seventy thousand other vehicles, every day, but what the hell.

'It was Oldham,' the SOCO confirmed, referring to the tyreprint.

'Have you done a comparison?'

'No. We don't have the file.'

'Fair enough, but let's have it done.' I dispatched people to talk to the neighbours and a couple of DCs agreed to have a word with local likely lads on the estates who might have heard something on the jungle drums. They have a system of communication that doesn't rely on wires or radio waves or satellites. It's a hotchpotch of rumour, gossip, lies, wishful thinking and wild imaginings. It spreads like chickenpox through an infant school but sometimes, just sometimes, there's a kernel of truth in it. It's a bit like satellite news.

'And you and me, sunshine,' I said, turning to Sparky as the others grabbed jackets and notebooks and filed out, 'we'll have a pleasant morning talking to the usual suspects.'

We blinked into the daylight and I wondered if some decent shades would help my image. 'We ought to be having the day off somewhere,' Dave said as we walked to his car.

'When we sort this,' I said. 'Big day out. Ingleborough, Hill Inn for a few bevvies, Chinky in Skipton. We'll hire a bus. Long time since we did something like that.'

'It'll probably be raining tomorrow.'

'Nuh-uh.' I shook my head. 'It's set fair for the foreseeable future. High pressure over North Outsera.'

'Day after tomorrow, then.'

We placed our coats on the back seat and I wound my window down. Dave started the engine. 'Tony's Antiques?' he suggested.

'Good a place as any,' I agreed.

But Tony had nothing to offer us. These days, he claimed, he'd lost contact with the old gang. Things were not the same; no honour any more; too much violence. He was respectable; all his mistakes were behind him; little woman saw to that. Just like he'd told us the last time.

'Sell many of these, Tony?' I asked, turning a twelve-inch bowie knife with a serrated blade in my hands. I held it to the light and saw *Made in East Germany* etched into the steel.

'Not many, Mr Priest,' he answered. 'One or two, to collectors. And 'unters, sometimes.'

'Hunters? What do they hunt?'

'Rabbits, that sort of thing. There's a fishing line in the 'andle.'

I pulled the end of the hilt and two yards of tightly coiled nylon line sprang out, thick enough to restrain a playful corgi. I imagined one of Tony's shaven-headed, pot-bellied customers chasing a rabbit across the moors, and concluded that Benjamin Bunny and his friends were not in danger.

'You'll be sure to let us know if you hear anything,' Sparky said, pushing his face close to Tony's. 'Won't you?'

'Er, yeah, 'course I will,' Tony promised, leaning away, his eyes flicking between us.

We were at the less prosperous end of town, where the mills and workers' cottages – better described as slums – once stood. Now it's a junction on the bypass, with a few run-down terraces left clinging to streets that terminate abruptly against the guard rail and don't figure in the council's road-sweeping plans. We came outside, squinting against the glare and the traffic-borne dust. An old man shuffled by using a Zimmer frame, slippers on his feet. He'd probably lived all his life within a hundred yards of that spot, in one of the few houses left standing. When he died, they'd knock it down and go back to their offices to wait for the next one. It's development by attrition.

'How's he supposed to cross the road?' Sparky wondered as we watched him dodder away.

'Cross the road?' I replied. 'Cross the road? Why would he want to cross the road? Roads are for cars.'

'Right. So where next?'

'Well, as we're talking about cars, let's go kick a few tyres.'

'Good idea. And why don't we walk?'

'Good idea.'

It's funny how second-hand car showrooms cluster together, challenging the would-be customer to find a better deal. There are three on the road out of town and over the years we'd had dealings with all of them. The dazzle as we approached the first one hurt the brain. A Ford Escort convertible, the hood invitingly down, stood temptingly in front of all the others, bait for the impulse buyer. *Car of the Week* was emblazoned across its windscreen.

'Why doesn't mine shine like this?' I asked the proprietor when he swam out from under his stone.

'I don't know what you drive, sir,' he replied. 'But these are all quality motors, and that's reflected in the paintwork. *Reflected in the paintwork!* That's a good one, eh? Are you particularly interested in a cabriolet?'

'No, not really.'

'So did you have anything in mind?'

'All of them,' I said, showing my ID. 'Do you have papers for them all?'

His expression fell quicker than a politician's trousers. 'P-papers?' he stuttered. 'Papers? Er, yes, in the office. Is there . . . is there a problem, Officer?'

'Not at all, sir,' I replied, smiling like the same politician when he realises it's only the wife who's caught him, and she's not going to derail the gravy train. 'I'm sure everything's in order. We'd like a word with you about another matter, though, in the office, if you don't mind.'

We were wasting our time, and the other two dealers were no help. They hadn't made any big cash sales recently, and nobody had offered them goods in kind or suggested any sort of dodgy deal. Business was steady and wholesome, even though customers these days knew every trick in the book and were determined to rip them off.

'My heart's bleeding,' I said as we walked back to the car.

'You were too easy on them,' Dave admonished.

'I think they got the message,' I replied. 'If they don't know anything they don't know anything.'

'Everyone knows something. We should turn one of them over, then ask again.'

'Sadly, it's not that easy, and you know it. Where next?'

'The tattoo parlour, then the Golde and Silver Shoppe in the town centre.'

'Right. I might have a discreet boudoir scene done on my left thigh while we're there.'

Unfortunately the tattooist was busy, so it would have to be another day. We dragged him away from the young girl who was having an iguana added to the menagerie on her scapula, but he didn't know anything, 'know what I mean?' The manageress of Ye Olde Golde and Silver Shoppe used language that would make a Cub Scout blush and threatened to report us to the Council for Civil Liberties. You'd never have believed her old man was doing four years for receiving.

We lunched on a bench in the square. Every town should have a square, a focal point. Ours has just been refurbished at monstrous cost, but it looks good and the office workers and shoppers certainly enjoy it when the weather's fine. We had ham sandwiches in oven-bottom cakes, and tea from polystyrene beakers.

A girl, about six feet two, clomped by on platform soles. She had the longest legs, the briefest mini and the skimpiest top I could imagine. Well, not quite imagine, but the longest, briefest and skimpiest I'd seen in a while. I turned my head to follow her, sandwich poised before my open mouth.

'You'll go blind,' Sparky warned.

'It's this warm weather,' I complained. 'It makes me feel poorly.'

'It certainly brings them out. What do you think of them?' He nodded towards the statue in the middle of the square.

It was a bronze, about half life-size, showing two doctors dressed rather differently; one Victorian, one Edwardian. J. H. Bell and F. W. Eurich lived in Bradford, when the woollen industry was at its height and employed hundreds of thousands of people. Of all the afflictions that beset them, woolsorters' disease was the most feared. A man might go to work perfectly healthy in the morning and be dead from it by supper-time. The French called it *la maladie de Bradford*. Dr Bell reckoned it was caused by imported fleeces and was a form of anthrax. Eurich took up the Petri dish and confirmed the link. He devised a way of treating the fleeces and the disease was eradicated. Pasteur was lauded for discovering how to protect animals against the disease, but the good doctors had gone unrecognised for their work with humans until Heckley decided to honour them.

'It's somewhere for the pigeons to sit,' I said.

'Did you vote?' Dave asked. The local paper, the *Gazette*, had conducted a referendum on who should grace the new square.

'Mmm.' I finished my sandwich and rolled the paper into a ball, trying to wipe my hands on it.

'Who for?'

'Them.' I nodded towards the doctors.

'Really? I'd never heard of them.'

'Neither had I until someone nominated them. Who did you vote for?'

'Denis Law.'

'Denis Law! A footballer, I should have known.'

'He gave pleasure to millions,' he retorted, primly.

'He was the best, but he didn't save any lives.'

Dave took my empty cup and wrapper and walked over to a bin with them. When he was seated again he said: 'Do you think we'll catch them, Charlie?'

The pigeons that had been strutting round our feet like battery-driven toys waddled over to the next bench to see if the pickings were any better there. 'We've got to, Dave,' I answered. 'Nigel thinks that someone might already be dead, sitting tied in their chairs because the message wasn't passed on.'

'I've thought the same,' he said. 'Maybe we should put out an appeal. *Check your neighbours, if you haven't seen them for a while.* Something like that.'

'I'll mention it to Gilbert. I'll have to get back, make some calls. Are you all right for seeing a few more miscreants?'

'I've a long list, but I'm not hopeful. This morning's been a waste of time.'

'So what do you conclude from that?' I asked him.

'Dunno,' he replied. 'They could be new boys in town. Or new to the job but clever with it. Or everybody's scared of them.

Or maybe they're from way outside the area.'

'All the jobs are centred on Heckley,' I said.

'What's fifty miles these days? They could be from the Midlands, travelling north for every job. Or from the north-east. It's probably too hot for them up there. Who knows?'

'Like I said, I'll do some ringing round.' I stood up and swung my jacket over my shoulder.

'Want a lift back?'

'No, I'll walk. Let's see what's happening.' I unclipped my mobile phone. 'Oops,' I said. 'Switched off. No wonder we've had a quiet morning.' I pushed the slider across to the red dot and pressed a memory button.

'It's Charlie,' I said. 'Anything happening?' There was a message for me. 'Did he say what he wanted?' He hadn't. 'Right,' I said, 'I'll ring him when I get back.'

I must have looked thoughtful as I clipped the phone back on my belt. 'Problems?' Dave asked.

'I don't know. Someone called Keith Crosby wants me to give him a ring.'

'The MP?' he asked, his eyes wide.

'Ex-MP. I'm not sure.'

'Bloody 'ell. It's been a long time since we saw him.'

'Hasn't it? I wonder what he wants.'

I was deep in thought as I walked back to the office. Keith Crosby had fallen from grace twenty-odd years earlier, and I'd been at the centre of things. The tall girl stepped out of Top Shop right in front of me and I banged into her. She told me to look where I was going and I said sorry. The tune blasting from within was Marvin Gaye's 'I Heard it Through the Grapevine', number one in 1969, and for a few seconds I lost track of time and place. It had been a long time ago, and was still unfinished business.

Chapter 3

I spent the afternoon on the phone talking to contacts in other regions and divisions. It's called networking these days, when everything has to have a name so that someone can do a PhD in it. I just call it normal. Our press office agreed to ask YTV and the local radio stations to put out a 'check your neighbours' warning when they reported the Joe and Audrey story. About four o'clock the troops came wandering back in, dragging their feet.

'The doctor gave me a couple of minutes with them,' Maggie told me as she pushed my door open with her hip and placed two mugs of tea on my desk.

'Thanks, you're a mind-reader,' I said, throwing my pencil down and clearing a space for the drinks.

'I asked the obvious,' she went on, sitting opposite me, 'but they were too shaken to be much use. Basically, it was a white van and there were two of them, carrying baseball bats and wearing masks. Near as I could find out it was about seven thirty, maybe a little later, and they stayed for a long time. The doctor made me leave it at that. He's a nice old dear. Joe, that is, not the doctor. Mrs McLelland is still in shock.'

'The famous white van,' I said, nodding my head.

The door opened again and Dave came in, carrying two

steaming mugs in his right hand. 'Oh, you've got one,' he said.

'Put it there,' I said, moving the first one a few inches to one side. Nigel Newley and Jeff Caton followed him in.

'Maggie's had a fruitful day,' I told them when they were settled. 'Baseball bats and a white van, as expected. Any luck with the videos, Jeff?'

'Yep. White Transit going on to the M62 at precisely oh-eight-thirteen yesterday. Phoney numberplate.' He spread a grainy ten-by-eight printout in front of me and laid two more alongside it. 'This is from the second robbery, in East Yorkshire, and this one is after the Penistone Road job. Can't read the numbers, unfortunately.'

Three white vans, coming towards the camera, an assortment of other vehicles around them. 'You reckon it's the same one?' I said.

Jeff pointed with a pencil, leaning across my desk with Maggie alongside him. 'Look at the similarities,' he told us, 'apart from the obvious ones, like they're all white Transits. See the radio aerial. It's on the driver's side, just behind him; not the normal position for a Transit. Usually they're just above the windscreen, one side or the other. The tax disc in the windscreen is halfway up the screen in all of them. It could have been higher, it could have been lower. And there's a mark at the top of the screen, there and there. Perhaps once upon a time there was a sun shield stuck across it with some lettering, and a piece got left behind.'

'Sharon and Wayne?' someone suggested.

'Yeah, maybe,' Jeff said, 'but it's the same van all right.'

'Well, that narrows it down,' Sparky declared.

'We don't know they did it,' I warned. 'Let's not jump in with both feet half cocked. Maybe this van is running up and down the motorway all day.'

'It's a start, though.'

'Oh, it's definitely a start, and we have a number to look for now. See if the whizkids can enhance those other plates for us, Jeff. Even if they can't give us a definite number they might be able to confirm that it's similar. Anything else, anybody?'

Sparky shook his head. 'Sorry, boss. Wasted day. The lack of information or even gossip must mean something, but I don't know what.'

'Right. Nigel . . .' I began.

He jumped to his feet and snapped me a salute. 'Yessir!' He thinks he's being humorous.

'Circulate all our friends, will you, with what we've got. Especially Traffic. The next time that van turns a wheel I want to know about it.'

'No problem.'

'Good, in which case I suggest we all have an early night, for once. Catch up on the gardening while the weather's good.'

'Tea on the patio,' Maggie enthused. 'Heaven.'

'Painting the mother-in-law's window frames,' Dave muttered. 'Hell on earth.'

'Cricket practice,' Nigel said. 'Absolute bliss, if it goes well.'

'Cricket practice!' I scoffed. 'It's wider bats you lot need.'

'Tell me something,' Maggie said. 'Where do these villains get their baseball bats from? Surely it would be much easier for them to use cricket bats?'

'Cricket bats!' Nigel spluttered, affronted. 'They wouldn't use a cricket bat!'

Sparky said: 'Somehow, a yob wielding a Stuart Surridge three-springer doesn't have the same menace, don't you think?'

In my PC Plod voice I said: 'Did you notice anything unusual about him, sir?' and then, in an upper-crust accent: 'Ye-es, Officer. His hands were too close together.'

'I thought it was a sensible question,' Maggie murmured, pretending to be hurt.

'It was, Maggie,' I told her. 'And the answer is: God knows.'

'Perhaps their counterparts in America use cricket bats,' Nigel suggested.

'Magnum see-mi-automatic cricket bats,' Dave added.

'Let's go,' I said, pushing my chair back from the desk. 'This is getting silly.'

'Did you, er, ring him?' Dave asked me.

'Who?'

'Keith Crosby.'

'Oh, no. I thought I'd wait for him to ring again. We've enough on our plates without resurrecting ghosts.'

'Keith Crosby? The disgraced MP?' Jeff asked.

'Not sure, but I imagine it's him.'

'What does he want?'

'I don't know.'

'He lives in Heckley, over near Dale Head.'

'So I believe. We had dealings with him a long time ago, didn't we, Dave?'

'You can say that again,' he replied.

'What did he do?' Nigel asked. He was from Berkshire, brought north by tales of streets paved with opportunity and warm-hearted women, and therefore unfamiliar with local folklore. He would also have been in short trousers at the time.

'Nothing,' I told him. 'He just happened to own this house in Leeds. Chapeltown. It burned down. Arson. Seven people inside were burnt to death.'

'Eight,' Dave corrected. 'Three women and five kids. It was a hostel for battered wives. First job Charlie and me ever worked together on, wasn't it, squire?'

'Mmm.'

'That was a sunny day, too.'

'I know. Somehow it made it worse.'

'Did he start the fire himself?' Nigel asked.

'Crosby? No, it was never pinned to anyone. There was a big stink about it and he was forced to resign as an MP.'

Maggie said: 'He has an MBE now.'

'That's right,' I replied, remembering. 'For his charity work. He started some sort of Samaritan organisation shortly afterwards. Rehabilitated himself, I suppose.'

'That's it, then,' Nigel stated. 'He wants a donation.'

'Very probably,' I agreed, standing up and unhooking my jacket. 'C'mon, or we'll be here all night again.' Sometimes I've just got to be firm with them.

Audrey and Joe McLelland were a pleasant old couple. She was still confined to bed when Maggie and I called to see them on Friday morning, but one of the nurses had found a wheelchair for Joe and he was parked alongside her. The bedside cabinet was covered in get-well cards and she was busy opening the pile that had arrived that morning. The woman in the next bed was fast asleep and snoring, her toothless mouth gaping like an oven door.

'A policeman and a police lady to see you. Aren't you lucky?' the nurse said by way of introduction, as if she were talking to two infants. 'Now be sure not to let them tire you out.'

'We won't,' I told her, and she dashed off to her other duties.

Audrey and Joe said they were feeling better and expecting to be going home later that day. Maggie told them to stay where they were and be looked after, if they could. I left her with Audrey and wheeled Joe out of the ward and into the lift. We bought two teas from the snack bar in the entrance and had them outside, me sitting on a low wall alongside him. Several other people were doing the same; relatives in summer clothes, patients oddly at ease in dressing gowns and slippers.

'I used to buy paints in your shop,' I told him. 'And 6B pencils. I think you got them specially for me.'

'We sold a few,' he replied, uninterested.

He confirmed what we knew about the van, and the baseball bats. The one he was threatened with had red stripes around it, as if it were bound together with insulation tape. Other than that he had nothing further to add. They had a son who was living in America and a daughter in Kent. She'd be coming up some time today if her husband could have time off work to look after their children. They'd decided not to tell the son. 'He's in computers,' Joe told me, as if that explained why.

We needed to know what had been stolen but didn't want to drag them out of hospital before they were ready. It would take weeks, even years for them to get back to anything like normal, and the bad dreams would probably be with them forever, but they were already over the initial shock. Whether they would ever feel safe again in their own home was doubtful, but I knew they'd both prefer it to Heckley General. Joe was reasonably well, but he'd be hopeless at telling us what had gone from where. We needed the woman's touch. I spoke with the doctor and he agreed that they could both go home the next day.

In the previous robberies the villains had taken any handy silverware and jewellery, plus the victims' credit cards. In the eight or ten hours' grace that they allowed themselves they'd stung the accounts for increasing amounts that were now up to the £3,000 mark. First of all, armed with PIN numbers, they took the daily limit of £300 from each account. Then, after practising the signatures, they did a tour of travel agents and bought themselves several £250 tranches of pesetas or dollars.

After that, it was credit card purchases of tyres, aluminium wheels, TVs and VCRs; stuff they probably already had orders for. It was like winning first prize in a game show – all you can stuff in your Transit before the shops shut.

We had photographs of one of them, the bright one, presumably, courtesy of the travel agents' CCTV cameras. He was burly and wore a hat and spectacles in a variety of styles. This time it had been a beanie hat and heavy rims. I turned my pad sideways and did a sketch of the crime scene, with Burglar Bill standing before the counter. If we measured the height of the camera from the ground, the height of the spot on the wall behind him level with his head, and the distance between the two, a bit of nifty geometry would give us his height. To the millimetre. As soon as we had the McLellands' bank account numbers and their consent we'd be able to follow the latest trail of thievery and tot up the damage. We'd compare the route the thieves had taken with the previous ones and see what we could deduce from that. The net was closing on them, but too slowly. Lives were at risk. We needed a break. Don't we always.

Joe gave us the permission we needed and Maggie spent the afternoon on the phone, talking to the banks and travel agents. We knew from experience that it would take days for all the transactions to be processed, but we were under way. I studied the other files, looking for inspiration, and spoke with the SIOs for the jobs outside our patch. No eager young detective came leaping into the office asking for a job so I went to the travel agent where the photograph was taken and took the measurements myself. I filled them in on my sketch and found some sine tables in the back of an old diary. It took me nearly an hour, but eventually I had a figure. He was six feet two tall, and built like a haystack.

* * *

The phone was ringing as I arrived home. I charged into the hallway and gasped: 'Priest,' into it, my jacket half off and every door behind me wide open.

A female voice intoned something like. 'Oh hello my name is Mindless Sally from Leaky Windows and we are doing a promotion in your area and require a show house for one of our conservatories all you have to do to receive a three million per cent discount is to agree for our photographer to take some pictures which we will use in our publicity material when would you like a representative to call to give you a no-obligation quotation?'

I said: 'Pardon?'

'My name is . . .'

'No, love,' I interrupted. 'I, er, already have a conservatory, thank you.' I didn't but it was unlikely she'd sue.

'Would you be interested in double-glazing?'

'Got it,' I told her, this time with conviction.

'A patio door? We have a special offer at the moment where . . .'

'No,' I insisted. 'I don't need anything like that, thank you. In fact, I'm moving next week.'

'What about your new house?'

'I'm going abroad. Puerto Rico.'

'OK. Sorry to have troubled you.'

I replaced the phone and pulled my other arm out of its sleeve, muttering: 'Then why did you?' to nobody in particular. She'd been the third this week. Six flies had come in through the open doors and were doing aerobatics around my kitchen. I found an aerosol of Doom under the sink and gave each of them enough to stun a Tetley's dray horse. With maximum prejudice, as the CIA say.

One minute earlier the next call would have dragged me out of the shower, and that would have meant big trouble for someone. I mean, like, BIG. As it was, I was dry but improperly dressed when I answered it.

'Sorry to bother you, Charlie,' the desk sergeant said, 'but a bloke called Mr Crosby has been on again. Asked me to ask you to call him. Wouldn't say what it was about, just that he knew you from long ago.'

'No trouble, Arthur,' I replied. 'You know as well as I do that the CID never sleeps. Give me the number.' I wrote it down and said: 'If we've met before it must be Keith Crosby. You remember him, don't you?'

'Our old MP? That was a long time ago. He got sacked, didn't he?'

'He resigned.'

'I remember now. Wasn't he caught dipping his bread in someone else's gravy? Nowadays they're all at it. What does he want?'

'No, he wasn't, and I don't know what he wants. Have a quiet night.'

'And you.'

Keith Crosby wanted to meet me, to tell me a story. That's what he said after I'd rung his number and introduced myself. 'I've seen your name in the paper several times, Mr Priest,' he continued, 'and I remembered you from all those years back. You impressed me. I thought then that you'd make a good policeman, and I was delighted to read of your successes.'

'Sadly, not in the promotion race,' I said.

'Ah, I suspect that has more to do with a lack of ambition, not any flaw in your ability,' he replied. I was growing to like him. 'You came to see me,' he went on, 'twenty-three years ago, after the fire. Do you remember?'

'Yes, I remember. I had a piece chewed off me by the DCI for interfering.'

'I'm sorry to hear that. He was convinced that the real target for the arsonist was a brothel in the next street, Leopold Crescent. A group of girls had set up a co-operative, working for themselves instead of the local pimps. He assumed the pimps were fighting back.'

'It's the sort of thing they'd do,' I said. 'It was the identical house, one street along.'

'But you didn't really believe it, did you?'

'I didn't believe anything, Mr Crosby. We gather evidence, see where it leads.'

'You found a piece of chalk, remember? Someone had marked the house earlier, so that there would be no mistake. That's what you thought, isn't it?'

'It was a possibility.'

'Will you see me, Mr Priest? It's a long story, I'm afraid, but I desperately need to tell it to someone. Someone who might understand.'

'I'll listen to what you have to say,' I told him, 'but I can't promise any action. We just haven't the time or resources to resurrect ancient crimes, especially if there is little or no public benefit. Perhaps an injustice was done, which is unfortunate for you, but that's how it works. Sometimes, as you know, the bad guys win.'

'But you'll listen, Mr Priest? That's all I ask.'

'I'll listen. I have a reputation for being a good listener. It usually hides my boredom.'

'So when can I see you? Do you work Saturdays?'

'Yes, but I'm busy in the morning.' Another sunny day off was slipping out of my grasp. 'Tell you what,' I said. 'I'll lunch at the Bargee. That's fairly near you, isn't it? I could eat about twelve, see you about half past. How does that sound?'

'It sounds fine, Mr Priest, but do you object to me having

lunch with you? They have a nice garden where we could eat and talk without fear of being overheard, if the weather stays fine.'

'OK, Mr Crosby. Tomorrow at twelve it is.' I didn't know what I was letting myself in for, and it had been a long time ago, but the photograph in the paper of little Jasmine Turnbull had lived with me ever since, and I'd have gambled money that Sparky could have named the other seven victims. The inquiry had turned nothing up, and a couple of months later all CID's resources were concentrated on finding the person who was going round knocking street girls on the head with a ball-peen hammer.

All that talk about lunches had reminded me that I was hungry. I looked at the bottom number on my telephone pad and dialled it. A husky voice repeated the numbers and I said: 'Hi, Jacquie, it's me. I've managed to escape early. Don't suppose you'd like to watch me eat, would you?'

There was a condition. There's always a condition. Jacquie would watch me eat providing she had a similar piled-up plate in front of her. 'I'll never be a rich man,' I sighed and arranged to pick her up in fifteen minutes.

We went to the Eagle, up on the moors. It had been taken over by one of the big chains since my last visit and the menu read like a government specification. We had overdone eight-ounce (uncooked) steaks with French fries as dangerous as broken knitting needles, succulent garden peas that were so green they looked radioactive, all garnished with half a tomato – cold – and a sprig of parsley. What are you supposed to do with parsley? We entered into the spirit of the place by finishing off with Black Forest gâteau and ten minutes in the bouncy castle.

'That was lovely,' Jacquie said, looking up into my face and laughing as we walked across the car park.

'Telling fibs doesn't become you,' I replied. 'It was dreadful. Six months ago it was all home-cooked and they did the best apple pie in Christendom. Sorry, love, I'll let you choose next time.'

'It was fine,' she told me. 'Don't worry about it. The alternative for me was washing my hair and phoning Mum.'

'And this was preferable?'

'Of course it was. No dishes to do.'

'Thanks. Get in.'

Jacquie came into my life when I was as low as I've ever been. I'll never be able to tell her how good she was for me, for I'd only be able to do that by comparing her with someone else, which would be unkind. She was eighteen years younger than me and had the kind of figure that ought to be included in the Highway Code. Watch out, deadly distraction ahead. Masses of wild fair hair framed a face that was full-lipped yet ingenuous, blue-eyed but smouldering. English Rose meets Sophia Loren. It was a potent combination. But . . .

'Let's go for a drive,' I suggested, starting the engine. 'I need my spirits lifting after that.' I took us on to the Tops, near Blackstone Edge, and parked with the nose of the car almost overhanging the drop into Lancashire. It's one of my favourite places, and Jacquie wasn't the first woman I'd shared it with. I sat with my arm extended across the back of her seat, my fingers running through her hair, and we talked about our days as the sun fell imperceptibly into Morcambe Bay. Jacquie owns a boutique, Annie's Frock Shop, in the new mall, and she told me about a difficult customer and the problems of ordering from the winter collections when the thermometer is in the eighties. I told her about the robbers and the ram-raiders.

'I knew you'd ring me tonight,' she said, 'although you left it a bit late.'

'I didn't know I could get away until the last thing,' I replied.

'It was in my stars.'

'Was it?'

'Yes. What did yours say?'

'That I'd buy a rabbit and fall off my bike,' I replied.

'Don't mock them,' she admonished, looking at me. After a few moments she declared: 'Leo. I bet you're a Leo, aren't you?'

'How do you work that out?'

'By studying you. You pretend to be relaxed, asleep, but you're always in charge, watching. That's a Leo characteristic. You have a wisdom, a self-confidence, but it's easily damaged and just as easily restored.'

'Yep, that's me,' I said. 'All it takes is a tickle behind my ears.' I pulled her closer until her head was resting on my shoulder. Her perfume was so delicate I hadn't smelled it until now, and it hit me like a fix.

'You're soft and cuddly,' she went on, 'but you have claws and you're not afraid to use them, if necessary.'

'Only on nasty people,' I said. 'And never on you.'

'So am I right?'

'Ssh,' I said. 'Watch the sun. Sometimes, just as it disappears, there's a flash of green light.'

The last molten blob of orange spread sideways and vanished, leaving a void in the sky that the stars would soon fill. 'How long does it take you to brush your hair?' I asked.

She turned her face towards me and said: 'As long as I've got. Two minutes? Ten minutes? It doesn't make much difference.'

'Doesn't it?'

She shook her head.

'I'd like to brush it for you,' I told her, burying my fingers and raking them through it. 'Two hundred times, and then another two hundred just for the hell of it.'

'That would be nice,' she replied, tilting her face upwards towards mine.

Her lips are everything I'd dreamed they'd be, are everything I remember. But lips are lips, promising all, then creating greater desires than the one they satiate. My free hand slipped around her waist and hers fell on to my forearm, halting its progress, like it always does. I buried my face in that hair, gritted my teeth and thought of England.

Maggie was sitting in my chair when I arrived at the nick Saturday morning. 'Morning, crimebuster,' I said as she moved into the visitor's place. 'Is the kettle on?' It was, of course.

'I've rung the hospital,' Maggie informed me. 'They're sending them home first thing, meaning nine o'clock, so I'll meet them there. Are you coming?'

'Do you need me?'

'No. I can manage.'

'OK. I want a word with Mr Wood, if he comes in. We need to know exactly what's missing: values; photographs, if possible; any distinguishing marks; you know the sort of thing.'

'It's going to be a really jolly morning,' she sighed.

'Yeah, afraid so. To be honest, I think you'll be better on your own. Look after them, Maggie, it's a tough time for them.'

She finished her tea, looked at her watch and decided there were a few minutes to waste. 'So, did you have a riotous Friday evening?' she asked.

'Went to the Eagle,' I replied. 'Don't bother going. It's a fun pub now.'

'The Eagle up on the moors?'

'Mmm.'

'They used to do decent grub.'

'Not any more.'

'That's a shame. Did you, um, go by yourself, or were you, um, accompanied?' Maggie takes a sisterly interest in my love life.

'I, er, did have a companion with me,' I admitted.

'The radiographer?'

'No.'

'The librarian?'

'She's not a librarian. I thought she was but she'd just gone in to see her best friend, who *is* the librarian. They were both behind the counter and when they saw me approaching they fought to decide who served me.'

'And the librarian friend won?'

'No,' I said with forced patience, 'Jacquie won.'

'Ah, it's Jacquie, is it? So what does Jacquie do?'

'She owns Annie's Frock Shop in the mall.'

'Really?'

'Really.'

'So she's a lady of independent means?'

'Let's just say she's doing better than I am.'

'Great, Charlie. I hope it works out for you. Tell me, why don't they call it Jacquie's Frock Shop?'

'I don't know. Maybe it's like Alice's Restaurant.'

Maggie looked puzzled, then said: 'So what happened to the radiographer?'

'She saw through me,' I replied.

I had an hour doing paperwork until I felt the need for another brew coming on and went upstairs to see Superintendent Wood. When we were settled behind our mugs and I'd brought him up to date on crime in a small Pennine town, I said: 'What can you tell me about Keith Crosby?'

He took that first tentative sip to test the temperature and replied: 'Keith Crosby? Our old MP? Why, what's he done?'

'Nothing that I know of, but he wants to see me. Says it's important. I thought you might have met him at one of your charity bashes, or the Freemasons.'

'How many times,' he sighed, 'do I have to tell you? It's the Rotary Club, not the Freemasons.'

'It's all the same,' I told him.

'No it's not.'

'You all piss in the same pot . . .'

'No we don't.'

'. . . while standing on a chair, with one trouser leg rolled up.'

'Do you want to know about Crosby or don't you?'

'Do you know him?'

'I've only met him briefly, but I know about him. He gets talked about.'

'Ah, so you go for the gossip,' I said.

Gilbert nodded in agreement. 'You'd be surprised what I learn, Charlie, when tongues have been loosened by the Macallan.'

I told him about me and Sparky being at the fire that caused Crosby's fall from grace. Gilbert hadn't known we were there. I was supposing that Crosby had some new evidence, and wanted to know as much as possible about him before we met.

'He remembers you from the fire?' Gilbert wondered.

'Yes.'

'It was sad, I suppose,' he went on. 'Poor bloke had only been an MP for a couple of years. Achieved his life's ambition, then, *splodge*, it's taken from him. Word has it that he'd set up a love nest with a gorgeous black girl, but I doubt if it's true. Anyhow, it cost him his job.'

'It was sad for the people burnt to death in the fire, Gilbert,' I said. 'Tell me how he's got to where he is now, if you can.'

'Well,' he began, 'you've heard of the Friends in Need organisation?'

'Yes. It was a forerunner of the Samaritans, wasn't it?'

'Not exactly. The Samaritans came first, I believe, but the Friends is slightly different. Crosby started it long before he became an MP. It was a counselling service intended primarily for the student population, but the idea is that you call them long before you reach the suicide state. He must have got the idea when he was at university himself. From small beginnings it spread to other universities, and now it's targeted at specific professional groups, especially the ones with high suicide rates. Doctors, for example. The theory is that each client also becomes a counsellor, so you are accountable to each other, if you follow me.'

'You mean, they'd introduce a doctor who was having problems to someone similar who'd pulled through, so they could counsel each other?'

'I think that's it. If you are responsible for someone else's well-being you are, hopefully, less likely to top yourself. I bet they had some really miserable phone calls, but we all enjoy a good moan, don't we? Anyway, he got an MBE for it, so somebody thinks it works. After resigning from Parliament he threw himself into it, but I don't know if he still runs the show; he must be nearly seventy now.'

'Where does he come from?'

'He's not English. Well, nationalised, not born here. Poland, Hungary or somewhere. I think he probably fled here with his parents during the war. When are you seeing him?'

I looked at my watch. 'Twelve o'clock. I've stung him for lunch.'

He was dressed differently but I easily recognised him. The

politician's suit was replaced by fawn slacks and a crumpled linen jacket, and he wore a straw Panama hat. The face was long and aristocratic, as I remembered it, with a nose designed for looking down or sniffing claret. Our Man in Heckley. I rose as he glanced around the pub garden, and he lifted a hand in recognition and threaded his way between the plastic furniture.

'This is pleasant,' I said as he seated himself next to me. The garden led down to the canal, and several narrow-boats were moored nearby. I fetched two pints of bitter while he composed his speech.

We sipped the froth off the tops of our glasses, and after licking his lips appreciatively he said: 'I'm very grateful for you seeing me, Mr Priest. I know you're a busy man.'

'We never close an unsolved case, Mr Crosby,' I replied.

'Right. I've been trying to decide where to start, not really knowing how much you already know . . .'

'First of all,' I said, 'how about telling me how you came to own a run-down house in Chapeltown when you lived in your constituency, Heckley.' If it was a love nest we'd better have it out in the open, then I could go home and mow the lawn.

He nodded, eager to explain. 'I think it would be better for me to begin there,' he replied. I turned my chair slightly towards him because the sun was slanting into my left eye. A dappled shadow from the hat's brim fell across the top half of his face and he gazed comfortably at me through watery blue eyes. I decided to buy a hat just like it.

'The house originally belonged to a lady I knew as Aunt Flossie,' he told me. 'She fostered me when I came to Leeds as a young teenager. Adopted me, almost. We drifted apart as I began to find my feet, because she clung to the old ways – she was orthodox Jewish – while I threw myself into being everything English. She couldn't understand that, Mr Priest, but I loved it here. England was like a dream come true for me.'

'Where did you come from?' I asked.

'Germany. A town called Augsburg, in Bavaria.'

A mosquito landed on the rim of my glass and another was irritating my neck. Al fresco has its problems. I wafted them away and took a sip. 'Go on,' I invited.

'In 1975 she died and left me the house, as simple as that. I was the nearest thing to any family she had. We'd kept in touch, it wasn't a great surprise to me. I put the house up for sale but nobody was buying houses at the time, and a little later a woman came into my Saturday-morning surgery saying that she had to escape from her boyfriend. He beat her up regularly and she feared for the safety of her little girl.'

'Jasmine Turnbull,' I said.

He paused, mouth still open, then said: 'That's right, Mr Priest. Jasmine Turnbull.' He had a drink of his beer and I waited for him to continue. 'Now,' he said, 'it seems unbelievably naïve of me, but at the time it was a perfectly natural arrangement. I owned a spare house, fully furnished, and Mrs Turnbull, Jasmine's mother, needed somewhere to go, desperately. We agreed that she could live there for a couple of weeks, see if it was suitable, and start paying me a small rent when she was eligible for benefits. I was horrified when my agent told me how it would look if the papers got hold of it. Mind you,' he said, with the first hint of a smile since he arrived, 'she was a beautiful girl. I think I might have been rather flattered by the accusations. To cut the story short, I had a word with Social Services and they moved another couple of battered wives in. That got me out of the frying pan, but . . .' He stopped, realising that his choice of phrase wasn't appropriate, and started again. 'Because the place was now regarded as multiple occupancy, we were in breach of the fire regulations. We were arguing about who was responsible – frankly, who paid – when . . . when . . .' He reached for his glass and turned it in his fingers. '. . . when thirty-two Leopold Avenue burnt down,' he said, very quietly, 'and eight lives were lost.'

A waitress hovered nearby and when he finished speaking she asked if we'd like to see a menu. I shook my head and she went away. 'And you had to resign as an MP,' I said.

He nodded.

'And now you have some new evidence?'

He gave a little start, as if just waking, and said: 'New evidence? Oh, I'm not sure.'

'So what is it you want to tell me?'

He took a handkerchief from a pocket and wiped his brow and neck with it. The forecasters had predicted the hottest day of the year and it was looking as if they were right. Three elderly women with pink arms protruding from flowery dresses stood debating where to sit and eventually arranged themselves around the next table. They looked like sisters.

'What do you know about John Joseph Fox?' Crosby asked.

Now it was my turn to be surprised. J. J. Fox was one of the top six entrepreneurs in the country, fighting it out with the others to be the next Murdoch or Rowland, but with half the population expecting him to be another Maxwell. He was a Flash Harry with the Midas touch, famous in the past for his golden Rolls Royces and platinum women, but nowadays courted by politicians of all persuasions because of his media interests. I shrugged my shoulders. 'Just what I read in the papers,' I said. 'What's he got to do with it?'

'Do you know how he started in business?'

'Mmm. He claims to have begun with a barrow in the East End, doesn't he?'

'As you say, that's what he claims. There may be a kernel of truth in it. His real beginning was when he won a boxer in a poker game.'

'A boxer?' I queried.

'A boxer, Mr Priest. A heavyweight with a glass chin. That didn't matter; you just backed the other fellow. He moved with a violent crowd in London in the late forties, early fifties. He expanded rapidly, from second-hand cars sold from bomb sites to bingo and discothèques when the cinemas began to close. J. J. Fox became an expert at turning one man's failure into his success. It's a lesson he has exploited to the full over the years.' He paused for a drink. The old ladies were leaning forward, studying menus, their heads bobbing about like cauliflowers in a cauldron. Crosby carefully placed his glass on the table and continued. 'Unfortunately, as he expanded he attracted attention from the gangs that were becoming a feature of life in south London at the time. He wasn't really a criminal, just a struggling businessman who had to be flexible with the rules. Ultimately he wanted to be part of the Establishment, not fighting it. So he assessed the situation and decided to move north, lock, stock and barrel. Manchester, Liverpool and Leeds were sitting ducks for someone with his talents.'

'He created the Reynard Organisation, didn't he?' I asked, trying to show off the little I knew about the man.

'That's right. He moved into the high streets, with a chain of boutiques; pop groups; music outlets; fast food. He had his finger on the pulse of the times and kept one step ahead of the trends. Now, as you know, he's big league. It's the FT100 and public utilities now, plus the two newspapers, if you can call them that, the football club and controlling shares in a television station. The Reynard bandwagon is unstoppable, and J. J. Fox runs it single-handed from a deck chair on a yacht somewhere in the Caribbean.'

'He built the big new hotel in Leeds,' I said.

'The Fox Borealis,' Crosby stated. 'And the office block across the river from it. Leeds is the fastest-growing financial centre outside London, Mr Priest, and Fox has a slice of the action.'

I knew it was, I'd read it in the papers often enough, but I didn't know what it meant. 'So where is this leading us?' I asked.

Crosby deflated with an audible sigh, drumming his fingers on the table as he gathered his thoughts. 'He hasn't changed,' he began. 'He still exploits other people's bad luck, but he manipulates their luck for them.'

I thought I was beginning to see where he was leading me. 'You mean insider dealing?' I asked.

He shook his head. 'No, it's much more than that.' He leaned forward, closer to me, and began to speak rapidly in a low voice. 'Two years ago, Mr Priest, there was a crash on the Northern and Borders Railway. One person was killed and it was put down to a signalling fault caused by vandalism. A month later two trainloads of commuters had narrow escapes when one train cut across the other. The passengers were hurled to the floor as their train braked and some of them saw the other train go by. Five seconds earlier and it could have been the worst disaster in British railway history. Again it was blamed on vandalism and hundreds of passengers vowed they would never travel by N and B again. Share prices plunged from over five hundred pence, Mr Priest, to below four hundred. Guess who stepped in to rescue the business? That's right, J. J. Fox. They now stand at five-eighty pence. Not bad, eh? Seven years ago they were giving away shares in the Alpha Brig oilfield after borehole samples were analysed and the predictions made the whole thing look like a white elephant. J. J. Fox bought up every available share and blow me if it didn't turn out to be a software fault and the samples were promising after all. Everybody agrees that the water companies have a licence to print money, but last year was the driest on record and things looked dodgy for a while. When a technician put a decimal point in the wrong place and tipped a hundred times too much concentrated aluminium sulphate into the Tipley Valley supply, five thousand people were made ill. Tipley Water shares plummeted but this year they are predicting a record dividend. Guess who suddenly became a major shareholder? I could go on and on and on, Mr Priest.' He sat back and waited for a reaction.

I wasn't happy. The midges were bothering me, my beer was warm and I didn't like his story. I had no doubts that Fox was a crook, but so what? Everybody in his position must have done something mean and nasty as they fought their way up the heap. Nice people didn't make it because they couldn't do it. Well, that was my excuse. 'So what's all this to do with the fire?' I asked.

'I'm sorry,' he said, leaning forward. 'I get carried away. It's all been bottled up inside me for so long. Back in 1975 Fox was just making his mark nationally. He'd been involved in several contracts with a certain company of planners working on town centre developments. I'd been looking into his activities for a number of years, when I was in local government, and didn't like what I was seeing. I asked questions in the House about him, and wanted him to appear before a select committee to explain his apparent good fortune. Proving what I knew was difficult, as I'm sure you appreciate, and I couldn't voice my allegations outside the House, but I wanted his replies on record. The fire, like so many events, came at a very opportune moment for Mr Fox.'

I wished that we had the power of parliamentary privilege to shelter behind, and said: 'You're saying he started the fire to discredit you?'

'Not personally, Mr Priest. He didn't start the fire personally. He has a network of recruits to do his dirty work for him, but he gave the orders. It's the only explanation. The technician with Tipley Water is currently on a Reynard management training scheme. The computer programmer with Alpha Brig escaped the sack and moved to a systems analyst post in the Reynard Organisation, until he died in an accident. Fox looks after his friends, one way or another.'

'Can you put all this in writing for me?' I asked. It's a simple enough theory. Someone pops in and gives you a lifetime's work, so you bounce it straight back at them by suggesting they put it all in writing. Often, you never hear from them again.

'It's all here,' he said, delving into his inside pocket and producing a bundle of papers and envelopes.

Ah well, I thought, it was never much of a theory. I pointed at his empty glass. 'Same again?'

'Oh, er, yes please.'

I meandered to the bar and ordered a pint of orange juice for myself. I'd tell him I'd ask around, do what I could, but I'd only be stalling him. Fox might be as guilty as hell, we might even prove it, but we'd never get near a conviction. His lawyers would tie us in knots, spin things out for years, cost the taxpayer a fortune and we'd be accused of wasting public money by pursuing a man who gave employment to thousands. He would be left whiter than white. Perhaps, they'd concede, some of his staff were over enthusiastic in their desire to see Reynard do well, but that was the unfortunate reverse side of loyalty . . . We were on a hiding to sod-all.

I placed his beer in front of him and sat down. The three ladies were poring over the menus again, their empty dinner plates in a considerate pile for the waitress to collect. The fence around the garden was lined with tubs of blooms, blazing with colour. Fat bees stumbled between them, overladen with pollen. 'The flowers are gorgeous,' I said, nodding in their direction.

'Geraniums,' he told me, although I was already fairly sure of it. 'They bring back memories for me.' He looked unhappy, his thoughts filled with oomphah bands and lederhosen, and thanked me absent-mindedly for the beer. After a silence he said: 'Did you see the television programme a few years ago about Fox's early life?'

'No.'

'It was a harrowing account, Mr Priest, even after making allowances for it being a Reynard production. It told of how the storm troopers came to arrest his parents a few days after the Kristallnacht, the Night of the Broken Glass. His name then was Johannes Josef Fuchs, he said, and his father was an outspoken lawyer, hated by the Nazis, and a Jew, of course. Young J. J. was bundled out of the back of the house with as much money as they had, plus a few items of jewellery, and told to find his way to France and then England. He was twelve years old. He caught a train that he hoped would take him to Strasburg, but a party of Hitler Youth boarded it at the next station and began to torment him. Eventually they beat him up, stole everything he possessed and threw him off the train. He walked the one hundred and fifty kilometres to the border, being looked after by several people on the way, farmers mainly, some gypsies, and eventually made it into France and then on to Britain. When he was settled here he Anglicized his name and became the John Joseph Fox we all know so well.'

I wasn't sure what the point of the story was. I'd been expecting a last attempt to win my sympathy, but this justified some aspects of Fox's character. 'In a way,' I said, 'it explains why Fox has turned out the way he has: determined to succeed; single-minded; responsible to no one. Experiences like that must be ingrained in your character for the rest of your life.' I had a good long drink of my orange juice. After the warm beer it tasted good. 'Tell me,' I went on. 'Why have you suddenly resurrected all this, after twenty-three years? What's happened to bring it all back again? What do we know now that we didn't know before?' I had a feeling he was using me, and that's a feeling I don't like.

'This came last Tuesday,' he said, extracting a crumpled envelope from the sheaf of papers. 'I made you a photocopy.'

I took the page he offered me and read it. There was a Welwyn Garden City address at the top and it went on:

Dear Mr Crosby

It is my sad duty to inform you that my older brother, Duncan Roberts, committed suicide four weeks ago. We found your address and telephone number among his papers and assume he had been in contact with the Friend's in Need society. May I take this opportunity to thank you for any help you may have offered Duncan, but unfortunately there was nothing anyone could do for him. Please accept this small cheque as a donation to help you in your good work.

Yours sincerely,

Andrew Roberts.

It was brief and to the point. Somebody was clearing up, doing their housework, after an untimely death in the family. You can excuse a surplus apostrophe in a situation like that.

'There was a cheque for twenty pounds with it,' Crosby informed me.

'So who was Duncan Roberts?' I asked, laying the photocopy on the table. I was growing tired of riddles.

'Four weeks earlier,' he explained, 'I was on holiday in Ireland. When I returned the Friends informed me that a man had been trying to contact me. He phoned three times, sounding desperate, but would not talk to anyone else. The calls were traced to a phone box in south London. In the third and final call he said: "Tell him I did it. I started the fire, and I'm sorry." Then he hung up and there were no more calls. A few weeks later this letter arrives. It must be the same person, Mr Priest. Duncan Roberts started the fire and it's been troubling his conscience all these years. I feel sure that it will be possible to link him to J. J. Fox.'

He certainly knew how to string me along, and he hadn't finished yet. My thoughts were a jumble of confusion. I wanted to help him, but what good could it do? Fox was an old man. We could hound him to his grave, but would we feel any better for it? Sometimes hatred keeps you going. Remove the object of the hatred and you've nothing left. Crosby had spent a lifetime pursuing J. J. Fox, for what? Because he bent the rules? Because, perhaps, some unknown people had died? It wasn't worth eating your heart and soul out for. Not even that.

Crosby read my mind and went for the jugular. He said: 'I adopted the name Keith Crosby when I came to this country, Mr Priest. Keith was an English pilot I met when I was hiding in France. Crosby was borrowed from Bing Crosby. I thought the name had a nice ring to it. My real name, the one I used for the first twelve years of my life, was Johannes Josef Fuchs. I was that small boy on the train, attacked by the Hitler Youth. 1940 was the worst winter in living memory. I should have died, they expected me to die, but I didn't. I don't know what happened to my parents. I went into Parliament to fight people like J. J. Fox, Mr Priest. Fox, whoever he was then, stole my clothes, my papers and my money, but most of all, Mr Priest, he stole my identity.

Will you help me get it back, please?'

I watched his eyes blinking back the tears, unable to comprehend what they had seen when they were in the head of a child. All we can do is try. His beer was untouched and a ladybird was mounting an unsupported expedition across the tabletop. 'What else have you there?' I asked, reaching for the bundle of papers.

Chapter 4

I walked across the car park with him to his battered Volvo – made in Sweden, the Land of Eternal Sidelights – and agreed to read his notes and have a think about what he'd told me. He shook my hand as if I'd promised to buy the vehicle from him and I said I'd be in touch.

I didn't mow the lawn. Closer inspection showed it would last another week, and it's not good to cut grass during a dry spell. Well, that's what my father taught me. I opened a can of lager, spread myself out on the garden seat and listened to the world turning on its axis.

I don't see much of Jacquie at weekends. She stays in on Saturday nights, doing her books, her hair and everything else that beautiful ladies do that we men know nothing about. Sundays, when possible, I like to go walking. Once, I'd suggested she come with me and you'd have thought I'd asked her to pose naked for the *Police Review*. 'Walking?' she'd queried. 'You mean . . . up hills? For fun?'

So I went on my own. This particular Sunday dawned blue-skied and filled with promise, and I watched a golden sunrise through my rearview mirrors as I headed towards the Lake District. I beat the crowds and found a parking place in the little park just outside Braithwaite. The Coledale Round is a tough walk and you're straight into it. You put the car keys in a safe pocket, hitch up your shorts, step over the stile and start climbing. The path stretches straight and true before you, to the summit of Grisedale Pike two miles away and 2,000 feet higher.

It's good thinking time. You stare down at the path six feet ahead of your boots and let your mind wander. Anything will do, as long as it takes it off the burning sensation in your chest and the wobbles in your legs. After twenty minutes I stopped and turned around to see how far I'd come. The village was like Toytown down below and beyond it the classically proportioned Skiddaw was bathed in sunlight. I took a few deep breaths, eased the straps on my shoulders and told my feet to get moving.

The whole Round was a bit too much for me on such a hot day. One of the pieces of knowledge that comes with the passing of the years is when to say: 'Enough!' I ate my sandwiches on a flat rock under Hopegill Head, sunbathed for an hour then dropped into the valley and followed the miners' road back to the car. It was a good day out. I didn't come to any conclusions about Crosby and Fox, but my legs were definitely a shade browner. Perhaps I'd go to work in my shorts tomorrow.

In the cold light of a Heckley Monday it didn't seem such a good idea, so it was back to the grown-up trousers. We'd had a fracas in the town centre after evensong, so all the cells were filled with rebellious D and Ds demanding their rights prior to appearing before the beak. It's the communion wine that does it. Nothing to do with CID, thank goodness, except that it had taken a big chunk out of the overtime budget. Maggie and Nigel went to circulate the list of property stolen from the McLellands while Jeff and Sparky went to talk to the travel agency managers and collect the names of any customers who'd been booking holidays when the raids took place. I spread the papers Keith Crosby had given me across my desk and started to read.

Everything was on a diskette, but he'd told me he used AppleMac, while I was strictly Microsoft. It didn't matter, as he'd provided hard copies of the important stuff and there wasn't much of it. Nigel was an AppleMac man, so I'd ask him to run off the full story. The main item was a list of about fifty companies that had fallen on difficult times and crashed in value. Fox had stepped in and bought low, which ain't a crime, and soon afterwards, miraculously, they all appeared to be doing quite nicely. Crosby had listed them in date order, with share price or company value fluctuations over the relevant period and number of shares bought by Fox. Other information was patchy. Against some he'd typed details of the troubles they'd been beset by, and occasionally there was a name. The first on the list was a small chain of betting shops that had suffered a couple of fires and a disastrous loss on the 1970 Grand National when the telephone lines went dead and they couldn't lay off some large bets. Gay Trip had cost them a fortune. Last on it was the Tipley Valley Water Company. It made interesting reading, very interesting, but I couldn't put it much stronger than that. Accidents happen, and anybody could have bought shares in the companies, though when Fox did it was usually enough to take control. I made a few notes, read the letter from Andrew Roberts again and extracted my road atlas from the bottom drawer. It was eight years old; I really ought to bring a new one in. Welwyn Garden City is nearer to London than I thought. I looked in my diary for a number and wrote it on my pad. Directory Enquiries gave me Andrew Roberts's, no problem. Just for the hell of it I did a person check on him and discovered he'd never come to our attention. There must be millions out there like that. I opened my diary at the week ahead and rang Gilbert on the internal.

'Are you likely to need me tomorrow?' I asked him.

'Umm, no, I don't think so,' he replied. 'Anything special?'

'I want to nip down to see Commander Fearnside.'

'Your friend at N-CIS?'

'Mmm.'

'Not going to accept that job he keeps offering you, I hope.'

'That's the nicest thing you've ever said to me, Gilbert. How could I possibly leave after that? No, I've a load of stuff I want to talk to him about. It might be something big, but it's more likely to be a waste of time. He sees the big picture, though. He'll give it a fair hearing.'

'OK. I'll be in most of the week. Arrange it to suit yourself and let me know what he says about it.'

'Cheers, boss.' I clicked the cradle and dialled again.

'Charlie!' Fearnside boomed after I'd manipulated my way past several flunkies. 'Long time no see. How are you, old boy?'

'Fine, Mr Fearnside. And you?'

'Counting the days, Charlie. Counting the days.'

'Aren't we all. I want an hour of your time, if you don't mind, soon as possible, about a long-running saga that's not going to go away. It's too big for me to handle without some authority from on high, but its source is an ex-MP, so I've got to take it seriously.'

'Right, Charlie. The wife's got tickets for the ballet tonight, but I could always tell her that something's . . .'

'Er, not that soon,' I interrupted. 'How about tomorrow?'

He sounded disappointed, but agreed to meet me at the Happy Burger on the M25, near Waltham Cross. He has a thing about their pancakes and likes to escape from the office whenever possible. Clandestine meetings at motorway services made him feel important, but we'd worked on a couple of big jobs together and I trusted him to know if Crosby was being paranoid or if there really was a case. I placed the phone back and wandered into the open-plan, feeling suddenly restless. The wheels were in motion. There was nobody to talk to, so I filled the kettle and switched it on. Somebody's tabloid was lying there. I looked at the ladies' bosoms, the front page and the sport, in that order. Rebecca, on page three, was studying law. A barrister's wig was perched on her head, improving her posture wonderfully, and the caption read: *All stand for the judge.* She was beautiful, as they always are. Humiliating the plain ones isn't any fun. Silly girl, I thought. Thumbing through the rest I came across the horoscopes and scanned the dates. July 23 to August 23, that was me. Leo, would you believe it. It said that I was drifting aimlessly, and ought to try harder to create an impression. I knew I should have come in my shorts.

'How much is on it?' Nigel asked much later after he'd listened to the story, turning the diskette in his fingers as if he'd never seen one before.

'Not sure,' I replied. 'Just do one copy to start with, please, for me to give to Fearnside. Then, if there's not too much of it, do another couple. Put something on your FIN33 to cover it.'

Sparky was sitting on the edge of my desk, perusing the list Crosby had given me. 'Bloody hell,' he concluded, offering it back to me.

'Is that your considered opinion?' I asked.

'I knew there was more to that fire than everybody thought,' he replied.

'Are you sure he's not a nutter?' Nigel asked. 'When we lived in Virginia Water we had a neighbour who claimed to be the last descendant of Walter Raleigh. Spent the family fortune trying to prove it and finished up in a mental hospital.'

'No, I'm not sure at all,' I replied.

'You mean . . .' Sparky began, '. . . there really is a place called Virginia Water?'

'Of course there is,' I told him. 'And very nice, too. It's close to Blackbush airport.'

'Blackbush airport,' Nigel echoed. 'How do you know about Blackbush airport?'

'I saw Dylan there in '79. Me and quarter of a million others.'

'You were there!' he exclaimed. 'With all the hippies! We couldn't get out of the avenue for two days.'

'Cultural event of the century,' I declared. 'Now here's what we do. We keep this under our hats. We three and Mr Wood are the only ones to know about it. Nigel, you and Jeff will have to run the everyday show, while I work on this when I can. I'll borrow Dave when I need another pair of eyes and ears. OK?'

'No problem, boss.'

'If anything goes off I want to be there,' Dave insisted, his tone as hard as millstone grit.

'I know you do, old son,' I assured him. 'And you will be.'

Tuesday morning someone hijacked the postman's van and ram-raided the Sylvan Fields newsagent with it. They escaped with four boxes of cheese and onion crisps and ten copies of the *Guardian*. We're looking for a liberal with a savoury tooth. I escaped by a nifty piece of delegation and headed south on the M1.

A lorry with a puncture in the middle of the roadworks near Northampton ate up the extra hour I'd allowed, so I arrived at the Happy Burger just about dead on time. Fearnside was sitting in his big Rover. He got out as I parked and we walked into the café together, without ceremony.

'It's good to see you, Charlie,' he said when we were seated in the smoking section, where it was quieter.

'And you, Mr Fearnside,' I replied. 'I just hope I'm not wasting your time.'

'Well, first of all, let's cut out this Mr Fearnside nonsense, eh? It's Roland. And secondly, you got me out of an accountability meeting, so you're definitely not wasting my time. So what's it all about, eh?'

They did pancakes with cherries, maple syrup or caramel sauce, and Fearnside ordered one of each. The little girl who took the order looked flustered. She might be an ace at French irregular verbs, but this hadn't been in her crash course on waitressing. 'You mean, all on one plate?' she improvised.

'Yes please,' Fearnside told her, beaming. I ordered a cheeseburger.

When she'd gone I said: 'In July 1975 we had an MP called Keith Crosby in Heckley. You may remember him.' Fearnside gave a hesitant nod. 'He fell from grace when an old terraced house he'd been bequeathed by an aunt burned down and eight people – women and children – were burned to death. He'd allowed the house to be used as a shelter for battered women and it was breaking the fire regulations. He resigned as an MP shortly afterwards.'

Our waitress was hovering. I stopped speaking and looked up at her. 'We don't do three pancakes together,' she told Fearnside, 'but you could have them on separate plates, if that's all right?'

'That will be fine, my dear,' he replied with a warm smile. He was growing benevolent in his old age. I decided he must be nearer to retiring than I'd thought. 'Go on, Charlie,' he prompted as she turned to leave.

'Keith Crosby is convinced that J. J. Fox was behind the fire, to deliberately discredit him. Apparently he'd been investigating Fox's background and business methods. Asking questions in the House.'

'J. J. Fox!' Fearnside mouthed, almost silently. '*The* J. J. Fox?'

'Of the Reynard Organisation,' I confirmed.

'Pardon me asking this, Charlie, but does he have any . . . you know . . . *evidence*?'

I pushed a manila envelope across the table. 'I'd hardly call it evidence, but it's all in there.'

'Bloody hell, Charlie,' he said. 'When I was with the SFO we had a file on Fox thicker than prep school porridge, but we never pinned anything on him. Not that that meant a lot; we had files on nearly everyone who earned more than the commissioner did.' He patted the envelope. 'I'll have to talk to a few people. You realise that, don't you?'

What he meant was that Fox would have friends in the force, and they might have fraternal contacts in Yorkshire. 'No problem,' I said.

The girl brought the food and Fearnside slid his pancakes, each complete with a blob of vanilla ice cream, on to one plate. 'There you go, my dear,' he said, handing her the two redundant plates. I cut my cheeseburger in half and wished I'd ordered it with fries.

We ate in silence and I continued the story over coffee. Fearnside dabbed his chin with his napkin and nodded at my words. At the far end of the restaurant a couple and their two children were eating. The older child, a teenage boy, was brain-damaged. He kept jerking his head around and waving his arms. His father fed him spoonfuls of food and wiped his mouth. Both of them were smiling, as if it were a game they played. I half-remembered a line from a poem; G. K. Chesterton, I believe: *To love is to love the unlovable, or it is no virtue at all,* and for a moment or two everything I was trying to do seemed second rate.

'Hell's teeth, Charlie,' Fearnside said. 'If you can land

something on Fox the SFO'll put your statue up in Elm Street.'

'So you think it's worth pursuing?'

'From what you've told me, most certainly, old boy.'

'Good. I'm just glad I haven't wasted your time.'

'Not at all. Not at all.'

I decided to have a little celebration and have cream in my coffee. As I fumbled with a plastic thimble of what passed for it I said: 'So how long have you got to go, then, Roland?' His reply took the wind out of my spinnaker.

'Um, allowing for leave, I'll be away a week on Friday.'

And then I'd be on my own, I thought.

I hadn't known what to expect of Welwyn Garden City, so it came as a pleasant surprise. I'd telephoned the Robertses after arranging to meet Fearnside, and Mrs Roberts had told me that her husband, Andrew, would be in any night after five thirty. Two junctions on the M25 and four short ones up the A1 and I was there, an hour early. The approaches to the town – it's not a city, that's just its name – were along an avenue with wide close-cropped verges and wall-to-wall trees. I followed the intermittent town centre signs and found myself on a one-way system that routed me into the shopping area, where my initial enthusiasm gave way to dismay. The planners had done a good job, with some decent open spaces, and it's probably a pleasant enough place to live and work, but the architect only knew one type of brick and one shape of window. He was working to a tight schedule, so he designed one building and rubber-stamped the rest. Couldn't see any of the famous concrete cows anywhere. Or was that Milton Keynes? Come to think of it, was it Milton Keynes where I was supposed to be? I decided it didn't make much difference either way. I thought about exploring the town centre, but a drive through sufficed. I found the street where the

Robertses lived and parked up for an hour, listening to the radio.

It was an ornate semi with jutting eaves in what was more like an overgrown jungle than a leafy suburb. Someone had overlooked the simple fact that trees grow. Their front garden boasted a giant flowering cherry, long past its best, and a wishing well. A Bedford Rascal with *Andrew's Carpet Fitter's* painted on the side stood on the drive, behind a fairly recent Saab and an elderly Fiesta. I was at the home of the phantom apostrophe bandit. The garage door was open and a teenage boy with lank blond hair and acne was working on a Honda trail bike. There was a nasty blank space behind the engine, with two suspicious-looking bolts projecting into it.

'Problems?' I said, to introduce myself.

He spared me a worried glance and said: 'Yeah, it's eight-stroking on the overrun.'

'That sounds painful.'

'It's the carburettor.'

'Will you be able to fix it?'

'I hope so. Are you looking for Dad?'

'Yep.'

'He's round the back. DAD! Your visitor's here.'

Dad wore his hair in a ponytail and had a tattoo, nothing extravagant, on each arm. He was wearing cut-down jeans and a Guns 'n' Roses T-shirt. Definitely not what I'd expected.

'DI Charlie Priest,' I said, extending my hand, 'from Heckley CID.'

He gave me a limp shake. 'Andrew Roberts. Pleased to meet you. I'm just lighting the barbecue, round the back.' He turned and led the way, me following behind.

It had just reached the God-will-it-ever-burn stage, with smoke billowing over the lapboard fence into the neighbour's yard. The back garden was mainly lawn, with those little apple trees that only reach five feet tall growing along one side and a greenhouse down at the bottom. They had a pond with a naked cherub piddling into it, and an ultraviolet bug-killer was already glowing on the wall, like a neon sign outside a house of pleasure. This was a no-fly zone. He poked his head into the kitchen to tell his wife I was here and invited me to sit on a plastic chair.

'First of all,' I began, 'can I say how sorry I am about your brother.'

'Fancy a beer?' he asked. I opened my mouth to say how jolly welcome that would be but he cut me off with: 'Oh, you're on duty, aren't you? Never mind, I'll get Shaz to make a pot of tea. Duncan? Yeah, it were sad. To tell the troof I hadn't seen him for years. He was free years older than me, went his own way, like. You said on the phone that it was somefing that happened back in 1975.'

'That's right. There was a fire, in Leeds. A short while ago Duncan, or someone we now believe to be Duncan, rang the Friends in Need people to say he knew who started the fire.'

'I wrote to them,' he said, adding: 'Well, I got DJ to.'

'DJ?'

He pointed towards the garage and said: 'Duncan John.'

'Your son?'

'Yeah. He's a bright lad. We've always called him DJ.'

'It was your letter that put us on to Duncan. Your brother Duncan, that is. The person who rang was obviously distressed, suicidal.'

'Jesus,' he hissed.

'Did Duncan know Leeds, back then?'

'Yeah. He was at the university there.'

A minute piece of the jigsaw fell into place. 'Tell me about him,' I invited. 'What was he like, before he went to Leeds?'

He fingered his left ear and I noticed the ring through it. 'He was my big bruvver,' he said. 'I looked up to him. Troof is, I worshipped him. At least I did until he went to Leeds. After that there was a lot of pressure on me from Mam and Dad to follow him, but I just wasn't bright enough. Before that, though, we got on well. All he was interested in was bikes. Push bikes, that is. He raced them, on the road, on the track, and he'd take me wiv him. He was good, and we had some fun. Then things went pear-shaped, and suddenly they didn't want me to follow him. They were quite happy for number two son to settle for an apprenticeship.'

'Pear-shaped? In what way?'

'He fell in wiv the wrong crowd. He did well his first year, kept up wiv his training and his studies, but then he started drinking a lot and got into debt. He bought a Claud Butler, he said, but I didn't believe him. We dreamt about Claud Butlers in them days. He used to write to me, all about the parties and how they'd drunk the pub dry. It sounded great at the time, but afterwards I realised that he was sliding. He kept sending home for money, first from Dad, then Mam, and then from me. He dropped out halfway through his second year, and we hardly saw or heard from him again after that.'

'You say he went to Leeds University?'

'Yeah.'

'To read what?'

'Chemistry.'

'Did you save his letters?'

He shook his head. 'No, sorry.'

'Did he mention any names in them?'

Another head-shake.

'Did he mention Keith Crosby?'

'The Friends in Need man? No.'

'Any girlfriends?'

'No.' He hesitated, then added: 'Come to fink of it, he did mention one, once.'

'Can you remember her name?'

'He didn't say. He just said he was going out wiv this bird but he didn't fink he'd ever dare bring her home. He raved on about her. Said she had purple hair and a ring frew her nose. In them days that was way out. From anuvver planet. I'd never even seen anyone like that back then. Not for real. I didn't believe him and he said he'd send me a picture, but he never did.'

'That's a shame,' I said.

It was a sad story, and it's a hundred times more common since drugs other than alcohol became freely available. After Leeds Duncan had moved to Manchester, vanished for ten years and resurfaced in Brixton, living in bed-and-breakfast accommodation. They'd last met at their mother's funeral. Andrew had tried to help him and lots of promises were made, but it hadn't worked out. The barbecue was glowing brightly and I could sense Andrew's impatience to be up there flourishing the giant pepper grinder. He didn't invite me to share a steak so I thanked him for his help and left. I never got that cup of tea and didn't find out who Shaz was. As I walked past the Rascal I resisted the urge to whip out my pen and draw a line through the offending apostrophe. 'How many effs in apostrophe?' 'There is no effin' apostrophe.' 'Boom-boom, thank you and good night.'

'Where is everybody?' I asked, surveying the empty desks and noting the absence of jackets, daily papers and items of food required to see a team of the force's finest through their strife-torn day. Job on, I was told. The chief suspect for the ram-raid had just had an early-morning call and at that very moment was standing in his summer-weight jimjams, explaining that he'd always been a *Guardian* reader; he bought it for the dog-racing tips.

I had my usual meeting with Mr Wood and started committing yesterday's story to print. I'd just reached the bit where the waitress at the Happy Burger kissed me goodbye and hoped I'd come again when the outer door burst open and the troops came laughing and jostling into the office. There was a knock on my door and Nigel entered, followed by Dave. I clicked *Save* and rocked my chair back on two legs. 'Success?' I asked.

'Yep,' Nigel said, with a self-satisfied grin.

'Go on.'

'Definitely a criminal type. Found a *Guardian* under a cushion on the settee.'

'Bang to rights,' I said.

'Oh, and about an ounce of what looks like herbal cannabis.'

'It gets better.' Herbal cannabis was suddenly turning up all over the place. I turned to Dave. 'Did he, er, behave himself?' I asked, nodding at Nigel. He has a reputation for impetuosity.

'He was OK,' Sparky replied.

'Only OK?'

'Well, I wasn't going to mention it . . .'

'Mention what?'

'Don't encourage him,' Nigel interrupted. 'He'll mention it, whatever it is. Believe me, he'll mention it. Nothing will stop him.'

'I don't know if I ought to . . .' Dave continued, feigning awkwardness.

'Now you've *got* to tell me,' I replied, my hands in an appealing gesture that I'd seen so many times in court.

'Well . . .' he went on, 'we brayed on the front door, like we do, and this little old lady opened it . . .'

'Mmm.'

'And . . . well . . . it's just that . . . to be honest . . . I thought *Freeze, motherfucker!* was a bit over the top.'

'I never!' Nigel exclaimed. 'Oh, forget it!'

'Little old ladies can be dangerous, David,' I warned him. 'Especially if they're carrying a handbag. Sometimes they have a jar of Pond's cold cream tucked in the bottom corner. Get sandbagged by one of those and it's like being hit by a flat-nosed .45. Anyway, it looks like you've saved us from a red face, so well done the boys.'

'What about you?' Dave asked.

I flicked the monitor with the back of my knuckles. 'Just putting it all down,' I replied.

'J. J. Fox had a mention on the YTV news last night,' Nigel said.

'What's he done?' I asked.

'Apparently that big new office block he's built near the river in Leeds is going to house Reynard Insurance, which will mean about a thousand extra jobs for the region. They're expecting him to come personally to cut the ribbon when it opens.'

'Really? Did they say when?'

''Fraid not, but they said he'll no doubt stay at the Fox Borealis, where the penthouse suite is permanently earmarked for him.'

'With a pad on the roof for his helicopter,' Dave added.

'How frightfully non-U,' I said. 'It sounds as if Leeds has adopted a new son. Maybe we'll get a chance to have an audience with him when he comes, so let's do our homework.'

The multiscreen was reshowing *Seven*, and I fancied watching it again, but Jacquie wanted to see the one about three girls from small-town America who vowed to stay friends whatever life threw at them, so that's what I bought tickets for. The willowy blonde married a millionaire, the husband of the perky brunette beat her up and the redhead caught cancer. I used the time to muse on Crosby's story, wonder where I fitted in life's big picture and reflect on the nature of the universe immediately before the Big Bang. Some professor of radio astronomy had been on *PM* talking about waves – ripples in space – that he had detected. He said they were vibrations from the Big Bang, still travelling outwards fifteen billion years later. In which case, I thought, how come we arrived here first? Maybe I'd write to him and ask. Everybody was in tears as we left the cinema, so it must have all worked out in the end. I hadn't expected it to still be light outside, but it was. We strolled hand-in-hand through the town centre, which was nice, and had a pizza, which wasn't. Pizza isn't on my menu. If the Romans had taken the recipe for Yorkshire pudding back with them we'd never have heard of pizza. Jacquie invited me in for a coffee and introduced me to the kitten she'd acquired. I tickled its ears while we listened to Neil Diamond and Jacquie fell asleep with her head on my shoulder. I used to like Neil Diamond, years ago. Now, I feel like throwing up. I sat through 'Sweet Caroline', for old times' sake, and said I'd better go. We had a short but torrid necking session behind her front door and I left. Another day over.

Leeds became a university city early in the twentieth century. The colleges upon which it was built rose out of necessity, not from the beneficence of a monarch with aspirations beyond his intellect and a weather eye on his place in history. The textile industry required chemists and the mines and railways needed engineers. Then, as the north burgeoned with industrial growth, all the incidental needs of the population grew apace with it. Doctors and priests; bankers and businessmen; entrepreneurs and charlatans: they were swept in as if by a spring flood, dragged along on the coat tails of steam, iron, coal and wool. The Parkinson Tower is a Portland stone monolith that dominates the skyline to the north of the city and marks the epicentre of the rambling campus. I drove by it and looked for a parking place.

The University Registrar and Secretary was called Hugh Roper-Jones and he'd been at his desk when I rang him. Unfortunately he was about to attend a briefing of potential undergraduates, but he told me he had to be free before twelve for a lunch appointment. I said it wouldn't take long and I'd be waiting outside his door.

I walked down the road past the departments of Civil Engineering, Mechanical Engineering and Electronics and Electrical Engineering and there it was – Chemistry. Duncan Roberts had been studying chemistry. I ran up the steps and through the wood and glass doors. Inside was a lobby but no reception desk. I scanned the notice-boards that lined the walls and decided that students hadn't changed much since my day. They still needed cheap accommodation and sold bicycles and went to concerts and piss-ups. A series of glossy posters advertised the department and listed some of its achievements. It reminded me that this was where they invented DFO. We use it to develop latent fingerprints, and I felt I was among friends. The next door led into a corridor with a lecture theatre facing me. A sign on the wall indicated that SOMS was on the fourth floor and LHASAUK on the second. Now I was way out of my depth. One thing I did know was that Roper-Jones's office was not in this block, so I left.

He was in the E. C. Stoner Building, and waiting for me. I told him about the phone call from Duncan and suggested that he'd possibly witnessed someone starting a fire, back in 1975, in which there had been a fatality. Perhaps, I was wondering, he had confided in a fellow student. If Mr Roper-Jones could furnish me with the names and last-known addresses of Duncan's classmates I could be on my way and leave him to lunch in peace.

'Ah!' he said ominously, fingering a cuff.

'Don't tell me,' I said.

'I'm afraid, Inspector, that our computerised records only go back as far as 1980.'

'Damn!'

'Before that, they are all on cards.'

'But you have them?'

'Oh yes. We can go right back to 1905, and before, for some departments.'

The door behind me opened and a female voice said: 'Oh, sorry!' I turned round and saw an elegant woman in a blue dress with white stripes, holding the door wide.

'Five minutes, Emm, please,' Roper-Jones told her and she left.

'If somebody could show us the cards I could supply a body to go through them,' I suggested.

'I think we'll be able to do better than that for you, Inspector,' he replied. 'Let me show you the students' office.'

He led me along the corridor to where it widened to make a waiting area, with a row of tellers' windows in the wall, like a bank. We went through a door into the large office behind the windows. It was cluttered with boxes and files and desks and terminals. They were running out of space. Would computerisation save them before they achieved meltdown and had to move to bigger premises? It was unlikely; there is no single recorded case in history of computerisation ever saving paper.

'Jeremy,' Roper-Jones said to a fresh-faced young man wearing wire-rimmed spectacles, 'this is Inspector Priest from the CID. He wants some information from the files. Would you give him all the help you can, please.' Turning to me he went on: 'Sorry to have to dash, Inspector, and it's been a pleasure to meet you. Jeremy's our archive expert; if the information is there he'll find it for you. And if we can be of further assistance, feel free to call us any time. As you'll have noticed, things are rather quiet at the moment. During term we haven't time to breathe. I'd be rather interested to know if you solve the case, Inspector. It's all grist for the mill, as they say.'

Or common room gossip, I thought. 'I'll keep you informed,' I promised, 'and I'm grateful for your co-operation.' We shook hands and he fled. He'd have something to tell Emm – Emma? Emily? – over lunch.

Jeremy had turned a chair around for me. 'Are you allowed to go for your lunch while the boss is out?' I asked.

'No problem, Inspector,' he replied with a grin.

'It's Charlie. Charlie Priest. C'mon then; let's have a quick look at these files and then I'll treat you.'

After I dropped Jeremy off I went for a drive round the city. The one-way system had changed but I just went with the flow for a while then followed the signs for the Royal Armouries. I knew the Fox Borealis was nearby, backing on to the River Aire. What I didn't realise was just how big it was; fifteen storeys, I counted, which must have made it the tallest building in Leeds. And directly across the river was the matching office block. The pair of them made an impressive gateway to the town for anyone coming up the river. They were almost all glass, which reflected the colour of the sky and made them look less intrusive. For once, the architects had got it right.

The hotel was open, doing business, but the finishing touches were still being added. A Coles crane was parked across the entrance, lifting a huge gilt fox, the company's emblem, on to the roof of the portico. I decided to pop in for afternoon tea and a workman in a hard hat directed me around the danger zone.

Inside was about par for the course: lots of pale wood, potted palms and low furniture; four businessmen in their shirt sleeves holding a conference around a paper-strewn coffee table; a lone woman tapping the day's sales into a laptop; and the Four Seasons playing softly in the background. Vivaldi, that is, not the American group. I sank into a settee and looked for a waitress.

The Coles crane was leaving at the same time as I was. As I walked out of the building I saw it turn on to the road, its yellow strobe light flashing and three cars already queuing behind it, and hoped it wasn't heading south. I eased out of my parking place and noticed the fox over the entrance, with two workmen tightening the holding-down bolts. It was in full flight, tail stretched out behind, and glancing back over its shoulder.

'How appropriate,' I said under my breath. 'How jolly appropriate.'

Friday morning a fax arrived giving the names of half of Duncan's fellow course members, with parents' addresses. We'd reckoned that if mummy and daddy had been in their forties when their offspring left the nest to explore the groves of academe they'd probably be in their late sixties now. Assuming that sponsoring one or more children through university had left them impoverished, there was a good chance that they hadn't moved far.

Monday morning another fax came with the rest of the names, giving a total of sixty-nine for me to be going on with. Jeremy had added a note saying that it would take him the rest of the week to list the students in the years above and below Duncan, and a long time if I wanted everybody at the university. He was throwing himself into this. I did a quick calculation. If the university had doubled in size since 1975 he was talking about 11,000 names. If I did four a day, without time off, it would take me nearly eight years to trace and interview them all. I faxed him back, thanking him profusely for his assistance but saying I had enough to be going on with.

Jeff and Maggie made a map showing the route the burglars had taken as they milked the McLellands' credit cards for all they could. Only one purchase had been made – two and a half thousand for a Hewlett Packard computer system from the Power Store – but cash withdrawals from machines and travel agents took the total to nearly five grand. Jeff had drawn the routes taken after the previous robberies in different colours, and had highlighted the places where the time-gaps indicated that they had possibly returned to base with the transit and transferred to something faster and less noticeable. It gave us a good picture of the general vicinity they operated from.

'They're somewhere in the Golden Triangle,' Dave stated. That's his name for the area bounded by Halifax, Huddersfield and Heckley.

'It certainly looks like it,' I agreed.

'So they're our babies. What are we going to do about it?'

'Can I make a suggestion, Charlie?' Jeff said. I spread my fingers in a *be-my-guest* gesture. 'Well,' he continued, 'I've been studying my Transits and this aerial behind the driver is really unusual. In fact, I haven't seen another like it, and a Transit passes you on the M62 about every fifteen seconds. They must be the most popular vehicle ever built. If we go public, say on *Crimewatch*, someone's bound to recognise it.'

Dave jumped in with: 'If we do that, we alert the villains too.

The Transit is the only decent lead we have. Going public will lose it for us.'

I stroked my chin and thought about it. 'I'll have a word with our friends,' I told them, when I'd made my decision. 'You might be right, Jeff, but for the moment I'd like to keep this knowledge within the team. If someone does finger the van for us we'll still need evidence to put them on the scene.'

Nigel had been quiet up to now. He broke his silence, saying: 'Has anyone else been receiving calls from double-glazing people?'

'Mmm, me,' I replied. 'What's that got to do with it?'

'I have, too,' Jeff added.

'I've had four calls in as many days,' Nigel told us. 'As I'm ex-directory I couldn't help wondering where they got my number from. I reckon someone has sold them a list of all our names and addresses and phone numbers. Maybe someone here, or maybe at the federation, or possibly the subscription list for the *Review*.'

'The point of your story being that we're as leaky as a wicker basket,' I suggested.

'Yep, and there's a good chance they already know what we have on them.'

You're both right, as always,' I agreed, 'but I'm using my golden vote to overrule you. We're supposed to be detectives, so let's find them our way.'

The phone rang, effectively rubber-stamping my decision. Fearnside didn't introduce himself, he just said: 'Can you be at the SFO at nine a.m. tomorrow?'

'Er, nine a.m.?' I queried, downcast.

'That's right.'

'Yes, I suppose so.'

'Good,' and he was gone.

I looked into the earpiece, as if expecting to see his face there before it receded back down the wires, and replaced the handset.

'Trouble?' Nigel asked.

Jeff didn't know anything about the Crosby case. I trusted him implicitly, but didn't want to go through the whole thing again. It always becomes awkward and embarrassing when you start keeping secrets from the team. 'Er, no,' I said. I'd have to set off about five o'clock and I was seeing Jacquie tonight. 'No trouble at all.'

The Serious Fraud Office is situated in NW1, which is about as accessible as Iquitos, Peru, to someone like me. I'd been before but couldn't remember the way, so I studied the map and jotted the route on a Post-it. Jacquie was content to go for a quick drink and afterwards didn't mind me dropping her off at the door. I half-heartedly suggested that she come down to London with me for the day, but she was seeing a buyer.

It was a dewy morning, the air as cool as that first sip of a well-earned pint. The blackbirds were singing and my pet blue tits were already scurrying between feeding ground and nest, their beaks stuffed with caterpillars and their feathers growing raggy with the non-stop effort. I brushed a spider's web off my face and wrecked the one adorning the wing mirror of my car, but not before the perpetrator had dashed for shelter behind the glass. 'I'll get you,' I murmured to it.

Early-morning driving can be fun, before twenty million bleary-eyed commuters stagger to their garages and swamp the roads. I did the first hundred miles in ninety minutes and at six twenty-five pressed the button on the radio, just in time to catch up with the sport and the news headlines.

Big deal. Manchester United had lost and there was a bomb

scare at Mount Pleasant sorting office, two streets away from the SFO. Traffic chaos was expected, and we were advised to travel in by public transport. I took the sissy's way out and abandoned the car at Cockfosters, not far from where I'd met Fearnside one week ago, and caught the tube.

'Ah!' said the receptionist, when I introduced myself to her at precisely eight fifty-eight. As Miss Jean Brodie said, I didn't wish to appear intimidated by being late, or early. She found a message in her log book and told me that the meeting had been put back one hour. 'It's due to the bomb scare,' she explained.

'Bomb scare? What bomb scare?' I replied.

I went for a walk and tried again at ten o'clock. This time they were in. Fearnside introduced me to Chief Superintendent Tregellis, who sat behind a huge oak desk and looked like all top cops should look. His fierceness was enhanced by a deep cleft that ran from the middle of his cheek down past the corner of his mouth, like a duelling scar, except that there was a matching one at the other side and he didn't look the type to turn the other cheek. He was big and angular, with a shock of spiky black hair, his rolled-up sleeves giving him an air of no-nonsense efficiency. We did our best to break each other's fingers as we shook hands, and he invited me to sit down.

'Two hundred miles you've had to come, Charlie,' he said, 'and you beat us here. We are duly chastened.'

'And quite rightly,' I replied.

He picked up a phone and dialled three numbers. 'Get yourself in here and bring some coffee with you,' he said into it.

Fearnside was hovering. 'I'll leave you with Mr Tregellis, if you don't mind, Charlie. I think he'll be very interested in what you have to say.' I jumped to my feet and shook his hand while wishing him a happy retirement and saying how much I'd enjoyed working with him. The poor bloke looked choked and we agreed to talk on the phone when this was all over, neither of us believing it.

When he'd gone Tregellis said: ''Bout time the old bugger was put out to grass. He's been cruising these last three years.'

'He's helped me a lot in the past,' I stated, matter of fact. If he thought I was going to start slagging Fearnside off he was wrong. The door opened and two men came in: a lanky one in a power shirt, bow tie and blue braces, and a dumpy skinhead. Dumpy was carrying a tray filled with jugs and cups; his pal looked as if he'd refuse to carry anything heavier than a figure on a balance sheet. Tregellis's desk was equipped with enough chairs for mini-conferences and they both sat on my right, with their backs to the window. I pulled a brand-new typist's pad from my briefcase and when Tregellis introduced us I wrote their names down. Dumpy was a DS and Lord Peter Wimsey was from the legal department.

'Right, Charlie,' Tregellis began when the coffee was poured. 'Tell us what you've got.'

It didn't take long and I only had one copy of the file to offer them. Dumpy took it to someone to get more. They were good listeners, I'll give them that. As I spoke Tregellis rubbed the blunt end of his pencil up and down the groove in his right cheek. I half-expected him to dislodge a couple of acorns, but he didn't. 'That's more or less it,' I concluded. 'If you tell me that Crosby's paranoid I'll believe you and drop the whole thing.'

Lord Wimsey's real name was Piers Forrester and that was as good a reason as any for hating him. 'Mr Crosby isn't paranoid,' he announced. 'J. J. Fox is as nasty a piece of shite as you'll ever step in. What you have here, Priest, is confirmation of what we already know but it doesn't give us any more in the way of evidence.'

Tregellis glanced at him in a way that spoke volumes and

leaned forward. There was a faded tattoo on his forearm that could have been an anchor. 'J. J. Fox owns SWTV, as you know,' he told me. 'He put in the highest bid when the franchise was offered, back in 1985, and because of his media experience his offer was accepted. Nothing wrong with that, you might say.' I nodded my agreement. 'The second highest bid was from a consortium of established media figures. Fox's bid, which beat the deadline by minutes, was one million pounds above theirs. All the other bids were miles away. Mary Perigo was secretary for the consortium. Spinster, fifty years old, but not bad-looking. While the bids were being calculated she found herself a boyfriend. Called himself Rodger Wakefield. Rodger with a "d" in the middle, she stressed, when she told a girlfriend all about him. This friend said he sounded urbane, suave and generous with his money. Two days after it was announced that Fox had won the franchise she was found dead in her car on the top floor of a multistorey. The car was burnt out.'

'Was their any evidence that she'd leaked information?' I asked.

'There were six in the consortium,' Tregellis continued. 'Some businessmen, some from the bright side of the footlights. They all knew the size of the bid, of course, as did Miss Perigo. Then they had partners, wives and mistresses, not to mention pals at the club, accountants, bank managers and the girl who typed the letter. We looked, Charlie, believe me we looked, but anyone could have leaked that figure.'

'Was she murdered?'

'Cause of death was never established, but the car had been torched deliberately.'

'What did Rodger Wakefield have to say?'

'We never found him. She'd told her friend his name, but otherwise was very coy about him. The friend had wondered if he was married. They were seen together at a charity "do" she'd help organise, in Newbury, and she'd named him as her guest, but according to acquaintances Mr Wakefield was unusually camera-shy. The *Berkshire Life* photographer was there, snapping away, but Wakefield only appears in the background of someone else's picture, a three-quarters rear view, I'm afraid. Several people saw him, however, and say they'd recognise him again.'

'Did he have an accent?'

'Public school northern, educated southern; take your pick.'

'How hard have you looked for him?'

'*We* haven't. Met CID circulated an E-fit. The usual; he was a murder suspect.'

'What's the state of play at the moment?'

'With Mary Perigo or J. J. Fox?'

'Fox.'

'There isn't one. What with bent pension funds and NHS scams and computer fraud we're up to here.' He waved a hand above his head. 'We've nobody working on it. Now and again someone writes us a letter and we put it on the file. Crosby isn't the only enemy that Fox has; five years ago the War Crimes Bureau contacted us and asked if we had anything on him. That's about it.'

'Did you help them?'

He looked grim. 'I suspect a copy of what we had may have fallen into their hands. Up to then we had never suspected that he wasn't a Jew. Crosby's story corroborates that.'

'Maybe Crosby was the one who tipped them off,' I suggested.

Tregellis pointed a finger at his head, as if shooting himself, and said: 'Of course.'

'So what do you want me to do?' I asked.

'Anything you can,' he replied. 'You're the murder specialist, we're only fraud. Find Wakefield for us. You're nearer to Fox's base than we are. See what you can dig up.'

'Bring us Fox's head on a plate, Priest,' Forrester said. 'That's what we'd like you to do.'

I finished my coffee and scanned the two lines of notes I'd made. Looking at Tregellis I said: 'So you reckon there's something in Crosby's story?'

He nodded.

'I'll be working on my own.'

'We're not expecting miracles.'

'Expenses?'

'Send them to me.'

'Right,' I said, nodding. 'Right.'

Tregellis stood up, rotated his head and rubbed his neck. 'I'm sure you appreciate that we're in shaky territory with this, Charlie, so the fewer people who know about it the better. I'll have a word with your people and N-CIS, and your contacts down here will be Piers and Graham,' he nodded at the others, 'but feel free to come straight to me if necessary. Anything else you need to know?'

'Not at the moment,' I replied, then turning to Piers and Graham said: 'But if I'm working with you two I'd better have your extension numbers.' They rattled them at me. 'Thank you. And your home numbers and mobiles.'

Forrester's glare had been honed by a thousand years of superiority since the days when it meant a sentence of death to some poor serf. Graham, on the other hand, was beaming like the sunrise over Dublin Bay. 'And I'd appreciate a copy of Rodger Wakefield's photograph and the E-fit,' I added, 'as soon as possible.'

Chapter 5

I'd done some digging about Duncan Roberts and discovered that he'd slashed his own throat with a Stanley knife and bled to death. The address was in Brixton, at the far end of the Victoria Line, which was convenient. Every town should have an underground system. I ticked off the stations, memorised the poem of the month and watched the people, grateful that this wasn't my patch. I'd have arrested every one of them. As I came out of the station a gang of seriously cool youths swept by on rollerblades, swerving in and out of the parked cars, and a consumptive skinhead jerked the lead of what looked like a pit-bull terrier as I passed him. Living in a city has certain attractions, even for a small-town boy like me, but I was damned if I could remember any of them as I strolled by the derelict tenements and corner shops with security grilles over the windows. Flyposters and takeaway trays were a major industry round here. A wino, sitting on some steps with a rubbish bag for a back rest, watched me go by, wondering if he could tap a white man for a drink, deciding against it. I saw the street I wanted and crossed the road.

The house could have been the one in Chapeltown. The door was open and the soulless, thump of a drum machine was coming from deep within. I hammered on the door in competition with it and smelled cooking. Spicy cooking. My stomach gurgled and sent a memo to my brain. It said: 'FEED ME!' I knocked again, but harder.

A giant West Indian ambled out of the gloom, a look of bewilderment on his face. He was grey-haired, wearing jeans and a vest the size of a marquee, and carrying a soup ladle. I decided to do it the proper way. 'Detective Inspector Priest,' I said, holding my ID out. 'Are you the proprietor?'

'What you want?' he asked, his face immobile.

'A word. Is this your place?'

'I am the proprietor,' he replied, and his expression developed a hint of pride. I'd given him a new title.

'You do bed and breakfast for DSS clients,' I said.

'Full,' he told me. 'No room.'

I know I dress casual, but I'd never thought it was that casual. 'I don't want a room,' I told him. 'You had a man called Duncan Roberts staying here until about two months ago?'

'No,' he answered.

'You did.'

'No.'

'He committed suicide.'

'Nobody of that name stay here.'

I repeated the address to him and he agreed this was the place. 'Well, he lived here,' I insisted.

'No.'

'He killed himself. Bled to death.'

'Nobody do that here.'

'I want to see his room.'

'He not live here.'

'What happened to his belongings?'

'He not live here.'

He was stubborn, unhelpful and pretending to be thick. I know the type; I'm from Yorkshire. I started again at the beginning, but it was a waste of breath. I thanked him for his time and headed back towards the station. The yob with the dog was coming the other way. He nodded a hello, I said: 'Ow do.'

Gilbert greeted me with: 'Ah! Just the man,' when I called in his office for my morning cuppa and to discuss tactics. 'What the devil did you volunteer us for at the SCOGs meeting?' He rummaged through his papers for the minutes of the meeting I'd attended.

'Er, nothing,' I replied.

'It says here . . . where is it? Oh, here we are, in Any Other Business: *Examination of all outstanding murder cases going back thirty years*, with *Mr Priest* typed in the margin. I know you don't like going to the meetings, Charlie, but if you think this'll get you out of them you're mistaken.'

I said: 'Forget it, Gilbert. We were just discussing DNA testing in old cases, and I suggested it could be taken further.'

'It looks as if you volunteered to do it.'

'Well, I'll un-volunteer.'

'Right. How did you go on yesterday?'

He wasn't too pleased when he learned that I'd be spending a large proportion of my time working for the SFO, but relaxed when I told him that they were paying my expenses.

'So where are you starting?' he asked.

'With the files. See what's on them that I never knew about. I was a humble sergeant at the time, and not on the case.'

I drank my tea and went back downstairs to review the troops. Nigel was due in court, Jeff and Maggie had appointments with various people on the robbers' circuit and Dave was hoping to talk to someone on the Sylvan Fields estate who had ambitions of becoming a paid informer. It's heart-warming when you hear of one of them trying to better himself, restores your faith in the system.

The West Yorkshire archives are in the central registry in the cellars of the Force HQ, or the Centre, as it is more usually called. Grey steel industrial racks, row after row, are bulging with brown folders stuffed with papers and photographs. Every written page is a testimony to man's indifference to the feelings of his fellows. There's not much joy down there, little to uplift the spirit when you consider that these are the unsolved cases. The ones we crack are usually destroyed to save space.

'1975, did you say?' the civilian archivist asked as he led me between the lines of Dexion shelving.

'July,' I replied. 'Possibly filed as Crosby.'

He turned down an aisle, read a label, went a bit further, read another, backtracked a few paces and looked up. 'We need the steps,' he said.

'I'll fetch them.' He walked with a pronounced limp and I was impatient. Our movements had stirred up fifty years of dust and the place smelled of old paper and corruption. I rolled the steps into position and locked the wheels.

The file was about two feet thick, in four bundles tied with string. I lifted the first one out and climbed down. 'I'll leave you, then,' he said.

'Thanks, you've been a big help. I'll put them back when I've finished.'

When he'd gone I scanned the letters and numbers on the next rack of shelves, looking for a name. I was certain this one wouldn't have been destroyed. There it was, next but one: a whole bank of shelves devoted to one villain, the biggest file we'd ever had. I ran my fingers over them, leaving a clean trail through the dust. In there were the names of thirteen women and fifty thousand men, and the contents had touched the lives of everyone in the country. One man's name was printed within those pages nine times, but he wasn't caught until a lucky copper found him with a prostitute in his car and a ball-peen hammer in his pocket. Peter Sutcliffe, better known as the Yorkshire Ripper.

I took the first bundle from the fire file to the desk near the door and untied the string. There were photos and a list of names and the coroner's report. Sergeant Priest and PC Sparkington, first on the scene, weren't mentioned. An hour and a half later I retied the string and fetched the next bundle. The prostitutes in the next street were convinced that they were the intended target and the CID went along with that. I broke off for something to wash the dust out of my larynx and some fresh air.

Bundle three was mainly interviews with the ex-boyfriends and minders of the girls. Their pimps, in other words. They all had alibis, which wasn't a surprise, and plenty of witnesses to say they were visiting their moms at the time of the fire, whenever that might have been. I was gathering a good picture of the investigation and where it might have gone wrong, but nothing that helped Crosby's case. Maybe bundle four would hold the key.

It was more of the same. The usual suspects had been rounded up, informants consulted, gossip listened to. It had been a crime that aroused passions, it's always the same when children are involved, and plenty of people had their pet theories. The local branch of the National Front denied any responsibility and expressed lukewarm regret, and the leaders of the Asian community demanded more protection.

I scanned the next statement briefly, turned it upside down on the pile I'd finished with and reached for another one. I was working on automatic. Something clicked inside my brain and I picked it up again. It was made by Paul Travis Carter to DC

Jones, four weeks after the fire. Carter lived at number twenty-seven Leopold Avenue, just over the road. Two days before the fire he'd gone on an expedition to the Dolomites with a party of schoolkids and had just returned. About a week before leaving he went for his customary takeaway, and as he locked the door he noticed a young woman approaching number thirty-two. She hesitated on the top step for a few moments and left. He'd assumed she'd put something through the letter box, although her actions didn't look like that. He followed her, because that was the way he was going, and she got into a posh car that was waiting round the corner and was driven away. The car might have been a two-litre Rover and the driver looked like a man, although his hair was longish and Carter couldn't be certain. 'I don't suppose it's important,' he'd told the DC, 'but I thought I'd better tell you.' The DC had obviously agreed with the *not important* bit; there wasn't even a description of the woman.

'Wait till I tell Sparky,' I said to myself, and made a note of Carter's details. He shouldn't be too hard to find. I put everything back and slapped the dust off my hands. As I turned to leave I took a last look at the Ripper files. We'd been misled on that one, gone off at a tangent, wasted thousands of man hours. Someone had made a big mistake with the fire, too, and I didn't think it was me.

Carter was a responsible citizen who conscientiously registered to vote. Two minutes on the computer upstairs in the HQ CID office and I had his latest address. Middleton, South Leeds. I thanked everyone for their help, flirted briefly with a rather attractive sergeant and left. Carter lived in a cottage along a dirt track near the golf course. It sounds nice, but a burnt-out shell of a Fiesta reminded me that just down the road was a rambling estate where middle-class meant having floorboards, and quiche was the plural of cosh.

He was in the garden, hacking at a grass jungle with a bargain-store sickle. A golf club would have done more good. His hedges were overgrown, heavy with honeysuckle and wild roses. It was a cottage garden gone mad, and it reinforced my belief that there is no such thing as a labour-saving garden. He looked up and demanded: 'Who are you?' the sickle held handy to deliver a forearm volley. I told him.

I'd decided that his wife had left him long before he poured it out. The garden; the state of his front room; having to wash two cups before he could offer me a coffee; they were all clues. I lived like that, once, before I reformed. Carter was wearing grey slacks, a striped cream shirt with the cuffs and neck fastened, and black brogues. His only concession to the weather had been to remove his tie. He told me he'd retired early and spent his time working for a Third World charity and trying to write a textbook on Roman England. He believed that Roman values were lacking in certain elements of our present-day society, and a return to them would be for the good.

Crucifixion? I thought.

He'd missed the fire, of course. First he knew of it was when he saw the boarded-up holes and smoke-streaked brickwork. He'd been shocked to learn that they'd all been killed, and disturbed by the matter-of-fact acceptance of it by his neighbours. They'd had a month to get used to the idea, and it's amazing how the human mind can accommodate disaster when it happens to someone else.

'It was twenty-three years ago,' I reminded him. 'Can you remember the girl you saw?'

'Oh yes, Inspector. I've thought about it so many times.'

'You said in your statement that she may have put something through the letter box?'

He looked uncomfortable. 'I know I did. She walked to the front door so purposefully, paused for a few seconds – much longer than it would have taken to put a letter through – and turned and left, equally purposefully.'

'Maybe she was checking the address on the envelope,' I suggested.

'I thought of that. It's possible, but her actions weren't right. I went through all this with the detective, you know.'

'OK,' I said, 'how does this sound? The woman walked up to the front door with a piece of chalk in her hand. The house was number thirty-two but the painted number had weathered away. She wrote thirty-two on the wall and left. Could that have been it?'

His eyes widened slightly and he nodded. His skin was sallow and hung in folds around his neck. He wasn't eating properly since she left. I didn't get this bad, did I? 'Do you know, Inspector, I believe you could be right.' He stood up and faced an imaginary door. 'The numbers were painted about here,' he said, raising his left hand to shoulder height. 'At least, mine was.' He went through the motions and said: 'Did she write it at this side?'

'Yes.'

'In that case, she'd have to lean over if she were right-handed, which she didn't. It would make more sense if she were left-handed.'

'We'll make a detective of you yet, Mr Carter,' I said. 'I'd come to that conclusion myself. Now what about her description? Do you think you can give me one?'

'Wasn't it on the file?'

'No, I didn't find it.'

'Well, I told the detective who interviewed me. It's a bit late, if you don't mind me saying so. It's lost its impact.'

'We appreciate that she'll be much older now,' I said.

'It's not just that. Punk was just starting, and now every other young person you meet has purple hair, but up to then I'd only seen it on television.'

I was up six times through the night. My neck itched, my wrists itched and my ankles itched. Big lumps came up in all these places. Now I knew why Carter kept his shirt tightly buttoned; he wasn't as dumb as I'd thought. I searched the bathroom cabinet for soothing gels but all I could find was some body lotion *pour hommes* that Nigel had told me contained pheromones and drove women wild. It didn't work, and wasn't any better on midge bites. I showered, dressed, wrecked the spider's web on the car door with great relish and went to work.

Sparky wanted to know all about it, and was as chuffed as a cock robin when I told him about the left-handed girl with purple hair.

'That's what we said,' he reminded me. 'When we found the chalk. How tall did he say she was?'

'About five feet, five-two.'

'Bloody 'ell! We ought to be detectives.'

'We are detectives.'

'So Carter saw this punk bird mark the house and Duncan told his brother he was going out with someone with purple hair? It's got to be the same one.'

'I'd have thought so. When did punk start?' I asked him.

'Umm, about 1980?' he suggested. 'Bit before, maybe.'

'Mid-seventies, according to the library. Their gazetteer says it "exploded" in 1976 and that's the year the Sex Pistols released "Anarchy in the UK". *Never Mind the Bollocks* was in '77. There can't have been too many of them around in '75 'specially in the provinces. Maybe she was before her time, like me. How do you fancy a day on the telephone?'

'Er, I don't,' he replied glumly, anticipating what I had in mind.

'But David,' I began, 'it's essential work, which may lead to the apprehension of a vicious criminal. It's not just the glamorous jobs, such as mine, that bring results. They also serve who sit in the office all day drinking vast quantities of machine coffee.'

'Gimme t'list,' he said, reaching for it.

If you go into any high street shop and buy something, a vacuum cleaner for example, the pimply assistant manager who takes your order will punch your name and postcode into his terminal and say: 'Is that Mr Windsor of Buckingham Palace Road?' and you say it is and your full name and address is printed on the invoice. Our system is nearly as good. If you have ever bought anything on credit, taken out a driving licence, voted in an election or owned a telephone, we have you on record. Or maybe you've joined a motoring organisation, a book club or the Mormons. Most of these sell each other volumes of names and addresses, and we're on the circulation list. When we get really desperate we consult Somerset House. If you've been born, married or died they'll know all about it. I gave Dave the three pages of names and addresses that Jeremy had sent me from the university.

'These are Duncan Roberts's classmates,' I told him, 'with their parents' addresses. It might be easier to see if mum and dad still live in the same place and ask them. Otherwise . . .'

'. . . otherwise, consult the oracle,' Dave finished for me.

'That's it, sunshine. And these . . .' I passed him another sheet, '. . . are names I extracted from the file yesterday. The three with the asterisks are the boyfriends of the women who died in the fire. Let's not lose sight of the fact that one of them might have started it. And then there are the names on the report that Crosby gave us. It wouldn't hurt to have a word with that lot.

I'll sort them out. If all else fails with the students, there's a department at the university called the alumni relations' office. Old boys' club to you. They might be able to help.' His hangdog expression gave me a pain in the left ventricle that I couldn't ignore. I said: 'You could, of course, give Annette a crash course in the system and leave her to it.' Annette Brown was a DC who'd been with us for a fortnight and had already fallen under Nigel's protective arm.

'I was going to ask you,' he replied, 'but it'll upset Goldenballs.'

'He'll recover. Anything else?'

'No. Where will you be if I need you?'

'Chemist's, to start with.'

'Chemist's? What for?'

'Something for bloody midge bites.'

It cost four quid and didn't work, and now I smelt like an apothecary's pinny. I came out of the toilets and went back upstairs to my office. Dave was busy on the phone, pencil poised over a half-filled page. I reread the list of Fox's shady dealings that Crosby had given us and extracted any relevant names. If they were really on Fox's payroll we'd need a jemmy to prise it from them, but it was worth a try. They'd be relaxed, not expecting a call from us. When they say they'll only talk in front of a solicitor you know you've struck paydirt.

Dave knocked and came in. He sniffed and said: 'Cor, have you been using fly spray? I've found a couple of locals, if you want to be getting on with it.'

'Who are they?' I asked, leaning back.

'Terence John Alderdice read chemistry at Leeds Uni with Duncan Roberts. He lives in Leeds and will be home after about six, according to his wife. And, wait for it, Watson Pretty, who was the ex-boyfriend of Daphne Turnbull, Jasmine's mother, now lives in Huddersfield, right on our doorstep. He's out on licence after serving five years for the manslaughter of one of his subsequent girlfriends. They had a quarrel and she fell down the cellar steps and broke her neck. Oh, and she had a ten-year-old daughter.'

'He sounds a right charmer,' I said. 'What do they see in them?'

Dave shrugged his shoulders. 'Want me to see Alderdice tonight?' he asked, but my phone rang before I could answer.

I listened, raising a finger to Dave to signify that this was interesting. 'Grab your coat,' I told him as I put the phone down and unhooked mine from behind the door.

'What is it?' he shouted after me as we ran down the stairs.

'Halifax Central have just arrested someone for using Joe McLelland's Visa card in Tesco. He'll be in their cells by the time we get there.'

If my geometry was any good he wasn't the one in the video. He had the build, but was only about five feet six. They brought him from the cell to an interview room and sat him down with his packet of fags before him. He was about twenty, wearing torn jeans and a T-shirt from the Pigeon Pie English Pub on Tenerife. They served Tetley's bitter and Yorkshire puddings and I could hardly wait to go.

'So where did you get the card?' Sparky demanded. I've told him before about being too circumspect.

'I found it.'

'Where?'

'In t'car park.'

'Which car park?'

'Tesco's.'

'When did you find it?'

'Just then.'

'Before you went shopping?'

'Yeah.'

'What were you doing in the car park?'

'Goin' shoppin'! What do you think I were doin'?'

'You had no money on you.'

'I'd left me wallet at 'ome. I didn't realise until I was in t'shop. I was goin' to 'and t'card in, but I'd filled me trolley by then and I din't know what to do, so I used t'card.' He whined his well-rehearsed story as if it were the most self-evident explanation in the world.

'You fell to temptation,' I said.

He swivelled to face me and jumped on my words as if they were a life raft. 'That's it! I fell to temptation!'

'Does your weekly shop normally run to four bottles of Glenfiddich?' Dave wondered.

'We's 'aving a party,' he replied, lamely.

'And six hundred cigs?'

'I'm a 'eavy smoker.'

'And two packs of fillet steak?'

'You've gotta eat.'

Dave was silent for a few seconds, then he asked him if he had form. He had.

'What for?' Dave asked.

'Thieving.'

'Have you done time?'

'Yeah.'

'How was it?'

''Orrible. I 'ated it.'

'You could go back in for this.'

'It was a mistake! 'Onest! I din't mean to use it, it just

'appened. Things just 'appen to me. Like 'e said, I was tempted.'

I clunked my chair back on all four legs. 'You made a good job of Mr McLelland's signature,' I said.

'I just copied it.'

'Whoever stole this card from Joe McLelland left him tied in his chair, and his wife, for ten hours,' I told him. 'They are both elderly. It's a miracle they were found. This was nearly a murder case. Now I'm prepared to believe that it wasn't you who tied them up. I'm prepared to believe that someone sold you the card. That's what I think, so if I'm right you'd better tell me a name, or we'll just have to assume you took it off them yourself. What do you say?'

His elbows were on the table, his fingers interlocked and both thumb-nails between his teeth. He chewed away for nearly a minute, then looked straight at me and said: 'I found it. If I'm lying may my little lad be dead when I go 'ome.'

It's always someone else they want dead. 'He might be,' I replied. 'Of old age.'

I pulled into the nick car park and suggested we have a fairly early night. Dave said: 'I could do another window frame round at the mother-in-law's, or I could cut the grass.'

'You're spoilt for choices,' I commented.

'Or . . .' he began, '. . . or I could nip into Leeds after tea and talk to Mr Alderdice, former student at Leeds University and erstwhile friend of Duncan Roberts.'

'Uh-uh,' I said, shaking my head.

'Why not?'

'Because I don't want your Shirley blaming me for you never being there.'

'I can handle her. I'd like to find out about this punk bird, fast as poss. It's niggling me.'

'I know what you mean,' I replied. 'Fair enough, you see Alderdice and I'll have a word with Mr Pretty. That'll be two names fewer to investigate. Do you want to meet in a pub afterwards and compare notes?'

'Er, no, if you don't mind. I know I said I could handle her, but there are limits.'

When he'd driven away I locked the car and walked into the town centre and had a teatime special in the Chinese restaurant. I enjoyed it, all by myself, with no one to entertain or worry about. Maybe this was my natural state, I thought.

But I didn't really believe it. Back in the car I rang Jacquie and told her I was on my way to a meeting. We could grab a quick drink later, if she wanted. I moaned about my midge bites and she said: 'Lavender oil.'

'Lavender oil,' I repeated. 'What will that do?'

'It's aromatherapy. Lavender oil will cool you down and de-stress you, then you need aloe vera to soothe the damaged tissue. I'll show you, when you come round.'

'Ooh! I can hardly wait,' I said.

Watson Pretty lived on the edge of Huddersfield town centre, not far from where I did my probationary training. Not much had changed. The main difference was that now both sides of every street were lined with cars; some worth much more than the houses they stood outside, some rusting wrecks standing on bricks, awaiting the invention of the wheel. The doctor's surgery was in the same place, but with wire mesh over the windows, and the greengrocer's was now a mini-market. I smiled at the memories and checked the street names.

He invited me in, speaking very softly, and told me to sit down. He was wearing pantaloons, a T-shirt with a meaningless message emblazoned across it and modest dreadlocks. He must have been fifty, but was refusing to grow up. The room was overfurnished with stuffed cushions and frills, and primitive paintings of Caribbean scenes on the walls. At a guess, it had belonged to his mother. He was out on licence, so I knew he'd be no trouble. One word out of place and he could be back inside to serve the rest of his sentence. Well, that's what we tell them.

'I'm looking for a girl,' I began. 'A white girl with purple hair.'

'I know no such girl,' he replied.

'How about back in 1975? Did you know her then?'

'No, I not know her.'

'You had a girlfriend called Daphne Turnbull.'

'Yes.'

'She died in a fire.'

'Yes.'

'And you didn't know a girl with purple hair?'

'Who is she, this girl?'

'That's what I'm trying to find out. You remember the fire?'

'I hear about the fire, but I live in Halifax at the time.'

He was a founder member of the Campaign for Simplified English. The first rule is that you only speak in the present tense. 'With Daphne?' I asked.

'We live together for a while, but she leave me.'

'Why did she leave you?'

He shrugged and half-smiled. 'Women?'

'Was her daughter, Jasmine, yours?'

'No.'

I'd read the interviews with him and knew he had a good alibi, but he could have hired someone to start the blaze. At the time he'd been my definite number-one suspect, although I'd never met him. Now I wanted to eliminate him, but I still wasn't sure. I rarely have hunches and don't trust my feelings about people. Evidence is what counts. I quizzed him about his relationship with Daphne and kept returning to the girl with purple hair, but he was adamant that he didn't know her. Talking about the fire didn't disturb him at all. It was just history to him.

I thanked him for his help and left. I'd parked at the top of his street and as I neared the car a woman came round the corner. There are some women you see and you think: Cor! She's beautiful; and there are others who deprive you of even that simple ability. You gawp, slack-jawed, and realise you are flatlining, but don't care, because this would be as good a time and place as any to drop down dead. Her hair shone like spun anthracite and she wore a white dress with buttons down the front. It was short, above her knees, and the seamstress had been very economical with the buttons. She turned to wait and a little girl with braided hair and a matching dress followed her round the corner, gravely avoiding the cracks between the flagstones.

I mumbled something original and amusing, like: 'Lovely morning,' and was rewarded with a smile that kicked my cardiac system back into action. In the car I gazed at the digital clock and wondered if there was any hope for me. It was seven forty-three in the evening. I sat for a few seconds, deciding whether to go through the town centre or do a detour, and started the engine. Neither. I did a left down the street parallel to the one Pretty lived in and a left and another left at the bottom of the hill. I pulled across the road and parked.

The woman and her little girl were now coming down towards me. Mum was tiring of the slow progress so she took her daughter's hand and led her for a while. They passed a few gateways then turned into one and mounted the steps. She knocked, the door opened almost immediately and mother and daughter disappeared inside. I stared at the door for a couple of minutes, long enough for a welcoming kiss and for her to settle in the easy chair I'd just left, and pointed the car homewards. Oh dear, I thought. Oh dear oh dear oh dear.

What would I do without Jacquie to come back to? She smiled and kissed me in a mirror-image of the scene I'd imagined forty minutes earlier. We had coffee and shop-bought cake and talked about our days. One of her assistants was causing trouble and the rents in the mall were going up. I rambled meaninglessly about what went off behind closed doors in this wicked world we lived in.

'You're stressed out,' she told me.

'I'm sorry,' I said. 'I'm not very good company.'

'How are the midge bites?'

'Agonising.' I smiled as I said it.

She went away for a while and returned carrying a box filled with coloured bottles, like a paintbox. She placed it on the coffee table alongside me and drew a chair up directly in front of mine. 'Prince Charles swears by lavender oil,' she said.

'Right,' I replied. 'Right.' If it was good enough for him it was good enough for Charlie Priest.

She lit three small porcelain burners about the room and turned the lights low. I relaxed. I had a feeling I was in for a treat. Jacquie sat facing me and took my hand. 'First the lavender, to absorb all your stresses,' she whispered. I watched her long fingers caress my wrists, her scarlet nails skimming my skin but not touching it. She did my fingers, one by one, and I discovered things about myself that I'd never imagined.

'And now the aloe vera,' she said.

I breathed deeply and closed my eyes, and wished this could go on forever. She removed my shoes and socks and stroked my feet, fingertips and exotic oils mingling together so I couldn't tell touch from smell, pleasure from torture, arousal from relaxation. I stopped trying.

'This is where the problem is,' Jacquie told me. She was massaging my neck now, harder than before, her thumbs probing muscle, searching for knots. 'You're tight here.' I let my head loll up and down in agreement. It could have been the most magical evening of my life, but it wasn't. She cured the itching and the stress; all I had now was confusion and frustration.

It was the hottest night of the year, which didn't help. I lay on my bed with just a sheet over me and the window open. When the blackbird on the roof started singing at about three thirty I got up and read a book. I don't mind him singing, but he will insist on tapping time with his foot, and he has no sense of rhythm. At seven I went to work.

Terence John Alderdice, Dave told me, remembered Duncan Roberts but was mystified about the girl. 'He reckoned Duncan was a right plonker,' Dave said. 'He was quite friendly with him the first year. They became mates on day one and were in the same tutorial group, whatever that means, then drifted apart as they found more kindred spirits, as you do. He said Duncan developed some repulsive habits. They were in a hall of residence, and Duncan took great pleasure in never washing his plate or coffee mug. He just used them over and over again.'

'Sounds delightful,' I said.

'In the second year,' he continued, 'Alderdice said Duncan just gave up studying. He lost interest and moved into a squat with a bunch of other dead-beats. Alderdice didn't see much of him again and never saw him with a girl and doesn't remember ever seeing one with purple hair. So there. How did you go on?'

'Similar. Waste of time. Except that the cycle is repeating itself. I saw Pretty's girlfriend come to visit, just as I left. Black girl, early twenties, with a little daughter, 'bout five.'

Dave said: 'Number three lining up for the chop. What can we do about it?'

'Not much. I'll have a word with his probation officer, see if he's any suggestions. She was gorgeous.'

'The little girl?'

'No, turnip brain, the mother. The little girl was . . . *little*.'

Chapter 6

The high pressure moved around a bit, bringing breezes from the north. The nights were clear and cold and early-morning mists rolled off the hills, causing havoc on the roads. Two people were killed in a fifteen-vehicle pile-up on the M62 and a golfer was struck by lightning in Brighouse. We made ten more contacts, some by telephone. It's all right having *carte blanche* with expenses, but driving a hundred miles for an interview takes a big chunk out of the working day. And although Nigel was running the big show there were some jobs I had to attend to myself and some I wanted to. Arresting Peter Mark Handley was one of the latter.

Handley was forty-four years old and taught physical development at Heckley High School, the local comprehensive. When I was a pupil there it was called the Grammar School and we learned PT. Because of financial constraints there was no games mistress as such for the girls, just a reluctant succession of uninterested teachers seconded to take a lesson when they could. The netball and hockey teams suffered, as did a group of girls who showed promise as swimmers. To prevent a further slide in the school's fortunes Handley had volunteered to take over as their coach, too.

We'd heard via an older girl who spent a week with us on a

job awareness programme that he subscribed to the touchy-feely training method. We held off while the school was in session to avoid rumours spreading, but as soon as the summer holiday came we put him under observation and started interviewing specially selected pupils. Another girl, called Grace and wise beyond her years, said he would give them group talks before a match, extolling the virtues of the East German training methods. He showed them videos of the 1936 Berlin Olympics and modern ones of powerful Teutonic maidens out-sprinting, out-throwing and out-swimming their mortal competitors. Winning was all, he exhorted. Any means of achieving victory was acceptable, and 'Simply the Best' became the unofficial team song.

Later, after the game, when senses were heightened and bodies pleasantly tired, he would offer a lift home to his current favourite. Let's have a McDonald's he'd insist. In the restaurant he'd tell her more about East German training methods. They had relied heavily on the administration of huge amounts of the male hormone testosterone. It was a wonderdrug for female athletes, and drastically cut down on the amount of training required to achieve international status. There could be problems, of course, if the dosage wasn't carefully controlled. He'd laugh, and suggest that some of the women shot-putters who'd taken massive doses now left the seat upright when they came out of the toilet. What it did for their sex lives he couldn't imagine, he said, studying the girl's reaction as he broached the subject.

In the car, near the end of her street, he'd park while talking about the game to hold her attention. His arm would reach across the back of the seat and his fingers caress her hair. There were other methods, he'd say. She was special. She could make it, right to the top. The coach-and-athlete relationship was like no other. The other way, his way, was the loving way. There were no tests for it, and anyway, it wasn't against the rules. His way of administering the male hormone brought only happiness and contentment, plus improved performance. And there were no unwelcome side effects. He didn't mention pregnancy.

Grace told him to go play with himself and slammed the car door so hard the mirror fell off. He never spoke to her again but she thought the next girl he approached fell for it. Two others gave us the same story but different names of girls they thought had had affairs with him. Three refusals, three successes, not a bad scoreline. A female DC had a quiet word with the girls we'd been told about and two of them admitted it. The other one told her to mind her own business.

Trouble was, they were over sixteen. A schoolteacher is *in loco parentis*, and is not expected to seduce his charges, but it ain't illegal. We could get him sacked, but that looked like all we could do. Then one of the girls mentioned the magazines he'd shown her and that was all we needed.

The good news was that his wife had left him about a month earlier. Whether it was related we didn't know, but she'd packed two suitcases and decamped to her mother's in Wombwell, near Barnsley. We have to tread delicately in cases like this, but with her out of the way we had a free hand to go round and put the shits up him. Thursday morning, nine a.m., me, Maggie Madison, Sparky and Annette Brown swung into the street of mock-Georgian link-detached dwellings and knocked on his door. The neighbour's sprinkler was drenching the shared lawn and a sunbed was deployed, all ready for duty. The forecast said thunder and a few big cumulus clouds were sailing overhead, but it looked unlikely.

Mrs Handley opened the door, which wasn't in the script. I stumbled through the introductions and suggested she let us in. Her husband was in the back garden, tinkering with a lawnmower.

'Peter Mark Handley?' I asked.

'Yes. Why?' He placed a screwdriver back in its toolbox and rose to his feet. He didn't look like a PT instructor. He didn't look much like anything right then, except a man whose past has caught up with him. Mrs Handley looked at us in disbelief and didn't even ask if we'd like a cup of tea.

'We have a warrant to search your house,' I said, holding the printed side towards him.

There was a green plastic picnic table nearby, with four matching chairs around it. He reached out like a blind man, feeling for a chair. When he located one he fumbled with it and lowered himself down. 'Search the house?' he repeated.

'Yes.' I turned to his wife. 'Would you like to accompany my officers while they conduct the search?' I said.

She ignored my question. 'What are you looking for?'

'We're acting on information suggesting that your husband may be in possession of pornographic material.' I nodded to the other three to get on with it and invited her to accompany them again.

'What's all this about, Peter?' she asked.

'I . . . I don't know, love.'

'I'm not leaving you alone with my husband,' she said. 'I want to know what this is about.' We sat down. Pornography is a vague definition. The tabloids and most women's magazines overstep the boundaries that our parents would have laid down. I'd wanted to have a chat with him, perhaps suggest he quietly hand in his resignation and take up welding or tyre-fitting. Something that wouldn't surround him with nubile young ladies. I couldn't have done his job. I wouldn't have fallen to temptation, like him, but I'd have slowly gone blind and mad.

'We didn't expect you to be here, Mrs Handley,' I said.

'I came back last night.'

'Why did you leave?'

'Is that relevant?'

'I don't know. Is it?'

'You tell me. My mother suffers from Alzheimer's, with other complications. The doctor wanted to put her in a nursing home. One for geriatrics. She has four daughters, so we decided we could look after her ourselves, staying with her for a few weeks at a time. I've just done my first stint. At a guess I'll have one more to do. I can't see her lasting much longer than that.'

'I'm very sorry,' I said. It wasn't much to offer, but I meant it.

'Boss.' I looked round and saw Maggie standing in the doorway. I walked over to her and she whispered: 'Upstairs.'

'Go sit with them,' I told her, and went inside.

The loft ladder was down, with Dave leaning on a rung and Annette standing nearby. 'Up there,' she said. It was his den. His private world, his space, his fantasy land that nobody else was allowed to enter. I couldn't stand upright, even in the middle, but there was room for a cheap desk and chair, with a TV and VCR.

Mr Handley liked pictures of young girls. Without their clothes on. He liked to see them posing. He liked to see them struggling. But most of all he liked to see them suffering. At a guess he downloaded stuff from the Internet and dealt in imported magazines. I looked at just enough to satisfy myself it was illegal and went outside, to the real world, where the sun still shone. President Truman was right: sunshine is the best disinfectant.

His head was in his hands. Normally I would have invited Annette to launch her career with his arrest, but I didn't. 'Peter Mark Handley,' I began, 'I am arresting you for the possession of material of an obscene nature. You need not say anything . . .'

I was aware of Mrs Handley rising to her feet as I droned the caution. 'Oh no,' she sobbed. 'Oh no.'

The three of them took him back while I waited for her to

lock up. We rode to the station in the patrol car we'd had standing by and I seated her in reception and told her about the allegations against her husband. It wasn't enough to stop her looking at me with hatred in her eyes, as if it were all my doing. Maggie would interview her, stalling for long enough for the porn squad to lift the stuff we'd found. I trudged upstairs to my office to read the mail and wondered if it was all worthwhile.

The ten ex-chemistry students we'd contacted told us very little, so we pressed on. After another couple of blips I decided to concentrate on the female members of the course, on the doubtful grounds that they'd be more likely to remember a male colleague and, being the more sentimental gender, might possibly have retained any photographs. Also, there were only sixteen of them. Also, if they went to university in 1975 they'd be in their early forties now, which is a dangerous age. I didn't mention that last reason to Sparky.

Four of them remembered Duncan, and confirmed the dropping-out bit. One supplied us with a first-year class photograph and a lady working for the EEC in Belgium said she had some pictures taken at a party. Duncan was there and he might have been with a girl, but not one with purple hair. She wasn't sure if she still had the pictures but would be going home in about six weeks. The others were all doing quite well for themselves: one had just resumed a career as an industrial journalist after rearing three kids, and we had accountants, an advertising executive, a megabyte of computer boffins and, would you believe, several chemists among the rest. All of which was about as much use to us as dog poo on the doorstep.

'How,' I said to Sparky, 'do you fancy going to university?'

'I'd a feeling this was coming,' was his glum reply.

'We're getting nowhere, and we need to know who the girl

with purple hair was. So far, all we've established is that Duncan dropped out. She was probably the reason but almost certainly wasn't on the chemistry course. She's the key to his problems and ours. I'll have a word with Roper-Jones, the registrar, and maybe you could have a day or two over there, going through the records of all the other students. For Christ's sake, surely someone can remember a girl with purple hair!'

'How many is "all the other students"?'

'There's twenty-two thousand there at present, but it would be a lot fewer in '75.'

'That's a relief.'

'Are you OK for tomorrow?'

'University, here I come. Wait till I tell Sophie that I've got there before her.'

Sophie is Dave's daughter and my goddaughter. She'll be starting university soon, when she decides where to go. Her results were brilliant and she's spoilt for choice.

'Tell you what,' I said. 'Why don't you take her with you?'

'You mean . . . to help?'

'I don't see why not, there's nothing confidential about the records. I'll mention it to Roper-Jones; he didn't strike me as being a job's-worth. If he doesn't agree she could always explore the campus or do some shopping.'

'Great. She'd like that. Do you mind if I tell her it was my idea?'

'Why?' I demanded, suspicious.

'I'm in her bad books. Not enough time to give her driving lessons.'

'Well, pay for them.'

'At twenty quid a throw? I should cocoa!'

When he'd gone I rang Jacquie and arranged to see her that night. I felt ready for another steak, possibly followed by a session of aromatherapy. She was telling me that too much could be dangerous for my health and I was clarifying whether she meant steak or pongy massage when my other phone rang. I said a hasty goodbye and picked it up.

'Pop up, please, Charlie, if you don't mind,' Superintendent Wood said.

He had Gareth Adey, my uniformed counterpart, with him, and they both had problems. Gilbert was catching hell from the Chamber of Commerce over the number of street traders who were selling fake jeans and T-shirts, and Gareth had double-booked three teenagers who were coming in to be cautioned. I agreed to do the youths and Gareth promised a blitz on the street traders at the weekend.

The first of the cautions was a young man with low aspirations; he'd been caught shoplifting at Everything a Pound. 'It says here that you are a thief,' I told him, waving his case notes. He was standing in front of Adey's desk in the downstairs office, his mother on a chair to one side. He nodded his agreement.

'Do you know what I normally do?' I asked him. He didn't. 'Well, I'll tell you. I chase murderers, and here I am wasting time because you stole a cheap musical box from a two-bit shop.' He didn't look impressed. 'Yesterday,' I continued, 'we had a meeting about you. Four strangers, round a table, discussing what to do with you. How do you think that makes your mother feel, eh?' He didn't know. 'Don't think you've got away with it,' I told him. 'The reason you are not going before a court, and possibly to a young offenders' institute, is because we decided it wasn't best for you. We decided to give you another chance because we don't want you to waste your life. What do you want to do when you leave school?' He shrugged his shoulders. 'Pardon?' I said.

'Speak to the inspector,' his mother told him.

'Get a job,' he mumbled.

'And what chance do you think you'd have with a criminal record?'

'Dunno.'

'If you had six people apply for a job and one had a record, who would you choose?'

'One of the others.'

'Right.'

I told him that shoplifting cost every man, woman and child in the country about a hundred pounds a year and ranted on until I reached the point where I was boring him. He signed to accept the caution and I kicked him out. His mother apologised and swore he wouldn't be back. Funny thing is, most of them don't come back.

The other two were much the same. I made a coffee with Adey's fixings and read the contents of his in-tray. That was much the same, too. There was a canister of a new CS gas in his drawer that he was supposed to be appraising. I gave a bluebottle on his window a quick squirt and it keeled over. Good stuff, I thought as I closed his door behind me, tears running down my cheeks.

Fresh air, that's what I needed. I cleared my desk and went for a wander round the town centre. I have a policeman's eye for detail, the unusual, and girls' legs. The warm weather certainly brings them out. The new mall has taken a lot of trade from the high street shops, and the place is a ghost town through the week compared to a few years ago. The only street vendor at work was O'Keefe, at his usual place near the entrance to the market. He'd be tall if he straightened his back, with a craggy complexion eroded by years of neglect and outdoor life. He plays the Old Soldier, unable to work because of the wounds he suffered in Korea and, later, the Falklands. Soon it'll be the Gulf.

His right eye has a wedge of white where it ought to be brown and it points off to the side. O'Keefe sells jeans and football shirts.

'Anything my size, O'Keefe?' I said.

''Ello, Mr Priest,' he replied warily. 'Didn't recognise you for a minute. All a bit short in the leg for you, I'd say.'

'How much are the Town shirts?'

'Eighteen quid to friends. Cost you forty-two at the club shop.'

'Are they any good?'

'Course they're any good. They're just the same. No middle man, that's the deal.'

'And no rates, rent, electricity, National Insurance and so on. How's business?'

'Pretty fair, Mr Priest. Pretty fair. And with you?'

'Oh, you know. It's a bit like sex. Even when it's bad, it's good. Or so I'm told.'

He threw his head back and guffawed, the afternoon sun shining straight into his mouth and illuminating his teeth like a row of rotting sea defences. 'You're a case, Mr Priest,' he said, wiping his chin with the back of his hand.

'Anything to tell me?' I asked.

'Aye, there is summat.'

'Go on.'

'Pickpockets, Saturday morning. About five of 'em. Not from round 'ere.'

'I'll send someone to have a word with you. What about burglars? Someone is causing me a lot of grief.'

'You mean, these where they ties 'em up? Old folk?'

'Mmm.'

'Nasty jobs, them, boss. I'll let you know if I 'ear owt.'

'Ask around, will you? They take orders for stuff they can buy on credit cards. Expensive stuff, like sets of alloy wheels and televisions. Washing machines, anything like that.'

'Right.'

'One more thing,' I began. 'Find another pitch at the weekend. We're having a crackdown. Spread the word if you want to earn some kudos, then ask about the burglars.'

'Yeah. Right. Thanks, Mr Priest. Thanks a lot.'

It was only half past four, but I went home. I rang the office, had a shower and set the alarm clock for seven. When it rattled into life I thought it was early morning and nearly went back to work, but the jaunty tones of the *Archers* signature tune saved me.

The prawn cocktail was tasteless, the steak dry and the mushrooms like bits of inner tube dipped in oil. I'd have preferred a curry but Jacquie doesn't eat them – she has her customers to consider. She had to be up early so I forsook the massage and dropped her off at the door. My ansaphone was beeping when I arrived home.

'Hello, Uncle Charles,' a female voice said. 'If you are home before midnight could you please give me a ring.' It was my favourite woman: Dave's daughter Sophie. Apart from my mother, my previous girlfriend was the only person who had ever called me Charles. Sophie had been as besotted by her as I was and almost as devastated when she left. Calling me by my Sunday name was an echo from the past. I sat down on the telephone seat and drummed my fingers on my knee, just for a moment wishing that things were different. But they weren't. Never would be. Never could be. I dialled Sparky's number.

His son, Daniel, answered the phone. 'Is that Mustapha?' I whispered.

He said: 'If you're another one who wants to know if the coast's clear, ring the flipping coastguard.'

I said: 'There were some very handsome camels for sale at the market today.'

He said: 'A handsome camel has a price beyond rubies.'

I said: 'Beyond Ruby's what?'

Sophie's voice in the background asked: 'Is that Uncle Charles?' and Daniel said: 'Hang on, Charlie, Slack Gladys wants a word with you,' rapidly followed by: 'Ow! That hurt!' He's four years younger than she is and a good foot shorter.

'Hello, Uncle Charles,' she began, 'did you have a nice meal?'

'Not really. That sounded painful.'

'Mmm, it did hurt my hand a bit. It was me who found her.'

'Found who?'

'The girl with purple hair, of course. She's called Melissa. Melissa Youngman.'

I loosened my tie and unfastened the top button of my shirt. Tonight I'd gone out smart. 'You found her?' I repeated.

'Just after lunch. It was looking hopeless, so I said to myself: "What course was a weirdo most likely to be on? Let's try psychology." I rang one of the postgraduates who still lives in Leeds and she remembered her, told us that she was called Melissa Youngman and had been the first punk at the university. Brilliant, aren't I?'

I told her she was. I wanted to take her in my arms and hug her, squeeze her to pieces, ask her to marry me, but she was only eighteen and there were three miles of telephone cable between us. And I'd have caught hell from her dad.

The weather was breaking. The Saturday-morning forecast said widespread thunder, followed by a cooler spell. I breakfasted early and gathered my walking gear together. I'd have a couple of hours in the office then hotfoot it up into the Dales for the afternoon. I was taking my boots out to the car when I saw him.

The spider, that is. It was a dewy morning and he was suspended in space, halfway between the wing mirror and the outside light, welding a cross-member into position. I pretended not to notice him as I sidled down the side of the house, then I struck. 'Yaaah!' I yelled and severed his web with a well-aimed karate chop. He fell to the ground, rolled expertly back on to his feet with a bewildered look on his face and fled for safety – under the front tyre. He was definitely having a bad hair day. I flexed my fingers but no damage was done. Weight for weight, spider web is six times stronger than high-tensile steel.

Dave came in and told me all about it over bacon sandwiches in the canteen. They'd been getting nowhere fast until Sophie had her brainwave. Jeremy in the students' office had taken her to the pub for lunch, much to Dad's disgruntlement, and she'd come back with the idea about looking for courses that might attract someone with purple hair. Psychology had been the first guess. Dave suspected it was really Jeremy who'd thought of it, but who cares? It had saved us ploughing through several thousand records.

'I'd better buy her a present,' I said. 'She's saved the tax payers a few quid.'

'Er, not another Alice Cooper CD, if you don't mind,' Dave requested.

'Why? What's wrong with Alice Cooper?'

'She's a bit noisy, for a start!'

'She! He's a he!'

'A he? Well why do they call him Alice?'

'Er, well, er, because Alice is an ancient abbreviation of, er, Alexander. Who, as you know, was a Greek. The name was popular among Greek immigrants to the States at the turn of the century and handed down through the male line.'

'Really?'

'Well, either that or he's living in Wonderland.'

I suggested Dave collect his boots and maybe the kids and come walking with me, but his mother-in-law's windows needed a final coat of Dulux gloss and Daniel had gone off with his pals. I didn't suggest Sophie tag along and neither did he. I bought a sandwich at the café across from the nick and drove to Bolton Abbey, about an hour away.

The Valley of Desolation is aptly named in winter, but in good weather it's a pussycat. I watched a succession of people crossing the Wharfe on the stepping stones, waiting for someone to come to grief on the low one in the middle. There's always one, halfway across, that's wobbly or slippery; it's a law of stepping stones. They weren't going anywhere, just crossing for the hell of it, determined to get the most from their day out. I decided not to risk it and used the bridge ten yards downstream. A rumble of thunder rolled down the valley, followed by a second of silence as every face turned towards the sky and noticed the black clouds above the trees.

In twenty minutes I'd left the tourists behind and was scrambling up the path that headed out on to the fells and towards Simon's Seat, a magnificent fifteen hundred feet above sea level. No chance of altitude sickness today. As I emerged above the tree line I saw a figure ahead of me, laden down with equipment, and shook my head in amazement at the amount of stuff some people take with them. They believe all they read about the dangers of walking on the moors.

It was a young woman. She stopped, looked around her, and decided this was the place. As I approached I saw that she'd been carrying painting equipment and I made a silent apology to her. She was struggling to set up an easel while holding her artist's pad under her arm, trying not to put it on the ground.

'Can I give you some help with your easel?' I asked with uncharacteristic boldness.

'Easel!' she gasped, red-faced. 'Easel! The man said it was a deckchair.'

I laughed and took the pad from under her arm. She was quite small, with fair hair pulled back into a short ponytail, and a mischievous smile. 'Lift that bit upright,' I said, pointing, 'and tighten that wing nut.' She did as she was told and turned the nut the right way first time, which was a surprise.

'Well done,' I said. 'Now pull the middle leg back and tighten that one.'

'Ah!' she exclaimed. 'Now I see how it's done. You're a genius.' She extended the legs and locked them in position.

'I've done it before,' I told her. 'Maybe you're not mechanically minded.'

She tested the easel for rigidity and said: '*A body will remain at rest or in motion until it is acted upon by a force*. Isaac Newton said that and I agree with him. You can't be more mechanically minded than that. Do you paint?'

'*A body will remain at rest until the alarm clock goes off*. I said that. I went to art school, many years ago.'

'In that case,' she told me, looking up into my face and smiling, 'I'm not starting until you are a mere speck disappearing over that hill.'

'I'm going, I'm going.' I hitched my bag on to my shoulder and said: 'You've picked a nice spot.'

'It's lovely, isn't it? Enjoy your walk and thanks for your help.'

'Thank you.'

She'd given me a new zest for life. I walked too fast, buoyed by her cheerfulness, and was soon puffing. Grouse flew up around me, clucking and whirring like clockwork toys before they dived back into the heather further away, and another roll of thunder sounded ominously near.

Big blobs of rain were staining the path by the time I reached the Rocking Stone, pockmarking the dust with moon craters. I made it to the top and sheltered in a shooting hut while I donned my cagoul. Then the rain came in earnest, dark and powerful, Mother Nature showing us that the brief respite we'd had was at her whim. The path outside the hut became a stream and visibility dropped to about fifty yards, grey veils sweeping over the moor, one after another. I leaned in the doorway, dry and warm, and marvelled at it.

Five minutes later the storm had moved along, leaving a rainbow and a steady shower in its wake. I had intended to do a circular route, but I wasn't sure of the way and now the paths were sloppy with mud. I pushed my arms through the straps of my rucksack and went back the way I'd come.

It had been quite a downpour. The lazy river had become a torrent and the stepping stones were submerged. The bridge hadn't been swept away, thank goodness, but all the tourists had vanished. I soon found them. They were in the café, drying off. I unhooked my bag and edged between the stools and pushchairs, looking for an empty place at a clean table.

I walked straight past and wouldn't have recognised her if she hadn't pulled my sleeve. Her T-shirt was now covered by a blouse in an ethnic design from one of the more mountainous areas of the world, Peru or Nepal, at a guess, and her ponytail had come undone so her hair framed her face. It suited her that way. She was tucking into a giant sausage roll and a mug of tea.

'Hello,' I said, unashamedly delighted to see her again. 'Did you get wet?'

'Managed to dodge most of it. And you?'

'The same.' I pushed my bag under a spare chair and nodded

at her plate. 'That looks good. Can I get you another?'

'No, one's enough, thanks.'

'Tea?'

She shook her head.

One might have been enough for her but I ordered two, with a big dollop of brown sauce. I bought a large tea, without, and two iced buns with cherries on top. 'I've bought you a present,' I said as I sat down beside her.

'Oh, thank you,' she replied, slightly surprised, and took it from the plate I offered.

'How many paintings did you do?'

'About a half, that's all. What about you? Did you have a good walk?'

'Brilliant. Not very far, but the rain added a different dimension. I don't mind it.'

'It doesn't help when you're trying to paint in watercolours,' she told me.

She was a schoolteacher, which I found hard to believe – she looked about Sophie's age – and was called Elspeth. Her number one subjects were physics and biology but she was hoping to move into the private, that is, public, sector of education and another talent on her CV would be useful, hence the painting. She'd taught for three years at a big comprehensive in Leeds without a problem, but was beginning to think her luck might run out. I confessed to being a policeman and she wanted to know if I'd ever caught a murderer. It's easier to say no.

We were in mid-chat about the Big Bang theory when she looked at her watch and said she'd better go. She had a bus to catch.

'A bus?' I repeated. 'You came on the bus?' I said it as if she'd announced that she'd arrived by sedan chair.

''Fraid so. We humble teachers have difficulties with

mortgages; there's nothing left for luxuries like iced buns and motor cars.'

'My heart bleeds,' I said. 'Where do you live? I'll give you a lift.'

She said no, like any properly brought-up girl would, so I showed her my ID and a CID visiting card. 'Ring Directory Enquiries,' I told her, shoving my mobile across to her, 'and ask for Heckley police station. Check the number with that.'

'OK, I believe you. Thanks. I'd be very grateful for a lift.'

'Uh-uh,' I said, shaking my head. 'Ring 192 and ask.'

She did as she was told and checked the number against my card. 'It's the same,' she agreed.

'Right, now dial it.'

She dialled, and when someone answered I took the phone from her. 'Hi, Arthur,' I said, holding the phone so she could hear I was engaged in a conversation. 'It's Charlie. I'm expecting a call, has anyone been after me?' Nobody had. I told him where I was and about the weather and rang off. I hadn't meant to frighten her, but there's no harm in it. Psychopaths and fraudsters go to great lengths to appear legitimate. A few forged cards and a false ID would mean nothing to them. I could easily have watched her get on the bus, followed her and set the whole thing up. There are some wicked people out there.

We put her stuff in the boot and drove up the hill and through the ancient archway, heater at maximum to dry our feet. When we'd exhausted the Big Bang we talked about DNA testing. She explained the difference between meiosis and mitosis to me and I told her about the retrospective cases we'd solved. I probably said a good deal more than I ought, but she was interested and I enjoyed showing off.

On the outskirts of Leeds I said: 'Usually, after a walk, I

indulge in a Chinese. Would you let me treat you?'

'Ah,' she replied.

'Ah?' I echoed.

'I was just thinking that going home and starting to cook was a bit of a drag. Trouble is, I had a Chinese last night. How about a pizza or something, but it's my treat. We're not completely impoverished.'

'Um, I'm not a great pizza fan. Do you like spicy food?'

'Yes. Love it.'

'Right, then stand by for something different.'

I headed towards the city centre then picked up the Chapeltown signs. 'I spent some time here,' I told her. 'Got to know every eating house in the district.'

We went to the Magyar Club. It started life as a big house, probably for a merchant or a surgeon. It's escaped the division into bedsits that has befallen all its neighbours and now the descendants of the local Hungarian population meet here to keep their traditions alive. The place was empty, but later would resound to balalaika music, the stomping of boots and the clashing of vodka-filled glasses.

'Do you still do the best goulash in town?' I asked the steward when he came to see who was ringing the bell.

'We certainly do, sir,' he replied, only his broad face and fair hair indicating his ancestry. 'Come in.'

It hadn't changed at all. We had the speciality goulash and a small glass of red wine each. Elspeth didn't know whether to believe me when I told her it was Bull's Blood.

'Phew! That was good,' she proclaimed, wiping her chin with the linen napkin and settling back in her chair. 'How did you find out about this place?'

'I was the local bobby for a while. You get to know people in the community.'

'And can anybody come in?'

'I suppose so, but we probably wouldn't fit if it was busy. You'd give yourself away when it was your turn to do the Cossack dancing with a vodka bottle balanced on your nose.'

'Ah-ah! Are you pulling my leg?'

I shook my head. 'No.'

I broke a few seconds' silence by saying: 'You haven't mentioned your boyfriend once since I met you. Where have you left him?'

The smile slipped from her face for the briefest interval. She sighed, and told me: 'Oh, I don't have one. I seem to pick all the wrong ones. What about you? You haven't mentioned your wife at all.'

She didn't mince her words. 'Similar,' I replied. 'She left me so long ago that I think of myself as a life-long bachelor. I'd have thought that in a big school there would be some handsome geography master wanting to whisk you away from it all.'

She gave a private chuckle and said: 'There is one. He took me for a drink last week. He's thirty years old and teaches maths. I wasn't too disappointed when he arrived wearing a football jersey. It was blue and green stripes and looked quite nice.'

'Sounds like Stanley Accrington,' I interrupted.

'Stanley Accrington! Trouble was, it said something like . . . I don't know . . . *Syd's Exhausts* across the front, which completely ruined it. And if that wasn't enough, when he went to the bar I saw it had a player's name across the back. Thirty years old and he was pretending to be someone else! Can you believe it?'

'He was trying to impress you,' I told her. 'That was his mating plumage.'

'Well he can go mate with a goalpost, that's what I say. Do you know how much those jerseys cost? It's a real racket.'

'Mmm,' I replied. 'Forty-two quid. I bought one yesterday. A red one, with number seven, *Georgie Best*, across the back and *Phyllosan* across the front.'

'Oh no!' she cried, pulling her hair. 'Now you *are* having me on! Tell me you're having me on!'

'Actually . . .' I leaned across the table conspiratorially, '. . . you can buy them at less than half price from the street traders. Except that today, in Heckley, we had a clampdown on them. Arrested them all and confiscated their stock. Or we would have done if somebody who shall be nameless hadn't tipped them off.'

'Who'd do that?'

'Don't look at me!' I protested.

'You didn't!'

I winked at her. 'In CID we adopt a you-scratch-my-back-and-I'll-scratch-yours policy.'

'Charlie, that's *awful*!'

We paid the derisory bill and I took her home. She lived in a nice semi in Headingley where trees grew in the street and gardens had lawns and flower borders. I parked outside and opened the boot.

'This is where the salary goes,' she told me.

'You could always take in a student,' I suggested.

'No way. This is my little castle. I come home at night and lock the door with all the world and its troubles on the other side.'

'I know what you mean.' I lifted the easel out and she took it under her arm. The artist's pad went under the other and I hooked her bag over her head. 'Can you manage?' I asked as I loaded her to the gunwales.

'I think so.' She looked up into my face and said: 'You made it a lovely day, Charlie. Thanks for everything.'

'I've enjoyed meeting you, Elspeth,' I replied. 'Thank you for your company. I believe it's called serendipity.'

'Yes, it is. Well, thanks again.' She hitched the easel further under her arm, tightened her grip on the other stuff, and walked across the pavement towards her gate. She opened it, then turned and said: 'You could come in for a coffee.'

I shook my head. 'No, I don't think so.'

'Right. Goodbye then, Charlie.'

'Bye, love.'

I watched her go in, struggling with her cargo, and she gave me a wave from the front window. I pushed a cassette home and drove off. It was Gavin Bryars, not quite what I needed. I ejected it and fumbled for another, something jauntier. This time it was Dylan's *Before the Flood.* Just right. He was launching into 'Like a Rolling Stone' as I approached Hyde Park Corner. A gang of youths ambled across in front of me, even though the lights were green. I wound my window down and turned the volume to maximum. *How does it FEEL*? Dylan howled into the evening gloom.

I watched a wildlife programme and listened to some more music until bedtime, helped along with a can or two. Sunday I cleaned my boots and used the washing machine. Non-colour-fast cotton, my favourite cycle. I took the car to the garage for a shampoo and set and filled it with petrol. Inside I could smell Elspeth's perfume. I hadn't noticed it yesterday. Lunch was courtesy of Mr Birdseye and in the afternoon I vacuumed everywhere downstairs. I wasn't expecting upstairs visitors.

In the evening I took Jacquie to a pub out in the country. We sipped our halves of lager 'neath fake beams and admired the horse brasses that were probably made in Taiwan. I told her a bit about my day at Bolton Abbey, just the geography and weather, and she described the tribulations of being in business. Apparently the popular colours this winter are going to be emerald green and russet. Outside her house, before she could invite me in for coffee, I said that I wasn't going to see her again.

She took it badly. I told her that I was wasting her time and that it would be better for both of us. I didn't love her, didn't think I ever would. She cried a little and her shoulders trembled. I put my arm around them as she dried her eyes.

'Is it because I wouldn't go to bed with you?' she asked when she felt better.

'No,' I answered truthfully. 'Of course not.'

'I would have done, you know. When I was sure.'

'In that case, you were right not to.'

'Would it have made a difference?'

I shook my head. 'No. It would just have delayed things, that's all. This way we can still be friends.'

Trouble is, I haven't had much practice at this sort of thing. Mostly, we drift apart. Mutual consent or something. A few women had dumped me, some badly, but this was worse. All we want from life is to be happy. All we do is make each other unhappy. Tomorrow it would be back to chasing villains. You know where you stand with them.

Chapter 7

'Have you heard about the woodentops?' Jeff Caton asked as he joined us in my office on Monday morning.

'What have they done now?' Nigel enquired.

'Used up this month's overtime to nab a busker and an old lady collecting for the Sally Army. Apparently they had a crackdown on the unlicensed vendors in the town centre, but unfortunately they appear to have had wind of it. They were all elsewhere and Adey's furious.'

Dave said: 'Charlie buys all his clothes off them, don't you, boss?'

'Not all,' I replied. 'I get some in the market.'

'What, fakes?' Nigel asked.

'They're not fakes,' I told him. 'They just have different labels. They're made on the same machines from the same materials to the same patterns as the designer ones that you fashion victims are daft enough to buy.'

'The quality isn't as good,' Jeff declared.

'Of course it is.'

'I don't believe it.'

'Neither do I,' Nigel added.

'Listen,' I began. 'How much would you pay for a pair of Levi 501s?'

'About forty quid,' Jeff said and Nigel nodded.

'Well, I bought a pair in the market last week for fifteen pounds.'

'Genuine 501s?'

'The real thing. They'd just made a slight mistake with the labels and rejected the whole batch.'

'So what did the label say?'

'Elvis 150s.'

'*Elvis 150s*!' they scoffed in unison. You try to help them, to pass on the benefits of your accrued wisdom, but they just won't listen.

'Any chance of talking about work?' Dave wondered.

'Right!' I said, clapping my hands together. 'Enough of the tomfoolery. It's time to get our act together. Jeff?'

'Yes, boss.'

'You may have become aware that Dave and I have been preoccupied with something.'

'I'd noticed you're never here when I want you.'

'Sorry about that. Nigel will fill you in with the details but you'll probably see even less of us for a while. I want you to take over the robbery job, with Maggie. Don't be afraid to give the others plenty to do and let them get on with it. Nigel will oversee the day-to-day stuff but keep up to date with this other job and liaise between us all. You can stay now, if you want, otherwise we'll have a meeting on Friday afternoon to swap notes. OK?'

Jeff nodded. 'Fair enough. I'll float off, if you don't mind. I've plenty to do.'

'Right.'

'I'll see you later,' Nigel called after him as he closed the door.

I opened a window to let some fresh air in and gathered the

papers on my desk into a tidy pile. 'We'll have a quick recap, for your benefit, Nigel,' I began. 'Interrupt if you require more detail. If we consider the fire, and forget all the conjecture about Fox and Crosby, we believe that, a) a girl with purple hair possibly marked the house that burnt down, b) Duncan Roberts knew a girl with purple hair, c) Duncan recently confessed to starting the fire, d) a girl with purple hair was on a psychology course at Leeds Uni at the right time. She was called Melissa Youngman.'

Nigel said: 'So it looks as if she put him up to it?'

'Mmm,' I agreed. Turning to Dave I asked: 'Are you on Melissa's trail?'

'You bet,' he replied. 'Had no luck over the weekend, everywhere was shut, but I've sent my feelers out. Should have something later this morning.'

'Great. Let me know as soon as anything comes through. Once we discover who she is we should be up and running.'

I was downstairs, talking to the beat boys, when the desk sergeant waved to me, his hand over the telephone. 'Somebody in a callbox, Charlie,' he said. 'Asking for you. Won't give his name.'

I took the phone from him and made a writing gesture. He pushed a pad under my hand and pressed a pencil between my fingers. 'This is DI Priest,' I said. 'How can I help you?'

'It's me, Mr Priest. O'Keefe,' came a gruff voice.

'Hello, O'Keefe,' I said. 'What do you want?'

'I might 'ave summat for you.'

'Information?' I asked, just to confirm that he wasn't talking about a pair of thirty-six-inch inside-leg Wranglers.

'Yeah.'

'Right. Fire away.'

'Not on the phone, and my money's run out. I'm set up in Halifax.'

'Near the Piece Hall?'

'That's right.'

'OK. I'll be with you in half an hour.' I put the phone down and shoved the pad back across the counter.

'O'Keefe?' the desk sergeant asked. 'You mean old Walleye who sells jeans an' things?'

'His name is Wally,' I told him.

'Yeah, but everybody pronounces it Wall-eye.'

'I don't,' I replied, turning to leave.

He said: 'Wait a minute! If he's working for you . . . I don't suppose it was you who . . . no, you wouldn't . . . would you . . .?'

But I was halfway up the stairs, going for my jacket, before he synchronised his thoughts and his power of speech, so I never discovered what I might or might not have done.

On the drive to Halifax I listened to Radio Four and caught a sketch about Groucho Marx trying to buy a wooden Indian. I nearly drove off the road. Halifax is a handsome town with an ugly past. They had the guillotine here long before France adopted it, and at one time the death penalty was administered for stealing a shilling's worth of wool. Not for nothing did vagrants pray: 'From Hell, Hull and Halifax may the good Lord deliver us.' The town is built of stone, out of wool. The fine buildings and institutions hide the fact that it was also built on slavery. Not the African sort, who were transported thousands of miles and sold like cattle. These slaves still retained a fundamental freedom: they could work or starve, the choice was theirs. The mill owner had no investment in them, and no responsibility for their welfare. When they didn't work, through age or injury, sickness or circumstance, they didn't get paid. There are no stone monuments to the thousands who died of the diseases of squalor, or who tangled with the new-fangled machinery. They grew crooked-boned and bronchitic from sixteen hours a day in the mill, and if they survived all that a new horror awaited them. They developed cancer of the mouth, from 'kissing the shuttle'.

The Piece Hall is built around a cobbled quadrangle, with archways to allow one into a scene straight from the past. The building itself is three storeys high and comprised of an endless series of rooms, each big enough, just, to hold a weaver's loom. In the eighteenth and nineteenth centuries the weavers produced 'pieces', hence the name, for display down below. Nowadays it's a market, selling everything from eyelash curlers to cylinder head gaskets. There's the odd cabbage and carpet there, too, and it wouldn't have been a surprise to find a wooden Indian.

But O'Keefe wasn't there. He normally sets up shop outside, safe from the protests of the stallholders who pay dearly for the privilege of being on hallowed ground, but he wasn't near either entrance. I saw a shady figure selling gold chains from a suitcase but decided not to ask him. I was strolling around the street outside the hall, half looking for him, half admiring the shadows on the stone buildings, when O'Keefe tapped on the window of a café and beckoned me in.

'Thought I'd missed you,' I said, sitting down.

'Sorry about that, Mr Priest,' he replied. 'Sold out. Just waiting for my supplier to make anuvver delivery.'

A waitress came and I ordered us a tea each with another ham sandwich for O'Keefe to go with the one he was halfway through. 'Business must be good,' I told him.

'Yeah, well, you know what I always say. It's a bit like sex. Even when it's bad it's good.' He laughed just as much as before, giving me another view of his stumps, but this time there were wodges of half-masticated bread and ham clagging the gaps between them and strings of saliva hung down from his top palate. I turned away and gypped.

'So what can you tell me?' I asked when I dared look back at him.

He swallowed and scavenged around the recesses of his mouth with his tongue. 'Mate o' mine,' he began, 'heard a conversation in a pub. Might be interesting.' He rubbed his thumb and forefinger together in a gesture recognised in every market in the world.

I said: 'Don't muck me about, O'Keefe. I saved you losing your stock on Saturday, not to mention appearing before the beak this morning. If you've got something for me, let's have it.'

'Fair enough, Mr Priest. Thought it was worth a try, that's all. This mate. He was in t'Half a Sixpence, in Dewsbury, about a month ago. He was at t'bar, getting a pint, an' three blokes were leaning on it.'

'Go on.'

'Two of 'em was rough-looking, he reckoned. Not mucky or owt, but tough. 'Eavies, you might say. T'other one was a bit of a wide boy. Smart suit, sunglasses, 'anky in his top pocket.'

'What did they say?'

'I'm coming to it.' The waitress brought the teas and sandwich. When she'd gone he said: 'One of the rough ones asked t'toff if there was anything else. He said, no, just the computer, and 'anded 'im a bit o' paper. The rough one looked at it and said no problem. Then one of 'em said: "I don't suppose you want any elephant, do you?" an' they all 'ad a good laugh.'

'Elephant? What's that?' I asked.

'I dunno. My mate thought it was maybe a drug. Don't you know?'

'It could be. They have all sorts of different names for them.

A computer was bought with the stolen cards from the last robbery, so I'm fairly certain you're on to something, O'Keefe. You'd better tell me who this mate is.'

'He's called Collins. "Wilkie" Collins, but he won't talk to you. He 'ates cops.'

'Would I know him if I saw him?'

'Doubt it. He only does Dewsbury and Leeds.'

'OK, you'll have to talk to him for me. Tell him that it's only a matter of time before somebody dies and he could help prevent it. Maybe that will change his mind. For a start, I want a better description of all three of them. What time of day was it, did he say?'

'Dinner time.'

'Right. You've done well for me. Find out what you can and give me a ring. If I don't hear from you I'll come looking, eh?'

'Glad to be of assistance, Mr Priest,' he replied, grinning.

I left my tea untouched and drove back to Heckley. I skipped lunch. O'Keefe, with his odd eye and bad teeth, had left me without an appetite. He could earn a good living hiring himself out to slimming clubs as an appetite suppressant.

The outer office was deserted except for Dave, crouched over his desk, telephone to ear. He raised his head and gave me a thumbs-up as I walked through. There was a sheet of A4 on my desk with a message on it to ring DJ Roberts, timed at eleven seventeen, with a number I didn't recognise. I was staring at it when Dave ambled in.

'Seen this?' I said, waving the page before his eyes.

'Yeah. One of the girls brought it in and I had a quick look. DJ's the son, isn't he?'

'Mmm. Wonder what he wants?'

'Give him a ring.'

'First things first. How've you gone on?'

'Pretty good,' he said, settling on to the spare chair and smoothing a sheet of paper on the desk. 'Listen to this. Melissa Frances Youngman was born in Anlaby Maternity Home on New Year's Day 1951. She attended Cathedral Grammar School, Beverley, where she became head girl and passed ten O levels and four A levels. I spoke to the school secretary, she was very helpful. Melissa passed her driving test in 1968 but has never registered a motor vehicle.'

'Probably given driving lessons for doing so well at school,' I suggested.

'If that's a dig then I resent it,' he snarled.

'Sorry.'

'I should think so. In 1969 she enrolled at Essex University to study palaeontology and her mother died shortly afterwards, in August 1970. She was only forty-two.'

'Did you find cause of death?'

'Accidental overdose.'

'That must have been unsettling for Melissa.'

'It must, mustn't it? Her father, incidentally, died in 1995. Melissa only did one year at Essex, but there's a note on her record to say she applied to Edinburgh and the Sorbonne for a place there. That's in Paris.' He spun the sheet of paper round and pushed it towards me, so I could read his notes for myself.

'I thought it was in Scotland,' I said, but he ignored me. 1969, Essex, I thought. Then Edinburgh or the Sorbonne, and Leeds in 1975 or 1974. 'It looks as if she decided to become a professional student,' I declared, adding: 'I wonder what her influences were? Why would a small-town girl like that, with a decent intellect, dye her hair purple back in those days, when it was considered pretty outrageous?'

Dave said: 'I'm only a couple of years older than her and

when I was at school loads of the kids had their heads dyed purple.'

'That was by the Nit Lady,' I reminded him. 'You had to have a dose of malt every day, too, for rickets.'

'No, we had some white powder for them.'

'Rickets, not crickets. So what do you think?'

'What do *I* think?'

'Mmm.'

'I think you want me to start all over again at Edinburgh University and the Sorbonne, but you want me to volunteer because you daren't ask me yourself.'

'That's about it,' I admitted. '*Man with dog never has to bark.*'

'I might have to recruit Sophie's help again with the Sorbonne. She *parlais* better French than me.'

'So do Interpol,' I suggested.

He nodded his agreement. 'Why didn't I think of that?'

'There's one thing we could check,' I said.

'I know! I know! I hadn't forgotten. Has she any form? I'll do it now.' He stood up and went out into the big office, where one or two of the others had returned from wherever they'd been. I looked at my piled-up in-tray, grimaced, and reached for the top item. It was a report predicting the benefits of synchronised traffic lights on road congestion in the town centre. I ticked my name on the distribution list and slung it in the out-tray. If only they could all be so simple.

Dave was smiling when he came back five minutes later. 'Two convictions,' he told me. 'Possession of a small quantity of a Class B drug, namely cannabis, in 1970, while living in Essex, and possession with intent to supply in 1974, when she was, believe it or not, a student at Durham University.'

I said: 'Durham! Jesus! She gets around.'

'Small fine for the first offence. Community service order for the second.'

'That's been a good day's work,' I told him. 'Well done.'

'Cheers. Have you rung him?'

'Young Duncan? No, I'll do it now.' I found the telephone number and dialled, convinced that the code was one I'd never used before. A girl answered almost immediately.

'Is Duncan there, please?' I asked.

'Duncan? You mean DJ?' she asked.

'Yes.'

'Who wants him?'

'He wants me. He left a message.'

'I'll get him.'

I put my hand over the mouthpiece and hissed: 'Woman; she's fetching him.' I pointed to a phone in the outer office, and dialled the number to make it a party line. Dave went out and picked it up.

'Is that Inspector Priest?' said a voice I'd last heard talking about carburettors.

'Yes. How can I help you, DJ?'

'I, er, was just wondering about my Uncle Duncan. My dad told me you came to talk about him, free weeks ago, when I was fixing the bike.'

'That's right. Did you get it going?'

'Yeah. No problem. It's just that, I, er, was a bit closer to my uncle than my dad knew, what with being named after him an' all. Went to see him now and again. I just wondered if you could tell me anyfing about how he died, and why. If you know what I mean.'

'You used to visit him at . . . his flat?' I said, narrowly avoiding saying 'squat'.

'Yeah.'

'I went to have a look for myself, about a week after I saw you. Nice place he had.'

'Yeah, wicked.'

'Mr Wong, the landlord, showed me round,' I lied.

'Did he?'

'Mmm. Right, DJ, I'll tell you what we know. Your Uncle Duncan telephoned someone just before he died, confessing to starting a fire in Leeds, back in 1975. Eight people died in the fire, and it's still on our files as an unsolved crime – it was arson, started deliberately. I've been trying to link your uncle with it but so far can't find anything at all to suggest he was anywhere near or had anything to do with it. He was a sick man, DJ. Maybe he knew someone who died in the fire, someone he loved, and thought he could have saved them somehow. It might have been preying on his mind all these years. Perhaps, in the phone call, he didn't say he *started* the fire, perhaps he said he was *to blame for it*, and the person he was talking to misinterpreted his words. Do you follow what I'm saying?'

'Yeah, I fink so.'

'I don't know if that helps at all. Anything else you want to ask me?'

'No. That's about it. Fanks for ringing.'

'No problem, DJ. And any time you want to talk, you know where I am.'

'If you find anyfing else will you let me know?' he blurted out as an afterthought.

'Will do.'

'OK. Fanks again.'

We all replaced our phones and Dave joined me again. 'You handled that very, er, sensitively, squire, if you don't mind me saying so,' he told me.

'Li'l ol' smooth-talkin' me,' I said. 'Trouble is, he was lying through his teeth. Someone put him up to that call.'

'Oh. Who?'

'I don't know. His dad? His mum?' I reached into a drawer for my planner diary and turned to the back page where I write new telephone numbers. I said: 'The code for his parents, in Welwyn Garden City, is . . . here we are . . . 01707. And the code for wherever I've just rung him at is . . . 01524. Where's that?'

'Hang on,' Dave told me and went back out. I watched him walk over to the bookshelf where we keep all the telephone stuff and extract some pages stapled together. He consulted them for a few seconds, put them back and retraced his steps into my office.

'Lancaster,' he said.

'*Lancaster*?' I echoed. 'He's in Lancaster?'

'It sounds like it.'

'What the chuff's he doing there?'

We were discussing possibilities when Nigel and Jeff came in. Jeff was carrying a rolled-up tabloid, which he spread on my desk, saying: 'Seen this, boss?'

We were on the front page, or the Transit was. *Find This Van* ran the headline, over a full-page picture of a Transit doctored to look like the one we needed. That took care of page one. Inside, we learned that East Pennine police were putting lives at risk by not disclosing details of the vehicle used by villains who had terrorised old people right across the north of England, tying them to their chairs in their own homes while they ransacked, violated and desecrated. It was powerful stuff; interrupted only by Angharad on page three who wanted to be a brain surgeon and had nipples that stuck out like a racing dog's balls. If we were indifferent to the safety of the people, it went on, they, the *UK News*, would gladly take that responsibility upon themselves by publishing full details of the vehicle used in these dastardly crimes. They offered a £10,000 reward for anyone who found it, providing, of course, that they weren't policemen and it led to a conviction.

'See!' I declared. 'I told you to go public.'

'Um, no, boss,' Jeff replied. 'The way I, um, recollect things, you used your golden vote to overrule us all.'

'Did I!' I exclaimed. '*Moi*!'

Dave said: 'Blimey! You could hang your cap and a walking stick on them.'

'It might work,' Nigel told us. 'Perhaps someone will ring in.'

'Don't hold your breath,' Dave told him. '*Yuk News* readers probably think they're talking about something on television. They'll all be looking for a Transit in *EastEnders* tonight.'

'So what do we do?' Jeff asked.

'Nothing,' I replied. 'If the other papers don't pick it up we might get away with it. Chances of the villains seeing it are fairly small, and the *Yuk News*'s credibility is about as low as mine at the moment. Give something bland to the publicity department for them to hand out if anyone asks.'

'Right,' Jeff said, rolling the paper up and tossing it into the bin.

'Are you happy with that?' I asked him.

'Sure. No problems.'

'OK,' I said. 'Here's another for you. What is elephant?'

'Elephant?' they replied, not quite in unison.

'That's right. Elephant.'

'Big grey animal,' Dave told us. 'Pulls bunches of grass up with its tail and stuffs them up its arse.'

I ignored him and related the conversation that O'Keefe's pal, 'Wilkie' Collins, had overheard in the Half a Sixpence. 'So what did he mean?' I asked.

'Horse is heroin,' Nigel said. 'Could be the same. *Elephant*, sounds reasonable. Or perhaps it's simply E for Ecstasy.'

'It must be drugs,' Jeff agreed. 'Herbal cannabis looks a bit like elephant shit.'

'Have you ever seen elephant shit?' I asked.

'Well, no, but it looks like it ought to look. And shit's cannabis.'

'Trouble is,' Nigel said, 'they change the names all the time. It's best to just use the proper name when you talk to them. If you try to be clever and streetwise you end up looking foolish.'

'It's not Ecstasy,' Jeff declared. 'It's too butch for Ecstasy.'

Nigel, thinking aloud, mumbled: 'Elephant . . . elephant . . . elephant . . . s'foot umbrella stand.'

We were getting nowhere until Dave made a contribution. 'It's rhyming slang,' he said.

'Go on,' I urged him.

'I don't know what for. Elephant something . . . then something else that rhymes with it, like, oh, er, horse and cart . . . fart.'

'Earthy as always, David,' I said. 'So keep going.'

He thought for a few seconds, then offered us: 'Elephant's trunk . . . um . . . skunk.'

'That's cannabis,' Jeff told us.

'Elephant's trunk, junk,' Nigel suggested.

'That's heroin,' Jeff confirmed.

I said: 'Sounds highly likely it's one or the other. Have a word with O'Keefe, Jeff, and see if he's anything to add. Have a few liquid lunches in the Half a Sixpence; they sound a distinctive trio, you might recognise them. And let Drugs know about it; maybe they'll have some ideas of their own.'

'Right,' he replied, adding: 'My money's on skunk. The place is flooded with it.'

* * *

Things were moving, and that gives me a good feeling. I'd have liked to have kept working on the burglaries but I had to let go and give Jeff a chance. If he caught them I'd still get the credit, but all the satisfaction of feeling their collars would be his. We now had a name for the girl with purple hair, and that would lead to other names, dozens of them, one of whom might hold the key to eight agonising deaths. I'd be more than satisfied if we could solve this piece of unfinished business.

Interpol came back to us on Tuesday afternoon. They had a file on Melissa Youngman because of her drugs conviction and some doubtful associates, and had faxed us a résumé. She'd attended seven universities, including the University of California, Los Angeles, but had never graduated. Not in any of the named subjects, that is. Her studies had given her foundation courses on palaeontology, very useful; modern languages; psychology; politics and business studies. No bomb-making, but a well-rounded education by any standards. The last bit was most interesting. When at UCLA she had contacted a right-wing group of militiamen and was believed to be currently living in the States. Consult FBI for further details, it said, which was all the encouragement Dave required.

'They're five hours behind us,' Dave reminded me when our paths crossed and he had an opportunity to tell me how hard he'd worked. 'Somebody called Agent Kaprowski is attending to it and will ring back. I'm taking the kids to the baths, so I've given him your home number and our office hours. Is that OK?'

'You've been a little beaver on this, Dave,' I told him, knowing that sitting in the office using the telephone was not his favourite style of policing. 'I appreciate it.'

'That's because I've a ghost to lay,' he replied grimly.

We'd never talked about me dragging him out of that burning building all those years ago. I'd always suspected that a little bit of him blamed me for not letting him try to rescue Jasmine Turnbull, but he'd never said anything. I didn't feel guilty about it; he hadn't stood a chance. 'I know, old son,' I said. 'I know you have.' I reread the fax and that old restless feeling began to swell inside me. We were on to something, I was sure of that. 'Some time tomorrow,' I said, 'have a word with Graham at the SFO and tell him where we're at. If we're dealing with the FBI and Interpol we should keep them informed, and no doubt they have some better contacts than us. Give him some of it to do, if you want.'

'Did you say he's a DS?'

'Yeah.'

'Right. No sweat.'

I called at the supermarket and bought a fresh trout and a ready-made salad, determined to improve my eating habits. Smothered in margarine and four minutes in the microwave and the trout would be delicious. The oven was pinging to say it was ready when the phone rang. 'DI Priest, Heckley CID,' I barked into it.

It was Loopy Lucille from Easybroke Windows. They were working in my area – again – and looking for a show house that they could fix at a huge discount PLUS offering four windows for the price of six and when could they start?

I said: 'Er, no thanks, love.' That trout smelled good.

'What about a conservatory?' she asked. They were doing interest-free credit on conservatories.

'Er, no, love.'

'A patio door?'

'I don't have a patio.'

'Our range of Victorian patios come complete with free dwarf conifers. When would you like our surveyor to call?'

'No thanks.'

'Plastic guttering, soffits and fascia boards?'

'No.'

'Imitation stone cladding?'

'No.'

''Block-paved driveway?'

'No.'

'Well, thank you for your time, Mr Priest,' she sang, unperturbed by rejection.

I couldn't believe it. She was about to put her phone down, allowing me to return to my meal, when I heard myself saying: 'Wooden Indians.'

'Pardon,' she said.

'Wooden Indians,' I repeated. 'I don't suppose you do wooden Indians. I've been trying to find a wooden Indian for years.'

'Wooden . . . Indians?' she queried. They weren't in her script.

'That's right.'

'I'll put you through to my manager. Hold the line, please.'

The New World symphony burst into my left ear as she briefed her manager. I remembered a little dodge I used to be good at when I spent some time on the front desk, and wondered if I could still do it. If one of our regulars rang the nick to complain about a domestic I used to make clicking noises like a loose connection on the line. I was young and irresponsible in those days. After struggling to be understood for a while they'd say: 'Oh, forget it,' and stab their husband with the potato peeler.

'Hello, Mr Priest,' came a cheery voice.

'Actually, it's the Reverend Priest,' I replied.

'Reverend Priest! Well, good evening, sir. How are you this evening?'

'Very well, *ck ck* you.'

'Good. And a lovely evening it is too.'

'It is, isn't *ck ck*?'

'This is a bad line,' he told me. 'Can I just check your number, Reverend Priest, and I'll ring you back.' I agreed that he'd got it right and held the bar down. The phone rang immediately.

'Ah, that's better,' he began. 'Now, could you please tell me what it was you're interested in, Reverend Priest. Lucille didn't quite catch what you said.'

'I told her I was considering *ck ck* a conservatory, if the price was *ck ck*.'

'Right, sir. I'm afraid this line is just the same.'

'I can *ck ck* you perfectly well.'

'Good. Good. So when will it be convenient for someone to come and discuss our range of Georgian, Victorian and Edwardian conservatories with you?'

'I'd prefer it if you could just give me an approximate *ck ck* over the phone. I may not be *ck ck* to afford one.'

'We're not really able to give prices over the phone,' he replied. 'There are so many different considerations, such as size and style and . . .'

'Oh, I *ck ck* the size,' I interrupted. 'It will have to be *ck ck* six inches long by *ck ck* six inches wide.'

'I didn't quite catch that, sir.'

'I said *ck ck* six inches long and *ck ck* six inches wide.'

'I'm sorry, sir,' he said. 'I'm only getting the six inches.'

'Ooh! You should be so lucky!' I told him and he called me a fucking wanker and we slammed our phones down more or less simultaneously.

Agent Kaprowski rang just after nine, while I was still basking in the warm glow of success. 'According to Officer Sparkington you're interested in a lady called Melissa Youngman,' he said, after the introductions. 'I'd be appreciative if you could tell me what your concern is, Inspector Priest.'

'Right,' I told him. 'First of all can I say thanks for ringing,

Agent Kaprowski. Do I, er, have to keep calling you Agent Kaprowski? I answer to Charlie.'

'Pleased to have your acquaintance, Charlie. I'm Mike.'

'That's better. OK, Mike, here we go.' I told him briefly about the fire and Melissa's possible involvement. I made it vague and general, and said we thought there might have been a political motive. I suggested that it gave us a window on to a much bigger picture, but at the moment it was dark out there. He made *uh-uh* noises at appropriate intervals. I finished by asking why the FBI had a file on her.

'Routine,' he replied. 'It was opened in '73 when she came to UCLA, presumably because of her drugs conviction. They were heady days back then, and all sorts of cuckoos were coming in and causing trouble. Miss Youngman, it says here, had friends in Paris who were believed to be attached to the Red Brigade. They were a bunch o' left-wing loonies based in Italy. She left the US a year later, re-entered in 1989 and immediately made contact with a militia group in Tennessee. That's about the size of it. Did you say this fire was back in '75?'

'Yes.'

'Gee! Don't you guys ever give up?'

'Just catching up with my workload, Mike. I thought these militia groups you have were *right*-wing.'

'Right-wing, left-wing, what's the difference? Do you subscribe to the theory that the world is round, Charlie?'

'Er, yes.'

'That's a concept that a farm boy from Iowa like me has difficulty grappling with. Apparently if you walk far enough in one direction you'll find yourself coming back the other way. It's just the same with these groups; they all widdle in the same creek. If the guns are big enough and it messes with the government, they'll join.'

'I get the message. Do you know where she is now?'

'Youngman? No, but I reckon we could find her without breaking a sweat. You want her back?'

'I'm not sure. We might one day, but at the moment we're only gathering background, acquaintances, you know the thing.'

'Well, just let me know if you do, and I'll put her on the next plane with a liddle label around her neck.'

'She sounds a delightful lady, I can hardly wait. Thanks for your help, Mike, and I'll be in touch.'

'My pleasure, Charlie. Adios.'

'Adios.'

Adios. I liked that. I replaced the phone and said it again. 'Adios. Adios. Adios, *amigo.*' So Melissa was in America, running through the woods with a bunch of rednecks whose wives had backsides bigger than their pickups and whose idea of entertainment was arm-wrestling with a bear. Should be right up the street of an ex-head girl of Beverley Cathedral Grammar School, I thought.

Chapter 8

The anticyclone re-established itself over the Bay of Biscay, pushing the threat of unsettled weather back over Russia, where it belonged. Dave finished his painting, the M62 was closed for two hours by grass fires, and I mowed my lawn. A judicious grass fire would have saved me the bother. Once again the bright tables and umbrellas sprang up all over the precinct, like toadstools in a book of fairy stories, and commerce slowed to a standstill. Crime didn't. Lust is mercury-filled; it rises and falls with temperature. Hot afternoons, scant clothing, walks in the meadows; it's a potent mixture. Add lunchtime drinking outside the pub with the new girl from Telesales and you have all the ingredients for rape, and we had several. Not by the inadequate loner, waiting for a victim, any victim, and striking violently. These were between semi-consenting couples who were carried away by the moment. Two of them were mothers complaining about the boys next door and their daughters, and one housewife thought that inviting the builder in for a beer was normal behaviour, even if she was wearing a bikini and had spent all morning sunbathing topless. We had a rubber stamp made that said: 'She was asking for it,' to speed up the statements.

The druggies changed their *modus operandi*, too. Open windows facilitated the taking of tellies and videos, but demand was down. Garden tools, barbecue furniture and big chimney pots, plants for growing in, became the new currency. It added some variety to the job and the woodentops had to learn how to spell some new words.

'Ta-da!' Dave fanfared as he came into my office on Wednesday morning, his smile broader than a seaside comedian's lapels.

'What?' I said, lifting the pile of papers in my in-tray and sliding the request for next year's budget underneath.

He sat down and grinned at me.

'Go on,' I invited, 'or is that it?'

'That Piers Forrester is a really nice bloke,' he told me.

'He's a supercilious twat,' I replied.

'He's been very helpful.'

'He wears a dickie bow.'

'Oh, so he's a supercilious twat because he wears a dickie bow, is he?'

'Yes.'

'And Graham's OK, too.'

'He's all right, I suppose.'

'Because he doesn't wear a dickie bow?'

'He wears Yves St Laurent short-sleeved shirts. That must say something about him.'

'Like what?'

'I don't know. You're the detective, I'm just the office boy. What have you found out?'

'Right,' he replied, eagerly. 'We've cracked it.'

'Go on.'

'Melissa went to grammar school in Beverley, didn't she?'

'Yep.'

'And then on to Essex University.'

'Mmm.'

'So Graham has paid them a visit to have a look at her classmates there, like I did for Duncan in Leeds. And guess what?'

'I'm all ears.'

'There was another girl enrolled there at the same time, from the same school in Beverley. She was called Janet Wilson. She's bound to have been in the same class as Melissa, don't you think? She must know her.'

I let my glum look slip, but only briefly. 'What do you mean by *was* called Janet Wilson?' I asked.

'She's married, that's all. She's now called Janet Holmes, and lives at the Coppice, Bishop's Court, York. We could be there in an hour.'

You can learn a lot about a person from the pictures they have on their wall. This one was a tinted drawing, larger than average, of a circular construction. It looked Moorish at first glance, and I expected it to be called something like *In the Courtyard of the Alhambra*, but when I looked closer I realised it was biological. What I'd taken as tiles or pieces of mosaic were individual cells.

'Do you like it?' Mrs Holmes asked as she came into the room, carrying a tray.

'It's not what it seems,' I replied, 'and that intrigues me. It's also very attractive.'

'Your sergeant's call certainly intrigued me,' she replied. 'Please, sit down.'

'Constable,' Dave corrected.

There was a caption and a signature under the picture. They read: *Ascaris lumbricoides* and *J. Holmes*. I said: 'Did you do this, Mrs Holmes?' sounding impressed.

'It's what I do for a living,' she answered. 'I'm a technical illustrator. I took a few liberties with the colour on that one, but it's not great art.'

'The inspector's into painting,' Dave told her. 'Went to art college. He does all our wanted posters.'

'Really?' she replied.

'He jests,' I told her. 'So what exactly is an ascaris whatsit?'

'It's a nasty little parasite that lives in pigs and occasionally in humans.'

''You mean, like a tapeworm?'

'Very similar, but they only grow to about a foot in length.'

'*Only* a foot!' Dave exclaimed. 'Blimey! So how long does a tapeworm grow?'

'Oh, the common tapeworm can reach twenty feet,' she told him.

'Urgh!' he responded. 'I'll never have another bacon sandwich.'

Mrs Holmes poured the tea and suggested we help ourselves to milk and sugar. 'Now, what is it you want to know about Essex University in the early seventies?' she asked. 'I'm totally fascinated.'

She was a good-looking woman, easier to imagine addressing a class or opening a fête than looking through a microscope. I sat down and took a sip of tea from the china cup. She'd also supplied scones which looked homemade and more in character with her appearance.

'Do you work from home?' I asked.

'Yes,' she replied. 'My husband left me two years ago, as soon as the children were off our hands. Traded me in for a younger model; and more streamlined.' She patted her hips, which looked perfectly reasonable to me. 'I'd always been an illustrator, which was considered something of a cop-out for someone with a degree, but now there's a bigger than ever demand for my services. I do lots of computer animation, too, of course, but a good animator can name her own price, almost.'

It explained a lot. The house was a four-bedroomed detached on a swish estate just down-river from the bishop's palace. We knew she'd lived there for nine years, so it must have been the marital home, but she'd managed to keep it. Working alone, in her studio, explained the hospitality, which was above that we normally received. Two handsome detectives were visiting and she probably hadn't spoken to anyone livelier than a checkout girl all week. Get out the decent cups and some buns.

'So,' she said, 'what's this all about?'

I reached for a plate and a scone and settled back in my easy chair, gesturing towards Dave. 'DC Sparkington will tell you,' I said, adding: 'The scones look good.'

'They're from Betty's,' she told me.

'And I thought they looked homemade,' I replied.

'No. I'm afraid I'm the world's worst cook.' Ah, well, I can't be right all the time.

Dave took a drink of tea and placed the cup and saucer back on the low table that was between us. 'You went to the Cathedral Grammar School at Beverley, I believe, Mrs Holmes?'

'Yes, that's right.' She leaned forward, interested, and interlinked her fingers around her knee.

'And from there?'

'From there I went to Essex University for four years, as you know.'

'Reading . . .'

'Biology.'

'Was anyone else from Beverley accepted for Essex?' Dave asked. I had to smile. A week ago he'd have said: 'What were you taking?' and: 'Did anyone else go to Essex?'

'Yes, there was one other girl,' she replied.

'Called . . .' Dave prompted.

'Melissa. Melissa Youngman.'

'How well did you know her?'

'Quite well. We weren't friends, but we were in the same classes at Beverley for seven years, plus a year at Essex.'

'Were you on the same course?' Dave asked, puzzled.

'No. Melissa read palaeontology, but some of our courses were combined for the first year. And we shared a house.'

'You shared a house? How did that come about?'

'Melissa's parents bought a little semi for her, and I had a room in it. It was normal for freshers to stay in a hall of residence, so we had to have a special dispensation, but it only lasted a year. I moved out and Melissa moved on.'

'Where to?'

'Melissa? I don't know.'

'Tell me about her,' Dave invited.

I put my empty plate back on the table and settled back to listen.

'Tell you about Melissa?' she queried.

'Yes please.'

Mrs Holmes's face looked mystified for a few seconds, then broke into a smile of realisation. 'It's Melissa you want to know about, isn't it?' she demanded, unable to contain her delight. 'What has she done now?'

'Her name has cropped up in an investigation,' Dave told her. 'We don't know if she is involved but we'd be grateful for anything you can tell us about her.'

'About poor Melissa? Good grief.'

'Yes please.'

'Well, let me see . . .' Mrs Holmes hadn't spoken to a soul for a fortnight, and now she was being given the invitation to gossip about her best schoolfriend, who she hated, by two people who were trained listeners with no intention of interrupting. It was a moment to savour. She gathered her thoughts, smoothed her flowered skirt and began.

Melissa was head girl, which we knew, and a brilliant scholar. Annoyingly, she was also good at games, and not considered a swot by anyone. She had long hair, down to her waist, and her parents doted on her. They were always in the front row at speech days and school plays, applauding their daughter long after everyone else had stopped. But something happened to her in that first week at university, and Mrs Holmes didn't know what it was.

'All sorts of societies organised meetings and parties for the new students, partly to entertain us and break the ice, partly to recruit new members. We went to one, I remember, about the rain forests, which weren't quite the *cause célèbre* in 1969 that they are now. Oh! The high life! Those were the days,' she laughed, and I noticed that she still had a girlishly happy face. Betrayal and disappointment hadn't left their mark. 'On the Friday,' she continued, ' – and this is still the first week - Melissa announced that we were going to a lecture about a man called Aleister Crowley. Have you ever heard of him?'

Dave said: 'No,' and I left it at that, although I had.

'He was the self-styled wickedest man in the world, apparently, although it all sounded harmlessly bonkers to me. He was a witch, a warlock, I suppose, who climbed Everest without oxygen or warm clothing and performed other fiendish deeds like that. He probably did spells and things, but the Everest bit is all that I can remember. Melissa was fascinated. Or maybe it was the lecturer who captivated her. He was a bit of a dish, if you like that sort of thing, but far too smooth for me. Afterwards she trapped him in a corner and wouldn't let him go. I waited for ages, sipping a half of beer and wondering why people drank the stuff,' she laughed again, 'until Melissa came over and told me that it was all right, Nick would see her home later.'

'Nick?' I asked.

'Nick Kingston, the lecturer. Apparently he also taught psychology at the university, although we didn't know that at the time. So I walked home all by myself and Melissa stayed out all night. I was shocked, but that was only the beginning.'

'Why? What happened next?'

'I didn't see her until she came in, late Saturday afternoon. She'd had all her hair chopped off and it looked a dreadful mess. I asked her why and she just said she was sick of it. The following week she had it dyed and she had her nose pierced. She was a different person.'

'What colour did she dye it?' we both asked.

'Bright red.' Ah, well, she still had six years to go purple.

'Was there anything else?' I wondered.

'Not really,' Mrs Holmes replied. 'We drifted apart after that. I knew I had to work hard, and I didn't want to let my parents down. I know it's corny, but they made sacrifices to send me to university, and I wasn't as gifted as Melissa. I thought she wasted her talents, and to be honest, I grew to dislike her.'

'Did she and this Kingston become a couple?' Dave asked.

'For a while,' Mrs Holmes answered, 'and then . . .' She covered her face with her hands and began to laugh uncontrollably. 'Oh my goodness!' she exclaimed as she recovered. 'I don't know if I should tell you . . .'

Her laughter was infectious. 'If you don't,' I said, smiling, 'we'll just have to arrest you and take you to the station to make a statement.'

She blew her nose on a tissue and concealed it somewhere in the folds of her skirt. 'It was awful,' she declared, but her expression said otherwise.

'What happened?' I asked.

'We went to a party at Nick Kingston's flat. It must have been after Christmas, because I'd taken my father's car back down there after the holiday. It was a Morris Minor, and he said I'd have more use for it than him. After that, I was invited to a lot more parties, because I was good for a lift. I remember! It was to watch a moon landing, that was it! *Apollo 13*, the one that had problems. We were all interested, history was being made, but Kingston knew everything about it. He was a complete show-off. Would you like some more tea?'

We would. She refilled our cups and I invited her to continue.

'Kingston was awful to Melissa. They'd seen a lot of each other up to then, but I could see he was deliberately ignoring her and chasing another girl. Melissa took her revenge by latching on to poor Mo.'

'Mo?'

That smile came back, but wistful this time. 'That's right, short for Mobo Dlamini. He was from Swaziland, that's in South Africa, and a lovely person. His father or grandfather was the king, and he came over here to study law.'

'Could you spell it, please?' Dave asked, and noted it down.

'I went home just as it was breaking dawn,' Mrs Holmes continued, 'but Melissa didn't come with me. I heard her and Mo arrive much later. Their giggles and antics woke me up. About lunchtime I had my revenge. There was a knock at the door and who should I find there but Melissa's parents, Mr and Mrs Youngman. They pushed past me and marched up to her room. Can you imagine their reactions? Not only was their darling daughter in bed with a man, but he was a *black* man. It was awful. I heard most of it and Mo told me the rest. They stormed out and drove away, and I don't think she saw them again. I gave Mo some aspirin and some breakfast and took him home.'

'This was early 1970?' I asked.

'Yes.'

'Melissa's mother died of an overdose in August of that year,' I said.

'Oh no,' Janet Holmes sighed. 'The poor woman.'

'Melissa sounds a right little charmer,' Dave declared. 'I'm not surprised you disliked her.'

'What happened to them all?' I asked.

She took a deep breath and thought for a few seconds. 'That was the end of our friendship, if you could call it that. I moved out and concentrated on my studies. Melissa didn't do the second year and I haven't heard a whisper of her until now. Mo joined a firm of solicitors in London and married an English girl. We kept in touch until I left university, but I don't know what happened to him.'

'And Kingston?' I prompted.

She hesitated before shaking her head and saying: 'I don't know.'

My tea was cold but I finished it off. Putting the cup down I said: 'You wouldn't happen to have any photographs, would you?'

Our lucky streak stayed with us. She sat upright, stretching her spine to its full extent, and said: 'Why didn't I think of that? Of course I have, somewhere.'

'We'd be grateful if you could find them.'

She said it would take a few minutes, but she knew where they should be if we didn't mind waiting. We passed the time by having another scone each and I studied the cross-section of the beastie above the fireplace. Seeing one of them down the pan would ruin your morning.

It took a little longer than we expected, and she had a smudge of dust on her nose when she returned, explaining that they were in the loft and she rarely went up there. 'Here we are,' she said, laying an album on the table. It said 'Essex' on the cover in ornate lettering.

There were only four that were relevant to our inquiry. Melissa, Mo and Mrs Holmes, or Miss Wilson as she was then, were in self-conscious poses with several other young people in the various stages of inebriation. 'Which one is you?' I'd asked after she'd pointed to Melissa on three of them.

'There,' she said, 'and there,' indicating a slim girl with long straight hair.

'You look like Julie Felix,' I said.

She blushed and said: 'I did a reasonable impersonation of her with the guitar, when pressed.'

'And that must be Mo.'

'A brilliant deduction, my dear Watson,' she replied. He was the only black person in the photographs.

'Elementary, Holmes,' I said, on cue, and she gave me a wistful smile, as if I'd stumbled into a private joke that she hadn't heard for a long time.

The pictures weren't the great breakthrough we'd hoped they might be. They were small, two and a quarter inches square at a guess, and black and white. The quality was excellent, but the poses were informal and not much use for identification purposes.

'Can we borrow these?' I asked.

'Yes, of course.'

'Is Kingston in any?' Dave wondered.

'No. He took them, but would never let anybody else handle his precious camera. It was the same as the first men on the moon used, he claimed. Another of his boasts. He did us all a set of contact prints, but would charge us for enlargements, if we wanted them. He wasn't famous for his generosity, just the opposite. Photography was one of his hobbies.'

'Along with witchcraft,' Dave suggested.

'Yes, and keep-fit and rock climbing. He was into everything. He was an interesting person, in a way, but weird with it. And slimy. I didn't like *him*, either.' She laughed again and said: 'I'm awful, aren't I?'

I assured her she wasn't and thanked her for everything. We placed our cups on the tray and I held the door for her as we walked through into the kitchen. Outside, there was a table on the lawn, with one chair against it, and the grass had been half-cut and then abandoned. 'Do you know where Melissa is?' Mrs Holmes asked.

'We believe she's in the United States,' I replied.

'I've always thought I'd read about her one day,' she said. 'She was a remarkable girl, but after that episode with her parents I decided she was heartless, capable of anything. Nothing Melissa did would surprise me.'

'You've dust on your nose,' I said, smiling.

'A talented lady,' Dave commented as we rejoined the A1.

'Mmm. And capable of anything, it would appear.'

'Who?'

'Melissa.'

'I meant Mrs Holmes.'

'Yes, she's a clever woman.'

'And nice, too.'

'What are you getting at?' I asked.

'Nothing, but you could do worse.'

'She can't cook,' I replied.

'I suspect she was being modest, and that's what takeaways are for.'

'She's not my type.'

'No? I bet that when we've had these photos enlarged you just happen to return the originals personally.'

'I might. The camera was a Hasselblad, by the way,' I said.

'I know. And the moon men left theirs at the Sea of Tranquillity. Shall we go fetch it tomorrow?'

'Good idea.'

We went to London instead. I'd wanted Dave to have a day down there to meet Graham and the team and compare notes. Our loose agreement was that we'd concentrate on the fire and they would resurrect the files on the other deaths that had accumulated on J.J. Fox's path to fortune. When we'd arrived back at the office I'd rung the SFO and Graham had quickly discovered that Mo Dlamini lived in Southwark, south London, and had carved himself a reputation as a worker for civil liberties. Nicholas Kingston was harder to pin down. I decided we'd both go; meet them mob-handed. Dave could drive us there while I snoozed.

Taking the car into town was a mistake. I'd timed it so we'd arrive about ten o'clock, but every hour is rush hour in London, and people were killing for parking places. We eventually muscled into a space and I took Dave into the hallowed halls of the Serious Fraud Office. A quick phone call told me that Mo Dlamini would be in his office most of the day and I left Dave discussing tactics with his new friends, Graham and Piers.

There was a tube train waiting at the platform, but I didn't know which way it was heading. I jumped on and risked it. At the next station I got off and looked for the down line. I'm just a country bumpkin at heart. Southwark is just across the river, according to the map, but it still took me nearly an hour to find his office. It was in a purpose-built Community and Resources centre, with graffiti on the walls next to posters about needle sharing and benefit cheats. Thursday was basketball, and two teams of youths were charging about in a huge gymnasium and getting nowhere, in spite of all having the proper gear. Looking the part is all. Their shouts and the shrieks of rubber against wooden floor were deafening. I watched them for a few seconds with the door ajar and decided he wouldn't be in there. A woman with two toddlers asked me where the toilets were. I'd noticed them when I came in, so I pointed and said: 'At the end.' If in doubt, ask a policeman. There were several other doors off the corridor, some padlocked, some open. One led to a kitchen where a youth with a shaved head and a bolt through his neck was mopping the floor. 'Where's Mr Dlamini's office?' I asked.

'Who?' he replied.

'Mo Dlamini.'

'Dunno.'

'Thanks.'

Fortunately for me a human being came round the corner, wearing a dog collar, and he told me that Mo's office was the last on the left. I knocked and a voice shouted:

'Come in!'

Everybody in this case is older than I expected. Not *old*, exactly, but more mature. In their prime. About my age. I imagined everybody as if frozen at the age they were in the seventies, before twenty-three years of striving to earn a living had taken their toll. Mo Dlamini's hair was seriously greying, but he was as big as he'd looked on the photos and the expression was just as open and confident. He was a lighter colour than I thought he'd be, and his features were soft, almost European. He shook my hand vigorously and introduced me to his son, Ainsley.

Ainsley was leaning on the wall because it was easier for him than contorting his frame into one of the little stacking chairs.

Including his hair he must have been nearly seven feet tall and was built like a clothes prop. 'Hi, Ainsley,' I said, peering at the discreet logo on the left breast of his dazzling white T-shirt as we exchanged handshakes. It said *calvin bolloCKs*, and I warmed to him immediately.

'Sit down, Inspector Priest,' Dlamini invited, 'and tell us what we can do for you. You're a long way from Yorkshire so it must be important.'

'Thanks.' I coiled myself into the chair he gestured towards and took a quick glance at my surroundings. It wasn't exactly the office of a hot-shot lawyer, with its transport café Formica table, bare walls and tiled floor. I decided that this was where he held his surgeries. The heavyweight bookcases, VDUs, coffee percolator and secretarial staff were elsewhere. I looked at Ainsley then back at Dlamini and said: 'Some of the stuff I want to discuss is of a confidential nature . . .' I left it hanging and they both took the hint.

'I'll see how the basketball's going,' Ainsley said, launching himself towards the door. 'Pleasure to meet you, Inspector.'

'Likewise, Ainsley,' I replied. 'Nothing personal.'

'Ring your mum,' his father shouted after him, followed by, 'Kids, who'd have 'em?'

'He's a big lad,' I observed.

'Big? I work the first three days of the week just to feed him. So what's this all about?'

I dived straight in. 'I'd like you to cast your mind back to 1970 if you can, Mr Dlamini. Can you remember where you were then?'

'1970? Jesus,' he replied. 'First of all, it's Mo. Everybody calls me Mo.'

'And I'm Charlie.' I told him.

'Right. Let me see . . . in 1970 I was gaining work experience on company law with a firm of solicitors in Colchester, Essex. Do you need any more than that?'

'No, that's fine. Do you remember going to a party in April of that year? It might be helpful if I tell you that the party coincided with the *Apollo 13* moon mission, which was the one that nearly ended in disaster.'

The corner of his mouth twitched, but I couldn't tell if it was a stifled smile or embarrassment or something else. He tried to speak, hesitated, and tried again. 'Party?' he mumbled, his thoughts miles and years away.

'*Apollo 13*,' I prompted.

'Yes, I remember,' he admitted, struggling to appear impassive.

'Can you remember anybody else who was there?'

He thought about it, but all he could remember was that he was a lawyer. 'No,' he replied, shaking his head.

'Maybe I can jog your memory. Did you meet a young lady called Melissa Youngman there? She was quite distinctive-looking. Had dyed red hair.'

The description was unnecessary because he was already holding his head in his hands. He pulled at his hair in a parody of despair and cried: 'A lawyer! My kingdom for a lawyer!' When he recovered from the shock he said: 'What's she doing? Kiss 'n' telling?'

'Not that I know of,' I replied. 'Her name keeps cropping up in our investigations and they brought us to you. What can *you* tell us about *her*?'

'God!' he croaked, grinning at the memories. 'If this gets out I'm finished. What can I tell you about her? Nothing, Charlie. Nothing at all.'

'Didn't you have an affair with her?'

'An affair! We had one night of rampant lust and that was it.

She left me gasping for release, trying to beat the door down to escape. I never went out with her or anything because I stayed well away. That's all.'

'I believe you were interrupted,' I said.

He suddenly looked grave. 'You know about that?' he replied. 'God, that was awful. Her parents came marching in. It was very unpleasant. I tried to be reasonable, said I loved her, we were engaged and stuff like that, but she didn't give a toss. *She* called *them* names. And her language . . . it was fucking this and fucking that . . . to her *parents*! Not a night or a young lady I choose to remember, Charlie. Thanks a bunch for reminding me.'

'It had to be done. So how did you meet her? Were you introduced?'

'Yeah. This so-called friend introduced me to her. I think she had been his girlfriend and he wanted rid of her. She looked interesting and she was bright, very bright. We both had a bit – a lot – too much to drink, and that was that.'

'What was this friend called?'

After a long pause he said: 'No. I've told you enough for the moment. You tell me a bit more about the reason for all this.'

'Fair enough,' I replied. I told him about the fire five years later, and the girl with purple hair that we thought was Melissa Youngman. If she'd put Duncan Roberts up to the fire, who was *she* working for? It was enough to convince him.

'OK,' he replied. 'The person who introduced us was called Kingston. Nick Kingston. He lectured in psychology.'

Kingston rides again, I thought. 'How did you meet him?'

Mo sat back in the chair, which was invisible under his bulk, and folded his arms. He raised a knee and pressed it against the table, which moved away from him so he had to put his foot back on the floor. 'Let me tell you about my background,' he began. 'You have, here before you, a member of the royal family of Swaziland. Now, before you are overwhelmed with respect and deference let me tell you that my grandfather, the king, had two hundred wives, of whom my grandmother was about number one hundred and seventy. He died in 1983 after ruling for fifty-two years, which made him the longest-serving monarch ever. I was a bright child, so I was sent to England for my education and was expected to take up a position in government after I'd qualified.' He held his arms wide and proclaimed: 'I could have been Prime Minister by now!'

'What happened?' I asked.

'Usual story. I fell in love with a white girl in the office. Couldn't really see her baring her breasts at the annual Reed Dance, so we settled here. She was a bit of a radical; espoused what our enemies call left-wing causes, as if that were an insult, and here we are.' He waved a hand at the walls. 'Business is good, as you can see.'

'That's interesting,' I told him, because it was. 'You have a colourful background.'

'But what's it got to do with Kingston? I'll tell you. King Sobhuza, my grandpa, was a very wise man. He embraced modern technology, where possible, but strove to maintain traditional values. Witch doctors – the ones who cast spells on people and dabbled in the black arts – were outlawed, but the more benign ones are still tolerated and even encouraged. For instance the iNyanga are herbalists, and the iSangona are foreseers of the future. I wanted to explore the psychology of traditional medicine and started attending Kingston's lectures. I'd approached him and he said it was OK, which I thought was very kind of him. Unfortunately, as I got to know him better, I changed my mind. He was more interested in the witch doctors than I was. He was forever asking me about their powers and the type of things they could do. He believed in astral travel and all sorts of oddball stuff, and thought they had the key to it and the knowledge would be lost forever if someone, namely him, didn't write it down. He saw me as his key to that knowledge.'

'Was this after the party?' I asked.

'Yeah, I suppose so. I was starting to have doubts about him by then, though.'

'In what way?'

'I realised he was strange. He was into keep-fit and martial arts, things like that. Yoga. He didn't feel pain. He could snuff out a candle with his fingers, very slowly. It was his party trick. And the same with cold. Christmas Day he used to join the swimmers in the sea at Southend or somewhere. I tell you, Charlie, Nick Kingston is a weird cookie.'

'It sounds like it. You don't know where he is now?'

'No, 'fraid not.'

'Did you fall out or just drift apart?'

'It was a fairly gradual process. I saw him one evening and Melissa was with him again. We fell into conversation, naturally, but it was obvious that she'd told him all about that night. They were laughing at me behind their hands, so to speak. I decided he'd been patronising me; I was just another backward nigger to him. They weren't my kind of people, so I split.'

'They sound a lovely couple.'

'Made in heaven, Charlie. I'll tell you who might be able to help you. A girl called Janet . . . Wilson, I think it was. She had been to school with Melissa. They shared a house. She was a lovely person, just the opposite of Melissa. I have an address somewhere, but it'll be twenty years out of date. God, she'll probably have a grown-up family by now.'

'I've met Miss Wilson,' I told him, unable to hide my grin.

'You've met Janet?'

'Mmm.'

'Did she . . .' A broad smile spread across his face, like the sun breaking through and illuminating the savannah. 'Was it Janet who put you on to me?'

I nodded.

'Hey, that's great,' he declared. 'How is she?'

'She's fine. Family grown up and her husband's left her, but she's doing nicely.'

'Fantastic! She was a lovely girl; a real sweet. Not like Melissa. Will you give her my number, please?'

'Sure. No problem.'

I thanked him for his help and left. Outside, I rang Dave on my mobile and told him that Kingston had dominated the conversation once again. He said he'd put his new friends on to it and agreed to meet me at the car.

He was waiting when I arrived, eating an ice-cream while sitting on someone's garden wall with his jacket over his shoulder, hooked on a thumb.

'Sorry I'm late,' I said.

'That's OK. Graham had a quick look at the Nicholas Kingstons; there's only a handful of them. Going by approximate DOB, making him in his fifties, the most likely one is a Nicholas James William Kingston who lives in Kendal. They're having a closer look at him right now. Anything else?'

I told him about Kingston's fascination with the witch doctors, and his indifference to pain. It was stop-start motoring along the Marylebone Road and no better along the Edgware Road, except that we were now heading north. Every junction was controlled by traffic lights and the bits in between were clogged with buses trying to get past parked vehicles, for mile after mile. It was nearly as bad as Heckley High Street when the school turns out.

I was hungry, and Dave can eat anything, any time. He's what they call a greedy so-and-so, unless he has a twenty-foot tapeworm eating away inside him. I said: 'They're paying, so which do you fancy; the Savoy Grill or the Little Chef?'

'If it's on the SFO,' he replied, 'we might as well splash out. Bugger the expense.'

'Right,' I agreed, 'so Little Chef here we come.'

All the postman had brought me was a credit card statement and there were no messages on the ansaphone. Dave's wife, Shirley, had invited me in for some supper when I dropped him off, but I'd declined. Sometimes they're just being polite. The all-day breakfast had been over two hours ago and I was peckish again, so I had a banana sandwich with honey and a sprinkling of cocoa. 'Condensed milk,' I muttered to myself. 'Why can't you find condensed milk these days?' The cut-and-thrust of the M1, plus three hours of near-total concentration, had left me on edge. I was stiff and tired, but knew I wouldn't be able to sleep. Jacquie's number was still on the telephone pad, and I thought about ringing it. For a friendly chat, that's all. Make sure she was all right.

But it would have been self-indulgent and inconsiderate of her feelings, so the phone stayed where it was. Part of me wished I'd gone in for that coffee at Elspeth's. It would have ended in tears, probably, but would that matter? Is ending in tears worse than never happening? I doubt it. In fact, I'm sure of it. I wondered if she'd finished her painting.

Dave was right. I'd make an excuse to see Mrs Holmes again. Time it so we could repair to the riverside pub for a ham sandwich, with salad and a glass of orange juice; unless she had eventually developed a taste for beer. Then, perhaps, she'd show me some more of her drawings.

Things were moving on all fronts, which is how I like it. I found my box of oil paints in the back bedroom and a stretched canvas, about two by two, which hadn't been used. All this talk of pictures had inspired me. I underpainted the canvas with a big red circle and then divided it into segments. It was going to be an abstract inspired by a cross-section of a tapeworm. I edged the segments in blue, didn't like it and tried orange. That was better. By one o'clock it was mapped out and I knew exactly how it would look. The circle had become broken and scattered, a jumble of interlocking triangles and rectangles. All it needed now was the colour piling on, thicker than jam. It was a happy and optimistic me that fell into bed, still smelling of natural turpentine, to dream of girls and art galleries and long student days.

Sparky was rapidly becoming the bringer of good news. I was having my morning coffee with Mr Wood when he knocked and came in, looking pleased with himself. 'Pour yourself a cup, David,' Gilbert invited. 'Not often we see you up here.'

'No thanks, boss,' Dave replied. 'I prefer it from the machine. It has this pleasant . . . *undertaste* of oxtail soup.'

'Don't know how you drink the damn stuff,' Gilbert declared.

'He doesn't drink it,' I said. 'He drinks mine. What is it, Dave? You came in grinning like a dog with two bollocks, so you've obviously something to tell us.'

He tilted his head to one side, thought about it for a few seconds and stated: 'Generally speaking, dogs do have two bollocks.'

'Not on the Sylvan Fields estate,' I snarled.

'Oh, right. Nobody has two of anything there. Nicholas Kingston. The one with a Kendal address, that is. Our little friends at the Serious Fraud Office have done the homework that I set them yesterday and scored ten out of ten. They've got better contacts than we have, that's for certain.'

'Go on,' I invited.

'Well, first of all, this Nick Kingston earns a respectable income as a university lecturer, which is what we had hoped for. Bit more than you take home, Charlie, but not quite as much as Mr Wood. The interesting bit is the university. He's at Lancaster.'

'Lancaster!' I exclaimed.

'Yep.'

'Struth!'

'What's special about Lancaster?' Gilbert asked.

'On Monday,' I replied, 'or perhaps Tuesday, we had a phone call from Duncan Roberts junior, known as DJ. He's the teenage son of Andrew Roberts, brother of Duncan senior who topped himself after putting his hand up for the fire in Leeds.'

Gilbert nodded, pretending he understood.

'He wanted to talk about his Uncle Duncan, see if we could tell him anything. His parents live in Welwyn Garden City,' I continued, 'but when we checked, young DJ was ringing from Lancaster.' I turned to Dave. 'Can you see if he's at university there, please?' I asked.

'Dunnit. He is, reading mechanical engineering.'

'Blimey!' I exclaimed. 'That's interesting. I don't know what it means, but it's interesting.'

'Could be a coincidence,' Gilbert warned. It's his job to remind us of the mundane possibilities.

It's mine to go off on wild flights of fancy; to soar with the eagles and wage war on the forces of evil. That's how I see it. I turned to Dave. 'Well done, Pissquick,' I said. 'You'd better take a day off this weekend.'

He pulled a glum face and said: 'But . . . don't you want to know what I came to tell you?'

'You mean there's more?' I queried.

'Just a bit. University lecturer is only one of his jobs.'

'Where did you say this info came from?' Gilbert interrupted.

'The SFO,' Dave answered.

'No, where did they get it from?'

'No askee,' he replied with a shrug, implying ask no questions, be told no lies.

'The Inland bloody Revenue, I bet,' Gilbert stated.

'Like I said,' Dave told him, 'they have better contacts than us.' The Inland Revenue's principal task is collecting taxes. They're not a reservoir of essential information for the law enforcement agencies. If it were common knowledge that they supplied us with details of their clients' finances it would hamper their tax-collecting abilities, so they don't do it. Anything an individual employee of theirs might pass on is strictly off the record.

'So what else did they say?' I demanded, impatiently.

'Apparently,' Dave continued, 'Mr Kingston also earns a healthy salary working as a freelance consultant. His main customer for this work – in fact, his only customer for the last few years – is . . . wait for it . . . something known as the Reynard Organisation.'

'The Reynard Organisation?' I whispered.

Dave nodded. 'Yep!'

'Reynard the Fox. Holy mother of Jesus!' That was it. We had the link. Duncan senior started the fire, Melissa put him up to it, Kingston was pulling *her* strings. Crosby owned the house and he was Fox's sworn enemy. And Kingston worked for Fox. QED, *quod erat demonstrandum*. 'Which was to be proved.' All we had to do now was the *demonstrandum* bit.

Chapter 9

I put the phone to my ear and nodded to Annette Brown, our swish new DC. She was seated in my office where I could see her through the window. We'd set up a telephone conference on the internals, with Dave, Nigel, Jeff and myself all listening in the big office.

Annette picked up my phone and dialled the Kendal number. After three rings a man said: 'Hello.' It's difficult to form an impression from just hello.

'Is that Mr Kingston?' Annette asked in her best little-girl voice.

'It might be,' he replied.

'Oh, hello, Mr Kingston,' she went on. 'This is Janine from ABC Windows. We're doing a promotion in Kendal at the moment, with fifty per cent off, and are looking for a show home in your area. Would you be . . .'

'What did you say your name was?' he interrupted.

'Er, Janine, Mr Kingston.'

'And do you have a boyfriend, Janine?'

'Er, yes.'

'So in that case why don't you piss off home and get him to give you a good stiff seeing-to.' CLICK!

The four of us in the outer office buried our heads in our arms and shook with laughter. When I looked up Annette was standing there, blushing. 'That was short and sweet,' she said bravely.

It wasn't politically correct, but I couldn't resist it. I flapped a hand towards the door and said: 'Well, off you go then.'

It was Friday and he was at home. I didn't want to wait until Monday, but we were supposed to be having a team meeting in the afternoon. Dave knew as much as I did about this case but we were both a week behind with the burglaries, although it was obvious that there had been nothing new to report. I decided to dash up to Kendal to try to catch Kingston at home while they held the meeting without me. Dave and I discussed tactics and at just after eleven I filled the car with petrol and pointed it towards Cumbria, formerly Westmorland, aka the Lake District.

First stop was Kendal nick. I had a long talk with my opposite number, who I'd never met before, and told him the minimum I could. He realised I wasn't being too forthcoming but had the good sense to know that I probably had my reasons and didn't ask too many questions. The main thing was that he offered his co-operation and gave me directions to Kingston's house.

Somebody once said that schizophrenics build castles in the air, psychopaths live in them and psychiatrists collect the rent. OK, so he was a psychologist, but he was doing very nicely. The house was the end one of three that a farmer had built in one of his fields in the middle of nowhere. How he'd obtained planning permission was probably a story in itself, but the proof was here in the security gates, the five- or six-bedroomed mansion and the sweeping views towards the mountains. I pressed the button and wondered what happened next.

There was a click and a hum and the big gates swung open. They were black with gold arrowheads and Prince of Wales feathers. I looked one way, then the other, and strode off up to the block-paved drive. I'd once had a quote to have mine done like this, but had thought £4,000 excessive and opted for tarmac again. Kingston's drive was about twenty times as long as mine. Loopy Lucille from Draughty Windows could have earned herself a holiday in Benidorm with the commission on this. When I reached the door I paused for breath and rang the bell.

It definitely wasn't the cleaning lady who opened the door almost immediately, her mouth already forming words which she cut off when she saw me. 'Oh!' she exclaimed, with what might have been a touch of disappointment. 'I, er, I'm sorry, I, er, thought you were the man from Wineways.'

She was about average height but that was the only thing about her that was average. Ash-blonde hair down to her shoulders and curves like Monza, fast and sweeping, demanding your full attention. She was under thirty, at a guess, and wearing a navy-blue pullover with a white blouse and jodhpurs. This was trophy wife incarnate. I took it all in with a trained policeman's sweeping glance, from the Hermès scarf at her throat right down to the gleaming riding boots with two spots of mud on the left and three on the right. She'd been out for a canter.

'No,' I said, offering my ID. 'I'm the man from the CID. Detective Inspector Priest. I was wondering if I could have a word with Mr Kingston.'

She quickly regained her composure and realised I really was just another tradesman. 'Mr Kingston?' she echoed, as if I'd asked for an audience with Barbra Streisand. I was two steps down from her so she had the advantage, whichever way you looked at it.

'Is he in?' I wondered.

'What's it about?' she demanded. 'He's very busy.'

'Are you . . . Mrs Kingston?' I risked. I suppose she could have been his daughter.

'Yes, I am.'

'Could you please tell him it's about a little matter that I'm sure he can clear up. I won't keep him more than a few minutes.'

'Well, actually, he's not in the house. I think you'll find him in the belvedere.'

'The Belvedere?' I queried. Where the hell was the Belvedere?

'Yes. He does his reading there.'

'Can you give me directions, please?'

She stepped down to my level and pointed to the corner of the house. 'At the bottom of the garden,' she told me. 'I'll tell him you're coming.'

I wandered down the side of the house feeling bemused. He had a *pub* at the bottom of the garden? Wow! Wait till I told Sparky! There was a BMW M3 convertible in one of the garages and a short hike away I saw a large summerhouse flanked by ornamental trees. As I approached it Kingston came to the door and held it open for me, for which I was mightily grateful. This, presumably, was the belvedere, and they had a telephone line to it.

They also had electricity and the security system coupled up. It was a double-glazed mahogany construction shaped like an old thrupenny bit, with a raised deck running all the way around it.

'Good afternoon, Inspector,' Kingston greeted me. 'My wife forewarned me of your approach.'

I entered, then waited for him to pass me because there was more than one room. He pushed a door open and said: 'In here, please.'

It was every grown-up small boy's dream. Windows on three sides gave a view of the hills, as if from a ship's bridge. Behind me, the wall was lined with bookcases and framed old Ordnance Survey maps. 'What a gorgeous view,' I stated.

'Mmm, it is,' he agreed. 'Goat Fell. We try to walk over it three times a week.'

'Both of you?'

'Of course. Just the thing to raise your, er, spirits.'

'It's beautiful. I envy you.'

'Do you know the Lake District at all?' he asked.

'Yes, I've done most of it,' I boasted.

'Really? Good for you.'

Leaning in a corner I noticed a high-powered airgun with a telescopic sight, and one of the windows was wide open. 'Shooting?' I asked, nodding towards the gun.

'Squirrels,' he replied. 'Grey ones, of course. Bloody menace they are.' Thirty yards away, hanging from a branch, were several bird-feeders filled with peanuts.

'Sit down, Inspector,' he invited, 'and tell me how I can help you. Francesca didn't catch your name . . .'

'Priest,' I told him, settling into a studded leather chair that matched the captain's he pulled out for himself. 'From Heckley CID. I believe you were a lecturer at Essex University back in 1969.'

'Good God!' he exclaimed, throwing his head back and guffawing. 'I knew I should have paid that parking ticket! You've taken your time, Inspector, if you don't mind me saying so.'

I didn't mind at all. My day would come. In some ways he was a bit like me. Tallish, skinny, with all his own hair worn a little too long. The years had treated us differently, though. My features have been etched by alternating stress and laughter into an attractive pattern of wrinkles and laugh-lines. Well, I think so. He'd grown flabby-cheeked and dewlapped from a dangerous combination of dissolute living and half-hearted exercise. He wasn't wearing well, in spite of his efforts.

I said: 'You lectured in psychology, sir, I believe.'

'That's right, Inspector. You are to be commended for your diligence; I can see you've done your homework.'

'Can I ask . . . why psychology?' There was no table between us and I carefully watched his reactions. He might have the book learning, but my knowledge of human behaviour was honed on the streets and in the interview rooms, with some of the toughest nutters and craftiest crooks in society.

He smiled and shrugged, saying: 'I've never been asked that before, Inspector. Is it part of your enquiry?'

'No,' I replied. 'I just wondered how a person goes from school into a subject like that. It's not as if it was on the curriculum in those days is it?'

'No, I suppose you're right.' He thought for a few seconds, then said: 'Girls.'

'Girls?' I repeated.

'Mmm. Girls. I'm a Freudian, Inspector. I think I went into psychology because: a) I would meet lots of girls, and b) I'd learn how to deal with them after I'd met them. Does that answer your question?'

'Did it live up to expectations?'

He bit his lower lip and nodded his head, very slowly. 'I think I can safely say that it did. It bloody well did. After all,' he continued, 'we're talking about Essex in the sixties. What more could a man want? What was it that poet said? Sexual intercourse was invented in 1962, or whenever?'

'Philip Larkin,' I told him. 'It was 1963, *after the something-something and the Beatles' first LP*.'

'That was it. Bloody wonderful time, it was. Did you go to university, Inspector?'

'Art college, about the same time.'

'Well then, you'll know all about it, eh?'

'Can you remember any names from that period?' I asked.

He pulled his feet in, just for a moment, then relaxed again. ‘Students, you mean?’ he queried.

‘Mmm.’

His right hand brushed his nose. ‘No, ’fraid not,’ he replied.

‘None at all?’

He did an impression of a thinking man before shaking his head.

‘I have a list of names,’ I told him, taking my notebook from my jacket pocket and opening it. ‘I’m supposed to ask if you can volunteer any, and if you can’t I’ve to prompt you with a few. Is that OK?’

‘Fire away, Inspector.’

‘Right.’ I glanced down at the notebook. ‘Have you ever known a girl called . . . let me see . . . Melissa Youngman?’

His hand went to his mouth in a pensive gesture and he said: ‘No.’

‘Are you sure?’

‘Positive.’

I put a cross next to carrots on last week’s shopping list. ‘How about Janet Wilson?’

This time there was no reaction. ‘No.’

‘Mo . . . Dlamini, would it be?’

He pulled his feet under the chair and said: ‘No.’

‘You never heard of any of them?’

‘No.’ He relaxed, stretching his legs again, and said: ‘I’m sorry, Inspector, but it was a long time ago, and to be honest, sometimes I couldn’t remember their names the next morning. Are you allowed to tell me what it’s all about? It must be serious after all these years.’

‘Something about a fire, I believe, in an area of Leeds called Chapeltown. It’s the red-light district. A witness has recently made a death-bed statement that has led us to this woman called

Youngman, but we can't find her. One of my chiefs has decided I haven't enough to do already and has given me the job of looking into her background and associates. We've got to look as if we're doing something, I suppose. I'm told that she went to Essex University and one of her classmates thought she'd had an affair with a psychology lecturer. That led me to you. Believe me, Mr Kingston, I've enough on my plate that happened last week, never mind twenty-three years ago. I suspect that it's to do with drugs, it usually is, but nobody tells me anything.' I closed my notebook and asked if there'd been much drug-taking at Essex.

It was there, he told me, for those who took the trouble to look for it. And if you were at a party the odd reefer might be passed round. He'd dabbled, of course – who hadn't? – but only with pot. Nowadays he didn't know what made young people tick. He sympathised with the dilemma the police and the government were in. Legalisation wasn't the answer; that would just make a fortune for the tobacco companies. Perhaps the new Drugs Tsar would make a difference? I stifled a smile. We call him Twinkle, as in *Twinkle, twinkle, little Tsar*.

'Well,' I said, 'if you've never heard of her or the others I don't think I need trouble you any longer. Thanks for your time, sir.'

'Not at all,' he replied. 'I'm only sorry I couldn't be of more assistance.'

I stood up as if to take my leave and glanced around. 'Is this where you do your studying?' I asked.

'Yes. This is my little den.'

I turned towards the bookcase. 'May I look?'

'Of course.'

They were the sort of books that are referred to by the names of the authors rather than title. Get out your Weber, Umlaut and

Schnorkel rather than your *The Perceived Differences Between Alternative Analytical Approaches to Clinical Investigations of Stress-Induced Syndromes in Western and Oriental Societies*. They made *Stone's Justices Manual* sound kid's play. I let my eyes flick over them, not paying much attention, until a familiar title caught my eye.

'Read one!' I announced triumphantly, pointing to *Zen and the Art of Motorcycle Maintenance*, which had been a cult read book in the seventies.

'Ah, the Pirsig,' he said. 'Did you enjoy it?'

'Mmm. Dabbled with Zen for a while afterwards. And caught up on my Plato.'

'Really?'

Further along I saw some more I had read. I was definitely down among the beer-drinkers now. 'And these,' I told him. 'The Carlos Castanedas.'

'I'm impressed, Inspector,' he replied. 'What did you think of them?'

We had something in common. I decided to milk it for every drop. 'I thought they were interesting,' I told him. 'Only last week I was walking in the Dales when the weather changed. I could feel it coming, long before it reached me. It was probably only a temperature drop, or the wind rustling the heather, but I thought of Castaneda and wondered about it. And I always look for a power spot before I sit down to eat my sandwiches.'

'Ah! Don't we all, but we are only looking for somewhere free from sheep droppings, eh, Inspector?'

'No, I think there's more to it than that.'

'You've surprised me,' he said. 'You're obviously a man with a great sense of the spiritual. You said you'd walked most of the hills in the Lake District, I believe?'

'Several times, over the years,' I replied.

'Have you ever done any at night?'

'No, not really. Camped out near Sprinkling Tarn a couple of times in my youth. That's all.'

'Well, I recommend you try it. The spirits are abroad after dark, Inspector. Late evening is a very special time. For a man with a soul it's a wonderful experience up there. Power is everywhere, believe me.'

'Isn't it dangerous?'

'Only for he that cannot *see*.'

'I'll have to try it some time. Thanks for your time, Mr Kingston.' I walked to the door and he followed me out.

'I'll take you through the house,' he said. We wandered down the path, making small talk, and entered through a back door inside a smallish porch filled with flowers I couldn't name. 'Darling!' he called when we were inside.

Francesca appeared and Kingston said: 'The inspector's leaving, dear. I wasn't able to help him, unfortunately.' He introduced us and we shook hands.

'Perhaps you'll stay for a coffee next time, Inspector,' she said.

Only if you make the offer first, I thought. We were in a passage, quite gloomy, that ran through the house. There were original watercolours of Lakes views on the walls, and in an alcove I noticed a display cabinet filled with cameras.

'Who's the photographer?' I asked, although I knew the answer.

'Oh, I used to dabble,' Kingston replied.

There was a full range, from ancient folding jobs with bellows, levers and spirit levels, right up to a Nikon with a complete set of lenses. He hadn't bothered with the latest electronic devices which did everything for you except choose the subject. Smack in the middle, with the others arranged round it, was the famous single lens reflex Hasselblad.

'I'd hardly call it dabbling,' I said, 'if you used one of those.'

He smiled with pride and agreed that he had been quite keen.

'I've never seen one before,' I admitted, adding: 'Neil Armstrong left one on the moon, you know.'

'Too heavy to bring back, Inspector,' Kingston replied. 'The cost was negligible compared with the rocks that replaced it. A cool million dollars an ounce, they said, to transport anything there and back.'

We parted like old mates and I strolled off down the drive. I had a moment of panic when I remembered the gates, but they'd opened them for me.

He was a liar, I was sure of that. He'd recognised the three names I'd mentioned. Salesmen are supposed to be suckers for a so-called bargain, and it looked as if something similar applied to psychologists. I'd been right not to forewarn him of my visit. That would have given him time to rehearse his answers and his body language. Taken off guard, he scored none out of ten.

I'd enjoyed the Carlos Castaneda books. The main character is a Mexican sorcerer who does wonderful things while blasted out of his mind on peyote. They're full of wisdom and insights, but otherwise total claptrap. Mind you, I really do look for that special spot, what he called a place of power, before I sit down to eat my sandwiches.

I went back to Kendal nick to give an informal report to my opposite number, in case I needed any favours from him, and drove back to Heckley. The meeting was over when I arrived, but Sparky was still hanging around. I was writing my thoughts down when he came in with two mugs of tea.

'He sounds a right charmer,' he concluded after I'd told him all about it.

'He is. What happened here? Anything I need to know?'

'Just one small item. There's nothing new on the burglaries, so you can forget about them. Except, of course, that it's a month since the last one, so they're due again. Jeff's alerted everyone. Graham rang, from London. He said that the FBI have located Melissa, and we can have her any time we want. Apparently she's over there on a non-immigrant visa, and has overstayed her welcome by several years.'

'That's useful to know. Have they talked to her?'

'No, and they won't unless we ask them. She's living in a trailer park just outside a town called Oak Ridge, in Tennessee. Graham thinks he should go over to have a word with her.'

'That might be a good idea,' I said. 'Do you fancy going with him?'

He shook his head. 'Nah, let him have all the glory.'

We pushed our chairs back. I put my feet on the desk and Dave balanced his on the edge of the waste-paper bin. 'First drink I've had since the one this morning,' I said.

He looked at me and told me: 'You'll be giving yourself an ulcer.'

'Through not drinking tea?'

'Through not eating regularly; not looking after yourself. What are you doing this weekend?'

'Haven't thought about it,' I replied. 'Do some catching up. Sleep, cleaning, gardening and the car, for starters.'

'Do you fancy going off somewhere?'

'No. I've too much to do.'

After a long silence he said: 'You still miss her, don't you?'

I put my mug down and replied: 'Who, Annabelle?' in my best see-if-I-care voice. She dumped me three months ago, after five years, and yes, I did miss her. Like a bird would miss its wings.

'Mmm.'

'I suppose so. Does it show?'

'Yep. You've become a miserable sod.'

'I'm sorry. I thought I'd covered it up fairly well.'

'I've known you a long time.'

'That's true.'

He finished his tea and said: 'How about having a day's fishing some time. It's years since we've been.'

'You mean, like, there's plenty of fish in the sea? Is that it?'

'I didn't say that,' he protested, grinning.

'But that was the train of thought. I'd have socked you if you had.'

'Bridlington, next weekend. We could take Nigel. We could all go.'

I nodded my approval. 'It might be fun,' I replied. 'We could bring a cod back for Gilbert, show him a proper fish.'

We talked about the case for half an hour and went home. We had lots of hearsay evidence but nothing substantial. Nothing forensic that would link Kingston with the fires or even with Melissa. If he denied ever knowing her there was little we could do to show otherwise. Witnesses might identify him as Rodger Wakefield, but in isolation that was worthless. In the absence of a rock-solid link we would have to build up a formidable amount of circumstantial evidence to show he was the man who did Fox's dirty work. We might not be able to pin anything on Fox himself, but we'd disgrace him. We'd have to settle for that, but it was going to be a long haul. I decided that a talk with Mr Big himself might be a good idea.

Three o'clock in the morning; the thunder and lightning woke me. I dozed until eight and had a leisurely breakfast while watching the rain flatten the peonies in the garden. At nine I strode into the police station to see what the mailman had brought.

'It'll wash the cricket out,' the desk sergeant grumbled after I'd said my good morning.

'Well, paint a door and watch it dry,' I suggested.

I read the night 'tec's report and the mail, but there was nothing worthwhile. I tried the SFO, to have a word with Graham about going to America, but they don't work weekends. I didn't bother with his home number. At ten I rang Janet Holmes in York.

'It's Charlie Priest, Mrs Holmes,' I began. 'Inspector Priest. I came to see you on Wednesday.'

'Hello, Mr Priest,' she answered, sounding quite pleased. 'This is a surprise. Was there something else you wanted to know?'

How about dinner one evening, for a start, I thought, but I decided not to rush it. 'Not exactly,' I told her, 'but on Thursday I was speaking to a friend of yours. Mo Dlamini. He asked me to give you his number.'

'Mo? That's wonderful. I'll write it down.'

I dictated the number then told her that we'd have to hold on to the photographs she'd loaned us, but I could send her copies if she was worried about losing them.

'Oh, keep them, Inspector,' she said. 'I've had to let go of a lot more than a few old snapshots lately. I, er, would like to know what happens, though. I don't suppose you're allowed to discuss it with a civilian, are you?'

'Not on the telephone,' I replied, smiling to myself. 'And not until after it's been to court, which could take years.'

'Oh, what a pity,' she replied.

'On the other hand,' I said, 'I've been on lots of other cases which *have* been to court and I'm perfectly free to discuss.'

'What are you trying to say, Inspector?' she asked, with a laugh in her voice.

'I'm trying to say, Mrs Holmes,' I began, 'that we are both grown up and on our own, and I would like to take you out to dinner one evening, if you'd be so kind as to accompany me.'

'I'd be delighted. You're very kind. Does your sergeant go everywhere with you?'

'Er, no, not everywhere. In fact, I wasn't thinking of bringing him along. Do you mind?'

'Not at all, Inspector. I'm afraid there is one small snag, though.'

There always is. Usually it weighs seventeen stone and plays rugby union. I invited her to tell me all about him

'On Monday I'm going to Greece for two weeks. Nothing exciting, I'm afraid. I'm accompanying my mother and a friend of hers, just to make sure they stay out of trouble. I don't want my inheritance going to someone called Popodopolopodis.' She laughed again.

'That's all right,' I said. 'I'm a patient man. Have a good time and I'll give you a ring in a fortnight or so.'

'I'll look forward to that. Thank you.'

Dumdy-dumdy-dumdy-dum. I put the phone down and sat back. *Dumdy-dumdy-dum.* She was a very pleasant lady, I thought. *Dumdy-dumdy-dumdy-dum.* And intelligent, too. *Dumdy-dumdy-doo.* I put the stuff on my desk in neat piles and went home.

The Reynard Organisation headquarters are in London's Docklands, in spite of what the people of Leeds are led to believe. The new office block would be one of Fox's satellites, and the thousand new jobs he promised would be young girls with telephone receivers glued to their ears, working round the clock.

Monday morning I asked Graham to investigate how I could get to see the man.

He rang me back just before lunch. 'The office block in Leeds is called Reynard Tower,' he told me, 'and Fox himself is coming over to cut the ribbon. He's on a run with the government at the moment, probably trying to ingratiate himself for a knighthood. Having sacked about a quarter of a million workers in the last twenty years these thousand jobs are his way of proving that we have turned the corner and are now in a leaner, fitter Britain. Opening day is two weeks tomorrow, so that's your best chance to see him while he's in Yorkshire.'

'How do I make an appointment?'

'Ring his diary secretary at the Docklands HQ. Then follow instructions.'

'Thanks, Graham. You've been a big help. Are you serious about going to America?'

'Oh!' he exclaimed. 'I could be. I definitely could be. What do you think?'

'I think you should,' I told him. 'I get the impression that Melissa and Kingston didn't part on friendly terms. Maybe she'd enlarge upon that. Or do a deal, who knows?'

'Their politics are poles apart. He's a militant capitalist and she sounds like an anarchist. Then there's the sex thing; a woman scorned and all that. You could be right.'

'Think about it. Have a word with Piers and Mr Tregellis. Tell them that I think someone should go over there and stir things up.' I'm a great believer in stirring things up.

'I'll do that, Charlie. Thanks. Thanks.'

I dialled the number he'd given me and a very polite female told me that I was through to Reynard London.

'I'm trying to fix an appointment with J.J. Fox,' I told her. 'Could you please put me through to his diary secretary?'

'What name is it, please?'

'Priest.'

'Mr Priest?'

'As in Roman Catholic.'

'I beg your pardon?'

'Sorry. Nothing.'

'I'm putting you through.'

It was Pachelbel's Canon in D. I hate Pachelbel's Canon in D, especially when it's played on a twenty-quid Yamaha organ. Fortunately I had only to endure two bars, which is all you need hear to know the work intimately, when another female sang: 'Secretaries; how can I help you?'

'I'd like to make an appointment to see Mr Fox when he comes to Yorkshire in a fortnight. Can you put me through to his diary secretary, please?'

'Mr Fox? We don't have a Mr Fox.'

'J.J. Fox, love. He owns the company.'

'Oh, *that* Mr Fox.'

After that it was personnel, then head of secretariat, with bursts of Pachelbel in between. By the time I reached the legal department I'd decided that a hatchet downsizing of his own administrative staff might be a good idea and that Pachelbel should have been burned at the stake.

'Did you say Detective Inspector Priest?' one of his tame solicitors asked me after I'd been shunted around the legal department.

'Yes. From Heckley CID.'

'And what's it about?'

'Before I answer that,' I said, 'tell me this: do you have the authority to make an appointment for me to see Mr Fox?'

'Yes, I do. Subject to his approval, of course.'

'Right then, listen up. It's about murder. I want to ask Mr Fox a few simple questions, and one way or another I *shall* ask them. It might be easier and less embarrassing for all concerned if you could make an appointment for me to see him on *his* territory, then I won't have to *insist* on seeing him on *mine*. Do I make myself understood?'

'I'll ring you back, Inspector.'

Phew! I'd enjoyed that last bit. It's not too often I get to tell a lawyer the facts of life. No doubt if and when I saw Fox he'd be surrounded by them and they'd have a conference about everything from whether to say good morning right through to having milk or sugar in their coffees. I'd learn absolutely nothing, but I'd have them worried, and that's worth a lot.

He kept his word. At four o'clock he confirmed that Fox would be opening the Reynard Tower in a fortnight. He'd arrive at the Fox Borealis Monday afternoon and stay for one night. Tuesday morning he was having a power breakfast with the Lord Mayor of Leeds and other dignitaries, and would see me at ten, before his next appointment at half past. I said my thank yous, like I'd been brought up to do, and wrote it in my diary, with a fluorescent marker-pen circle around it. We were on our way!

I'd been neglecting Keith Crosby, so I rang him from home, after chicken pie and new potatoes. I didn't give him any details or names, but assured him I was working full-time on the case and the Serious Fraud people were interested and involved. He thanked me profusely. After that I finished most of the painting that I'd started on Thursday night. Every summer the police put on a gala in the park to raise money for the children's ward of the General. The dogs and the horses show what they can do, and we stage a mock bank raid, with flashing lights and cars skidding on the grass. One of the stands is for paintings by cops or their families. Most of them are of the Dales, some amateurish, some extremely skilled, but all slavish to the scene as viewed. The PC who has organised the show for the last ten years brought me a wad of entry forms for the troops and I told him to put me down for a couple of paintings. If I could knock up a couple of big abstracts I'd enter them, just for the notoriety. Anything for a laugh, that's yours truly. And Janet would be back by then; perhaps she'd come with me.

When I saw Kingston he'd talked about walking in the dark, and the more I thought about it the more it appealed to me. Most of the time it would be ordinary, like walking in fog, but if you did it often enough you'd eventually have one of those magical experiences that make all the dull trips worthwhile. I could imagine being above the clouds, with the stars blazing across the sky like you'd never seen them before. I'd have to give it a try, when all this was over.

Tregellis was on the phone at eight thirty next morning and kept me talking for nearly an hour. It was worthwhile, though. He agreed that Graham should go to America and thought that Piers should accompany him. If Melissa agreed to kiss and tell about Kingston he could reassure her that she was safe from prosecution, or if he thought that that was out of the question and she insisted on having a team of hotshot lawyers present he could stop them running rings around poor Graham. The legal staff employed by the SFO have a special status. A Prosecution Service solicitor would never visit a client, but one with the SFO can because he is part of the investigative team, and the SFO can order a suspect to answer questions. There's a downside to that. A cornerstone of British law is that a suspect is not expected to incriminate himself, so any information extracted this way cannot be used in court. It'll be different in America, of course, so Piers would have to do some swotting on the plane.

Meanwhile, we agreed I'd talk to J.J. Fox on the pretext of

gathering information about Kingston, who we knew worked for him. At this point we were displaying no suspicions about Fox himself. We'd nail his minions first, then see how they sang.

'What if,' Tregellis asked, 'my two trusty manservants go all the way to the US of A and Melissa denies all knowledge of Kingston? She was never in one of his classes, was she?'

'No, but I've been thinking about that,' I replied. 'How does this sound?'

When I'd finished he said: 'Right, I'll have a word with the brass in Cumbria and tell them to liaise with you.'

I put the phone down, rubbed my ear and rotated my shoulder. Who'd be a telephone girl? Maybe I should be more sympathetic to them in future.

Eight a.m. on the Thursday morning a contingent from Cumbria Constabulary led by my oppo from Kendal arrested Nicholas Kingston on suspicion of defrauding the Inland Revenue. Eight a.m. was a compromise. They'd said seven, I'd suggested ten. Sparky, myself, one of their DCs and our photographer sat sipping coffee from a flask in Dave's car at the end of the lane as Kingston was lifted.

'There's seven of us for Saturday,' Dave said.

'Saturday?' I queried. 'What happens Saturday?'

'Fishing. Don't say you'd forgotten.'

'What? To Bridlington?'

'That's right. Nigel and myself are going with you, and Jeff's got a car-full.'

'Oh. Right.'

'They're coming,' Dave hissed, and I ducked down out of sight. I didn't want the Kingstons to associate me with this. I was from another force, miles away, and on a different inquiry.

'They've gone,' he said, and I sat up.

'Got the warrant?' I asked, twisting round. The DC waved it in front of my face and I said: 'Right. Let's go.'

A WPC had been left with Mrs Kingston to ensure that she didn't destroy all their records before we arrived. That was the story. The main thing was that she ensured that the gates were open for us. Dave parked right in front of the door and bailed out, followed by the other two. I spread myself across the seats, lying low again, and waited.

I opened my eyes as the door was wrenched open. Dave said: 'They've taken her down to the gazebo. We've the place to ourselves.'

'It's not a gazebo, it's a belvedere,' I told him, arching my back and stretching my legs.

Inside the house the photographer was standing beside the camera cabinet, green with envy. 'I haven't touched anything,' he said, 'but I asked her to unlock the door.'

'It's OK,' I told him. 'Stick your film in it and shoot away.'

He extracted the Hasselblad with professional ease and unclipped the back. In a few seconds the roll of film, huge by modern standards, was on the spools and the camera was back together again. He shot off half of it against a mahogany door and then went outside and took some pictures of the sky.

Dave went for a wander around the house while I watched through the back window for the others returning from the belvedere. I was in the kitchen, which was white-tiled and reminiscent of a high-tech operating theatre, with lots of stainless steel and glowing digital displays. Only a half-eaten bowl of muesli and a mug of cold coffee on the breakfast bar spoiled the image. I doubted if Mrs K spent much time in there. Beyond the belvedere, Goat Fell looked benign and welcoming in the morning light. They'd miss their walk today. I pushed the coffee mug nearer the centre of the bar and placed the muesli spoon at a more natural angle. That was better. Now they could let the *Vogue* photographer take his snaps. A black and white woodpecker landed in the garden, pecked at something and flew off, rising and falling like a small boat on a rough sea. 'Look out,' I whispered after it, 'or the man will get you.'

'Bloody hell!' I heard Dave say behind me as he wandered into the room. 'Talk about how the other half live.'

'Does it meet with your approval?' I asked.

'I'll say. Wouldn't mind a week here myself. Do they take boarders, do you know?'

'I doubt it, but with luck it'll be on the market, soon. See anything interesting upstairs?'

'Not really. He has a telescope poking out of a window.'

'He's into astronomy.'

'Is he? Then why is it focused on the bedroom window of the farmhouse?'

I sighed. 'Like you said, Dave, he's a charmer through and through. Everything he does is bent.'

'So let's make it his undoing.'

'We will. And I'll tell you something else about him. Given plenty of time his planning is immaculate. If he's done the jobs we think he has then he hasn't left a trace. He's a clever man, but he can't think on his feet. When I interviewed him he was floundering, sent out all the signals that he was lying. Ask him a question that was irrelevant and he'd dictate you a textbook on it, then come to the point and it was one-word answers.' I turned away from the window and said: 'Keep an eye out for them. Did I see a loo along the corridor?'

'It's, er, out of order,' Dave replied, stepping after me and placing his hand on my arm. 'Use the one upstairs. You've never seen anything like it. The tiles are right up your street. Top of the stairs, on the left.'

I'd seen an enamel sign, probably Victorian, on a door. It read *WC*. Underneath, in matching letters, blue on white, was one saying: *Gentlemen adjust your dress before leaving the urinal*. I took Dave's advice and used the one upstairs.

It was nothing special. Toilet, bidet, huge free-standing iron bath, full-length mirrors that made you look sunburned and enough towels to cushion a stuntman's fall. It could have been mine. The tiles were a mural of a classical scene. Aphrodite tempting Lesbos or something, with a swan taking an unhealthy interest in the proceedings and only a few vine leaves keeping it this side of depraved. A high-tech exercise bike with more dials than a light aircraft stood in a corner and two black satin dressing gowns hung behind the door. I had a slash, washed my hands, smiled at myself in the mirror, decided that a tan suited me and went downstairs.

I walked past the downstairs loo, then changed my mind. It was hard to imagine anything in this house being out of order. I bet they sent for an electrician to set the video. I read the sign, checked my flies and pushed the door open.

There was no window, but the light switch was handy, operated by a china bauble dangling on a string. For a downstairs loo it wasn't bad, about the same floor area as my upstairs one. The sink was full-size, not one of these miniatures added as an afterthought, and there was a shower cabinet in the adjacent corner. I flushed the low-level toilet, which worked, and washed my hands again. The towel warming on the heated rail had the letter C woven in gold braid in the corner. *Claridges*? I wondered. I shook my head in disbelief and turned to leave.

There were three tiny pictures on the wall alongside the door, and they attracted me like marmalade to carpet pile, as pictures always do. At first I thought they were abstracts, but then I saw they were the wings of something like a dragonfly. I lifted one off its hook and took it under the light.

I need spectacles. It comes to everyone, with the passing of years. I peered at the caption in the bottom right-hand corner until my head ached. The microscopic letters read, I think, *Aeshna grandis*, whatever that is. The signature in the other corner was easier. It said *J. Wilson*, who we now know as Mrs Holmes.

Chapter 10

'He's got a dirty muriel on his bathroom wall,' I announced, strolling into the kitchen.

'Not bad, is it?' Dave replied.

The photographer had joined him. 'Oh, can I go look?' he asked.

I shook my head. 'Sorry, Pete, it's against the rules.'

'Shirley would love this,' Dave said, waving at the appliances. His wife is the best cook I know. 'Poggen . . . pohl? Where are they from?'

'Why the kitchen?' I asked. 'She'd probably love the bedroom or the television lounge or every other room in the house.'

'Women like kitchens, Charlie,' he stated. 'Maybe that's where you go wrong.'

'Could be,' I replied, 'but this is not for us. Give 'em a click, Dave, and let's go.'

He unclipped his radio from his belt and clicked *transmit* three times, as we'd agreed. 'We'll wait at the gate,' I said, 'just in case she comes to the door to wave goodbye.' The photographer followed me out and we took the car to the bottom of the drive. Five minutes later Dave, the local DC and the WPC piled into the back seat and we drove back to Kendal nick. On the way we told them that they could let Kingston go.

The fraud boys calculated that Kingston was living way beyond his legitimate income. He appeared to receive frequent but irregular sums of money from somewhere, and he said that he gambled at a casino in Blackpool. Checks they made later showed that he was a member, but nobody there recognised him from his photograph. He must have been the most successful player of roulette ever, but he claimed he had a system, which he had to be careful not to give away. He was, he said, very cautious and low-key when he played. Casino winnings are not tax-deductible, so they let him go and even managed a strained apology. Kingston was happy, because he thought he'd fooled us, and we were delirious because he was happy. Like they say, nowadays we're a service, not a force. The local team took us to the pub and we had a long lunch, sitting outside in the sun, and Mr Snappy took a picture of us all.

I was sitting at my desk, just before seven, when Pete the photographer rang me. 'We've something to show you,' he said.

I pulled my jacket on and ran down four flights of steps to the basement, where the darkroom was. I knocked and he opened the door. With him was a scientist from the Home Office lab at Wetherton. We'd met before and exchanged pleasantries.

'This is proper photography,' Pete said. 'There's no arguing with this.'

'How do you mean?' I asked.

'Well,' he explained, 'with this digital stuff you can fake it. The picture is converted to a million bits of information, little electrical impulses, passed down wires and through silicon chips, then reassembled into something that hopefully resembles what you started out with. With the Hasselblad, the image falls directly on to the negative and from that directly on to the print paper. What you see is what you get.'

'He's right,' said the scientist, whose name I'd forgotten. 'A thousand-pound-a-day barrister would get digital evidence kicked out of court.'

'That's something for us to think about,' I said. 'So what have you found?'

'OK,' the scientist began. 'Pete shot a roll of 100 ASA through the Hasselblad and printed it on medium-grade glossy fibre paper. The prints you supplied are on similar paper. The border of each picture, as you know, is an image of the frame in the camera that the film is held flat against. Ideally, we should see four dead-straight black edges all the way round. In practice, when seen under the microscope, there are minute blobs of paint and specks of dust that make it irregular. Let me show you.'

He switched on an overhead projector and placed a slide under it. The images on the screen jerked around as the shadow of his hand manipulated them, its movements magnified by the apparatus. I could see two black right-angles which he eventually placed side by side. 'We took some negatives from your pictures,' he said, 'and this is a typical comparison. It's not as clear as under the 'scope, but you can see here . . .' He pointed to something on the slide, then realised that it was easier to show me on the screen and jumped to his feet. 'Here,' he continued, 'and here. These are probably dust particles stuck to the paint that the camera interior was treated with. As it is matt paint we can also show how irregular that looks. See here, and here.'

'They look similar,' I said.

'That's right. There are also some scratches across the negative, caused by dust in the camera. Similar scratches can be seen on the photographs.'

'So what's the bottom line?' I asked. Sometimes the cliché is the easiest way of expressing it.

'The bottom line, Inspector, is that I am quite prepared to

stand in the box and say that the pictures you supplied of the groups of partygoers and the film that Peter says was shot through a Hasselblad earlier today were taken on one and the same camera. No doubt about it.'

'You'll do for me,' I said. 'You'll do for me.'

We could prove that Melissa and Kingston had met, in spite of his denials. I rang Tregellis's home number from my office and told him the good news. 'Great!' he said. 'Leave it with me.'

The young lovers shuffled forwards in the queue, tightly holding hands. Rows twenty-one to thirty were boarding flight BA175 from Heathrow to New York, and their seats were 22A and 22B. They worked for British Airways, in the accounts department, and this was the first time they had used the generous concession on fares that their employer offered. It was also to be the first time he had ever been abroad and the first time she had been to New York. And slept with a man. It was to be a short stay, two nights, so they only carried hand luggage. Hers contained a selection of tasteful underwear and a transparent nightie; his held enough condoms for the crew of a nuclear submarine on shore leave in Saigon. Expectations were high and sightseeing wasn't in the itinerary.

He offered their boarding passes to the stewardess at the mouth of the tunnel that would transfer them magically on to the jumbo, and wondered why the man with her was peering over her shoulder and paying so much attention to the passes.

'Ah!' the stewardess said, showing a pass to the man.

'Ah!' he responded, saying to the couple: 'Could you just step to one side, please. I'm afraid your seats have been taken and we'll have to bump you off this flight.'

They turned tearfully away and never noticed the two men

who came running through the departure lounge to join the back of the queue. One of them was short and bulky, with an Adidas holdall over his shoulder, and the other, the one with the bow tie, carried a leather Armani flight bag. Both of them were puffing with the exertion. Graham and Piers were on their way.

I did some travelling too, but slower and lower. Friday afternoon, on a whim, I drove 190 miles to Welwyn Garden City and at five forty-five pressed the bell at the side of the front door of Andrew Roberts' house. It was called Sharand. I hadn't noticed that before. Shaz, is wife, must be Sharon, I thought. How clever. The Bedford and the Saab were on the drive, but the Fiesta was missing.

He opened the door, still wearing his Guns 'n' Roses and cut-downs. 'Hello, Mr Roberts,' I began. 'DI Priest. I was just passing. Been to a meeting, you know how it is, and thought I'd call to give you the latest.'

'Oh, er, right,' he replied. 'You'd, er, better come in.'

The carpets were deep and well-laid, as you might expect, but the colour was out of your nightmares. Day-glo orange and browny-orange in geometric patterns that shimmered and swayed like a Bridget Riley painting. The fireplace with its copper canopy dominated the room and the pictures on the walls were numbers one to five in the World's Most Sentimental Prints. The kid with a snotty nose, the Malaysian woman who's just eaten a badly cleaned puffer fish, and so on. Shaz was curled on the settee in a fluffy pink cardigan, watching TV and looking like an inflatable Barbie doll with a slow leak. I rested my eyes on the fish tank bubbling in the corner and sat down.

'Hope I'm not disturbing you,' I began, 'but I thought you'd like to know what's happening.'

'No, that's all right,' he replied. She threw me a smile, on and straight off, and made a token effort to pull the hem of her miniskirt towards her knees.

'There've been a few developments,' I began, 'but we're still working on it.' I was competing against a peroxide-blonde creep who had a good line in third-form humour and a tits fixation. 'Whether your brother Duncan started the fire is uncertain, but if he did he was most certainly put up to it by a girl. We're convinced he was just being used. She's in America at the moment, but we'll be having words with her. The house belonged to Keith Crosby at the time of the fire, and he was sacked. He was an MP, as you know. Apparently there was some bad blood between him and a prominent businessman, someone really famous, but I can't tell you his name just yet. We're talking to him a week on Tuesday and hoping he'll throw some light on things. He's promised to give us his full co-operation. One theory is that the girl did it to please him. So . . .' I stood up to leave, '. . . watch the news on telly and hope that he keeps his promise.'

'Right,' he said, rising. 'Fanks for coming.'

At the door I turned and said: 'Isn't young DJ at home?'

'No,' he replied. ''E's at college.'

'I thought it was the holidays.'

'Yeah, well, you know how it is. 'Spect he has a bird up there or somefing. He's at Lancaster University. Takes after his uncle in that respec', not me.'

'What's he studying?'

'Mechanical engineering. He's a whiz wiv anyfing mechanical.'

'He rang me,' I told him, 'to ask about Uncle Duncan.'

'Who? DJ?' He sounded surprised.

'Mmm. I think he cared about him more than you realised. I was hoping he'd be here, so I'd be grateful if you could pass on what I've told you.'

'Yeah, right, I'll give 'im a bell an' tell 'im.'

'Week on Tuesday,' I said. 'Watch the papers.'

'Will do. Fanks.'

I started the engine and did a three-point turn at the end of their cul-de-sac. He'd gone in before I drove by so I didn't wave. That's put the Fox amongst the chickens, I thought. This hadn't been in the game plan, and Tregellis would probably eat his desk if he found out, but sometimes it helps to stir things up a little. I tried to blink away the green spots that were swirling before my eyes and headed back towards the M1.

'That's where Percy Shaw lived,' Sparky said, presumably pointing down a lane end we'd just passed.

Here we go, I thought. He's in one of those moods.

'Who's Percy Shaw?' Nigel asked, dead on cue. He'll never learn.

'Percy Shaw? You've never heard of Percy Shaw?'

'I'm afraid not.'

'Blimey, and I thought you were educated. Percy's a local hero, and his product is used on nearly every road in the country; in the world, probably.'

'Oh, I know who you mean,' Nigel realised. 'The Catseye man. He was clever, no doubt about it.'

Sparky was driving my car and I was dozing in the back. We were making our way towards the M62 and then on to Bridlington. It was six thirty a.m., the sun was shining and in the North Sea the fish were swimming on borrowed time.

'He was more than clever, Nigel,' Dave asserted. 'He was a genius.'

'Well, I wouldn't say a genius,' Nigel argued.

'Of course he was. It was on this very road that he had his inspiration. He was driving along, one foggy night, and this cat was coming towards him. Percy saw how its eyes glowed in his headlights and when he got home he invented the Catseye.

Nigel didn't comment, but Dave was undeterred. 'Next morning,' he continued, 'he was driving back from the patent office when he saw the very same cat, but this time it was walking away from him. Percy dashed straight home and invented the pencil sharpener.'

I'd heard it eight times before but I had to smile, or maybe Nigel's guffaws were infectious, or perhaps it was just that I was pleased they got on so well together. At first, when Nigel joined us, it was open warfare between them. Then they learned each other's strengths and weaknesses and now they ganged up against me. I regarded it as one of my successes. Dave went through my selection of cassettes, ejecting each after a short burst. 'God, you don't half listen to some crap,' he pronounced.

The rustling of paper told me that Nigel was struggling with the *Telegraph* we'd had to stop for. After a while he said: 'Hey, this sounds a bargain! P & O are doing two on the ferry from Portsmouth to Santander for seventy-nine pounds, and that includes a car!'

'Sounds good,' Dave agreed. 'I wonder what sort of car it is?'

I wasn't going to get any sleep so I opened my eyes and sat up. Nigel folded his paper and offered it to me, but I declined, so he stuffed it in the door pocket. We were on the motorway, south of Leeds, overtaking a string of lorries through the semi-permanent roadworks near the M1 junction.

'Speed cameras, Dave,' I warned. 'Slow down, or the bastards'll get you.'

'No,' he stated, 'they'll get *you*.'

'*Well slow down then*!'

He slowed down. We left the roadworks behind and Nigel

was admiring the view. 'What are those?' he asked, looking out of his window. 'I seem them every time I come this way and wonder what they are.'

Dave glanced across and I peered out of the back window. 'What are what?' Dave said.

'Those buildings, in that field.'

Long and low, red brick with slate roofs, they were a familiar sight to me, but to Nigel, from Berkshire, they were a novelty.

'Tusky sheds,' Dave stated.

'Tusky sheds?'

'Rhubarb sheds,' I explained. 'They grow rhubarb in them. Norfolk has its windmills, Kent has its oast houses, and we have rhubarb sheds.'

'Right!' Nigel exclaimed. 'Right! And I suppose that's a toothpaste quarry over there, and that old mill is where they used to make blue steam!' He pulled the *Telegraph* out again and started reading the obituaries.

'They're rhubarb sheds!' Dave snapped at him. 'Like he told you.'

'Just once,' Nigel pronounced, 'just once it'd be nice to get a sensible answer to a sensible question.' He read a few more deaths then pretended to be asleep.

'Nigel,' I said, assuming my mantle of authority. 'They are rhubarb sheds. It grows best in the dark. This area south of Leeds is the country's major producer of rhubarb.'

'Have you ever had rhubarb crumble?' Dave asked him.

'No,' he snarled.

Dave glanced back over his shoulder. 'Ring our Shirl,' he told me, 'and tell her to get a rhubarb crumble out of the freezer. Nigel's in for a treat.'

The arrangement was that the three of us were going back to Dave's house for fresh-caught fish, and chips made with his home-grown potatoes. I asked Nigel to pass me my phone and dialled Shirley.

We'd forgotten it was not quite seven in the morning, and Shirley wasn't too pleased at being disturbed again. She's a pal, though, and soon forgave me, but couldn't help with the crumble. They were out of them. 'Bring some rhubarb back with you,' she suggested, 'and I'll make him one.'

The east coast suffers from what are known as sea frets. One hundred yards inland it can be a scorcher, but a thick mist rises off the water, blotting out the sun and turning July into November. Today we had a mother and father of one.

We groped our way along the pier, between plastic-clad holidaymakers forced to desert their rooms while the maid changed the sheets, and were accosted by the touts who work for the boats. Seven blokes in scruffy clothes hadn't come to sample the funfare, and we were putty in their hands. Dave put up a struggle, giving nearly as good as he got, and insisted that we go in a boat that was only half-filled. Just before we cast off, however, we were ordered to switch into the boat tied alongside, which was also half-full, so now we were in one that was crowded.

On the trip out I explained to Nigel how to put a bunch of mussels on his hook and how to feel for the bottom with the big lead weight. Because of the weather, and because it was just a three-hour trip, we would only go into the bay. We shivered, shoulder to shoulder, and waited for the boat to stop.

The skipper switched the engine off and gave the order to start fishing. The boat, bristling with rods, looked like a floating hedgehog. I felt my weight hit the bottom, reeled in a couple of turns and showed Nigel how to do the same.

'Now wait for a bite,' I said.

'And then what?'

'Strike and haul it up.'

'That simple.'

'Yep.'

The first tangle came after about ten minutes of waiting. Someone at the other side of the boat started winding in, a chap along from me struck and started winding, then Dave, me, Nigel and everyone else in the boat.

'Stop reeling in!' yelled the skipper.

It took him nearly fifteen minutes to unravel the ball of spaghetti that we eventually lifted out of the water. We repeated the exercise six more times and that was the three hours up. 'Is it always this much fun?' Nigel asked.

The other four made straight for the pub while we went looking for a fishmonger. 'I don't suppose you have any cod with the heads and tails still on?' Dave asked in the most promising one.

'Sorry, sir,' the man replied. 'It's all been filleted.'

'Oh. In that case, can I have six large portions, please?' Shirley and their children, Daniel and Sophie, would be eating with us.

I noticed that the salmon was only ten pence dearer than the cod. 'I think I'd prefer a piece of salmon,' I said.

Dave turned on me. 'You can't have salmon. We've supposed to have caught it.'

'Well, I caught a salmon.'

'They don't catch salmon.'

'Of course they catch it. Where do you think it comes from?'

'It comes from a farm. They farm it.'

I turned to the fishmonger. 'Was the salmon wild?' I asked him.

'It wasn't too pleased,' he replied. Everybody's a stand-up comedian these days.

* * *

We couldn't find a rhubarb shop so we joined the others in the pub and let them have a smell of our fish. Dave and Nigel had a couple of pints and I settled for halves because it was my turn to drive. They talked about the job most of the way home while I concentrated on staying awake. 'So were you two on the Ripper case?' Nigel asked.

'*On it's* putting it a bit steep,' Dave replied. 'We were there, that's all.'

'So what were you doing?'

'Stopping cars, mainly. Anybody out late at night got used to being stopped. Other crime fell dramatically.'

'And how long did it go on for?'

'Oh, about two years. I'm not proud of it, but the Ripper paid the deposit on my first house.'

'We worked hard, Dave,' I said. 'Some paid for their entire houses and did a lot less than us.'

'Mmm, I know.'

'You were lucky, weren't you, when you caught him?' Nigel asked.

'Dead jammy,' Dave agreed.

'It was good policing,' I argued.

'We could do with a bit more luck like that,' Dave said.

After a silence Nigel asked: 'So why haven't you ever gone for your stripes, Dave?'

Dave didn't reply. 'You're on a touchy subject, Nigel,' I warned.

'Why?'

'I don't know, but he has his reasons, daft as they probably are.'

'So why haven't you?' Nigel persisted.

'Leave it,' I told him. Dave has fluffed his sergeant's exam several times, but I don't know why. He claims he just freezes in the exam room, but I don't believe him. I've seen him take on more than one whizkid barrister and do all right.

We were passing a sign saying the next services were ten miles ahead. 'Wouldn't mind stopping for a pee,' Dave said.

'Me too,' Nigel added.

Nigel was explaining to Dave how J.J. Fox gained control of various companies even though he had less than fifty per cent of the shares. 'He has a reputation second to none for making companies profitable,' he said. 'OK, so he sacks people and asset-strips, but the shareholders don't mind if they are reaping the benefits. If he has, say, thirty-five per cent of the shares, he can attract the proxy votes of the smaller shareholders who can't be bothered to vote themselves. This might give him, say, a sixty per cent holding, so he's effectively in control.'

'Shareholders want to see their investments doing well,' I said as I cruised past the slip road to the services. 'You can't really blame them for ignoring the man's ethics.'

'Not only that,' Nigel added. 'Most of the investors are probably pension schemes. They're obliged to strive for the best available for their members, so they can't afford to be choosy.'

'Aargh! You've passed them!' Dave complained.

Five minutes later we were back in the rhubarb triangle. 'How desperate are you?' I asked.

'Quite,' Nigel said.

'Bloody,' Dave added.

Away to my left I could see a pair of sheds, side by side in the middle of some allotments, with a Land Rover standing outside them. 'Right,' I said. 'In that case we'll kill two birds with one stone.' I pulled across into the slow lane and indicated that I was leaving at the next exit.

'Where are we going?' Nigel asked.

'To some rhubarb sheds,' I replied. 'There was a Land Rover outside. You can have a pee and I'll see if he'll sell me some rhubarb.'

I took left turns until I was driving back alongside the motorway, and turned left again down a cobbled street that looked promising. We were between two rows of terraced houses, left isolated for some reason when the area had been cleared. They were occupied and looked tidy, with clotheslines across the road and some children kicking a ball about. We'd stepped back in time.

The cobbles gave way to a dirt track that led through the allotments, fenced round with a mishmash of old doors, wire netting and floorboards. Blue smoke drifted up from a pile of burning sods and a piebald pony tied to a stake reached for fresh grass outside the bald circle it occupied.

'There they are,' I said, nodding towards the rhubarb sheds. There were two of them at the far side of an area of uncultivated ground, backing against the motorway embankment. More gypsy ponies were tethered nearby, but the Land Rover had vanished.

'He's gone,' I said. 'Never mind.' I drove up to the sheds and stopped. We all got out and Dave and Nigel wandered round the back to relieve themselves.

Several abandoned cars were strewn down one side of the buildings, like wrecks on the seabed, slowly returning to nature. A Morris Minor had almost rotted away, its oil-soaked engine putting up the only resistance. Tall grass and willow-herb grew through tyres that were scattered around, left where they fell. I kicked one and two goldfinches flew up from a patch of thistles.

The door at the front of the first shed was wide enough for a trailer to be backed through, and written on it in cream paint that had dribbled was the name *J. Nelson and Sons*, with a telephone number. The padlock on the door was a big Chubb made from some exotic steel that must have cost about a hundred pounds, and a picture of a Rottweiler's head bore the legend: *Make my day*. Rhubarb's a valuable crop, I thought.

I heard Dave call my name so I walked round the side. He emerged from behind the building, at the far end, and shouted: 'Come and look at this.'

I picked my way through the nettles and debris and joined them at the back of the sheds, up against the embankment. 'What have you found?' I asked.

There was a post-and-rail fence marking the boundary of the motorway, and Dave pointed at a rail. 'See that,' he said.

The rail was sawn through, almost all the way, close to the post.

'So?'

'And here, and here.' All three rails were similar. 'It's the same at the other end,' he told me.

I walked the four yards to the next post to see for myself. 'What do you make of it?' I asked.

'Someone might want to get away in a hurry,' Nigel said. 'They could charge straight through the fence and up the bank on to the motorway.'

'Now why would they want to do that?' I wondered. There was a junction five hundred yards away, with a choice of five different directions for them to flee down.

'Come and listen,' Dave said, adding: 'But mind the wet grass.'

I followed him to the boarded-up window in the back wall.

'What can you hear?' he asked.

'Traffic.'

'No, from inside. Listen.'

I cupped my hand around an ear and put it close to the window, sealing the other with a finger. There was a low hum coming from inside. 'Sounds a bit like a generator,' I said.

'Why would he want a generator?'

'Lighting?'

'Rhubarb grows in the dark. So do mushrooms.'

'Heating?'

'It's the hottest summer on record, and generators are not that powerful.'

'Right,' I said. 'So maybe we should take a closer look. The lock on the front door looks as if it came from Fort Knox.'

'Leave it to me,' Dave said, and wandered off to rummage amongst the wrecks. He came back in less than a minute carrying a half-shaft.

We were in a secluded spot behind the buildings, out of sight of the traffic or the nearby houses. What we were doing was illegal, there was no excuse for it, but we did it just the same. Every pane of glass in the window was broken but it was boarded up on the inside. Strands of barbed wire were stapled around it as a further deterrent. Dave took a swing at the end board and a dog inside started barking. It sounded big, and fierce, and very angry.

'Blimey, I'm not going in there,' I said. I worry about dogs.

The more Dave hammered the more demented the dog became. It sounded as if it might rip us limb from limb. 'Don't make the hole too large,' I pleaded. 'It might leap out.'

When the first board had moved a little he used the half-shaft as a lever. Nails screeched as they were uprooted. Dave knocked some bits of glass out and moved higher up the plank of wood, feeling for a new purchase.

'Let's have a look,' I said. He stepped aside and I peered through the triangular gap. 'It's light inside,' I told them. 'Looks like fluorescents, take it right out.'

One minute and a ripped shirtsleeve later the plank fell to the floor. The dog barks had subsided to a hoarse staccato, but no slavering face appeared at the gap. It must have been tied up.

'Bloody hell!' exclaimed Nigel. 'Is that what I think it is?' Inside was a jungle of foliage, illuminated from above by bluish strip lights.

'I knew it!' Dave declared triumphantly. 'I knew it! Cannabis! *Cannabis sativa*. At a guess the variety commonly known as skunk.'

'Ah,' I said, 'but what's that I can see at the far end, just inside the doors?'

'Friggin' heck!' he exclaimed. 'A white van.'

'Of the variety commonly known as a Transit,' Nigel added, and his grin made Sparky's ruined shirt completely worthwhile.

Everybody agreed that the fish and chips were superb. There was no substitute for fish taken straight from the sea. It made a big difference. We were late, but Shirley's annoyance soon evaporated when she saw our buoyant mood.

'So who caught them?' asked Daniel, Dave's son, as he pushed his empty plate away.

'I did,' his father replied; 'We caught one each,' I said; 'We bought them,' Nigel confessed, all more or less simultaneously.

Nigel had left his car outside my house. He came in with me and we did some phoning. James Nelson was sixty-three years old and had no criminal record. It was different for his sons, Barry and Leonard. They'd been in trouble all their lives, starting with shoplifting and progressing right through to burglaries, via a couple of fracas. Up to then they'd concentrated on breaking into industrial premises and shops, which is regarded as a less serious offence than burgling domestic premises, and carries a lighter sentence. They'd had the lot: cautions; probation;

community service; fines; and extended holidays at the Queen's expense. Sometimes the system doesn't work.

Or perhaps it did. They'd both kept out of trouble for over two years, which were personal bests. Alternatively, perhaps they'd paid attention to what their teachers said at the Academy of Crime, and thought they were now a lot cleverer. If so, they were mistaken. Jails are filled with the failures, the ones we catch; the smart ones we never even know about.

I rang Jeff Caton to tell him the good news, but his wife told me that he wasn't home yet.

'Not home!' I exclaimed. 'Not home! We've been home *hours*.' She agreed to tell him to phone me as soon as he arrived.

When it's on my patch I have the final say, so we met at ten on Sunday morning. Dave and myself went to see James Nelson while Nigel, Jeff and a DS from the drug squad met at the rhubarb sheds, armed with a search warrant.

Nelson lived in a run-down farmhouse just a few hundred yards from the row of terraced houses. More abandoned vehicles littered the yard and a German shepherd dog, chained to a wheel-less Ford Popular, gave an early warning of our approach. Judging from its teats it had just had pups. I moved to the other side of Sparky as we passed it.

'Are you James Nelson?' Dave asked the leather-skinned man who opened the door. He looked at least seventy, so we couldn't be sure. He wore a vest and dangling braces, and wouldn't have looked out of place in a documentary about Bosnian refugees.

'Aye,' he replied warily.

'I'm DC Sparkington from Heckley CID, and this is my senior officer, DI Priest. I think you'd better let us in.'

My senior officer! Dave was at his Sunday best and I was impressed.

The inside of the house was all Catherine Cookson. Not the

wicked master's house, and not that of the poor girl who is left orphaned and has to dig turnips every day with only a broken button-hook to raise a few coppers to feed her six younger brothers and sisters and keep them from the lascivious clutches of the master. This belonged to the stern but kindly blacksmith who throws her the odd horseshoe to make soup with, who is in love with her but knows that she is really the master's illegitimate daughter and can never be his.

There was a big iron range, with a built-in set-pot and a fire glowing in the grate. Pans and strange implements hung from the beams and two squadrons of houseflies were engaged in a dogfight around the light bulb, which was on because the curtains were closed. The temperature must have been in the nineties. We sat down, and a black cat which I hadn't seen bolted for safety from under my descending backside.

'Are Barry and Len in?' Dave asked.

Mr Nelson shook his head.

'Where are they?'

'They'm don' live 'ere. What they'm done now?'

'Is there a Mrs Nelson?'

'No. She passed away, twelve years sin'.'

'I'm sorry. So where do Barry and Len live?'

'Abroad. Tenerife.'

'How long have they lived there?'

''Bout two year, why?'

'Do they ever come home?'

'Oh, aye, now an' agin.'

'When were they last home?'

'Dunno.'

'How about six weeks ago?'

'Aye, about then, I suppose.'

'And about a month before that?'

'It could o' been.'

'What do they do for a living in Tenerife, Mr Nelson?' I asked.

He switched his gaze to me and clenched his hands together, squeezing and relaxing his fingers, as if milking a cow. 'They'm 'ave shares in a bar, or so they'm tells me. Dunno for sure.'

'When are you expecting your sons home again?' I said.

He shrugged his shoulders and glanced at his hands and back to me. 'Dunno.'

'Do they write or phone to tell you?'

'No, they'm just turn up.'

'Without warning?'

'Aye.'

'Do you look forward to their visits?'

He didn't answer.

'You had to raise them yourself,' I stated.

'I did me best.'

'But they gave you a hard time?'

No answer. His fingers were long and swollen at the joints, and one nail was blackened and about to fall off. He wore a wedding ring, but it had been relegated to his pinky because of the swelling. And all the time he squeezed and relaxed his hands, as if the rhythm gave him some comfort.

'Mr Nelson,' I began. 'Do you own the rhubarb sheds that back on to the M62?'

The kneading increased in fervour. 'Aye,' he replied, his head down.

'What do you grow in them?'

'Rhubub,' he replied, looking up at me. 'I grows rhubub. My boys, Barry and Len, they'm use the other 'un. Don' ask me what they'm grows in it.'

'But you've a good idea, haven't you?'

He lowered his head again. 'Aye, I suppose so.'

'What do you think it is?'

He shrugged his shoulders.

'Pardon.'

'Drugs, I reckon.'

'So why haven't you reported it to the police?'

He looked at me as if I'd asked him if he ever sniffed when his nose dribbled. ''Cos they'd do for me,' he replied.

'Are you scared of your sons?' I asked.

He looked at his hands and didn't answer.

'Do they knock you about?'

He mumbled something I didn't catch. 'Could you say that again, please,' I insisted.

'They've given me a tap, now an' again,' he said.

I looked across at Dave. He said: 'Put the rest of your clothes on, Mr Nelson. We have a warrant to search the sheds and we'd like you to come with us.'

If only to hold the flippin' dog, I thought.

The other three were scattered around, looking for birds' nests or that long-lost part of the vintage car. As we pulled up they emerged from the greenery and congregated around us. Jeff and the others had arrived home from the fishing trip after midnight, and his eyes resembled the proverbial piss-holes in the snow. In the car Mr Nelson had explained that he came every day, to feed the dog and fill the generator. There was an automatic irrigation system, so he never had to touch the plants.

The dog leapt about with joy when he unlocked the door, and after a great deal of fussing it settled down with what looked like a dustbin lid full of cows' feet. I measured the length of its chain and added a yard for safety.

'Oh my Gawd!' exclaimed Jeff when he saw the Transit. He pointed at the aerial, the tax disc and the mark on the windscreen.

'Oh my Gawd!' he repeated, then: 'It's it. This is it. You jammy so-and-sos.'

'Good policing,' I told him. 'Jammy's nothing to do with it.'

'I'll ring for a SOCO,' he said, producing a mobile phone.

The plants were in orderly rows, close together and about chest height. We spread out and walked between them, trailing our fingers through the fronds and all wondering what they were worth and if there was any harm in it. At the far end Dave hammered some new nails through the loose plank so the local youths couldn't steal the evidence. Jeff rejoined us. 'He's on his way,' he said.

I pulled two leaves from a plant, gave one to Jeff and popped the other in my mouth. 'Make you feel better,' I told him. Strolling back through the rows I plucked another. At the far end Jeff emerged from the adjacent row and poked his tongue out at me. On it was a chewed-up ball of what might have been spinach. I did the same to him and we both giggled like schoolgirls in an art gallery.

Dave and I took Mr Nelson back to the station. Some use the Nice Cop and Nasty Cop routine; others rely on the bastinado, beating them on the soles of their feet until they co-operate. We seduce them with a bacon sandwich and a mug of hot sweet tea. After that, he'd have told us anything.

He didn't know when his sons were coming back, but agreed to tell us as soon as they did. If he had the opportunity. The burglaries had coincided with their visits and he had wondered if they had committed them. We assured him they had, and he shed a few tears.

When Jeff and Nigel returned we sat Mr Nelson in an interview room with another sarni, making a statement to a nice police lady, while we had an operations conference in my office. I wasn't happy about asking him to grass on his sons. Blood, as they say, is thicker than prison soup.

'The alternative,' Jeff said, 'is to put out an APW on them and hope someone tells us when they come into the country, or mount an observation operation.'

'One's unreliable and the other's expensive,' Nigel said.

'We could just watch out for the van moving,' Jeff suggested.

'Still expensive,' Nigel countered. 'We could be waiting weeks. I think we should rely on Mr Nelson.'

'We're asking him to shop his sons,' I said. 'It doesn't seem fair. Plus, he might not get the opportunity. Or he might change his mind; he's obviously scared of them.'

'Let's ask the technical support boffins to fit the van with a bug,' Dave suggested.

'Sadly, it belongs to Len,' I said. 'If it's not Mr Nelson's van he can't give us permission.'

'We could say we didn't know.'

'It would be inadmissible,' Nigel told him.

'So what? We'll still nab them.'

'And it'll get kicked out!'

'*We* can't fit a bug,' I said, 'but there is a way Mr Nelson could.'

They all looked at me.

'He could just happen to drive the van into Electronic Solutions on Monday morning and ask them to fit it with a Tracker,' I explained.

'Who would pay?' Nigel asked.

'We would,' I replied.

'They cost about two hundred pounds.'

Dave turned on him. 'If you don't mind me saying so, Nigel,' he began, 'you're growing into a right management cop.'

'Nigel's right,' I said before an argument could develop. 'Money's tight, but I'll make a case out for it. Jeff, how much would a surveillance operation cost?'

'God knows!' he gasped.

'Think of a number.'

'Er, ten thousand pounds.'

'That'll do. Two hundred for a Tracker is a bargain. Have a word with Electronic Solutions in the morning, see if they'll do it cost price. Or, better still, free. Tell them we'll take our fleet business away from them if they won't. Then ask Mr Nelson to take the van in.'

Electronic Solutions are auto electricians in Halifax. They tune our pursuit cars and fit various gizmos to them. The Tracker is a patented device that is more usually fitted to top-of-the-range vehicles like Porsches and Jags. It is secreted away somewhere and is completely passive until activated by a signal from a tracking station. If the car is reported stolen the signal is transmitted to it, and from then on its movements can be followed to within five yards. According to the literature some owners have had their vehicles found within minutes. Sadly, we're not allowed to plant bugs in vehicles without the consent of the owner. It's regarded as unsporting. Going to court with evidence gathered in such a manner would be misguided and overoptimistic, like ringing the Scottish Assembly and asking to reverse the charges. These days we're not allowed to gain evidence by trickery, subterfuge or deviousness. Confessions are acceptable, most of the time, but not always, and video evidence is good. Courts love video evidence, because TV doesn't lie. Get a decent tape of a crime in progress, show it on *Look North*, and the villains queue up to shout: 'It's me!' They're the same inadequate souls who appear on afternoon TV shows like Ricki Lake and Jerry Springer, confessing to owning a Barbour coat or having sexual relations with an armadillo. After that, putting your hand up for blagging Barclays Bank is positively high class. No, we couldn't fit the Transit with a bug, but Mr Nelson could.

'It's not continuous monitoring,' Nigel warned. 'They need alerting that the vehicle is on the move before they activate the bug. And they'll want a crime reference number.'

'Give them the last burglary number,' Jeff suggested. 'And once it's activated it should run forever. It's connected to the battery, I think.'

'OK,' I said. 'Let's go for belt and braces. First of all, find out exactly how the Tracker works, Jeff. Then, if you think it necessary, put out an APW on the brothers. That might give us some notice that they are in the country. Lastly, if you're still not convinced, ask Mr Nelson to give us a nod when they are around. OK?'

'Yep.'

I sent Mr Nelson home with the WPC. His home, that is, not hers. As I walked to the door with them I said: 'I believe you told us that your sons held shares in a bar in Tenerife, Mr Nelson.'

'Aye, so they'm tell me.'

'Any idea what it's called?'

'Aye, it's called t'Pigeon Pie.'

'Really?' I said. You could have knocked me down with a Sally Lunn.

Chapter 11

It was back to being a small-town DI for a week. We had an average quota of muggings, fights and burglaries, and Gilbert asked me to go to his Chamber of Commerce meeting to talk about security cameras. In other words, to tell them that if they wanted them they'd have to pay for them. Highlight of the week was when the owner of a Toyota pickup caught a wheelclamper in the act and made a commendable attempt to force the clamp where most of us can only fantasise about. The Toyota owner appeared before the beak and the clamper appeared before a surgeon for some stitches. The good news was that they did his piles at the same time.

We were hanging fire with the Fox job. A lot was resting on my meeting with him. I talked to Tregellis a couple of times and we discussed possibilities. Fox employed Kingston but might deny knowing him personally. If they were buddies we'd concentrate on Kingston, suggesting that he might be involved with several crimes, including the fire, and encourage him to tell us what he knew about the man. If he said he didn't know him personally we'd switch tack. I'd bring Crosby into the conversation and tell Fox that we were looking into his ancestry, which was true. Tregellis had asked the War Crimes Bureau, which had extensive German-Jewish connections, to try to find any surviving relatives of a certain Johannes Josef Fuchs who fled Germany in 1940, aged about twelve. I'd asked Crosby to call in at his convenience and donate six hairs from his head, so we could do a DNA comparison with any relatives they located back in the Fatherland. Maybe I'd ask Fox if he wanted to make a similar donation.

After that we'd talk to Kingston. We were flapping around in the dark, spreading shit and not knowing where it might land. We didn't even know if they talked to each other. The fallback plan was to arrest Fox and ask him some searching questions. We'd get no answers and have to release him, but there'd be leaks of information and the papers would sit up and take notice. Every one of them would put a specialist team on the Fox story and they'd turn up more dirt than we could dream about.

Thursday morning Piers rang me from his home. They'd landed at Heathrow three hours earlier and he'd just staggered in, jet-lagged and weary. I imagined him with a five o'clock shadow and his bow tie askew and wondered what they'd thought of him in Hillbilly Land.

'Have you brought Melissa back with you?' I asked.

'No, but she said she'll come,' Piers replied. 'Those photographs were crucial. At first she denied ever knowing Kingston, but with them we were able to convince her otherwise. When she realised that the crap was about to hit the fan in a big way, and we were willing to make a deal with her, she became more co-operative.'

'What's she offering?'

'First of all let me tell you about where she lives. It's a shanty town of trailers, not unlike some of those places you see from the train in north Wales, except it's not raining all the time. She lives with an older man who is supposed to be some kind of revolutionary poet or something. They have ties with a ranch up in the hills, and spend a lot of time there. I think it's probably where their redneck friends hang out. They're into the gun culture in a big way, the place was bristling with them.'

'Did you feel safe?' I asked. It sounded dodgy to me.

'Not really, Charlie,' he replied. 'Even though we had the deputy sheriff with us each time we visited them. They have some mean-looking neighbours.'

'How well off is she?'

'Hard to say. Not very, at first glance, but they have plenty of possessions: the trailer, big Dodge pickup, huge television, freezer, air-conditioning, you name it. I'd say their main problem is cash flow. Melissa is having problems finding the money to have her teeth fixed.'

'Her teeth?'

'That's right. This is the good bit. Their belief in self-sufficiency and disrespect for the establishment precludes having health insurance, it would appear, and Melissa is suffering from impacted wisdom teeth. They're giving her a lot of trouble.'

'Sounds painful. How does that help us?'

'Like this. Melissa IDs Kingston for us and signs a statement saying that he told her to mark the number on the house in Leeds and show Duncan Roberts which it was. She thought he was just visiting there, or something. She swears she knew nothing of any plan to burn it down.'

'She's a lying little madam,' I said.

'That's as may be,' Piers replied. 'Her story is that she was a nervous little student and Kingston was a charismatic lecturer. She was under his spell. Our side of the bargain is that we fly her to England with her boyfriend, house them for a week somewhere cheap but cheerful up near you, and arrange for her to have her teeth fixed. What do you think?'

I thought for a few seconds before replying, then said: 'I think you've done well, Piers. That's about as much as you could possibly achieve, but it means she's getting away with murder. We only know about Leeds. What happened, who did she recruit, in Durham or Manchester, California, Paris or wherever?'

'I understand your feelings,' Piers told me, 'but I think it's the best we'll do. We don't know how she fits into the scheme of things; whether she was a leading light or a tiny cog; and you can't catch 'em all, Charlie.'

America had done him good, loosened him up. He was calling me Charlie. After a long silence he said: 'There is one little titbit I've been saving. It might upset all our plans, but on the other hand, it could be useful. How does this sound?'

When he'd finished I said: 'Right. I'm convinced; let's do it.'

Piers went home and slept for fourteen hours. On Friday he briefed Tregellis, who had no objections, and on Monday he phoned Melissa and said we were trying to make an appointment for her to have her wisdom teeth fixed. That was my job. The appointment, that is, although I was quite willing to tackle the teeth myself, with the pliers from my little toolkit.

Over the weekend I tidied the garden, did some washing and took my shirts to the lady who irons them for me. She's a widow who lives a few doors away. Before her husband died he was the only friend I had in the street. The others don't like me because my dandelion seeds blow into their gardens. And I'm the law. I stroll round the cul-de-sac and pretend to look at their tax discs, and as soon as I've passed they dash out to check them. We had home-made lemonade in her garden, with carrot cake, and I paid for it by making her laugh.

I bought three broadsheets on Sunday and scanned the business pages for news of Fox and Reynard. All of them told the story about him opening Reynard Tower, in Leeds, which would be the new seat of his insurance empire. The jobs, the spokesperson assured us, would be real ones.

Monday I gave Annette the job of negotiating with our contacts at Heckley General to see if they would be able to do Melissa's teeth at short notice. It would cost us, but a specialist said he could fit her in, after hours. In any other profession it's called moonlighting, using the boss's tackle, and would result in the sack. In the NHS it's normal practice. Can you imagine Kwik-Fit allowing their mechanics to fit exhausts to the cars of their private customers after five o'clock? Not on your Nelly, José.

I had a long session with Nigel; questions and answers, role-playing. He's good at stuff like that, and it was useful. We lunched at the Chinese and Nigel tested me on my knowledge of the Reynard Organisation. I scored ten out of ten, but I'd done some swotting. Tregellis rang to wish me luck and Sparky poked his head round the door to say the same thing. I felt as if I was about to fight Mike Tyson. I emptied my in-tray and went home, slightly disappointed that there was no postcard of the Acropolis in there.

Tea was a tin of sardines, full of essential oils – no, that's aromatherapy, but they're good for you; followed by a piece of my neighbour's carrot cake that she'd insisted I bring home. I wondered what her apple pies were like. After that I found two big pieces of hardboard and painted them with white emulsion. The art exhibition was two weeks away and I was behind schedule. I did some sketches and by the time I went to bed I'd developed a couple of ideas.

I've interviewed people who've strangled wives, stabbed lovers, shot strangers, smothered babies. Some filled me with rage, others made me weep. All of them had a story, some redeeming feature, that reminded me of the old saw: *There but for the grace of God* . . . Well, nearly all of them. But Fox was different. He was from a mould that is rarely used, thank heaven. If what Crosby had told me was true, his goals in life were self-preservation and the accumulation of wealth and power. Vast wealth. Monstrous power. The tools he used in the pursuit of these were murder and a cold indifference to the lives of anyone else. He'd had fifty years to hone his skills, and tomorrow I was meeting him. One thing was certain; I wouldn't come away from that meeting much wiser than when I went in. But I'd know my quarry. I'd have seen him on his own patch, surrounded by his imperial guard of lawyers. I'd know what I was up against the next time we met, and I was sure there'd be a next time.

The weather changed through the night, as the forecasters had predicted. The summer was over. Flurries of rain rattled against the bedroom window like handfuls of gravel tossed by a lover. I sat up with a start. Perhaps it wasn't rain . . . but the sound of water running along the gutter told me it was. I sank back into my pillow and tried to sleep.

And then there was Kingston. If Fox was the Führer, then Kingston was the head of his Gestapo. I was sure of it, but I had my own reasons for wanting Kingston. Private reasons.

I'd set the alarm to give me an hour's lie-in, but when it beeped into life I couldn't understand why I was late. Then I remembered; today was the day that Mr Fox would snip the ribbon and create a thousand new jobs. And a city would be grateful and honour him. How many he'd lost that city over the past twenty years was incalculable. A thought struck me, as I lay in that never-never land when my stomach wants feeding but my legs refuse to swing out of bed. It was self-evident, but had completely eluded the last government. *Every time a company streamlines itself by destroying a job, ten other businesses lose a customer*. Not bad for seven on a Tuesday morning, I thought, and my legs kicked themselves from under the duvet and the day began.

I put on my charcoal suit and a blue tie with a pink stripe that added a dash of frivolity. I wouldn't take my briefcase, I decided, or even a notebook. We'd have a chat, man to man, nice and informal – if I could see him for lawyers – and I'd try to drop a little bombshell just before I left. Something to put them in a panic. I buffed my shoes with the soles of my socks and we were ready.

Traffic into Leeds at that time in the morning is like any normal big-city traffic. A great time to read *War and Peace* or study Mandarin. I timed my run so I'd just miss the nine o'clock peak, if there was such a thing, and hopefully arrive far too early. Perhaps I'd have time for a coffee in the restaurant. We were stop-going on the M621 when I thought I'd catch up on the mornings news. The M621 used to be the only motorway in the world that terminated at a set of traffic lights. Now it peters out in a forest of traffic cones, but it'll be good when it's finished. I pushed the *power* button and a familiar voice finished a story about natterjack toads. 'Police in Yorkshire . . .' she continued.

'That's me!' I thought.

'. . . are trying to identify a man who threw himself off the Scammonden bridge over the M62.'

He was, she told us, the umpteenth suicide there since the bridge was constructed. That'll be a great consolation to the relatives, I thought. A BMW in the fast lane decided he wanted my bit of the slow lane and cut across me. Fifty seconds later he'd done just the opposite. I braked and cursed him but he was too engrossed in his telephone conversation to notice.

'And a piece of late news has just been handed to me,' she was saying. 'The businessman J.J. Fox, head of the Reynard Organisation, has been found dead in his hotel room in Leeds.

We'll let you have more on that as soon as we receive it.'

I swung on to the hard shoulder and yanked the handbrake on, but she'd passed us over to the sports presenter, who was saying that our *numero uno* tennis player had lost in straight sets to a nine-year-old from Utah. 'You should have strangled the little bastard,' I hissed at the radio as I switched it off and reached for my phone.

I rang the nick and then Tregellis, but it was me breaking the news to them, so I decided the best place to be was at the Fox Borealis. I indicated right and an artic flashed me out.

The foyer of the hotel was filled with people standing in little hushed groups. There'd been a PC at the entrance, making a note of all visitors, which meant that the death was regarded as suspicious. He told me that Superintendent Isles was in charge and let me in. My old mate Les; that made it easier.

Another PC was guarding the lifts and two detectives were trying to organise the guests into a queue so they could take their names and then let them out to do their selling or conferencing or whatever it was that had brought them to this place on this day. Technicians and reporters in T-shirts and jeans, were wandering around with microphones and tape recorders, talking to anyone who looked as if they might be able to string two words together. A TV person with a big camera was speaking to head office on his mobile. 'Can you get one of the body?' they'd be saying.

I introduced myself to the PC at the lift and told him I needed to see Mr Isles. He explained that there was an express lift, for private use, that went straight up to the penthouse, on the fifteenth floor, where Mr Isles was. However, that was out of bounds and only one of the other lifts was in use. I could go up in it but it only went to the fourteenth floor. I thanked him and he pressed the button.

I stepped out into a moderately large foyer with a blue and gold carpet and several easy chairs. Four figures turned to see who the newcomer was and Les Isles said: 'Good God! What are you doing here?'

'Look in his diary,' I replied. 'I've an appointment to see Mr Fox at ten o'clock.'

'You were seeing Fox? What for?'

'To ask him some questions. Is it murder?'

'We don't know.' He introduced me to the pathologist and a DI, telling them: 'When Charlie appears, you know you have trouble.'

'So what's happened?' I asked.

'Maid found him, 'bout six thirty,' Les replied. 'He's half on the floor, hanging from the bedhead with a dressing gown cord round his neck. At first glance it's a sex game gone wrong, but that might be the intention. The SOCOs and scientific are in there at the moment. I want every fibre, every latent footprint on record. Nobody goes in without an Andy Pandy on. We should have a video in a few minutes. Right, now you're up to speed, how about telling us why you're here.'

I told them about the fire, Melissa, Kingston and the link with Fox, and left it at that. 'I was hoping Fox might tell me something about Kingston,' I said, 'seeing as he employed him.'

A SOCO came down the stairs carrying a video cassette. He was wearing a white suit that completely enveloped him. Presumably Andy Pandy dressed in a similar manner. Only a nose protruded, beneath a pair of rimless spectacles. Les took the cassette and said: 'Thank you, Carol.' He was a she.

The DI was speaking on his radio. 'The caravan's set up,' he said as he switched off, 'but the BT engineer's still working on the phones.'

'In that case find the manager and ask him if there's anywhere we can watch this,' Les told him, waving the cassette. The DI made for the lift and the pathologist excused himself and followed.

When we were alone I said: 'There's a lot more to this, Les. I'm seconded to the SFO and they're looking into Fox's affairs. I'll fill you in when we have the chance, but meanwhile I'd appreciate it if you could let me sit in on things.'

He ran a hand through his hair and sighed. 'I knew it. As soon as I saw you I knew it. You're bad news, Charlie, did anyone ever tell you?'

I grinned and said: 'I know, but it makes death more interesting, doesn't it.'

The manager switched the video on and told the DI which button to press on the remote control when the tape had run itself back to the beginning. He hovered until Les told him, very politely, that he'd have to leave. It might have been his office, with a huge mahogany desk, three-piece suite and Atkinson Grimshaw prints on the walls, but this was a murder inquiry and he'd have to go. I assumed they were prints, but you never know.

The SOCO had given us a wide-angle overall view of Fox's suite of rooms that constituted the penthouse. She'd panned around and wandered from room to room as if making a film for architects or interior designers. The main room, presumably the one intended for his waking hours, had a glass wall with a view over the city, and outside was a bank of mirrors that could follow the sun and reflect it in. Furniture was sparse but luxurious, with lots of white fur, and a few antique pieces struck a discordant note.

After the grand tour the SOCO pulled back the lens and got down to the nitty-gritty. Fox's clothes were in an unhasty pile in a Queen Anne chair with a pair of striped boxer shorts on top. The huge bed was crumpled and the pillows had been pushed to one side. It was built in, with lights and speakers in the headboard and a bank of controls for things I could only wonder about. The man himself was half-kneeling, half-sitting on the floor near the top of the bed. His head was at an awkward angle and a cord led from his neck and was looped behind one of the hi-fi speakers. The cameraman zoomed in with ruthless disregard for taste or propriety. This was strictly after-the-watershed stuff.

Fox was naked apart from pyjama trousers, which were round his ankles. His eyes were closed, and he looked reasonably peaceful, although a ribbon of saliva had run down his chin and chest. His winkie was relaxed, small and red, with a condom hanging off the end like an old sock. If that's safe sex, I thought, God save me from the dangerous sort.

An hour later we saw the real thing, just before he was hauled away for dissection. I didn't feel sorrow for him, not an ounce. Around his bed the pong of cheap perfume hung in the air like petrol fumes on a foggy morning, and that, as much as anything, convinced me what a sordid little man he was. Les still insisted we wore paper suits and bootees and we trudged from room to room, me concerned with the man's lifestyle, Les looking for anything that might throw some light on how he met his death.

A feature of the living room was a pond containing several large koi carp. As we approached they rose to the surface and followed us with their bulging eyes.

'They need feeding,' the DI stated.

'So do I,' Les told him.

In another room I found a bank of televisions, six of them, all glowing silently, their screens alight with columns of names and numbers. They were showing stock market prices from all around the world: the Dow Jones, Hang Seng, Nikkei; plus exchange rates and commodity prices. If that's what it took to become rich, I'd rather not bother.

'Look at this, boss,' I heard the DI say, and wandered out to see what he'd found. He was holding a fishing rod, about four feet long, complete with reel, line and hook.

'Where was that?' Les asked.

'Under there,' the DI replied, pointing to a window seat. 'It lifts up. I was looking for some fish food for them.'

'That's one way of doing your fishing,' Les said. 'Beats standing out in the rain for hours.'

I went back to Heckley and did some typing. Les promised to keep me informed about the post-mortem and I arranged to see him in the morning with a synopsis of Fox's affairs. He rang me late that evening, just after I'd stood under the shower.

'Cause of death was asphyxia by strangulation,' he said, bypassing the normal formalities. 'Time, about eleven p.m.'

'Foul play?' I wondered.

'Difficult to tell. We've told the press that it looks like a sexual experiment that went tragically wrong. He was over twice the driving limit with alcohol and there were traces of coke on the bedside table. Haven't got the results of the blood test yet. What did you say that character was called who worked for Fox?'

'Kingston,' I replied. 'Nick Kingston. Why?'

'I thought so. Because an N.J.W. Kingston was booked in the Fox Borealis for Monday night, but his bed wasn't slept in.'

'That sounds like my man,' I said.

'One other guest is unaccounted for,' Les continued. 'A young lady called Danielle LaPetite, also booked in for Monday night only. Her room was number 1403, Kingston's was 1405, next door. Both rooms were booked on Reynard's account, so there were no bills to pay.'

'Danielle LaPetite,' I said, 'sounds like a hooker.'

'She does, doesn't she? We're checking her out.'

'Les . . .' I began.

'I know what you're going to say,' he replied.

'What?'

'You want to talk to Kingston.'

'So how about it?'

'See me in the morning, as planned, and we'll discuss it then.'

'Fair enough, and thanks for ringing.'

'There's one other small point you might find interesting,' he said before I replaced the phone. 'Guess what Fox's last meal was?'

'No idea.'

'Sushi.'

'Sushi? Raw fish?'

'That's right. With oysters. About nine o'clock the chef went up to his room and prepared a freshly-caught carp for Mr Fox and his guest. She was a tall and beautiful half-caste girl. The chef is Japanese, and his English is rather basic. He said she was dressed like a prostitute.'

'Yuck,' I said.

Superintendent Isles was happy for me to interview Kingston. I knew the man, was intimate with the story, and could put my mileage expenses on the SFO's account. One of his own detectives would have been limited to the usual did-anyone-see-you-there questions; I could try to get under his guard. I rang him in Kendal from Les's office.

'It's DI Priest from Heckley CID,' I said. 'I came to see you a fortnight ago.'

'I remember, Inspector. The Carlos Castaneda man.'

'That's me. First of all, I suppose you have heard the bad news about J.J. Fox?'

'Yes, just caught it on the radio. What a tragedy.'

'We've just been going through the guest list at the Fox Borealis where he died,' I told him, 'and have noticed that there is a N.J.W. Kingston on it, with your address. Were you at the Fox Borealis on Monday night, sir?'

'Well, yes, as a matter of fact I was, Inspector. I had a meeting with J.J. that evening. I do consultancy work for the Reynard Organisation: psychometric testing of job applicants; motivational lectures to senior management; that sort of thing. He wanted to discuss some ideas he had. I assure you he was fit and in good spirits when I left him.'

Les was listening on another phone. He pulled a nice-work-if-you-can-get-it face and nodded for me to carry on.

'In that case, Mr Kingston,' I continued, 'we will need a statement from you and some samples, with your permission, so we can identify you amongst any others we find. Elimination purposes, as we say. I'd like to drive over now and see you at Kendal police station, if that's all right.'

'Of course, Inspector. Anything to help, anything at all. Can I ask, though, why you are on this? I thought you were with Heckley CID.'

'I am, sir,' I told him, improvising like a non-swimmer in the deep end. 'But I also work for something called SCOG; Serious Crimes Operations Group. We all get roped in when something like this happens.'

He put on a good show of sounding incredulous. 'Serious crime? Crime? You mean . . . you mean . . . it wasn't natural causes? Are you saying he was m-m-murdered?'

'We're not sure,' I told him. 'It was probably an unfortunate accident, but we have to treat it as a suspicious death, and with him being such an important person we're giving it all we've got. You know what the papers will say if we're negligent. I'll set off now and ring you from Kendal nick at about . . .' I looked at my watch, '. . . about twelve thirty, eh?'

'Fine, Inspector. I'll wait for your call.'

'Just one other thing, sir,' I said. 'Could you please wear the same shoes you were wearing on Monday night?'

We replaced our phones and Les said: 'Well done. He had it all off pat; he was expecting someone to ring him. Do you want a coffee before you go?'

'No thanks,' I said. 'I'll be stopping for a pee all the way.'

The A65 leads through the Dales and on to Kendal, Windermere and the Lake District. Long stretches of it are single carriageway and queues of slow-moving traffic are the norm. Lorries bring limestone from Settle and hurtle back at breakneck speed where conditions allow. They're no problem. It's the coaches and caravans and mothers taking the kids to school in the next village with the Range Rover stuck in first gear that cause the hold-ups. I hate the road. The only consolation is that although thousands of tourists head this way, thousands more are deterred. I did the eighty miles in two and a half hours and rang Kingston. He was with us in fifteen minutes.

I explained to him more fully why we wanted samples of his DNA, and he enthusiastically allowed the police surgeon to extract six hairs, by the roots. That's where the DNA lives. I boasted expansively about ESFLA, electronic footprint lifting apparatus, or something like that, that enables us to track a culprit across a carpet, and he happily surrendered his shoes to the force photographer. He admitted that he'd been in Fox's room, so he had nothing to hide.

I took him into an interview room but didn't bother with the tape. I wanted it to be nice and informal; he was among, if not friends, a bunch of half-witted coppers who didn't know their batons from their buttons. He told me that Fox had asked to see him about some ideas he was having. 'As I said on the phone, Inspector,' he continued, 'I analyse information from tests about the suitability of staff members. Management staff, that is. It's not regular work, about two hundred hours per year. I also devise the tests. J.J. is – was – a great believer in a scientific approach to staff selection and promotion. He puts great store by loyalty. That and competence were the attributes my tests were designed to highlight. Lately, though, he'd become paranoid. He was considering placing bugs in places where staff congregated, so he could see what they were saying about him behind his back. That's what he wanted to discuss with me. It would be my job to listen to the tapes and report directly to him. I discouraged him, of course. Said that just because someone might say something disparaging it didn't mean they were disloyal. We all go over the mark in private, I said. I think I talked him out of it.'

'What time did you leave him?' I asked.

'About eight o'clock. I had a workout in the gym and came home.'

'You didn't stay in your room overnight?'

'No, Inspector, I prefer my own bed.' He gave a little smile and I thought of the delightful Francesca.

After a long silence I said: 'Did you see anything of a dark girl who was staying in the room next to yours? She's called Danielle LaPetite.'

He heaved a giant sigh, leaned heavily on the table between us and drummed his fingertips on the top of his head. It was a gesture he'd seen on *How to be a Psychologist* videos, when the patient runs out of patience and is considering whether to slot the doctor. He'd obviously practised it. 'I might as well tell you,' he said, looking up at me, his face a study of embarrassed guilt. 'You'll find out, one way or another.' I sat back and waited for the revelation.

'Danielle is J.J.'s mistress,' he began. 'She's a dancer with a Manchester theatre group called Zambesi. I met her off the eighteen fifty-two train and took her to the hotel. J.J. trusts me, you see. We had a drink in the cocktail lounge, and I came home.'

'Did you find Danielle for Fox?' I asked, avoiding the word *procure*.

'I introduced them, if that's what you mean,' he replied, almost offended.

'Was she a student of yours?'

'What if she had been, Inspector? She was the same as lots of others like her; expectations way above their intellects. Thick as two short planks and wanted to be a doctor. She's a good dancer and good in bed; I encouraged her to develop what talents she possessed. J.J. pays her a thousand pounds a night and she enjoys her work. Where else could she earn money like that?'

'And what was your cut?' I asked.

'I didn't take a penny off her. J.J. paid me well, extremely well, and . . .' He shrugged and smiled.

'And what?'

'Like I said, she was a good dancer and good in bed, and nobody misses a coconut off a fruit stall, do they? J.J. liked her to put on a show for him and I was the warm-up act. I didn't need any money from him. Shagging the boss's ladyfriend just before he does has a certain appeal all of its own, don't you think, Inspector?'

'I wouldn't know,' I said.

Going home it was the M6, M61 and M62 all the way and I

never dropped under ninety. If a traffic car had followed me I'd have given him the secret signal that says: 'I'm a cop in a hurry,' and he'd have dropped back. You just switch your hazard lights on for three flashes and dab your brakes, that's all. Try it some time. The local chippie opens at teatime on Wednesdays, so I had them again. They were all right, but nowhere as good as the ones Shirley had cooked for us. By six o'clock I'd washed my plate, made a pot of tea and the full evening stretched before me.

I laid a blank piece of hardboard on the drive and started flicking blue enamel on it, *à la* Jackson Pollock. It's a lot harder than it looks, and time-consuming. It doesn't start to work until the entire field is thickly covered in splashes and squiggles and spots and dribbles. This would give the exhibition judges something to think about, and might even make the *Gazette*. I'd have to think of a name for it, and for its partner, when I'd finished the pair of them. I reached for my tea and found it had gone cold.

I was taking the lid off the red when a sound behind me caused me to turn. Young Daniel, Dave's son, was freewheeling his mountain bike through my gateway, closely followed by his dad on a lady's pink model with a basket on the handlebars. Dave was wearing a Heart Appeal T-shirt and jogging bottoms.

'Hi, Charlie,' Daniel greeted me. 'Whatya doing?' He saw the painting and went: 'Wow! It's fantastic!'

Dave dismounted, saying: 'It's *Uncle* Charlie to you, young man,' for the thousandth time, followed by: 'Good God, it looks like a bag of maggots.'

I knocked the lid back into place and stretched upright, my vertebrae creaking in protest. 'Visitors!' I exclaimed. 'This is a pleasant surprise. Let's have a drink.'

'Can I have a go on your computer, please, Uncle Charlie?'

Daniel asked. 'I think Dad wants to talk cop talk.'

'Sure,' I replied. 'C'mon, I'll set you up.' I left him with a glass of LA lager and lime, zapping aliens, and carried two cans of real beer and two glasses out into the garden, where Dave had made himself comfortable on the seat.

The cans went *psssss!* as we broke the seals. Dave said: 'It's just two small messages. First of all Les Isles rang to say that Danielle LaPetite is a tom from Salford, and she hasn't turned up yet. Aged twenty-two, several convictions for soliciting. But the big news is from Tregellis. He rang just before five to say that Melissa is on her way, with her boyfriend. They arrive in Manchester at nine a.m. tomorrow, and can you arrange for someone to meet them?'

'Brilliant,' I said. 'It's all coming together.' I looked at my watch. 'I ought to ring Tregellis,' I said, 'tell him about today.'

'He said to tell you not to bother,' Dave replied. 'He's out tonight; it'll do in the morning.'

'Good.'

Dave took a long sip, held the glass to the light and turned it in his fingers. A blackbird landed on the fence, looked affronted by our presence in his garden and took off again. High above us a jumbo jet filled with holidaymakers did a course-correction, leaving a bent trail across the sky. The sun glinted under its wing as it levelled out.

'There is one other thing,' Dave said.

'What's that?' I asked.

He shuffled and crossed his ankles. 'You remember Peter Mark Handley?'

'The games master who touched up little girls?'

'He did more than touch them up, but not any more. He's dead. Monday night he jumped off Scammonden bridge.'

'Oh God,' I said.

'He didn't leave a note or anything. He should have appeared before the magistrates that morning, but he didn't. They issued a warrant. He wasn't identified until this afternoon.'

'We drove him to that,' I said. 'Or I did. And I caused Fox's death, too. I put pressure on him and Kingston. Kingston probably killed him to silence him, thanks to me. Judge, jury and executioner, all in one. Sometimes I hate this job, Dave. When we're old, do you think we'll be able to sleep at nights?'

'You're talking soft,' he replied. 'Handley was a pervert and Fox a monster. We'll never know how evil he was. They were both all right when they were picking the fruits, but when it came to paying the bill they didn't like it. We're the law, Charlie. We just catch them. If they can't hack it, it's their fault. What is it they say? "If you can't do the time, don't do the crime."'

'"If you deserve it, serve it." Handley's wife didn't deserve it. She seemed a pleasant enough person, and loyal to him. Now she's a widow.'

'And how many little girls will never trust a man again? How many of them has he left damaged? Don't waste your regrets on either of them, Charlie, save them for more deserving causes. God knows, there's plenty.'

I fetched two more beers and left another LA with Daniel. He was playing Battle Chess against the computer. The sun had fallen behind next door's roof but it was still a warm evening. A flock of swallows were diving and swirling like tea leaves used to, before they invented teabags. I topped up both our glasses from one can. The first vapour trail had been dispersed by the jetstream, but another plane was following the same course, pumping millions of cubic feet of burnt hydrocarbons into the ozone layer. Seven miles above us two or three hundred rat-tempered passengers were wrestling with seat backs and folding tables, or standing in embarrassed queues for the toilets.

Bring back airships, that's my opinion.

Dave took a sip, sighed, and balanced his glass on the uneven top of the wall round my little rockery. He sat on his hands and kicked his feet up and down. 'You remember when we were going to Bridlington?' he said, when he was good and ready.

'Mmm.'

'Remember what we were talking about.'

'Percy Shaw?'

'After that.'

'Rhubarb crumble?'

'You don't make it easy for me, do you?'

'I'm sorry, Dave,' I said, 'but I haven't a clue what you're on about.'

'Nigel asked why I hadn't made sergeant.'

'Oh, that.'

'Yes, that. Have you ever wondered why?'

'Once or twice, but not lately. You could have walked it if you'd wanted. With a bit of effort you could have made inspector, and you'd have been a good one. I just assumed that you were happy as a DC and didn't want to spoil things. You had a family to consider. There's plenty of others feel the same way.'

'I am happy, but there's more to it than that.'

'Is there?' I wasn't going to ask. He'd tell me, if that was what he was leading to.

'I had a revelation.'

'A revelation? You found God?'

'No, I found my limitations. That day, at the fire.'

'Leopold Avenue?'

'That's right. When I saw her at the window, little Jasmine Turnbull, I knew I had no chance of saving her. But the alternative was worse. Just standing there, watching, until the fire or the smoke got her. I could never have lived with myself if I hadn't tried. Halfway up that first staircase I was in trouble. I was going to grab one more breath and press on, but you tackled me and dragged me out. I'd never have made it; I knew that. For a while, I wondered if you did what you did because you hadn't the bottle to go after her. But not for long. I soon realised that if it had been the other way round, if I'd been the sergeant and you the PC, there'd have been ten deaths in that fire, not eight. And we'd have missed all this.' He waved a hand at the garden. 'So,' he concluded, 'I suppose you could say I'm not cut out for authority.'

'Now *you're* talking soft,' I said. 'How many times has a situation like that risen since then? None.'

'But it might, tomorrow.'

'And you'd do what was necessary.'

'Well, it's too late now.'

I shared the fourth can between us. 'There's more in the fridge . . .' I hinted.

'Better not. What's the limit for riding a bike while in charge of a minor?'

'No idea. Cheers.'

'Cheers.'

It was good beer. The froth clung to the side of the glass, all the way down. That's how you tell a good pint. It's nothing to do with the taste. The widget was the greatest scientific breakthrough since Archimedes invented the overflow.

'I saw the pictures,' I said.

Dave licked the froth off his top lip and said: 'What pictures?'

'The ones in Kingston's loo, that you didn't want me to see.'

'Oh, those pictures.'

'That's right. By Mrs Holmes. She knew him better than she pretended, don't you think?'

'You can't say that. They might have been a Christmas present or anything. Maybe Melissa bought them off her and gave them to him. There's a thousand possible explanations.'

'I suppose so,' I admitted, but I knew different. It had all started at that party to watch the *Apollo 13* mission on television. Kingston had been awful to Melissa, Janet had told us, and chased another girl. She'd been that other girl, as sure as Satan made female Morris dancers. Why should Melissa have all the fun? she'd thought, and Melissa had reacted by taking a tilt at Mo, which was what Kingston had intended all along. I'd been to a few parties like that myself. Then it was back to the bedsit and the Leonard Cohen records.

'It was a long time ago,' Dave said. 'She was young. We all make mistakes.'

Daniel came out of the open doorway, saying: 'I've logged off, Uncle Charlie. Thanks for letting me play on it. We ought to be off, Dad, before it gets dark.'

'Kids,' Dave muttered to me, standing up. 'Who'd have 'em?'

I watched them pedal away in an impromptu race, and thought: I would.

Chapter 12

Thursday morning Manchester airport told me that Delta flight number DL064 from Atlanta was delayed two hours, which suited me just fine. I had long sessions on the phone with Les Isles and Tregellis, and a progress meeting with Mr Wood. I was working for three bosses and it was hard to juggle things so everyone was equally informed and no feelings were hurt. Fortunately, Tregellis was a long way away, Les trusted me and regarded me as an extension of his team, and Gilbert gave me a free hand, so I was able to do what I wanted.

One of our motorcyclists was waiting for me when I returned from Gilbert's office. He was nursing two videos. 'Ah, well done,' I said as I took them from him.

'My pleasure, sir,' he replied with a grin.

'Nice little ride, was it?'

'Smashing.' His helmet and leathers were shimmering with the carcasses of dead flies.

'Well, take it steady, and thanks.'

The old idea of an identity parade, with the suspect lined up alongside seven other short, bald-headed men, is rapidly fading. They were always a pain to organise and expensive in time and money. Video film and links are taking over. We can use recordings of the suspect, mixed in with images of similar-looking characters off the files, and let the victim examine them at his or her leisure. They don't even have to be in the same city. The security cameras in Kendal nick had captured Kingston's likeness on tape during his two visits, helped by a little careful manipulating of his position. The ID team had produced a video for me showing several stills of him, together with an assortment of similarly built policemen in civvies, visiting solicitors, and various friends, relatives and villains. I posted one straight off to Tregellis, via the internal mail, and watched the other in the main office. It was good.

I'd intended to take Annette with me to Manchester because I wanted her to be our contact with Melissa and her boyfriend, but Gilbert had asked her to produce some figures for a survey about overtime and sick leave. The Home Secretary had been given warning of a question he was about to be asked in Parliament, so everything had to stop until we had an answer. The sun was still shining, but the temperature had dropped by quite a bit. It was bright and pleasant, rather than oppressive. I gave myself plenty of time and stopped for a chicken burger at the services. As usual, when I used the loo I found that someone with pubic alopecia had beaten me to it.

I was still early. I called in at the Immigration office and they confirmed that Melissa was on the flight, which was a pleasant surprise. Piers had told me that she didn't seem to realise that once she had left the USA it was unlikely that they'd let her back in. He hadn't tipped her off about this small point and we were looking forward to breaking it to her after she'd given us what she wanted.

I wandered up to the spectator's gallery to watch the big jets taking off, and caught myself humming 'In the Early Morning Rain'. There's a shop up there that sells aviation magazines, spotters' guides and plastic models of famous crashes. Hanging in a corner was a sheepskin flying jacket, *circa* WWII, marked down from £300 to £199. Wow! I thought, this'll work wonders for my image. I'd wear it to the office tomorrow, regardless of the weather.

But the sleeves were miles too short. The rest of it fitted, but I held my arms forward to demonstrate the problem and exchanged disappointed smiles with the sales lady. I went back to Arrivals and stood with the blank-faced straggle of people waiting for flight DL064. Shifty-looking taxi drivers held boards under their arms with scrawled names across them, and a well-dressed elderly man in a chauffeur's cap stood patiently to attention. Once he'd been the terror of the parade ground, and now he was someone's lackey. That'd be me soon, I thought. The rest were bleary-eyed sons-in-law or parents, come to pick up their loved ones after yet another holiday of a lifetime.

I'd have recognised her at half a mile, but she still took my breath away. I stepped forward in front of them, and the immigration official shadowing them gave me a nod and peeled off. 'Miss Youngman?' I said.

'The former Miss Youngman,' she said, almost smiling. 'Now I'm Mrs Slade. Meet my husband of twenty-four hours, Jade Slade.'

'How ya doin'?' he said.

'Fine,' I lied. 'DI Priest.' Shit fuck bugger, I thought. She's done us.

The extravagances of the seventies had been toned down, and of course, our tastes have developed over the years. Her hair was red again, cropped short and carelessly styled, but nothing that you wouldn't see any day in any small town. She wore a nose ring and extravagant eye make-up – not heavy lashes and shadow, but paint and speckles all around them – with black lipstick. Underneath the muck was one of those faces that can launch a young girl to fame and fortune or blight her life with a string of wrong men because the decent ones don't think they stand a chance. She was beautiful, and ageing well, and I could understand anybody falling for her. Nancy Spungeon had become Zandra Rhodes.

He was something else. Short, pot-bellied, with one of those hillbilly beards that looks as if it's just been shampooed. He wore faded denims held up by a broad belt heavily inlaid with silver and turquoise. She was in a brown leather suit. I led them to my car and told them about the Station Hotel, in Heckley, where we'd booked them a room for the week.

'Do they have a pool?' he asked.

I apologised for the lack of a pool.

On the motorway I said: 'I understand you write poetry, Mr Slade.'

'That's right,' he replied.

'Will I have heard any?'

'Do you read redneck poetry?'

'No.'

'Then you won't.'

I told Melissa that she was booked into Heckley General Hospital tomorrow at about four thirty, to have her teeth fixed. Then, if she was up to it, we'd do a taped interview with her the following day, Saturday. All leave was cancelled for the first team. She mumbled responses in the right places and we rode the rest of the way in silence. He said: 'Jeez!' under his breath when he saw the Station Hotel, and that was the sum total of our conversation. I didn't mind; I had no desire to be on first-name terms with either of them. I wrote Annette's name and number on a page of hotel notepaper and left them to unpack.

Back at the nick I rang Tregellis but had to settle for Piers. 'The eagle has landed,' I said. We talked for a while about tactics and when he'd hung up I rang Les Isles and had the same conversation all over again.

Agent Mike Kaprowski wasn't in his office but a colleague introduced himself and told me that he was familiar with the case. 'I just met Melissa Youngman off the plane,' I told him, 'except that she's not called Youngman any more because she's got herself married. To this poet feller, Jade Slade.'

'Aw, shit!' he exclaimed. 'You know what that means?'

'We'll have to buy them a present?'

'Yeah, and that, goddammit! OK, Charlie, thanks for letting us know. I'll tell Mike and he'll get back to you. Adios.'

'Adios.' I put the phone down.

'*Adios*!' said a voice behind me. '*Adios*! Who was that, Speedy Gonzales?'

I half-turned and grinned at Sparky. 'Just my friends in the FBI,' I told him.

He flopped into the spare chair. 'What did they want?'

'They've run out of white chalk, wondered if we had any to spare. Actually, I rang them. Melissa's arrived, but she married her boyfriend in a touching little ceremony in the airport lounge just before they left the USA.'

'What difference does that make?'

I told him.

'The crafty little cow,' he said.

'It does look as if we underestimated her,' I admitted.

'Charlie . . .' he began.

'Mmm.'

'When you interview her . . . what's the chances of being in on it?'

I looked at him and said: 'I wouldn't have it any other way, Dave.'

He gripped his knees and said: 'Thanks.'

'But just remember she's co-operating with us.'

'I will,' he replied, 'but I still reckon she's in this up to her ears. She's gonna get away with murder, probably literally.'

'I think you're right,' I replied, 'but it's the only way we'll get Kingston, and he's the senior partner.'

'I've been thinking about Kingston,' he told me. 'If he killed Fox to silence him, I wouldn't be surprised if he didn't kill Danielle whatsername, the hooker, too, for the same reason. In the past he killed, or caused people to die, for financial gain. Now he's killing to save his skin. He's in a panic, thinking on his feet.'

'And that will be his downfall, Dave. Do you think he might have a go at Melissa?'

'Possibly. Does he know she's over here?'

'We haven't told him.'

'But she might, if she knows where he lives. Just for old times' sake.'

'Great,' I said. 'We'd better keep an eye on her.'

We booked a DC into the Station Hotel, posing as a travelling Punch and Judy man, and Annette went round to introduce herself to our guests. Friday afternoon she took Melissa and Jed Clampitt to the hospital to get for free what would have cost them a fortune back home. It was a cloudy day and I spent it in the office, typing my notes and memories into a more accessible format. Six of us had pie and chips for lunch in one of Heckley's more traditional pubs.

Nine o'clock in the evening Annette rang me to say that Melissa had been through the wringing machine and they'd decided to keep her in overnight. She'd be discharged in the morning, no problem, but an interview might be asking too much of her.

'In that case,' I decided, 'tell her Monday morning, at Heckley nick. You make sure she's there, please, Annette.' I rang the others to tell them that they could have the weekend off after all.

Saturday I did an hour in the office, then went home to finish the Jackson Pollock painting. It took me until ten at night plus two visits to B & Q for materials, but it looked smashing. If JP had done it you'd be talking above five million for it. I'd ask for fifty quid, for the kids' ward, and probably not get it. Sunday I completed the one that had originally been inspired by the tapeworm drawing done by Janet Holmes. It was ragged blocks of oranges and yellows, with a jagged flash of lime green coming up from the bottom left corner that danced before your eyes. I was pleased with that one, too. They'd look great surrounded by all those scenes of Malhamdale in autumn.

She still hadn't sent me a postcard.

Monday morning I rose early. I hadn't slept very well, worrying that Melissa might be taking us for a ride. After a cup of tea I decided that it was unlikely. We were, after all, offering her immunity from prosecution on charges of God-knows-what. I was just running the shower when the phone rang.

'It's Jeff,' it said, breathlessly. 'The Transit's on the move.'

'It can't be,' I complained, looking at my watch. 'I've an appointment at nine.'

'We can manage. I've scrambled the chopper and alerted the ARV. Now I'm just rounding up the troops.'

I was going to miss this, and I was annoyed. 'OK,' I said. 'Take everybody you need, plus a few more, but not Sparky and Annette; and alert our neighbours. We can't afford to lose them, so the more the merrier. Lift them whenever it's convenient. In the garden but before they enter the house would be ideal, but on no account let them get in the house. It would be nice, though, to know what their target was. Nobody hurt, that's the priority, Jeff, unless, of course, it's them. No, I didn't say that. Anything you want me to do?'

'Not at the moment, boss.'

'Get on with it then. I'll be in the control room if you need me.'

Dammit, I thought. Dammit. I'd wanted to scramble the chopper. Jeff had decided that the best thing was for him to ring Mr Nelson at seven o'clock every morning. If the boys were there, he'd say wrong number; if they'd come home and left the house Jeff would tell him to report the van stolen and give him a crime number. Mr Nelson then had to ring the Tracker people and report it missing. They would double-check with us before activating the transponder in the van, enabling the receivers in our vehicles to pinpoint it. Tracker only acted after a report of theft; we didn't have *carte blanche* to follow anyone who had the device fitted.

I had a hasty shower and nearly broke the speed limit on the way to the nick. The car park was surprisingly devoid of police cars but Dave's Escort was in its usual place.

He was in the control room, listening to the action. 'We could put Melissa back an hour,' he suggested, temptingly.

'No,' I replied. 'They can handle it.'

The radios were on talk-through, so we could hear everything. 'Target heading south,' someone said, which was bad news, because everyone had gone straight to the motorway, which was north. Jeff came on and directed all the unmarked cars in the right direction, sharing them out between the different routes. At this stage they just wanted to be close. The pandas and the ARV were told to take their time.

'Zulu ninety-nine, we have contact with target,' came over

the airwaves, against a background of the chum-chum-chum of the chopper's blades. 'On A616, just beyond Debberton, travelling slowly.'

Jeff asked for the positions of his cars, and rerouted where necessary. We studied the big map and the duty sergeant made a guess about some posh houses between Debberton and Holmfirth. I told him to pass it on to Jeff.

Zulu ninety-nine told us that the van had stopped in a lay-by and they were veering off to avoid being spotted.

'Lima Mike. Just passing target.' That was Maggie.

'Ten twenty.'

'Lima Oscar, we have target under observation. Zulu ninety-nine stay away until they move again.'

'Ten twenty. Do you copy, Zulu ninety-nine?'

'Zulu ninety-nine, ten twenty.'

'Lima Mike standing by.'

Gilbert came in and asked for an update. I showed him where they were on the map. 'Unlike you not to be out there, Charlie,' he said.

'Oh, you know how I like to delegate,' I replied.

'Lima Oscar, target on the move.' We all turned to the control desk, as if looking at the loudspeakers would give us a picture of the scene.

The Transit drove about a quarter of a mile and turned up a gravel track. 'They probably stopped to put their masks on,' Dave suggested.

'Zulu ninety-nine, we have them. T2 out of vehicle, opening gate to a house. Suggest you go-go-go.'

Accelerators were flat to the floor, tyres were squealing, but we could see none of it. 'Zulu ninety-nine, T2 has seen us. He's back in the van and they're aborting.'

'Lima Mike, I'm turning into the lane, Lima Oscar behind

me. We'll block the lane.' A silence, then: 'Lima Mike, they're out and running. Giving chase.'

We all laughed and relaxed. Gilbert went up to his office and I rang Annette at home, in case she'd forgotten what day it was. Five minutes later a breathless Maggie panted: 'Lima Mike to XL.'

'Go ahead, Maggie,' the controller told her.

'We have a ten twelve. Will bring T1 and T2 to Heckley, out.'

Jeff came on, saying: 'All units ten three. Thank you and good morning.'

'Let's go,' I said to Dave. 'We can't stand here all day listening to them playing cowboys and Indians. What's all this ten twenty stuff?'

They were half an hour late. Annette brought them in, apologising, and Dave set eyes on Melissa for the first time. She was wearing no make-up, which was a shock, and her cheeks were swollen. I suspected that the dark glasses were to hide black eyes. Nigel's wisdom teeth had been removed, and he said it gave your face quite a hammering. Jade Slade was with her, wearing an embroidered shirt, jeans and cowboy boots, like he was expecting line dancing. The duty solicitor looked a treat, as always, in his blue suit and regimental tie.

'Are you fit enough to answer questions?' I asked, because I was concerned about the quality of her answers, not her health.

'Let's get on with it,' she said.

'Okey-dokey.' I set the tape running and did the spiel and asked everyone to introduce themselves. Dave and I were at one side of the table, Melissa and the solicitor at the other, with Slade rocked back against the wall near the video player I'd asked for. He was holding one of our polystyrene beakers, and at first I thought he'd bought a coffee from the machine. When I saw him lift it towards his mouth and spit into it I thought: It's not *that* bad. When he did it again, a few moments later, I realised he was chewing tobacco.

'Mrs Slade,' I began, 'did you attend Essex University in 1969?'

'Yes.'

'And after that did you attend Paris, Edinburgh, Manchester, Los Angeles, Durham and Leeds universities?'

'If you say so.'

'What do *you* say?'

'I say this has fuck-all to do with why I'm here.'

'Did you meet a lecturer called Nick Kingston at Essex?'

'I might have done.'

'Did you?'

'I don't remember. I met him somewhere.'

'But you already knew him when you moved to Leeds?'

'Yes.'

'What was the nature of your relationship?'

'Were we fucking, you mean? Of course we were.'

Dave shuffled. When he was settled again I said: 'Have you contacted Kingston during this visit?'

She looked uneasy and turned to the solicitor. He shrugged, not knowing if this was relevant to anything. Slade said: 'Is this part of the deal?'

'What deal?' I asked.

'You know, the fuckin' *deal.*'

I turned to Melissa. 'Mrs Slade, to have it on the record, could you tell us what you are expecting from this meeting.'

'I'll tell you what she's expecting,' Slade shouted. 'She puts the finger on this Kingston, and you give her immunity from prosecution. That's the fuckin' deal, ain't it?'

I told Slade that we'd make better progress if he let his wife answer the questions. We weren't interested in his comments or opinions. She smiled at him and he spat into the cup and let his chair plop down on to all four legs.

'What are you expecting, Mrs Slade?' I asked again.

'What he said,' she replied. 'I tell you about Kingston and you let me go.'

'I have no power to grant you immunity from prosecution,' I explained. 'Nobody has. However, I can assure you that this force and two others involved with the Kingston case will not actively pursue any charges against you or follow up any evidence relating to these offences that may implicate you. Is that clear?'

'Yes.'

'Would you like your solicitor to discuss it with you?'

'No.'

'Very well, what can you tell us about Nick Kingston?'

'I've got a statement,' Melissa said, bringing a page of Station Hotel notepaper from the inside pocket of her jacket. She unfolded it and we sat back, listening.

'In June or July 1975,' she began, 'I was having a sexual relationship with a university lecturer called Nick Kingston. I was infatuated with him and completely under his spell. He was a very charismatic man. He told me that he was renting a house in Chapeltown, Leeds, to use as a postal address for a mail-order business he was just starting. The number on the house had worn off, so he asked me to write it on again, in chalk, so the postman would find it when the orders started coming in. He said he couldn't do neat numbers. He took me there one evening and I wrote the number thirty-two on the wall. A few days later he asked me to show a boy where it was. He was going to work for Nick, pick up the orders, or something. About a week after that the house was burnt down and some people lost their lives.' She refolded the paper and slid it across the table towards me.

I placed my pen on it and pushed it back, saying: 'Could you sign it, please.'

She unfolded the statement, took the pen in her left hand and scrawled her signature across the bottom. I didn't look but I just knew that Dave's eyes had flickered my way.

We sat in silence for a while, then I said: 'What colour was your hair then?'

She looked flustered, and turned to her solicitor. He decided it must be a leading question and came out with the usual is-it-relevant response.

'I'd like to know,' I replied.

'I can't remember,' she said.

'Was it purple?'

'I don't know.'

'Was the boy you took to the house Duncan Roberts?'

'I'm not sure. Duncan rings a bell, but I never heard his surname.'

'Are you sure he wasn't your boyfriend?'

'Positive.'

'You didn't have an affair with him?'

'Not that one, but I had lots of boyfriends. It was never a problem for me.'

I wanted to grill her about her relationship with Duncan, but managed to hold off. She'd already been threatened with the little we knew, when Piers and Graham saw her in America. That's why she was here, and I didn't want to reveal how fragile our case against her was. I asked Dave to start the video and explained to the tape recorder what we were doing.

The first image appeared, a still taken by a CCTV camera,

with the number 1 in the corner. 'If you recognise Kingston please say the number,' I told her.

'That's him,' she said, after a while.

'Number?'

'Eight.'

There were sixty-five pictures, and seven of them were Kingston. She got all seven.

'Thanks,' I said. 'I think that's everything. We'll try to get you on a flight on Wednesday, if that suits you.'

'The sooner the fuckin' better,' Slade said, and flung his cup of spit into the waste bin.

Annette was waiting upstairs. Dave went to put the kettle on and I told her that Bonnie and Clyde were finding their own way back to the hotel. She was relieved of baby-sitting duties. 'Thank God for that,' she sighed. 'They're the most thoroughly disagreeable couple I've ever met. Give me the Sylvan Fields lot any day.'

'What did you find out about the telephone?' I asked. We were paying their bill, so the hotel had no qualms about feeding us the information.

'Ah! You're not going to like this. They've spent every waking hour on the phone. Several calls to Directory Enquiries, but we can't tell who they asked for; more to various parts of England, as if she's been renewing acquaintances; and several long calls to the USA. I've asked for a printout. It's as if they've deliberately run up the bill, because we're paying.'

'They're anarchists, Annette,' I said. 'That's what anarchists do. They'll probably put the plugs in and leave the taps running when they check out. I'd better have a word with BT.'

Dave shouted: 'How many sugars, Annette?'

'None, thank you,' she called back.

'Listen, Annette,' I said, quietly. 'I'm sorry I didn't ask you to sit in on the interview, but Dave's been in on this since 1975. It's personal.'

'That's OK, Mr Priest,' she replied.

I'm growing to like Annette. She's a good sport and has a pleasant nature. That *Mr Priest* never fails to put me in my place, though. Dave came in, carrying three teas, which says a lot for my department. I found some custard creams and we told Annette all about Kermit Shermit and his filthy habits.

The others came filtering back, high on adrenalin and braggadocio. Maggie had socked one of the Nelson brothers and the other had fallen into a stream. Good living in Tenerife had not equipped them for cross-country running. Masks and baseball bats were recovered from the Transit and a hand-drawn map was found showing directions to the house they'd intended to rob. Somebody was doing the leg work for them. Jeff sent the map to fingerprints.

We all shared in the success, and a bonus was that I didn't have to do the paperwork. In the middle of all the laughing I heard my phone ringing.

'CID, Call It Done,' I said into it.

'Is that Inspector Priest?'

'Yes.'

''Morning, Mr Priest. It's Sergeant Watson from Division. As you know, the ACC leaves at the end of the week, and there's a presentation to him on Thursday night. I understand that you sometimes do cartoons for these events, and was wondering if you could knock one up for him?'

'Gosh, that's three whole days away,' I replied. 'I would think I could knock one up in that time. I could probably knock up a Sistine Chapel ceiling in three days.'

'Oh, right, Mr Priest. You'll send it over, will you.'

'Will do.'

I looked in my drawer to make sure the one I'd done three weeks earlier was still there. I didn't particularly like the ACC, so this had been a good opportunity to embarrass him. Not many people knew this, but a long time ago, when he was a humble superintendent in another division several hundred miles away, he had too much to drink at a chief constable's leaving bash and messed his trousers. He rang his wife to ask her to bring him a spare pair and skulked in the car park until she arrived with them. He took them from her, thanked her profusely, and sneaked back into the toilets to change. He took off the offending garment, stuffed it out of the window and removed the new one from the bag his good lady had handed him. It was a skirt she'd collected from the cleaner earlier in the day. My drawing recaptured the incident in all its bladder-wrenching humiliation.

It also reminded me that I needed two frames for the abstracts I'd done. One of our uniformed PCs is a dab hand at woodwork and has a nice little sideline turning out doorstops and wooden apples that he sells for charity. No wooden Indians, though. I rang him and he promised to make the frames for me. He pointed out that the exhibition was next Sunday and I'd left it a bit late. I'd thought it was weeks away.

We had a debriefing in the afternoon, eating ice creams that we'd sent out for. Barry and Len Nelson had been interviewed and fed into the sausage machine for processing. They were looking at twenty years each. I deflated the euphoria by saying that we'd missed a vital opening. The bar they part-owned was called the Pigeon Pie. 'And the yob we arrested for using Joe McLelland's credit card was wearing a Pigeon Pie T-shirt.' I said. 'We should have asked him about it.'

'T-shirts from pubs in Tenerife are ten-a-penny,' someone stated.

'Fair enough,' I agreed, licking the runny bits from round the edges, 'but it was still a link, and we missed it.'

Jeff sid: 'Ah, but with luck like yours, boss, we can afford the odd mistake.' He pulled the chocolate flake out and used it as a spoon.

'What do you mean, luck?' I demanded, with mock affront.

'Going to the rhubarb sheds like you did. That was dead jammy.'

'Luck had nothing to do with it. Good detective work, that's what it was. Right, Dave?'

'Right, Charlie,' he mumbled with his mouth full.

'So how did you know to look there?' Jeff asked.

'In the rhubarb sheds?'

'Mmm.'

'I'll tell you. Remember what O'Keefe said about elephant?'

'Mmm.'

'So what did we call rhubarb when we were kids?'

'Tusky,' someone chipped in.

'There you go, then.'

Jeff shook his head in disbelief.

Later, as we left for home, Dave said: 'You didn't *really* make the link between tusky and elephant, did you?'

We were in the car park. I looked over my shoulder, then under my car and behind his. When I was absolutely sure we were alone I leaned closer and said: 'I might have done.'

I called in the supermarket for some ready meals and filled up with petrol. It's over three pounds a gallon now. That's something else not many people know. My favourite checkout girl was there but I went to someone else just in case she's beginning to wonder about me. Three times in a month is stalker territory.

The council had written to me to ask my address and if I still lived alone. I put ~~Yes~~ ~~No~~ ~~Yes~~ ~~No~~ ~~Yes~~ No. An insurance company reminded me that I was at a dangerous age and somebody else thought that I'd benefit from listening to the best bits of every piece of classical music ever recorded. Nearly two years of it, for only £149.99. No postcards. I had chicken korma, a currant square and tea, followed by a short snooze in an armchair.

Action is the best antidote for lethargy so I washed the car. The next-door neighbour couldn't believe his eyes and sent for his wife to come and see. 'There's no hosepipe ban, then?' he whined.

'It's odd numbers this week,' I explained.

'Oh,' he said, and nodded knowingly.

I was flicking round the channels, trying to decide whether to watch TV or stand on one leg for a couple of hours, when the phone rang. 'Charlie Priest,' I intoned into it, almost absent-mindedly.

'Charlie, it's Arthur.' Arthur's the duty sergeant.

'Hello, Arthur,' I said. 'What's gone wrong now?'

'Bloke been after you. Said I'd give you his number. He's called Nick Kingston; do you know him?'

'Kingston? Yes, I know him. Fire away.'

I didn't ring him immediately. I went over all the possibilities in my head and rehearsed the answers. Les Isles was planning to see him and I concluded that Kingston wanted to grill me about that. Les and I had agreed that he'd say we were involved in two separate inquiries; him into Fox's death, me into the fire of 1975.

He must have been waiting by the phone, and answered with a cheery: 'Nick Kingston.'

'DI Priest,' I said. 'You've been after me.'

'Charlie!' he gushed. 'Thanks for ringing. Have you seen the forecast?'

'The forecast? What forecast?' I asked.

'The weather for tonight,' he explained. 'Bright and clear, but best of all, it's a full moon, and it rises at just after one. It'll be another world up there, Charlie. Francesca and I are going up Helvellyn. Fancy coming with us, eh?'

'Helvellyn?' I mumbled. This hadn't been in my expectations.

'That's right. High enough, but nice and straightforward. We'll see the stars in all their glory, and then the biggest moon you've ever seen in your life will come over the horizon. It's a perfect night, I guarantee you'll never forget it. Power will be in the air. Shall we wait for you?'

'Oh, er,' I stumbled. 'Er, it'll take me a couple of hours to get there.'

'Good man, Charlie. You're in for a treat. Shall we say the car park at Patterdale, at midnight?'

I looked at my watch. 'I've my boots to find,' I said. 'I might be a few minutes late.'

'We'll wait for you. See you soon.'

I knew exactly where my boots were. Right where I took them off last time. The kettle had just boiled so I made a flask of coffee and pushed it into my rucksack with a packet of biscuits and a sweater. I donned a thicker shirt and my Gore-Tex jacket and turned the lights out.

First stop was Heckley nick. I punched the code into the lock on the back door and let myself in. We were in the lull before the pubs shut. The front desk was deserted and the station was as quiet as I've ever heard it. No cheerful banter from the cells, no drunken snoring from the locker room. Behind the desk, the door to the sergeants' office was firmly shut, which was unusual. I tiptoed over to it, paused, then threw the door open.

Chapter 13

A fat man was standing there, bent over. His trousers were round his ankles, copious shorts enveloped his knees and his arse was as big and white as the harvest moon I was expecting to see later. Arthur was standing in front of the man and a PC was kneeling behind him, applying black ink to that backside with one of the little rollers that the fingerprint boys use. Arthur's jaw dropped as the door crashed open and the PC's eyes bulged like gobstoppers. The man's resigned expression didn't change – he was already as low as he could go. We stared at each other for an eternity until I said: 'My office,' to Arthur and turned on my heel.

I pulled my big diary from the drawer and opened it at today. I wrote: *See Nick Kingston in Patterdale car park at midnight. Climbing Helvellyn.* It was just in case. As I put it back I saw my handcuffs there. I picked them up, weighed them in my hands, and slipped one end down the back of my trousers. Like I said, just in case.

Arthur came in, looking contrite. 'What the fuck are you playing at, Arthur?' I demanded.

He shuffled about from one foot to the other. We have a good, casual relationship, but he knew that I was the boss and could only allow so much. 'He, er, he was caught, earlier this evening,' he said. 'Act of gross indecency.'

'Like what?'

'Buggery. Shit-stabbing. He was stuck up a youth in the Park Avenue toilets. Probably underage.'

'Where's the youth?'

'He ran away.'

'But Fatso didn't make it.'

'No.'

'So what were you doing?'.

He heaved a big sigh and said: 'We just added a line to the PACE conditions. We told him that in cases of indecency between males we have to take an anal print as well as fingerprints. That's what you caught us doing.'

'*Jeeesus Christ*!' I hissed. 'You know, don't you, that if he complains they'll hang you from the town hall clock by your bollocks? And not just you; all of us.'

'His sort are not in the habit of complaining, Mr Priest.'

'He might. And cut out the Mr Priest. Let him go, Arthur. Clean him up and let him go.'

'Right, Chas. Thanks. What shall we do with the print?'

'Destroy it. No, leave it on my desk. No, destroy it.' I opened the door and turned the light out.

'Shall we destroy the others?'

'*The others*!' I exploded. 'How long has this been going on?'

'Since PACE came out,' he replied. 'We've quite a collection.'

I shook my head in disbelief, but couldn't help laughing. 'Better hang on to them,' I spluttered. 'You never know, this might be pioneering research.'

At the bottom of the stairs I said: 'I want something from Gareth Adey's office.' The CS gas canister was still in his drawer. They're quite tiny for an aerosol, about the size of a tube of mints. It wasn't noticeable in the pocket of my anorak.

Then it was just a matter of a two-hour blast towards the setting sun and the Lake District, the heater blowing cold because I was overdressed, and the cuffs reassuringly sticking into the base of my spine.

Helvellyn, at just over three thousand feet, is the third highest mountain in England. Imagine you are in bed, with your knees drawn up and the duvet draped over them. That's what it looks like. The top is flat and unimpressive compared with its cousins like Scafell and Skiddaw, and the far side slopes gently down to Thirlmere. At this side it drops a clear thousand feet to Red Tarn, but there's no dramatic clifftop that you can peer over. It's just a gradual steepening of gradient until you are beyond the point of no return. In winter, when fresh snow lies on frozen, that point can come horrifyingly early. In summer, it's a pussycat. From Patterdale there are two approaches to the summit: Swirral Edge, up your right knee, which is a steep and narrow path; or Striding Edge, up your left, which is a jagged spine of rock like an iguana's backbone.

Kingston was leaning on the boot of the BMW when I swung into the car park. 'Hello, Charlie,' he greeted me. 'Glad you could make it.'

'Where's Francesca?' I asked without ceremony.

'Oh, she decided not to come. She doesn't like me wandering about on my own, but as soon as I told her I'd be in your capable hands she said she'd prefer to have an early night. We're having a dinner party tomorrow, so it will be a busy day for her.'

'Right,' I said. 'Just the two of us.' I poured a coffee and sipped it.

'I'm not bothering with a 'sack,' Kingston said. 'The weather is settled. Just stick a Mars bar or something in your pocket.'

'Good idea,' I told him. 'I always feel that we carry too much anyway.'

'Excess baggage, Charlie, in more ways than one. Travel light, like a warrior; free, fluid and unpredictable.'

'Let's go,' I said. I wasn't in the mood for philosophical discussions.

It's a two-mile walk-in, then you have to decide which path to take. Normal practice is to go up one and down the other. Common sense said up Swirral and down Striding Edge, when dawn would be breaking, but at the fork Kingston veered to the left.

'Striding Edge?' I said. 'Is that wise?'

'We'll be OK,' he assured me. I wasn't convinced. He walked fast, and I was stumbling along behind him, blindly placing my feet in black patches that might have been potholes or shadows, for all I could see. That's when I started worrying. Kingston was lots of things that I despised, but he could withstand cold and fire and was probably convinced that he had supernatural gifts. Some murderers, the real nutters, believe that when they kill someone their own life is enriched, their powers are enhanced. They are endowed with all the qualities of the victim. Like I said, I started worrying.

I'd intended staying behind him, but didn't have any choice. He clambered on to the rocks at the start of the Edge and waited for me. 'OK?' he asked as I caught up with him.

'Just puffing a bit,' I said. 'You set a brisk pace.'

'This bit's slow going; you'll soon get your breath back.'

He could see in the dark. He was soon fifty yards ahead, striding from boulder to boulder with all the confidence of a mountain goat. I measured each step, feeling for solid ground before I transferred my weight, and fell still further behind. When it came to walking, I was out of my class. If I fell it wouldn't be far, it's too rough for that, but on these rocks eight feet could kill you, no problem. This was for crazies.

I made it to the end. The last bit is the worst; a ten-foot step, with a narrow foothold halfway down. He was waiting for me. I sat on my backside and groped for the ledge with my feet. He extended his hand and I took it, gripping it in a butcher's hold. I stepped off, landed on firm ground and said: 'Cheers.' He turned and started on the final climb to the top.

It was just a steep slog from then on, levelling off as we reached the summit plateau. The sky was hazy, with no stars visible. A breeze blew from the north, and as it came over the brow it condensed into clouds above us. I wondered if he'd been lying about the forecast, and the moon.

He slowed and I caught up, but stayed about three yards behind him. There's a cairn marking the top, and a wall to give some shelter. Kingston moved to his right, approaching the wall in a curve, which struck me as curious.

Our feet crunched and scraped on the ground, and although we didn't speak our progress was noisy. When we were ten yards from the wall a figure rose and stepped out into the open. He was tall and gangly, and a rucksack hung from his hand.

'Hello, DJ,' I said. 'Come to watch the moonrise with us?'

He reached into the bag and produced what looked like two short walking sticks. They were bent at one end, sharpened into chisel points and wrought from steel. In the tool catalogues they are called wrecking bars, but they are universally known as jemmies. Kingston reached out and DJ handed one to him, bent end first so it would be difficult to pull it from his grasp. They're a formidable weapon. One blow and I'd be down. It didn't have to be the head. An arm, shoulder, knee or foot, it was all the same. They separated, shepherding me towards the slope that went on and on, all the way down to Red Tarn.

'You won't be watching the moonrise, Priest,' Kingston said.

I walked backwards, glancing from one to the other. The breeze was on my right cheek, flapping the collar of my jacket against my ear. 'This is a surprise,' I shouted above it. They didn't answer, just moved towards me in slow steps.

'So how did you two meet?' I tried. The book says keep them talking. It wasn't a bestseller. 'It's a reasonable question,' I argued. 'How did you meet?'

'You wouldn't understand,' Kingston replied.

'Try me.'

'DJ found me.'

'Found you?'

'Yes. Something brought him to Lancaster and I saw his name on the list of the new students.'

'What were you doing?' I demanded. 'Trawling for likely candidates you could corrupt?' The slope was growing steeper and I was aware of a big black nothingness behind me.

'I said you wouldn't understand.'

'A coincidence,' I said. 'You were looking for girls with fancy names and you came across Duncan Roberts. It rang a bell, so you looked him up. That's it, isn't it?'

'There are no coincidences in this life, Priest. We make our own destinies. Fate brought DJ to me because he understands that there is more to our lives than the average person can see. He was looking for something, a way to take control. Like I said, he found me.'

I turned to DJ. 'Hear that?' I yelled at him. 'You're listening to the words of a madman; a raving lunatic.' DJ raised the jemmy. The slope was so steep I had to twist my feet sideways to stand up. 'His half-baked ideas killed your uncle, DJ,' I went on. 'He hooked him somehow, sex and alcohol at a guess, then used him to do his dirty work. What's he supplying you with, DJ? Coke?

Heroin, and a nice bit of stuff that's thrown herself at you? She wasn't called Danielle, was she? Sex, drugs and promises of wealth and power. Is that it?'

'Danielle?' DJ said. 'He knows Danielle?'

'Don't listen to him,' Kingston argued. 'He's a cop. He's been spying on you.'

'Danielle's vanished,' I shouted. 'She worked for Kingston and we think he's killed her, like he killed your uncle.'

'I never met DJ's uncle,' Kingston shouted.

'Your girlfriend did. Melissa. She picked him out as a likely candidate, and between you you destroyed him.'

'He's lying, DJ,' Kingston protested. 'Duncan was a good person. He'd have been all right if they hadn't hounded him to his death, always keeping him down, moving him on, never giving him a chance. The pigs killed your uncle, DJ. *He* killed him. We're doing this for him. Remember that.'

I couldn't go any further and the wind was still on the side of my face. Duncan was holding the jemmy by the bent end, resting it on the palm of his other hand. I took a side-step up the hill towards him, and he raised his arm.

Maybe I could afford to take one blow. I felt in my pocket for the CS canister and turned it in my fingers, groping for the flat side of the button. If I whipped it out and pressed, and it squirted up my sleeve, I'd be in big trouble. DJ hesitated, the jemmy still aloft, ready to strike. Kingston, to my left, kept coming nearer and lower, slowly moving downwind, where I wanted him.

I pulled the aerosol from my pocket, took four quick steps towards DJ and ducked. I heard the jemmy hiss through the air and felt it thud into my back as I let fly at Kingston with the CS. He screamed and clutched his face, his weapon falling to the ground. DJ had swung himself off-balance and he stumbled to his knees, dropping the jemmy as he scrabbled to stop himself going over the edge. I'd fallen too, but was facing uphill and was soon back up. DJ recovered but he saw Kingston's agony, didn't understand what had happened and jumped away from me. I pointed the CS at him but he was upwind and I'd have got the lot if I'd pressed the button. The threat was enough and he turned and fled. I chased him for about thirty yards, but the gradient and the years were against me. He vanished, crashing and stumbling, into the darkness. I walked back to Kingston and picked up both jemmies, holding them around the middle.

He was on his knees, rubbing his eyes, and he called me a bastard. I gave him another short burst, at close range, just for the hell of it, and he rolled over, screaming like a pig on a spear. I handcuffed him and walked about twenty yards up the hill. I sat down with my arms around my knees and watched and waited. The moon came up, mysterious and majestic, bigger than I'd ever seen it, with Ullswater like a silver boomerang in the valley. He hadn't been lying about the moon.

When the sobbing subsided I grabbed a handful of Gore-Tex and hoisted him to his feet. 'Walk!' I ordered. He stumbled a few feet and sank to his knees. I yanked him up again and kicked him. 'Walk!' I yelled. 'Walk! Walk! Walk!'

We made slow progress. When dawn broke, bright and new, we were only halfway along Swirral Edge. Kingston fell to the ground and said he could go no further. I grabbed him by the hair and stuffed the end of the CS canister into his left nostril. 'Get this,' I hissed at him. 'You can either walk out of here or you can be carried. But if I have to carry you the first thing I'll do is empty this up your friggin' nose. So get up on your feet and *walk*!'

After that we made better progress. On the bridle path leading into Patterdale a group of walkers approached us. They were all fairly elderly, out to enjoy a day on the fells. As we reached them Kingston turned to one, his shackled wrists held forward in an appeal for help. I grabbed his arm and steered him past them with a communal: 'Good morning.' They all turned to watch us go by, mumbling their greetings, not believing their eyes. This was the Lake District, after all. When we were past them the first one to recover her senses called: 'What's he done?' after us.

'Dropped a crisp packet,' I muttered without looking back.

The cars were still there. I found my mobile in my rucksack and dialled 999. It was the only number I could remember. Fifteen minutes later a Cumbria Constabulary Vauxhall Astra pulled into the car park and two PCs with bum fluff on their chins climbed out with a battle-weary, what's-this-all-about air.

I showed them my ID. 'DI Priest, Heckley CID,' I said. 'I want him taking to Kendal nick.' I pushed Kingston back against their car and wished Sparky could have heard this next bit. 'Nicholas James William Kingston,' I began. 'I'm arresting you for the murder of Jasmine Turnbull. You need not say anything, but it may harm your defence if you do not mention, when questioned . . .' I couldn't be bothered. 'Oh, take him to Kendal,' I said. 'I'll see you there.'

'But we're from Keswick,' one of the PCs protested.

'If you lose your way, ask,' I said. I took a towel from my car boot and dried my face and blew my nose on it. That CS gas gets everywhere.

I doubted if we'd run Kingston for little Jasmine, but we'd done our best for her. Found her some justice at last.

The jemmies went to have prints taken from them and I went for breakfast in their canteen. I was having my second tea when the DI that I'd dealt with before came in and joined me. 'We've just had a report,' he said, 'of a casualty on Striding Edge. Male, early twenties, with a broken leg. Anything to do with you?'

'Good,' I replied. 'Good. My cup runneth over. He's called Duncan J. Roberts and I want a statement from him.'

'Patterdale rescue team are on their way,' the DI told me, 'and the Air Sea Rescue helicopter's standing by. He'll be in hospital in half an hour.'

We agreed that he'd interview DJ, if possible, before the morphine wore off. I suggested that the threat of an attempted murder charge might further loosen his tongue. Kingston was making a full and frank statement, we'd tell him, and blaming everybody but himself. Meanwhile, I'd try the same thing with Kingston.

DJ fell for it, Kingston didn't. He couldn't remember Melissa, didn't know anything about 32 Leopold Avenue, and stuck to his story about Fox. We brought Francesca in for questioning and searched the house. Thoroughly, this time.

In the garage we found a rubber dingy. Not a super-duper neoprene job with a wooden floor and mountings for an outboard, like we might have expected. This was a cheapo plastic one, bright yellow, like you see on garage forecourts for parents to cast their offspring adrift in. But Kingston had no children. It was deflated, and pools of water were trapped in the folds, so we took a sample and sent it for analysis. Apart from that and a couple of grams of coke, we didn't find much else. I rang Les Isles and told him of my adventures. He said: 'I'm coming over.'

It was ten o'clock in the evening when I arrived home, sustained for the drive by adrenalin and canteen tea. I cleaned my teeth, switched the alarm off and crashed out for ten hours.

'Where've you been?' Dave demanded when I wandered into the office, clean-shaven and crisp-shirted, carrying a Marks and Spark's prawn sandwich for brunch. I told him all about it. My back hurt where DJ had whomped me, and my left arm was stiff. I could have had the bruises photographed as evidence, and filed a report, but I didn't bother. Screwing DJ wasn't on my agenda.

I did the paperwork and rang Tregellis. It's always easier to do things that way round, then the decks are clear if you are landed with another job. He was delighted, and had some news for me, too.

'Graham's been doing the rounds with the video you sent us,' he told me. 'He's shown it to three people who were at that charity bash at Newbury, and they all ID-ed Kingston as the man who accompanied Mary Perigo.'

'Rodger-with-a-d Wakefield,' I said.

'That's right. The case is building up nicely. Melissa's fingered him for the fire, you say this DJ character is spilling the beans on him, he's had a go at you and now we can link him with Mary Perigo. It's looking good.'

'But it's all circumstantial,' I said. 'He'll spend his time in prison writing books about the injustice he's suffered, about the conspiracy against him because the Establishment regards him as a danger to their way of life. I want him nailing, bang to rights.'

'Circumstantial evidence can be overwhelming, Charlie,' Tregellis replied. 'I'll settle for that.'

'I suppose so.'

'When does Melissa go back?'

'Tomorrow.'

'Shame about the wedding. Piers said he couldn't believe his ears when she agreed to come over. Now that she's married they'll have to let her back in.'

'I know, but she was stringing us along, acting innocent, all the way. She's got away with it.'

'Win a few, lose a few, Charlie. Don't take it personally.'

'I'll try not to.'

After that it was Les Isles again. 'Thought you'd still be in bed, Charlie,' he said.

'Dangerous places, beds,' I replied. 'People die in them.'

'Thought you'd like to know the good news and the bad news about the dinghy. The water was tap water. He'd either used it in the bath or hosed it off, so we can't tell anything from that. But we know where the dinghy came from, and when. Kendal have traced it to a filling station in Windermere. The girl there knows Kingston by sight; he buys a lot of petrol and can't resist flirting with her. She recognised him as the man who bought it a week last Sunday, which was just before Fox died.'

'Start dragging the lakes, Les,' I said. 'He dumped Danielle's body from it. He used her to set Fox up, and now he's silenced her. He's a hard man and a midnight swim would be nothing to him. She'd have to be weighted, so he'd need some assistance to keep her afloat until they were over deep water. She's in one of them somewhere, I'm sure of it.'

'And he couldn't abandon the dinghy because he knew we might find it and trace it back to him.'

'Like you have done. Exactly.'

'The frogmen are out, and we've asked our amateur friends to help. You know what they're like; bloody bunch of enthusiastic ghouls. They'll find her.'

I put the phone down. Tregellis was right. We might not go to court with anything that could be called forensic, but overwhelming circumstantial evidence was just as damning. I could imagine the phrase rolling off the judge's tongue, and the jury sitting a little straighter as that word *overwhelming* helped them come to terms with the thought of locking a man away for the rest of his life. Just the same, a little more evidence would be useful. Wanting to find the body of a young girl made me feel uneasy. 'I hope she's not dead,' I said to myself. 'I truly hope and pray that she's not dead. But if she is, I hope we find the body.'

Nigel came for me after work, with Dave already in his car, and we went for a few bevvies in one of the pubs high on the moors. These days you can have an animated conversation in one with little fear of being overheard. Cheap booze from the Continent keeps the punters at home, sipping Australian lager from the can and watching Australian soaps on TV until the blue kangaroos coming down the chimney tell them they've had enough. The landlord blinked with surprise at the sudden influx of trade and tried to remember the prices.

The inquiry had fizzled out, that was the problem. Fox was dead, Kingston was in custody and Melissa was going home. We'd never know the full extent of their evil. Crosby had met the War Crimes people and told them all his early memories, right down to the colour of his grandma's cat. If it were proved that he was the original Johannes Josef Fuchs it would give us a good insight into Fox's character and the papers would go into a feeding frenzy at his expense. And that was about it.

'Where's Annette?' I asked, after a good long sip of proper beer.

'Out on a date,' Nigel replied, glumly.

'Oh. Do we know who with?'

'He sells computers.'

'That could be anything from Bill Gates's chief executive to behind the checkout at Computers-R-Us.'

'He rings her on his mobile.'

'Sounds a right prat,' I pronounced. 'Doesn't he, Dave?'

Dave was studying a miner's lamp hanging in a little niche. 'Er, sorry?' he mumbled.

'I said he sounds a right prat.'

'Who?'

'Oh, go back to sleep. Just leave your wallet handy.'

'I was thinking.'

'Well, no wonder you're tired.'

'She's got away with it, hasn't she?' he said.

'Annette?'

'No! Melissa.'

'Got away with what?'

'I don't know, but she has.'

I said: 'It's normal to be reasonably specific about the offence before we put someone before a judge and send them to jail. Juries take a dim view if we just say that we don't know what they've done, but they must have done *something*.'

'Listen,' he began. 'Mrs Holmes painted a bleak picture of Melissa. Said she was capable of anything. So did the black lawyer you met . . .'

'Mo,' I interrupted.

'Him. And look how awful she was with her parents. For God's sake, she drove her mother to her death. Then there's her friendship with Kingston. She's admitted that she was at Leopold Avenue with him, and that was six years after they met. Six years! What were they up to in between? She and Kingston were partners, equal partners, I'm sure of it. She's as bad as him, maybe worse.' He underlined his words by picking up his glass and draining it. 'And she's got off, scot-free.' He plonked the glass down on the formica table to indicate that he'd said his piece.

I looked at Nigel and he gave me a brief shrug of the shoulders, as if to say: 'He's been like this all day. What more can we do?'

I went to the bar for refills. 'Quiet tonight,' I said to the landlord.

'It'll liven up later,' he replied.

Dream on, I thought. A blackboard behind the bar said that Friday was quiz night, with free beer for the winners. Free beer for the losers would have stood a better chance.

I carefully placed the glasses on the beer mats and sat down. They both took sips and offered the customary salutation. 'We needed Melissa's evidence, Dave,' I began. 'Without her we'd never have got off the ground. We're not prosecuting Kingston for all the crimes he might have committed for Fox, we're doing him for the ones he committed to cover his tracks. Without Melissa we couldn't have linked him to the fire, or to Duncan.'

'She still gets away with it,' he complained.

'We tried,' I said. 'We thought she'd be refused readmission to the States. That would have hurt her, but she was one step ahead of us.'

'She's mixing with some crazy people over there,' Nigel said. 'There's a good chance one of them will shoot her, one day.'

'That's something to look forward to,' Dave agreed. He pushed his glass a few inches across the table and wiped condensation from it with a thumb. 'I'm sorry, Charlie,' he said. 'You've done brilliantly, and I sound ungrateful. It's just that . . . I wish we could have got Melissa. It doesn't feel finished. Tomorrow she'll be back with her hillbilly friends, and . . .' He lifted his glass and left it at that. And live happily ever after?

'I know how you feel,' I told him, raising mine to join him in a drink. 'And why. I was at the fire too, remember. We've only done half of the job, but something tells me we haven't heard the last of Melissa Youngman.'

'Slade,' Nigel said. 'Melissa Slade.'

'Don't remind me,' I hissed at him across the top of my glass.

* * *

I had the beginnings of a hangover, which wasn't a surprise. It was a cool, dull morning, and showers were promised, which didn't mean a thing. It might rain all day in Heckley and be fine in Halifax, or it could be vice versa. Either way, the weatherman would claim a success. A familiar little Nissan Micra with fat tyres pulled out in front of me and the sight of it raised my spirits. It swung a left and so did I. Then a right, into the station car park, and I pulled up alongside it.

'Morning, Annette,' I said. 'You're bright and early.'

'A lot to do, boss,' she replied, 'if you want me to deliver you-know-who to the airport.'

'If you don't mind,' I replied, holding the door open for her. 'Then they're off our hands. You don't have to talk to them.'

'Thank goodness for that. What's the latest from the Lake District?'

I was telling her about the dinghy and the divers as we climbed the stairs. Halfway up we had to stop to one side to avoid the desk sergeant on his way down. 'Ah, Charlie,' he said. 'Just left another message on your desk.'

'Another?'

'There was one already there.'

'And I was hoping for a quiet day,' I complained.

'I'll fill the kettle,' Annette said as we entered the outer office.

'Let's see what these messages are,' I suggested. 'Maybe they've found something.'

Two official message forms were on my desk, held down by my empty coffee mug. Someone was determined I'd find them. On the top one the spaces for *From, To* and *Time* were all ignored. It read: *Body found. Looks like her. PM this afternoon. L. Isles.* I passed it to Annette and read the one underneath.

I read it again, then folded it and put it in my pocket. Spots of rain were falling against the window.

'That was quick,' Annette was saying, offering the first note back to me.

'It was, wasn't it? What time did you say their plane left?'

'Two thirty, but they have to be there at eleven thirty.'

'Don't you worry about it, Annette,' I told her. 'I'll take them to the airport.'

'But I don't mind,' she protested.

I raised my hands, palms towards her. 'If you don't want to take them, that's OK,' I insisted. 'Never let it be said that I'm not considerate towards my staff.' She went to make the tea and I rang Les.

'Wast Water, is it?' he said.

'Obvious choice,' I replied. 'It's the deepest lake in the country. She's not the first to be dumped in there.'

'So I'm told. The amateurs found her. They said she was on a shelf, and if he'd taken her another twenty yards out she'd have gone down three hundred feet. Five house bricks were strung on a piece of what might be climbing rope and tied round her waist. They've gone for examination. They must have come from somewhere. Do you want to sit in on the PM? I've bet my sergeant a fiver that her last meal was sushi.'

'Thanks all the same, but much as I'd like to, I'll decline, if you don't mind.' PMs on sinkers are not pleasant. 'Apart from which,' I continued, 'I've said I'll take Melissa to the airport.'

'They're going back today, are they?'

'Mmm.'

'Shame about the wedding.'

'Isn't it just? Give me a ring, will you, please, Les, as soon as you have something.'

'Will do.'

After that we'd have a big meeting with Tregellis and the prosecution service to prepare the case against Kingston. That was something to look forward to. If I allowed an hour to Manchester airport I'd have to pick Melissa up at about ten thirty. Call it ten to be on the safe side. I went up to the top floor to tell Gilbert as much as he needed to know.

They were waiting for me, eager to be back in the Land of the Free, where the streets have no pavements, and you have to carry your driving licence with you and a disapproving look given to a skateboarding youth can end in gunfire. I pressed the lever to unlock the boot and Slade lifted it open. I got out and walked round the back but he didn't need any help. He wouldn't have received any, but he didn't need it. They were wearing the same outfits they arrived in, which was reasonable enough, you need to be comfortable when faced with a long plane ride, and she was made up like a Kikuyu warrior. They both climbed in the back. I could see the edge of his face in my rearview mirror, but she squeezed into the corner, out of sight.

I thought about taking them the scenic route, but decided not to. The M62 was quicker and that's all I was interested in. Cruising at seventy in the middle lane, I tilted my head to see him better and asked: 'You been to England before, Slade?'

He glanced at me in the mirror and replied: 'Nope. First and last visit, God willing.'

'You don't sound impressed.'

'You goddit.'

'What didn't you like?'

'The beer's like warmed-up hoss piss, the beefburgers rot your brain, you've never heard of air-conditioning and the women're ugly.'

I had to chuckle. Well, I did ask. 'Melissa's not ugly,' I said. 'There's an English rose lurking underneath all that muck she covers herself with.'

'Just fucking drive, Priest,' she snapped. 'We gave you what you wanted, now get us out of this dump.'

I stretched my neck but she was ducked down and I couldn't see her. What I didn't know was that she was holding one of the blades from the little feminine razor that she shaves her temples with, and was systematically slashing my back seat with it. I discovered that three days later, when I found the razorblade she'd thoughtfully left embedded in the upholstery. I wish I'd known; it would have helped me make a decision.

Meanwhile, the hangover had gone and I was feeling almost light-headed. 'We arrested Kingston yesterday,' I said.

'Congratulations.'

'Thought you'd like to know.'

'You were wrong.'

'Oh, and Mo Dlamini asks to be remembered to you.' He'd prefer to forget all about her, but I was in a mischievous mood.

There was a silence, then she said: 'Mo?'

'Mmm.'

'You've talked to Mo? About me?'

'That's right.'

'What did he say?'

'I wouldn't dream of repeating it.'

'Who else have you spoken to?'

'Just about everybody you went to school and university with. Everybody remembered you. Maybe it was the purple hair.'

After another pause she said: 'Did you speak to Janet? Janet Wilson?'

'Er, I'm not sure,' I lied.

'It was her, wasn't it?' she declared. 'She put you on to me, the two-faced cow. She tried to come between me and Nick, but it didn't work. She was just another notch on his bedpost, and she's hated me ever since.'

I'd asked for that. I was in the outside lane and traffic was bunching up on my left. A big blue sign flashed by before I noticed it, and I said: 'I think this is ours.' I squeezed across into the slow lane behind a minibus loaded with suitcases and didn't speak again until we were lifting theirs out of the boot.

It could have been different. She might have said: 'Look, Priest, I don't like you and you don't like me, and that will never change. I admit I've done some bad things in the past, things you'd never believe, but it's all behind me now. This is a new start for me, and I'm going to make the best of it.' That's what she might have said, but she didn't. She was arrogant, unrepentant and vindictive, all the way. And the decision I had to make was that much easier for it.

I parked in the short stay and Slade found a trolley for their luggage. 'We can manage from here,' he said. 'We've done airports before.'

'I'll see you aboard,' I told him. 'That's my orders.'

'*Just obeying orders*, hey, Priest,' she said. 'Always do as you're told, do you?'

'It makes for an easier life,' I replied.

'Do you know what the best bit was?' she went on. 'Do you know what made this trip worthwhile? I'll tell you. It was the look on your face when you learned that we were married. I'll cherish that for a long time.'

I shrugged my shoulders. 'Win a few, lose a few,' I said. 'It's just a job; we don't take it personally.'

'Ah, but you do, Priest, don't you?' she asserted. 'Well, tough shit.'

I followed them at a polite distance through checking-in and into the departure lounge. He had a beefburger and coffee, she sipped a mineral water. All those brains, I thought, all that talent, and the intelligence of a woodlouse. I found a seat and watched people for a small eternity.

The Air 2000 charter flight we'd squeezed them on was called through into the boarding area and I showed my ID to the immigration officer and followed the crowd. I stood with my arms folded as the seat numbers were announced and watched groups of tourists rush to be first on, as if their bit of the plane would take off before the rest of it. They were a cross-section of working-class Britons and their offspring, off for a fortnight of fast food and fun. Football shirts were the dress of the day, with a good smattering of back-to-front baseball caps. And these were the dads. They carried surfboards, deflated li-los, raster-blasters to annoy the neighbours and rolled-up windbreaks. *Windbreaks*! I almost wished I were going with them.

An indecipherable announcement was made and Melissa and Slade rose to their feet, hoisting hand luggage on to their shoulders. Melissa saw me and couldn't resist coming over. 'Just thought I'd tell you,' she said, 'that it hasn't been a pleasure knowing you. Goodbye, Priest. I hope all cops die in pain.'

'*Au revoir*, Melissa,' I replied.

'It may be a small comfort to you,' she went on, 'to know that seven hours crushed in a plane with all these ghastly people is my idea of hell, but it's worth it to escape from this dump. You're paying the fare, after all.'

'Oh, it's a large comfort,' I told her.

She went back to Slade and put her arm around his waists. He put his across her shoulders and they moved towards the girl at the desk and showed her their boarding passes. She gave them a well-used smile and they stepped into the gangway.

I moved across so I could watch them follow the file down the boarding tunnel. They stood behind a little knot of passengers until it was their turn. The hostess looked at the seat numbers on their cards and pointed, and they vanished from view. Ten minutes later the plane door was closed and the gangway pulled back. I turned and made my way up to the observation area.

It's a curious mixture of bracing fresh air and kerosene fumes up there. There's a theory that enthusiasts for old cars and aeroplanes and other things mechanical are really addicted to hydrocarbon vapour. I don't believe it. There's a romance in watching the big jets surrounded by the service vehicles, like worker ants around the queen. They replenish it with fuel, evacuate the waste and restock the kitchen with four hundred meals: two hundred of them chicken; one hundred and ninety-nine beef; and a vegan for the Hindu in row six. One by one they move away until the queen stands alone. A tiny figure with headphones makes a hand signal and you see the pilot return it. That's the bit I like best; the romance of travel captured in a single wave. The engine note rises to deafening and she edges backwards.

I elbowed a youth with a thousand-millimetre lens to one side and leaned over the rail. Strange vehicles, each designed for one specific task, were scurrying back and forth haphazardly, yellow lights flashing. The BA 767, next stop Miami, followed one of them at a snail's pace out on to the expanse of concrete. I watched it creep towards the far end of the runway and vanish from sight. Five minutes later it reappeared, gathering speed. They were on their way. *Hear the mighty engines roar* . . . The engines, on full power, were a distant rumble as it lifted off, climbed on stubby wings and banked into the clouds. *See the silver wing on high* . . . I looked at my watch. They were bang on time.

'You again,' the immigration officer said as I entered his office. 'You'll be asking for a job here next.'

'I couldn't stand the excitement. Do you mind if I make another telephone call, please? It's to America, I'm afraid.'

'Business, I presume.'

'No, I want to tell my mother-in-law that it's twins.'

'That's all right then. Help yourself.' He pointed to a vacant desk.

'Thanks.'

I pulled the second message from my inside pocket and dialled the number I'd written on it. I'd no need to. I could have screwed the sheet of paper into a ball and tossed it into a bin, and that would have been the end of it. But I dialled the number. This time the message form had been fully completed. It was from FBI Agent Kaprowski and addressed to me. It read: *Reference Jade Slade, aka Wes Wesson, born Norman J. Lynch. Married in 1979 at Dade County, Florida. Not divorced, wife still alive, two children. Has gone through two more marriage ceremonies since then, in 1989 and 1993. Both partners still alive, no divorces, several children. Marriage to Melissa Youngman therefore bigamous and invalid. Hang in there. Mike.*

'I'd like to speak to Agent Kaprowski,' I said to the telephonist who answered. After a delay I was told that he was in a meeting. I know all about meetings.

'I'm Detective Inspector Priest,' I told someone else, 'and I'm speaking from England. It's important and I'd appreciate it if you could get him to a phone.'

They found him. 'Hi, Charlie,' he said. 'Didya get my message?'

'I certainly did, Mike, and I've just seen her take off. I hadn't the heart to break the news to her myself. She'll land in Miami at about four thirty your time.'

'Righty-ho. I'll have a word with immigration and they'll put her straight back on board. Seems a waste of a return ticket.'

'Not a bit of it,' I assured him. 'If anybody grumbles I'll pay for it myself. If they just happen to take a video of her face when they tell her, I'd appreciate a copy.'

'Ha! I like your style, Charlie. I'll see what they can do. Listen, I've been asking around and we've had a few queries raised over here about J.J. Fox's business methods. Any chance of letting us have a copy of the file?'

'No problem. I'll sort something out and put it in the post.'

'That'd be great. Unless you wanted to bring it in person. We could easily fix you with accommodation.'

'That sounds inviting,' I said. 'I might take you up on it.' I could go jogging in the woods, and take pot-shots of cardboard effigies of Al Capone as they popped up, and practise my diving roll. Maybe not, but I would like to visit Arlington, to pay my respects to JFK. I'd think about it.

I drove home the scenic way, which was a mistake. It's a twisty road and my shoulder started aching. I saw a chemist's in Tintwistle and bought some paracetemol. They did the trick. There's a country-and-western song called 'I'm Just an Okie from Muskogee' that's a satire on redneck values. The Committee to Re-elect President Reagan didn't recognise it as a piss-take and adopted it as their official campaign song. So a Texan singer/ songwriter called Kinky Friedman penned an alternative version, worded so that there could be no mistake this time. It's called 'I'm Just an Ass-hole from El Paso', and that's the only line I know, but I sang it continuously, all the way back to Heckley. Most of the time it was silently, in my head, but occasionally out loud, and I launched into the full Pavarotti once in a while.

Sparky was holding court when I arrived back at the office, telling a story about this chap who died and went to hell. 'So he sat there with the sewage over his ankles, and they dealt him a hand of cards, and he thought: This isn't too bad, I can bear this for the rest of eternity. But just then the door opened and the Devil walked in. "Right lads," he said. "Tea break's over for this century. Back up on your heads."'

'Hi, boss,' he greeted me as I sat down with them. 'We were just discussing the possible effects of European union on sentencing policy.'

'Great,' I said. 'And what have you decided?'

'We're agin' it. Did you see her off OK?'

'You bet.' They were all drinking coffee, but there were no spare cups. I took Kaprowski's message from my pocket and handed it to him. 'Read that while I fetch my mug,' I said.

It was on my desk, where I'd left it, and laid alongside was a roll of big sheets of cartridge paper that I didn't recognise. I slid the rubber band off and spread them across my desk. The top one was a symmetrical blur of black ink, with a white line, an axis, down the centre. It was the anal print, and there were three similar ones. They reminded me of Rorschach images, which was disturbing. I rolled them up again and went back into the main office.

Annette took the mug from me and I said: 'Thanks, love.'

Dave had passed the message to Nigel. 'Does that mean . . . she's not an American?' he asked.

'That's right.'

'So they won't let her back in?'

'No way. Immigration have been tipped off to watch out for her.'

'So what'll she do?'

'I don't know. Either spend the rest of her life in Arrivals at Miami airport or fly somewhere else. Back here, I assume. She won't be having grits and pancakes for breakfast with the Waltons, that's for sure.'

'That's fantastic!' Nigel exclaimed, passing the note on.

'Bloody 'ell!' Dave added.

The DC reading the note said: 'Some of us don't know what all this is about. You've been a bit secretive lately, boss, if you don't mind me saying.'

I held my hands up to show contrition. 'For which I apologise,' I told him. 'It was all a bit sensitive and we wanted to keep it out of the papers. Tell you what. It's been a good week, first the burglars, then this. How about a full team night out, Friday?'

There was a mumble of approval. 'Chinky and the social club,' someone suggested.

'I reckon the firm should pay,' Nigel said. 'There ought to be at least some commendations in this for you and Jeff.'

'Oh, I haven't room on my wall for another commendation,' I told him.

'And I'd like to say,' Jeff began, 'that any commendation given to me is only because I'm the figurehead. It will really belong to all of you.'

'Golly, how kind,' they muttered.

The phone in my office was ringing. I rose to my feet but the DC grabbed his own phone and said, 'I'll pick it up, Charlie.' He tapped in the appropriate number and listened. 'Heckley CID,' he said. His eyes widened and he smiled. 'Yes, he's here. I'll put him on.' He covered the mouthpiece and hissed: 'This is it! The Chief Constable's secretary wants a word with you. Commendations here we come!'

I took the phone from him, composed myself and said: 'DI Priest,' in my most authoritative voice.

'Hello, Inspector Priest,' a husky female replied. 'This is Miss Yates, secretary to the Chief Constable.'

'Hello, Rita,' I boomed into the mouthpiece. 'Long time no see.' Rita goes through chief constables like Eurostar goes through the Chunnel. 'How can I help you?' The others were hanging on my words.

'I'm just preparing the agenda for the next Serious Crime Operations Group meeting,' she told me, 'and I've noticed that at the last one, item eighteen, you offered to look into unsolved crimes going back thirty years. Shall I put you down for a presentation at the next meeting?'

I took a deep breath, puffed my cheeks and exhaled with a *pooffff*, like a beachball deflating. 'Er, no,' I stated.

'What would you like me to put?'

'Nothing. Can't you just forget it?'

'No, Inspector. I'm afraid that's not possible.'

'Well, just say . . . say I'm working on it. Nothing to report at this stage.'

'I'll have to put it on the agenda, and you can tell the meeting yourself. Will that be all right?'

'If you say so.' She rang off and I handed the phone across the desk, my displeasure apparent for all to see. They stared, blank-faced, waiting for a pronouncement. It broke my heart to disappoint them all. 'That's it, lads,' I said. 'Tea break's over. Back up on your heads.'

Author's Note

This story is fiction and all the characters in it are imaginary. I have used some real places and institutions to give a sense of location and distance, but any implied criticism of these is without foundation. Throughout the writing of this book I was received, as always, with courtesy and cooperation wherever I made my enquiries.